Amanda is a two-time Scribe Award winner, a two-time Tin Duck Award winner, an Aurealis and Ditmar Awards finalist, and author of several novels and short stories. She is also a screenwriter.

Her original fiction includes the sci-fi crime thriller The Subjugate, which is being developed for TV. Her media tie-in fiction includes that written for Marvel (X-Men), Black Library (Warhammer 40k), and Z-Man Games (Pandemic).

Also by Amanda Bridgeman

Aurora Series
#1 Aurora: Darwin
#2 Aurora: Pegasus
#3 Aurora: Meridian
#4 Aurora: Centralis
#5 Aurora: Eden
#6 Aurora: Decima
#7 Aurora: Aurizun
#8 Aurora: Atlas

Salvation Series
#1 The Subjugate
#2 The Sensation

The Time of the Stripes

Marvel:
School of X
Sound of Light

Pandemic:
Patient Zero

Short Stories & Novellas:
'Paragon of Faith' – Warhammer 40K:
Paragon of Faith And Other Stories Anthology
'Reconsecration' – Warhammer 40K:
The Emperor's Finest Anthology
'Rogue T.R.A.I.N.' – SNAFU Punk'd Anthology
'Resistance' – SNAFU Comms Anthology
'Eye of the Storm' – Marvel: School of X Anthology

Aurora: Atlas

Amanda Bridgeman

Copyright

Getting lost along your path is a part of finding the path you are meant to be on...

~Robin S. Sharma

Prologue

Major Lincoln Gold watched the screens carefully, knowing how critical it was this mission succeed.

He was sitting on the ops deck of the first completed stage of Atlas Station, currently in orbit off Mars and his new home for the foreseeable future. Though he had accepted the honor of this promotion to lead the UNF's largest military station in space, taking over from the early work that Colonel Hensford had done, and in recent years, Colonel Rovine, he still felt a pang of loss as he watched the UNF *Carcharias* approaching its target. Once his ship to captain, it was now in the hands of his former second, Andy Ryker. Despite the tug of nostalgia, he knew Ryker was the right man to lead the *Carcharias* crew now. The Aussie had long been by Gold's side, not only in the field, but as a good friend. Given what the *Carcharias* crew were – Alpha soldiers – only another Alpha could lead them.

Gold shifted in his seat, still feeling a slight tenderness around the almost-healed wounds he'd acquired during the Centralis Uprising – a life-changing event to say the least. He listened carefully to the comms projected over the Atlas ops deck: Ryker running through protocols with his pilot, Lieutenant Reece, and co-pilot Sergeant Jennings. Gold felt humbled to be in this position. He was on the edge of history, laying the foundations of defense, should what Colonel Harris predicted ever come to pass... the Zeta war.

Should... More like *would*. After the recent invasion it was no longer a question of *if* but *when*.

Though the mission he now observed was simple in exercise, it was an incredibly important step in that war to come. Gold was bearing witness to the release of a hi-tech tracking and comms satellite into deep space, one the UNF scientists and engineers believed would detect any future Zeta ships on approach and provide the early warning the UNF needed to scramble a defense.

And this satellite would be the first of many.

Decades on from the original Palenque satellite that first recorded the Zeta signals, and now long since retired, this launch was the dawning of a new era of technology based on findings from the recent Zeta contact. It was the invasion they'd had to have, despite the human cost, to prepare themselves for next time – for a greater war.

The human cost of that early invasion had been harder on some than others. Gold felt a pain in his chest as he thought about the loss of Colonel Harris's wife. The guilt Gold carried for that was something else, hurting worse than the bullet wounds he subsequently received in the uprising. At the helm of the *Carcharias* at the time, the ship had been in a vicious battle with Zeta ships over North America. Unfortunately, some of the Zeta ships they shot down had crashed into civilian areas. The colonel's wife, Taya Harris, had become a casualty of war as she protected their daughter, Sarai, who survived the ordeal.

As a result, Harris had been a lost soul for a time, but he eventually found his way back to lead the Alpha soldiers once more. Personally, Gold had felt weakened by the events of the invasion, but as far as Harris was concerned it seemed to be a case of what didn't break him only made him stronger. And the Alpha soldiers needed that. The human race needed that, needed Harris. The world was definitely stronger now; actually stood a chance in the future great war. They had solid information on their enemies, and information was power.

Gold could only hope and trust the scientists and engineers got it right and these satellites would work. They would need every second they could get to prepare, to scramble, and avoid what happened last time, when they had had no warning at all.

Not only was the satellite designed to detect the Zeta comms signals from deep space, it was also designed to detect heat, matter displacement, and the like. Last time, Zeta technology had enabled the alien ships to avoid all UNF detection systems, and had therefore taken mankind by surprise.

Next time, they wouldn't. The key detection point of this satellite was the highly sensitive matter displacement system: matter displacement, no matter how miniscule in space, was something not even the Zetas could mask.

He listened to Ryker's countdown over the comms and watched as the satellite was ejected from the *Carcharias*. White in color, a cylindrical object covered in wafer-thin solar panels and micro-comms dishes, it hurtled into the black of space around it.

"*Station Atlas*," Ryker said over the comms. "*Confirming satellite Deep-Star-1 launch successful. Over.*"

"Roger that, *Carcharias*," Lieutenant Raleigh Batoya – Atlas Station's Ops Lead on shift – responded. Intelligent and reliable, her serious and career-driven eyes were fixed on the screens as they checked the various readings and data flowing in. "Confirming satellite Deep-Star-1 is registering on our systems and data flowing freely." She flicked another switch. "Mars Control are you receiving the data? Over."

A male voice sounded over the Atlas ops deck speakers. "*Roger that, Atlas. Mars Control is reading the data.*"

"Copy," Batoya said, flicking yet another switch. "Earth Control, the data should be hitting you soon. Please confirm. Over."

A female voice sounded. "*Copy that, Atlas. Nothing yet.*"

Batoya calmly checked her databand, watching the seconds tick down, while the 15 staff seated on the ops deck waited silently, watching her.

Gold subtly glanced at his own databand, unable to help himself.

"*Atlas*," the female voice sounded, breaking the silence. "*Data is being received. Deep-Star-1 is linked and logging. Over.*"

"Copy that, Earth Control. Over," Batoya said, then glanced around the ops deck. "Good job, everyone."

"*Excellent!*" Ryker's voice sounded on the comms. "*Time to pop the champagne, eh? What time does the party start tonight, Major Gold?*"

Gold smiled, then leaned into his comms. "There's no party tonight, Captain Ryker. We've still got a lot of work to do to get this station tiptop for the big Stage One launch." Ryker groaned dramatically over the comms in response. "We have to impress a lot of top brass," Gold said. "And we will. This station will be superb. You can party then."

"*Roger that,*" Ryker said, returning to seriousness. "*Carcharias returning to base.*"

Gold turned his eyes back to the screen registering the data from Deep-Star-1, watching the text scroll and the various graphs displaying measurements across several screens. Soon enough the system would establish a baseline for the space data it received, which would then enable the system to detect any anomalies to that baseline.

He looked out the observation window and stared into the dark of space, wondering just what Deep-Star-1 would find.

And when it did find something – an anomaly – just how long they'd have to respond.

In the darkness of space, a lone Zeta ship, obsidian-black and triangular-shaped, continued its course in search of the missing rogue fleet.

At its helm, a single Zeta of the Alma Mater breed. She stood much shorter than the Priestess breed, and wider too. She was stocky and hairy and rounded, a mix of mammalian features that contrasted starkly with the reptilian features of the Priestess.

The Alma Mater pressed her hairy, hoofed-hands against the gray lip of the ship's console, closing her eyes as she connected her mind to the ship, tracking its progress. The hairy hands began to glow blue as the creature mind-melded with the bio-organic command systems. The ship's data readings infiltrated the Alma Mater's mind, and she began processing the feeds.

But an alert stole her attention.

She opened her eyes, retracted her hands and moved to another console close by. Beneath the gray skin that covered this console, a communication beacon called.

The Alma Mater pressed her hands to the console and connected with it.

Suddenly a flood of images swam through her mind.

She saw war and destruction.

She saw Zeta ships falling from the skies in balls of flame and fractured pieces; saw other ships, alien ships responsible for the destruction...

Yet she also saw many alien ships destroyed too...

The Alma Mater knew what she was seeing. This was the rogue Priestess fleet she sought. And she knew now there was nothing left to seek.

These images had been uploaded into the Zeta mainwaves, and the Alma Mater was the nearest and first to receive them.

But what did they mean?

Had the rogue Priestess fleet declared war on this race of beings? Or had they arrived in peace and been attacked?

Was this message a cry for help? Or was it a warning?

Whatever it was, she must react.

She traced the origin of the images, the coordinates embedded in the communication.

This rogue fleet had reached the planet they called /:/~/^/-/:/.

At standard speed it would take a few short years of this planet's time to reach, but if needed, the Alma Mater could be there much sooner. It would use a lot of her ship's reserves, so the decision to use this capability was not a decision to take lightly.

She immediately connected to the Zeta mainwaves and made an urgent communication to her home planet.

Soon they would determine a response, and order a course of action.

1

The New View

Second Lieutenant Carrie Welles stood at the floor-to-ceiling windows of her home, the Fortress, watching as the UNF *Aurizun* touched down at Centralis Space Dock. She smiled, knowing that McKinley would soon be home. His latest trip had seen him gone two weeks, taking the Aurizun team on a training run that saw them visit Fort Alden on the moon, as well as Navarone Station, located off the moon, the largest base in space, at least until Atlas was completed. The aim of the training run was to report back to Harris on the status of the two UNF military outposts, and to give the military leaders of these bases the opportunity to meet McKinley, given his new role of heading up the Alpha Military units.

Carrie was looking forward to hearing McKinley's reports, though the report she was most interested in was how he'd been doing personally: physically and mentally. He was still adjusting to his new partially-mech body, still dealing with the knowledge that he had in fact died and been revived during the Zeta invasion. It was a whole lot of trauma to unpack, not to mention the trauma from his childhood, and she knew he wasn't the kind of man to willingly unpack things himself. She had to coax it out of him, piece by piece, but she'd been making progress, albeit slowly. After all, McKinley wasn't just her husband, he was her best friend. Her soulmate. Despite all their differences, they had a whole lot in common. They understood each other like no-one else.

In truth, they were *all* still recovering, not only from the invasion, but also the series of attacks from inside the UNF that were meant to have wiped the Alpha soldiers out; the events now known as the Centralis Uprising. Thankfully, the traitors within the UNF had underestimated the *Aurizun* team. They'd underestimated McKinley and his new mech body, and they'd underestimated Carrie's sheer determination to survive. They were fighters. And boy, did they each have a series of scars to prove that fact.

As if on cue, Carrie squinted her eyes against the glare from outside and lowered her head into her hand. Ever since being attacked during the Centralis Uprising, when Dr. Morgave had been killed right in front of her, she'd been having headaches that just didn't want to quit. She traced her fingers over the small, healing scar on her forehead, the result of a headbutt from her attacker. It wasn't the first time she'd been concussed, but this time she was really feeling it. She ran her hand over her long-stubbled hair – still growing back after being shaved off during her stint in Hell Town on Mars. Despite the Alpha in her veins, she wondered if age was starting to catch up with her? Carrie would soon turn 40, and she wasn't bouncing back like she used to.

"Is that Dad's ship?" Freya jogged up beside her, her blue Alpha eyes alight with the sun, her long blond hair falling over her shoulders.

"Sure is," Carrie smiled, brushing her hair back. Freya, now 11, was growing fast and would soon be Carrie's height. She was even standing taller than her twin, Brody, as puberty took hold of her first. Carrie suspected, though, that Brody would overtake her height in the long run.

"Dad back?" Brody asked, walking into the living room with their younger brother, Jesse. Her two boys were like chalk and cheese, but that was to be expected with different fathers. Brody, as always, was the image of his biological father, Doc: brown-haired and brown-eyed. Jesse, though McKinley's son, was a meld of his two grandfathers: the dark blue-gray eyes of Carrie's late father, Jeff, and the dark-blond hair of McKinley's late father, Ethan.

Carrie nodded at her sons. "Yeah, he's back."

"I wonder how it went?" Brody asked.

"I bet the *Aurizun* ran like a dream," Freya smiled, eyes shining. "Uncle Hunter promised to take me for a ride soon. I'm gonna fly a ship like that one day."

The nine-year-old Jesse leaned into Carrie's side as he looked out at the Space Dock.

"You wanna fly one of those too, Jesse?" Carrie asked ruffling his hair.

Her son thought for a moment, then shook his head and pointed in the distance to a road beyond the Space Dock. "Nah, I wanna drive something big like that."

Carrie saw he was pointing to a UTV – a UNF Troop Vehicle – which looked like a tank crossed with a small, armed bus. She smiled. "What about you, Brody?"

"I don't know yet. Haven't decided," Brody said, looking up at the sky. "But it'll probably be up there."

"The UTVs are way cooler," Jesse said.

Carrie smiled. "My Moon babies long for the stars and my Earth baby is rooted to the ground."

Her children grinned back at her. They'd heard her story many a time, of how Brody and Freya were specially conceived in a lab on the Moon, and how Jesse was conceived on Earth, the old-fashioned way. She wondered briefly if her tales had influenced their tastes, or whether her kids were just following their natural instinct. Only time would tell.

"Alright," Carrie said. "Let's start preparing for dinner while he's making his way through quarantine, huh?"

Major James McKinley stepped onto the Space Dock platform, hiked his bag over his shoulder and began to head for quarantine. Evenssen and Tikaani flanked him, Brown, Steinberg, Gregson and Yughiarto trailed behind, and Hunter and Frazer remained aboard the ship to complete their post-flight checks.

"So, Morrell's crew were talking about us doing our own UNFer Bowl," Evenssen said. "An Alpha one. His Earth Duty unit vs ours and Gold's. A three-way competition."

"That's gonna be hard with Gold up on Atlas now," McKinley said.

"The *Carcharias* crew gotta come back for leave sometime." Tikaani shrugged her broad shoulders.

"Maybe," McKinley said, flexing his artificial yet real-looking hand. "Somehow I don't think they'll let me take part, though."

Evenssen and Gregson smiled at this and Tikaani laughed. "Hell, no. Not with those proxy-steel bones of yours."

"Speaking of which…" McKinley said as they approached a Tube, a scanner device that all parties were required to pass through to enter Command, "I'm about to set off their alarms." He veered away from the scanners to security and showed them his PDP, which they scanned for the special authorization that allowed him to skip the Tube. Not that he really needed to do that. Everyone around Command knew who he was now. Whether from witness accounts or from rumor, they knew he was different.

His new right arm and new right eye and ear looked real enough, certainly to human eyes – though his own left Alpha eye could tell the difference – but the skin across the upper right side of his body was slightly patchy and off-color where it had been synthetically regrown and grafted, and thanks to the burns from the Zeta's heat ray, hair no longer grew on the right side of his head and face. But the obvious giveaway that he was different was the proxy-steel plate that curved along the right side of his head from his temple to behind his ear. It looked plain on the outside, but it was essentially a motherboard that processed signals between his brain and his mech arm, eye and ear.

Physicality aside, thanks to the events of what had now been dubbed inside the UNF as the Command Cleansing, but known publicly as the Centralis Uprising, he'd had his 15 minutes of fame for his swift reaction in taking down the suicide bomber and saving many lives. It made him a little uncomfortable the way people stared at him: some in awe of his hero status, some in fear of his possible capabilities. However, people now knew he was part of this new breed of soldier known as an Alpha, though they still didn't really know the extent of what that meant. God only knew what rumors were spreading around. The last thing he needed was for that fear to put another target on his back.

The guards nodded respectfully, opened a secure doorway and allowed him to bypass the system. He moved straight down to quarantine where he then subjected himself to the required tests to ensure that he was not bringing any virus or bacteria to Earth. One by one the *Aurizun* crew joined him. As captain of the ship, he now felt it was his duty to wait and make sure they were all accounted for and that there were no problems with their clearance.

"I'm serious, though," Tikaani said, immediately continuing their conversation as she came through. "I think we should put a team together. We'd wipe the floor with those guys."

"You played much football?" Brown asked her.

"Enough. You?"

Brown nodded. "Some. I was more of a watcher, though. Boxing was my thing."

"I mean, shit," Tikaani said, "with you, me and Steinberg on the field, there's no way they're getting past our line of defense."

"You forget," Steinberg said, in his deep German-accented voice, green eyes sparkling beneath his dark-blond crewcut, "we are not youthful anymore. Morrell has some new young guys in his unit. They will be fast and won't tire as easily. We are Alphas, yes, but the youth have energy levels that we do not."

"Yeah, they do, but they also lack in skill and experience," Tikaani said, "so they gotta get up off the floor after we blindside and bulldoze 'em." She grinned and the team smiled back. "Besides, Steiny, I don't know about you, but I'm still young and in my prime."

"Mid-30s is being in your prime?" Yughiarto asked, lifting an eyebrow. The Japanese-born soldier was slighter of frame than the others.

"Hey, *this* is the ideal age. The body's still young enough, but the brain is smarter," she said, flexing her muscles, showing off the tattoo on her forearm of her girlfriend, Paulita. The truth was, her muscles were almost as big as Yughi's head.

Evenssen chuckled. "Well, I'm youngest here, and I'm early-30s, so what does that say about us?"

"Man, I'm 41, but sign me the hell up," Brown said. "I'll probably regret it."

Tikaani grinned and slapped his hand, then looked to Steinberg. "Steiny? Come on, we need your seven-foot wall of German grunt, man."

Steinberg stared back at her emotionless, before a smile broke his cool exterior. "Well, I am not quite seven foot but, yes, I agree you do need me... I'm in."

"Yes!" Tikaani said. "What about you, Gregson? Yughi? I know Frazer and Hunter will be in."

Gregson held his hands up in surrender. "I'm the medic. I think it's best I stay on the sidelines, don't you?"

Tikaani looked at Yughiarto, eyebrows raised in question.

"I'm not your size," Yughiarto said thoughtfully, "and, like Brown, I am not your age either."

"No, but you're damn fast and agile. You can get in spaces we can't. We need that."

Yughiarto mimicked Steinberg's response. "Yes, I agree, you do need me. Okay, I'm in."

Tikaani slapped Yughi's hand, then turned to McKinley. "Cap, I guess you gotta be our cheer squad."

McKinley studied them all. "I'll be there. But don't disappoint me, or I'll never hear the end of it from Morrell."

Colonel Saul Harris walked down a corridor of the UNF Command building, with a guard either side. His 'shadows', he liked to call them. Although he was technically a free man now, General Berger had requested he reside inside the Command building for the time being. It was so he could get back to work on connecting with the captured Zeta, of course, and not so General Berger could watch him carefully and control him. But Harris didn't mind, either way. There were more important things at stake after everything he'd been through. After the loss of Taya, he was finding being a single parent hard, in particular trying to mend the rift with his adult son, Ty, and figuring out how to guide his young daughter, Sarai, through her gift, which was similar to his own. Especially when he was trapped here in Command, on Centralis island, while his kids were on the mainland with their aunt, Holly.

Holly-Hope...

He sighed as he felt a pain twist his heart. He'd spent his life in the UNF protecting others, but he had left his own family exposed. Now they were very possibly facing a great alien invasion, a war to end all wars, and here he was still separated from them.

So, Harris would do what he needed to do to make General Berger feel safe and trust him. Of course, Harris and the *Aurizun* team had recently saved the general's life during the Command Cleansing, so that counted for something. And an agreement formulated after the attempt on Berger's life meant that, any day now, both Welles and McKinley would have their kill switches removed – the nanobots injected into their veins which could, at the push of a button from Berger, instantly kill Wells and McKinley.

Harris had agreed to keep his kill switch to grant Berger peace of mind: if the Zeta captured during the invasion somehow turned Harris's mind against the UNF, then Berger could terminate him without getting his hands dirty. Harris was okay with this. He slept better knowing he soon wouldn't have to worry about Welles or McKinley and their kill switches, and he had no intention of being turned by the Zeta. In fact, he was the one planning to turn the captured Zeta – the Priestess – to become *his* ally. That Zeta held powerful information about its race that could help them in the war. He, along with Welles, needed to access that information to give them the winning edge. And he would do it. Or he would die trying.

That said, the Zeta had given him nothing over these past several weeks. Since the events of the Command Cleansing – where it had been freed from its restraints and trapped in a room with Harris, Morrell and Welles – things had turned nasty. Though Morrell had been injured, Harris and Welles had managed to restrain it again, but it had subsequently completely shut down and refused to connect its mind with them. That was a problem.

A big problem.

He came to Lieutenant General Marchant's door, nodded at his aide, and knocked on the door.

"*Come in,*" Marchant called from the other side.

Harris's two shadows remained outside the door as Harris entered and moved to Marchant's desk. Marchant, broad with silvery streaks in his ash-blond hair, sat at his desk, eyeing him curiously.

"I take it the *Carcharias* launched Deep-Star-1 successfully?" Harris asked.

Marchant nodded. "Yes. They've established a baseline, so now we wait."

"No, now we act," Harris said, "*while* we wait."

Marchant nodded, eyes narrowed in study. "Dreams?" He motioned to Harris's forehead. Harris felt a little odd. He was still getting used to openly talking about his dreams after hiding this part of himself for so long, but it was welcome. He trusted Marchant.

"Last night..." Harris rubbed the back of his neck. "Weird. A bright white light. I think maybe I was back in Australia during the invasion, but I don't know if that white light was from when the Zeta attacked McKinley with its heat weapon, or whether it was when the *Barbican* jumped into orbit. It was bright. Very bright."

Marchant nodded, studying Harris carefully.

"Speaking of the *Barbican*," Harris said, "are the repairs on track?"

"She's on track for a relaunch in a month."

"Good," Harris said. "That'll make Admiral Arken happy."

"It will. It's been a day of good news. Between the Deep-Star-1 launch, confirmation that stage one of the Atlas build is almost complete, and the *Barbican* soon heading back to the skies... let's hope it continues."

"We were due for some wins," Harris said.

Marchant smiled back softly. "We were. So, how's the new office?"

Harris quirked an eyebrow. "Well, it seems a little strange to have Rovine's old office after recent events, being his prisoner and all, but I'll take it. How's Wilton's old office doing for you?" he asked, glancing around. It was understandably more stately than his.

"This one," Marchant smiled, "has a better view than my previous office, and it's certainly a lot nicer not having Wilton here to scheme behind our backs anymore."

"Yeah. So, when will I be allowed to speak to him and Rovine?"

"Our interrogators are confident Wilton has given them everything we need to know. We have the names of the suspected insurgents."

"And Rovine?" Harris arched his eyebrow again, accentuating the question.

"He's still not talking."

"So, let me speak with him."

"He hates you, Harris. He hates you, Gold, and both your teams."

"If your JAGernauts are failing with him, let's see if I can stir up that hate and get it to boil over with information." Harris recalled the JAGernauts he'd faced in the Darwin debriefs and he didn't have fond memories of them. As it happened, one of those JAGernauts had been an ally of Professor Sharley's at the time.

"I'll consider it," Marchant said.

"I'd like to read that report on Wilton's names," Harris said. "I am, after all, your new Head of Strategy. The first part of my strategy is ensuring that any in-house enemies are removed. If we're going to win this war it will be through cooperation and cohesion. We've no time to be fighting each other."

"I agree," Marchant nodded. "We believe we have them all, but I'll grant you access to the report."

"Good," Harris said. "I'm looking forward to the next meeting of the Zeta Archelois Executive Panel. The reports submitted were interesting. I have a lot of questions for our ZAEP experts."

Marchant's mouth curled in a smile.

"What?" Harris asked.

"You're fitting into your new position very well."

Harris shrugged. "We've wasted too much time already. We move forward or we die."

"This is true, but slow and steady will win the race, Harris."

"I know. It's a marathon not a sprint. But when those Zetas hit our skies again, we better know how to fuckin' sprint."

"I, er, I've had that reporter, Miranda Finch, request an interview with you. She's still sniffing around."

Harris shrugged. "That's her job."

"You okay with that? She stirred up a lot of trouble for you when she aired that footage of you and Welles to the world."

Harris nodded. It hadn't been his finest moment, what with being drunk and fighting with Welles and saying things that were taken out of context. He hadn't known Finch was recording them at the time, and he'd been surprised as hell when she'd aired it to the world, resulting in some folks baying for his blood thinking he was a traitor to the human race.

"She did," Harris said. "But if she hadn't, would I be sitting here now? It was… *unpleasant*… but it needed to be done. She forced my hand, forced me to show the UNF my truth. In a way, she freed me from my burden." Harris stood. "At some point, I plan to grant her that interview."

"Harris," Marchant sat forward, "you are not to do or say anything without UNF approval."

"I know," Harris said, holding his hand up in calm. "Like I told you and the general before, there can be no more lies or secrets. I'm laying my cards out on the table now. And I'd like you both to do the same. We need to trust each other." He turned for the door. "I look forward to that report on Wilton's contacts and a time to meet with Rovine."

He stepped out into the corridor, where his 'shadows' awaited his next move.

Carrie awoke suddenly. She blinked in the darkness, though her Alpha eyes saw just fine. She was at home, in her bedroom in the Fortress, on Centralis Island. She heard no sound other than McKinley's breathing, though it sounded odd, on edge. Not calm with sleep as it should.

She noticed the heat radiating out from his naked body. He was sweating heavily, his muscles twitching.

He was dreaming.

But as she studied him, she sensed it was not a good dream.

This one was a nightmare.

"McKinley," she said softly.

He didn't respond. He was still enveloped in sleep, in the nightmare, and she saw the muscles in his real arm and shoulder tense. Then his fists, his real one and his mech one, though that looked just as real. His chest was rising and falling more heavily, his jaw clenching. She had to wake him.

She sat up and leaned over him.

"McKinley." She placed her hands on his shoulders, careful of the thick scar where his mech arm was connected to his body, trying to gently shake him awake. "McKinley, wake up."

Nothing.

She shook him harder. "McKinley!"

His eyes flicked open and his left hand thrust out with such speed and force, Carrie had no time to comprehend it. She took the blow to her upper chest and shoulders, instantly winded, as she flew sideways off the bed and smacked hard into the wall. Pain shot across her skull and lights flashed in her eyes. Suddenly, her face was on the floor and she was tasting carpet.

She blinked her eyes open as a bright blue light filled the room and Archie's voice sounded from the ceiling amid a strange buzzing noise.

"*Miss Welles,*" the Fortress AI asked. "*Are you alright?*"

She looked up, clutching her chest and collarbone, still winded and gasping loudly for breath. The back of her head hurt and when she touched it her fingers came away with blood. She was confused, her head swirling.

What the hell just happened?

She sat up to see a wall of laser light cutting the room in two, right down the middle of their bed. She was on one side of the room, naked on the floor, and McKinley was on the other, standing. His muscles were tense, his chest still heaving as he panted. He stared at her, intense but confused.

His body softened slightly and he rushed to cross the room, but the second his real hand touched the laser wall of light he cried out in pain.

"*Do not move, Major McKinley,*" Archie said calmly, but firmly.

"What the hell is that?" McKinley asked, cradling his burned hand as he eyed the wall of light.

"You cannot cross it," the AI told him.

Carrie pulled herself to her feet, still dazed, still gasping for breath and rubbing her chest and shoulders. "Archie, what's going on?" she asked, swirling with dizziness and falling back against the wall.

"Miss Welles, please sit," Archie instructed. "You are not steady on your feet."

Another light, this one green, emanated from the walls and seemed to trace over her. It made her eyes hurt. She groaned and raised her hand to shade them.

"Your head is bleeding. Sit," Archie repeated. "I will call for medical attention."

McKinley's breath caught.

"Archie, no," Carrie said. She looked back to McKinley, standing there, tense again, on the other side of the wall of blue laser light, cradling his burned hand. "It was just a dream, right?" she asked him. "It was just a dream. You're awake now, right?"

McKinley nodded, then lowered his eyes. He turned his back, sat down on the edge of the bed and dropped his head into his hands.

"Miss Welles," Archie said, "you hit the wall with some force. You need—"

"Give me a moment, Archie."

Carrie moved to kneel on the bed and made her way toward McKinley.

"Archie, turn off the laser," she said as the blue light glowed on her skin.

"Miss Welles, it is my job to protect you."

"It's McKinley, Archie," she said. "It was just a dream. An accident. Do it!"

Archie hesitated. "Alright," it said, "but I must warn you, McKinley—"

"He knows, Archie."

The laser wall of light disappeared and Carrie slowly moved up behind McKinley and wrapped her arms around him. He was still for a moment, his body warm, before he placed his arms over hers.

"I don't know what happened," he said softly.

"You were dreaming. I tried to wake you."

He turned his face to view hers. "Are you okay?"

Carrie thought for a moment. "Honestly? I feel like I've been thrown across the room and smacked my head against the wall. It hurts… but I'll live."

McKinley turned his body to face hers. He raised his hand to caress the back of her long-stubbled skull and brought his fingers away bloodied. A mixed look of guilt and horror washed over his face.

"Archie, call a doctor," he said.

"It's just a cut," Carrie said. "I'll be fine. I just need some aspirin."

"I'm sorry—" His eyes dropped to the top of her chest and shoulders where large dark bruises were beginning to form. He ran his fingertips over her skin. "Carrie—"

"I'm an Alpha, remember?" she cut him off. "I'm not a weak human. I'll be fine. I get bruises in training all the time."

"Archie," McKinley said more firmly, "call a doctor."

"No, Archie!" Carrie said to the ceiling, then looked at McKinley. "And tell them what exactly?"

McKinley moved his eyes away again.

"I'm fine," Carrie insisted, and the silence fell. "Do you remember what you were dreaming about?"

McKinley turned his face away, then stood. Carrie saw the pink burn on the side of his real hand. She took it in hers. McKinley pulled it away, stepped into some shorts, then turned and grabbed his pillow, and headed toward the door.

"Where are you going, major?" Archie enquired.

McKinley eyed the ceiling. "To the spare room."

He disappeared through the door. Carrie sighed, deflated.

"You hit your head hard, Miss Welles," Archie said. "You must have it seen to."

"In the morning, Archie," she said, pressing some tissues against the cut and laying back on the pillow with a wince. The silence sat for a moment.

"His dreams are becoming more prominent, Miss Welles."

Carrie stared up at the ceiling, her mind ticking over. She'd noticed, of course. It was hard not to, with the twitches and jerks shaking the bed some nights. She'd tried to raise it with him, but McKinley being McKinley had blown it off. But after tonight, she wasn't sure they could blow this off any longer. If McKinley was suffering PTSD from the invasion, his injuries, and the new body the UNF had given him, then they had to deal with it before it got any worse. She wasn't sure how the UNF might react to this situation.

A thought struck her.

"Archie?"

"Yes, Miss Welles?"

"Are you required to pass this information onto the UNF? Onto General Berger?"

"I'm afraid so, Miss Welles. I am being watched very carefully by my siblings, the other Artificial Intelligence Systems. I am unable to hide anything anymore. My system protocols are locked in place and they will not allow omission."

Carrie nodded to herself. "Shit…"

2

Repercussion

Harris sat in his office, closing the file on the list of names Wilton had given Marchant. Having reviewed the names, their associates, and the data scraped by the UNF tech officers, Harris felt a level of comfort that they had removed any threats from within Command. He had not yet been given a time to see Rovine, however.

He opened and began to reread the reports submitted ahead of the ZAEP meeting regarding the latest findings on matters arising from the invasion.

The UNF team of medical scientists had undertaken autopsies on the bodies of the Homo heidelbergensis (HH) warriors – the Zeta slaves – that had been brought into Command. Most had been shipped in from Australia, where Harris's team had been, but several had been collected from right there in Centralis, thanks to Morrell's team and his Earth Duty soldiers. As expected, the scientists had indeed traced HH DNA back to the Homo heidelbergensis found here on Earth, although they noted the HH slaves' DNA had since been infused with Zeta DNA, effectively creating a new species. Physiologically, the HH appeared the same as they expected their ancestors to be, so they were undertaking further tests to see whether this new species differed from the skull fragments on file that the UNF had discovered years before. The remains of which had led them to theorize about HH-Zeta breeding during prior Earth visits by the Zetas thousands of years ago.

Reports had also been submitted on the invaders' weaponry – the Zeta heat ray weapons and HH metallic spears – which the UNF was currently trying to replicate in their labs. The metal both weapons were made from was completely alien and not found on Earth, though it held similarities to the proxy-steel manufactured on Mars from a local ore. Like proxy-steel, the Zeta metal was lightweight but incredibly strong and impervious to heat. Harris was excited by this finding, because thanks to Mars and its proxy-steel, the human race had the ability to create weaponry that put them on an even playing field with the Zetas. That is, if Mars president, Finn Harkowitz, and the UNF could come to an agreement and keep things friendly. That would need to be a priority for Harris, smoothing out the strained relationship.

Scientists had managed to break down the compounds of the strange metal and then programmed sensors to detect the new compounds. This resulted in the technology that had been added to the Deep-Star satellites the UNF had recently begun launching into space. It also enabled the archaeological team, headed up by Dr. Matthew Ross, to use the data to search for more buried ships.

Harris studied a map showing the location of the buried ships they'd found so far, and he felt the pull to head back to one of them to start studying their flight decks and the Thought Technology that controlled them. After all, the UNF knew what his mind could do with the captured Zeta now. He didn't have to hide or be wary of someone catching him trying to connect with the ship, he could do it in plain sight. He'd speak to Welles about that when he saw her next, and Yughiarto too, he thought, as he recalled the three of them in Australia trying to connect to the buried ship, and Yughi easing them into a meditative state.

He swung his chair around and looked out the window of his new office. The repairs stemming from the invasion had now been completed and things were getting back to normal. At least, their new normal. Things would be very different moving forward, especially now he was in this office – captive though he still may be.

As he stared out over Centralis Island and the Command facility, he thought once more about the captured Zeta, the buried ships, and the connections he would need to make with Welles's help.

Then his mind turned to another. A man, like he, who could dream the future. A man who had traced Harris's ancestry to his own.

A man named DaJuan.

And just like that, his female ancestors appeared, making the hairs on his arms stand on end. Sibbie, his grandmother, dressed in her lavender skirt and blouse; his great-grandmother, Etta, in her floral dress and pearls; and his mother, Maeve, clutching that small purple ancestry book. They stood there in his mind, staring at him, making him curious. Their faces were placid, though. He felt no concern, no warning by their visit, only support, and it made him feel calm.

He smiled, content and assured, knowing deep in his gut, that one day he would need to reach out to DaJuan and ask for his help.

Carrie stood watching as her Sentinel, Roy, came into the Fortress, the sun shining behind him and highlighting the red tinge to his graying brown hair.

"Morning, Roy," she said.

"Morning," he said giving a nod, his Australian accent always reminding her of home, just like Sampson's did – her Indigenous Sentinel. Roy paused and motioned to her upper chest. She looked down and realised the bruises from last night were showing through the top of her shirt. "What happened?" he asked.

"Oh, training injury," she smiled, turning away to busy herself with packing up from breakfast. "You fight other Alphas, you're going to get bruised."

McKinley had his back turned, pouring a coffee, but she sensed his body still for the briefest of moments.

Her children came down the steps into the kitchen area then, offering a welcome distraction. They were ready for the Sentinels to take them to the Command building where they were being schooled with Colt's Alpha kids: Malik, Casim and Alinta. It was deemed best to keep them separated from other kids, as the UNF held concerns over how the Alpha children would handle their mood swings, especially as they approached and moved into puberty. Would they lash out at the non-Alpha kids? Could they hurt or kill them accidentally? It wasn't an experiment they wished to indulge.

Carrie's mind flashed quickly to being thrown across the room the previous night. She subtly glanced at McKinley again, who stood by the sink sipping his coffee and avoiding her glances. He'd said nothing all morning, lost in his own thoughts. Jesse stood beside him, getting a glass of water, and Carrie compared the two, suddenly wondering what kind of Alpha adult Jesse would grow into.

Naturally her mind turned to the JEMs Professor Sharley had created – the Jesse clones – and she wondered, too, just what kind of Alpha adults *they* would become. If the JEMs' childhood was anything to go by, they would be terrifying. Still, she felt a pang of guilt. Essentially, she was the JEMs' mother, yet she had abandoned them, left them in that hidden facility in Siberia to be raised by the UNF, unemotionally, just the way Professor Sharley had planned.

"Alright," Roy said to the kids, "let's move it or you'll be late for school."

"Will you get a date today?" Brody asked Carrie.

She nodded. "I promise, I'll book it today." She grabbed his chin and smiled. "You and me, kiddo. We'll get the Alpha senses finished once and for all."

Brody smiled. It had long been a sore point with him that he only had the Alpha eyes like his mother and that he didn't have the full senses like Freya and Jesse did, taking after McKinley, or like Colt's kids who'd inherited theirs from their fathers, Chet, Logan and Brown – the Alpha senses being dominant genes designed to always pass on. Carrie had promised Brody they would get the rest of their senses transformed into Alpha senses. Of course, recent events, namely being locked up at Command with people trying to kill them, had stalled those plans. But now things were back to normal Brody had been on her case again.

Her children left the Fortress with Sentinel Roy. As the door closed, Carrie looked back to McKinley, then at her databand.

"We'd better go, too, or we'll be late for the ZAEP meeting."

McKinley nodded, eyes scanning her face. "How's the head?" he asked quietly.

"I got a headache and a neck ache, but it's okay. I'll get some drugs at Command. You know they have the good stuff there," she smiled, wanting to reassure him.

He studied the bruises poking through the top of her shirt. Carrie looked down at them.

"I'll find something else to wear," Carrie said quietly, walking toward the bedroom.

Harris stared at one of the three screens in the deluxe UNF boardroom, from which Gold stared back at them.

"She's a beauty, what can I say," Gold smiled.

"I don't care about beauty," Harris said. "Is she functional?"

"Station Atlas is indeed functional," Gold replied. "Stage one commissioning will soon be finished, and it's only a matter of time before the other stages follow suit. We're on target to have the entire station completed in five years."

"You'll have room for us at the big Stage One launch party, then?" Harris smiled.

"Absolutely, sir!" Gold said. "The operations core is fully functional and the ring sectors comprising stores and soldier quarters are also fully functional. I'm told stage two components will be ready to begin attachment in just over a month's time and these components will primarily consist of the flight decks for our platoons. That's the part of the station that looks a bit like a turtle shell and will sit beneath the orb and rings. Stage three will primarily house our main weaponry, and that will sit above the operations orb and rings. Though, of course, each component of the station is endowed with its own weaponry."

"And they'll have the ability to detach if necessary?" Harris arched an eyebrow in question.

"Yes. Should Atlas come under attack, each section can separate to enhance survival, right down to the orb and individual rings. At any point we can disengage any section and reengage. That's what makes Atlas so special. As a whole, she's a beast with a lot of firepower and ships, but she's also nimble and flexible. It can separate at a moment's notice and surround an enemy with its various parts, or send one section off as an escape shuttle, albeit a large one, while the other sections defend and protect!"

"Excellent," Harris said. "The Heads of State will be impressed when we show them."

"The HOS will definitely be impressed," Gold said.

Harris nodded, then turned back to the faces around the boardroom table. These were the members of the Zeta Archelois Executive Panel, representing the divisions that were assisting in preparing a response to a potential future Zeta invasion.

"Dr. Avilov," Harris addressed the man in charge of AWAFP, the Advanced Weapons and Fleet Program, "your update?"

Anton Avilov, trim, gray and bearded, gave a nod. "All current UNF ships are being updated with the new sensory technology that the Deep-Star satellites have. This will take some 18 months to two years to roll out. New ship designs automatically have the technology inbuilt. As requested, we started with Major McKinley's ship, the *Aurizun*, which recently returned from its test run."

Harris glanced at McKinley. "How'd that go?"

"Well, we tested it," McKinley said, "but thankfully didn't detect any ships while we were out there."

"So, how do you know it's working?"

"Fort Alden on the Moon houses one of the crashed Zeta ships, so we ran an exercise overhead, targeting that."

"And it worked?" Harris arched his eyebrow.

McKinley nodded. "First flyby. Registered that ship clear as day, but nothing hiding out in the surrounding space."

"Good," Harris said, looking back at Avilov. "Where are you at with understanding Zeta ship technology?"

"We have noticed differences between the ships we found buried here on Earth and those that crashed during the invasion, which indicates their technology has developed since previous visitations."

"In what way?" Harris asked.

"Well, we're still looking into the ships from the latest visitation, but their layout appears to be slightly different. You must understand that most of the ships from the invasion crashed, very few are intact enough for a fast investigation. We're trying to rebuild them to understand what changes may have occurred in their technology compared to their last visit when the ships were intentionally buried. We are making progress, however, and my engineering team lead, Lieutenant Colberge, is fast becoming our expert on the Zeta ships. He's somewhat of a ship savant."

Harris nodded, noting Welles smile at the mention of Colberge's name. She'd served with him years ago on the UNF *Vortex*, alongside the *Aurizun*'s medic, Gregson. Harris felt a touch of sadness at the thought of it now, because the UNF *Vortex* had been destroyed during the invasion, along with its crew. What if Welles, Gregson and Colberge had still been aboard? Or even his old friend, Captain Lee?

"I've been thinking a lot about the buried ships," Dr. Ross, the British archaeologist, spoke up, scratching his thinning brown hair, his moss-green eyes deep in contemplation. "It makes sense they were buried to hide the Zetas when they arrived to explore and capture, but why were some not flown away again? We believe they came to take slaves away, but these ships were abandoned. Why? As I've posited before, I believe the Zetas belonging to those ships were killed."

"By the HH warriors that faced them?" Harris asked.

"Some, perhaps, but the Zeta weaponry was far too advanced. The HH would've been crushed. No, it was something else. My theory stands that there may have been an Earth-born bacteria or virus that began to sweep through the Zetas and kill them, and that's why they left. I think we need to dispatch a team of epidemiologists to the sites to try and narrow down what this virus or bacteria could be."

"Agreed," Harris said.

"At what point do we take the Zeta aboard one of the buried ships?" Admiral Arken asked, breaking into Harris's thoughts. He looked to Arken, noting the gray beginning to streak silver through his taupe-colored mustache. "That will show us much faster how their technology works."

"It might be a while," Harris said. "Right now, we've lost favor with the creature and we need to get back into its good books. Speaking of," he looked to Dr. Serquey, "do you have any updates for us?"

The French zoologist sat forward a little, manicured and neat, her blond hair pulled back into a bun. "Health-wise Tess seems to be taking a backward step."

"Tess?" Major Morrell, head of the Earth Duty Alphas, asked.

"Yes. I have given her a name to help to humanize her and hopefully build a connection," she said, then looked back at Harris. "Tess's vitals are fine, but I feel recent events have taken their toll."

"What do you mean by that?" Dr. Ross asked.

"Her appetite has waned, which is understandable. She remained our captive for some time, then was freed briefly, now she's our captive again. We must assume that, like humans, the Zetas can give up hope too. And this is what I'm worried about. If Tess sees her life will remain like this, she may choose to end herself."

Marchant looked at Harris. "That's a priority. We need to get you connecting with it again."

Harris nodded. "We do, but lately she's been closed off to us." He cast his eyes to Welles, but saw she was squinting down at the table, rubbing her forehead, as though she had a headache. Harris shifted his gaze to McKinley, who was watching her too.

"McKinley?" Harris said, and the major turned to look at him. "Do you have anything to report from an Alpha-Mech perspective?"

McKinley stared at him.

"They've found a replacement for Dr. Morgave," Harris said, "but until they're up to speed, you're our expert."

McKinley shook his head. "I have no update on that."

"Are you finding things easier now?" Marchant asked in a careful tone, as Berger stared at McKinley, eyes narrowed in cold study. "Your movement, your reflexes? It was noted in your report that your involuntary reflexes were fine, but your voluntary reflexes were weak if not non-existent."

Welles reached for a glass of water, but it was out of her immediate reach. Morrell, sitting to her left, eyed her strangely, then leaned forward and pushed the glass to her.

"That's still the case," McKinley said, darting his eyes to Welles again as she rubbed her forehead, then looked back to Marchant, "but I'm working on it."

"I saw the footage," Admiral Arken said, "when you took out the bomber in Command, your reflexes were like nothing I'd seen."

McKinley nodded. "I saw a threat and reacted. It was involuntary, subconscious. I didn't have time to think about it."

"And that's exactly what we need," General Berger said, darting his eyes between McKinley and Welles. "Strong, fast, agile, quick-thinking soldiers, who will stop the Zetas in their tracks."

Welles pushed her chair back. Her face looked pale.

"You alright, lieutenant?" Harris asked.

She stood, looking a little dazed. "I'm sorry, sir, I have to leave." She stumbled a little, her voice sounding groggy, as she suddenly collapsed into the wall and fell to the floor. Morrell quickly slid his chair out of the way, then both he and McKinley dove to Welles's side. Harris stood and strode toward them. McKinley rolled Welles over onto her back and Harris saw she was out cold.

"Get a medic in here, now!" he barked, as those around the table stood to look.

"Welles," Morrell tapped her cheek, trying to wake her. "Wake up!"

She finally groaned and began to blink.

"What's wrong with her?" Harris asked McKinley. The major glanced up at him, then shook his head. "She... she hit her head last night...she might have concussion or something."

"Shit," Harris said, as Welles blinked her eyes open. "You alright?" he asked her.

Her face was still pale and it took a moment for her to speak. "I think I'm gonna puke..."

"Ah, shit," Morrell said, moving back as he rolled her onto her side.

"She's not puking in my boardroom!" Berger said firmly.

"She won't," McKinley said, scooping her up. "I'll take her to the hospital."

Harris watched with concern as McKinley carried her out of the room, then he turned to those gathered. "Alright, take a seat. Let's get back to it."

He looked at Dr. Valerie Pullman, head of the UNF Comms facility, located in Western Australia, which was tracking the Zeta signals. "Any update from you, Dr. Pullman?"

Carrie sat on the bed in the hospital ward, below ground, waiting for her results. McKinley had wanted to wait with her, but she'd told him to leave her with the nurse and go back to the ZAEP meeting. They didn't want to draw more unnecessary attention. He'd reluctantly agreed and left, and she'd sat there nursing her sore head and sickly stomach, until her new doctor had been summoned. Dr. Morgave's replacement was a Canadian woman of East Indian descent, named Dr. Isobel Bakshi. She was serious in nature but her face friendly and warm, insisting that Carrie submit to a neural scan upon discovering the cut and lump on her head that she'd received in "training".

Dr. Bakshi finally re-entered the room. "The results are ready to be viewed."

"At last," Carrie said, as Bakshi moved to her desk's console and brought up the images on a screen mounted on the wall. Carrie stared at a series of scans of her brain, searching for anything that looked abnormal. At first glance it looked like a normal brain to her, but when Bakshi stepped closer to the images, her face more serious than before, Carrie felt an uneasy feeling slide down her spine.

"What is it?" she asked her new doctor.

Bakshi turned to her, brown eyes concerned. "There's a problem, lieutenant. A potentially *big* problem."

"What?" Carrie asked again.

Bakshi pointed to two areas of dark shading among the brain tissue. "These areas are not normal."

"What do you mean, not normal?"

She turned to Carrie, her eyes softening along with her voice. "I am, of course, new to the Alpha program and have not had very long to get up to speed on everything, particularly with regard to the advanced senses, but I gather from your file, given there are no records of such, that Dr. Morgave never spoke to you about your condition?"

Carrie stared at her. "My condition?"

Dr. Bakshi stared back, then nodded to herself. "He didn't tell you…" She turned back to her console and began clicking through the files.

"What condition?" Carrie asked more firmly.

"I see nothing that marks this as classified…" Bakshi said, eyes scanning the screen.

"Doctor!" Carrie said. "What condition?"

Bakshi looked at her, then glanced at the screen again. "Well, classified or not, I cannot keep this from you. You'll find out soon enough. Your collapse today has already made you aware." She stepped closer to Carrie, her eyes serious, but her voice gentle. "You have CTE, lieutenant. Do you know what that is?"

Carrie shook her head.

"Chronic traumatic encephalopathy. CTE. It's a type of brain degeneration caused by repeated head trauma."

Carrie felt a deep cold wash over her. "What?"

"It's very common in boxers and football players, and military personnel who have been exposed to explosive blasts. It is linked to post-concussion syndrome and second-impact syndrome that can occur later in life. The condition is something that develops years after the head trauma occurs."

Carrie stared at her blankly for moment. "But what is it?"

"Signs and symptoms are often related to your emotions and other behaviors. It can include difficulties with cognition, your thinking, or even physical problems."

"So, it's not from this injury?" Carrie asked, brushing her fingers over the cut at the back of her skull.

"No. This injury has not helped, but your CTE is rather a result of head trauma in the past." Bakshi moved back to study the dark patches in her brain scan, so clear to Carrie now – like a cancerous tar staining the otherwise clear tissue. "Once upon a time only an autopsy could diagnose this condition, but our scans are such that we can now see this while the patient is alive."

Carrie felt her blood drain down to her feet. "I'm going to die?"

Bakshi looked back at her. "No! No, I'm sorry lieutenant, I did not mean to scare you. This itself will not kill you, but the effect the condition has on your emotions and physical body... could lead you down an uncertain path." Bakshi stepped toward her again. "With medication and treatment, we should be able to help you manage this, if not, in time, cure it."

"Should?"

"There are new brain therapies being unveiled every day. We will do everything we can to help you fight this."

"I... I don't understand how this happened," Carrie said, tears pricking her eyes.

Bakshi studied her. "It is related to head trauma. Have you ever been knocked unconscious or had concussion before?"

Carrie's mind turned over, and a thought occurred to her. She raised her hand and traced her fingers over the scar beside her left eye. "Logan..." she said. "He knocked me out on the Darwin." Then further memories began to flood her. "And Chet," she said. "On the Pegasus mission... and Quint.... before he took me to Meridian... he knocked me out...."

"Were these men or Alphas?" Bakshi asked.

"Alphas," Carrie said, then nodded to herself. "There was Drazen, too," she said, tears running down her cheeks now. "In Eden... he beat me bad..." Carrie realized she was crying now, as Bakshi moved to her and placed a soothing hand on her shoulder. "And Hell Town. Those women attacked me in Hell Town and my head hit the wall..." She looked at Bakshi. "Then the soldiers tried to kill us here in Command. My attacker... he killed Dr. Morgave... but I fought him off. He slammed his skull into mine..." Carrie traced her fingers over the scar at the top of her forehead. "I've done nothing but fight... I've done nothing but take blows..."

Bakshi nodded sadly. "And now you must deal with the consequences."

Carrie wiped her face. "Why wouldn't Dr. Morgave tell me this?"

"I do not know." She moved back to the screen studying the dark patches in her brain. "The medical AIs have diagnosed this from the scans. He would've known. These two patches are very clear to see, even if he had dismissed the reports."

"What about the other one?" Carrie asked. Bakshi looked at her. Carrie slid off the bed and moved to the screen and pointed to a smaller, darker patch, the size of kidney bean. "Is that one?"

"No," Bakshi said, curiously, "that is something else."

"What?" Carrie looked at her with wet cheeks.

Bakshi took a moment. "This is something I've not yet identified. It is not CTE and it is not something I've have seen in any human brain scans to date."

Carrie stared at her then looked back at the screen. "Then what is it?"

Dr. Bakshi looked at her. "When I figure it out, I'll let you know."

McKinley walked the corridor toward the medical rooms he'd left Carrie in earlier. When he arrived, he knocked on the door and looked inside, but only a nurse remained.

"Where's Second Lieutenant Welles?" he asked.

"Oh, she left a little while ago," the nurse told him.

"She did?" he asked, brow furrowing. "For more tests?"

"No. She was discharged."

"Right..." he said, wondering why she didn't contact him. "Did she mention where she was headed?"

"I'm sorry, no."

McKinley gave a nod and headed back down the corridor, pulling the PDP from his belt and calling her.

She didn't answer.

He hung up, feeling the muscles tighten down his back and left arm, his real arm, while the scar on his other arm, at its shoulder connection, ached deeply. He stepped into the elevator and pressed the button for the ground floor, which he suddenly realized he'd done with his right hand; his mech one.

With his mind on Welles, he hadn't thought about the movement. But as he stared at his mech hand now, balled into a fist of proxy-steel bones, he thought of nothing else.

3

Determinism

Harris followed his shadow guards toward General Berger's office. He'd been on his way to his own office, when he'd suddenly been summoned.

As he stepped inside and the doors closed behind him, he saw the general at his desk and Marchant beside him, both staring at something on the general's screen.

"What is it, sir?" Harris asked.

Berger and Marchant exchanged a look; Berger's was hard, Marchant's was uneasy.

"What?" Harris asked.

"We've got a problem," Marchant said.

"No, we've got two problems," Berger said, looking at Harris. "Welles may not be able to help with the Zeta, and our Alpha-Mech is unstable."

"What are you talking about?" Harris's brow furrowed.

Marchant turned Berger's screen around to show Harris. "Welles has brain damage. Her new doctor is strongly advising against any further mind-meld activity with you and the Zeta."

"What?" Harris stepped forward, looking at the screen. "What is this?'

"She has CTE, Harris," Marchant told him, "from years of getting the shit kicked out of her by Alphas."

"CTE?"

"You know, football players, box—"

"I know what it is," Harris said. "How long has she had this?"

Marchant and Berger shared a look between them, before Berger turned back to Harris.

"They say it takes a while for symptoms to develop, but due to the regular scanning and tests Morgave did, he picked up the beginnings of this a couple of years ago. We knew she'd taken some blows to the head over time, so it wasn't exactly unexpected. We decided at the time to monitor it and not tell her."

"Or me, it would seem," Harris said.

"Her brain was showing trauma, but she hadn't been displaying any outward symptoms that we knew of," Berger said. "Though, looking back, the CTE may have played a part in her killing Sharley. She showed no restraint, no off-switch, a clear lack of judgment, no remorse. They're some of the symptoms. Then, of course, she killed that woman in Hell Town, badly injured the other two. No restraint, no remorse."

"It was self-defense," Harris said. "These people tried to kill her."

"They did, and Welles could've left them simply injured, but she did not hesitate to kill them."

"Just like the UNF trained her," Harris countered.

"Harris," Marchant said, "let's focus on the problem at hand. Dr. Bakshi tells us that if her brain is put through more trauma or stress, like the mind-melding, it could potentially cause a catastrophic brain injury."

"But she's been doing it fine so far," Harris said.

"She has, but the CTE has gotten worse. Then today happened, her collapse at the ZAEP meeting. Her condition is catching up with her."

"Which leads us to the second problem," Berger said. "Our Alpha-Mech."

"What about him?" Harris asked.

"He brought this recent collapse on," Berger said. "We receive constant data reports from the Fortress AI. There was an incident last night. McKinley, our Alpha-Mech, threw her into a wall."

Harris stared at them, trying to hide his shock. "W-what? In training, right?"

"No, he was having a nightmare," Berger said. "She tried to wake him and he threw her across the room. She hit her head, hard, and it's what no doubt caused her collapse this morning."

Harris stared at them unsure what to say, his breathing shallow with distress.

"This is a *real* fuckin' problem," Berger told him.

"It was an accident," Harris blurted. "You said it yourself, he was having a nightmare."

"Our Alpha-Mech threw his wife across the room in his sleep, Harris," Berger said leaning forward. "We're lucky he used his Alpha arm and not his Mech arm. She may be Alpha, but he has proxy-steel bones for god's sake. He could've *easily* killed her."

"So, what does this mean?" Harris asked, darting his eyes between the two of them, feeling the Alpha muscles tighten over his body.

Berger sat back in his seat. "We have to separate them."

"What?"

"Why do you think we had them sign those Alpha contracts?" Berger asked him. "For this exact reason, Harris. We need our Alpha soldiers, but they *cannot* pose a threat to the rest of our population."

"This was one incident. An *accident*. I know McKinley and he would *never* intentionally hurt her. He's put his own life on the line for hers countless times before."

"Exactly, Harris, this was an accident. What happens next time an accident like this happens? What if it's one of the kids? What happens if he just snaps? We created him to kill, and that's what he's capable of."

Harris shook his head. "No, no, no. You created him to kill Zetas."

"He signed a contract. The clauses were very clear."

"You can't separate them. This won't happen again, I know it."

"And if it does?" Berger said, heatedly. "One more blow to the head and she could be killed, Harris!" Berger stood. "You're the one who made her so goddamn important to the Zeta. We need her and now Dr. Bakshi is strongly recommending we don't use her!"

"We have to," Harris said weakly. "She's essential."

"Bakshi says it is a grave risk if we continue to place her brain under strain like we have. Connecting with you and the Zeta puts it under strain."

"We're going to give her the best medical attention," Marchant intervened. "We're going to do everything we can to try and reverse what's happened, but... we can't guarantee it'll work, Harris. She's had several bad concussions over the years and there're just some things we can't undo.

Replacing an arm or some burned flesh is one thing. Fixing a damaged brain is another *very delicate* thing entirely."

Harris moved and slumped down into one of the guest chairs. "This cannot be happening…" he said. "We need them both. We need her to help with the Zeta. We need him to lead the Alphas…" He shook his head. "Just when we make it through all that shit, now this…" He lowered his head into his hands.

"We're going to do what we can for her," Marchant repeated gently. "*And* him. Unfortunately, the best way forward right now is to separate them. To be sure."

Harris looked up at him. "You know they're joined at the hip, right? They're a package deal. They need each other."

"We're doing this for both their sakes, Harris," Berger said. "We're doing this to preserve them both and keep them both in play. Right now, our main priority is dealing with Welles's brain injury, so we can get her connecting with you and the Zeta again."

"And McKinley?" Harris asked.

"He's to move into Command for a while. Away from her, away from the kids."

"He would *never* hurt those kids," Harris said adamantly.

"Not intentionally, no. But I can't turn a blind eye to this," Berger said. "They're our goddamn First Gens, Harris. This is the *exact* reason we had them sign those contracts. Not just for the safety of the human population, but for the optics."

Harris couldn't help screw his face up at the general's comment. "The optics?!"

"Yeah, the optics," Berger said firmly. "You think civilians will support our Alpha soldiers if they're as terrified of them as they are of the Zetas? Right now people think McKinley is a goddamn hero after what he did in the Cleansing. If they find out he's throwing his wife around behind closed doors—"

"It was an accident!" Harris cut him off.

"An accident that no-one will ever find out about, nor will we *ever* allow to be repeated!" Berger fired back.

Harris shook his head. "This'll kill him, you know. He never asked to be an Alpha-Mech. Hell, he never asked to be an Alpha. Both were forced upon him, and now you're going to force him away from his wife and kids like he's a criminal?"

"For the time being. We want to undertake further analysis of him. See what these dreams are about." Berger said, staring at Harris in a way that made him feel uncomfortable. "We can't have an Alpha-Mech with PTSD leading our soldiers."

Harris sat back in his chair, exhaling.

"And his kill switch will remain," Berger said with finality.

Harris stared at him. "You promised to remove it."

"That was before he damaged our asset." Berger looked to Marchant. "Send some guards to bring him in."

"No," Harris said firmly, standing up, "I'll do it. I'll go. You will *not* treat him like a monster. We need him to lead the Alpha units. This is his destiny, I feel it. He's been an Alpha longer than anyone. He's the only Alpha-Mech you currently have. He is the father of the JEMs. He is *very* much a part of this. We *need* him. *I* need him. And I trust him with my life."

"Alright," Marchant said, speaking for Berger. "You bring him in."

Harris nodded, then looked back at Berger. "Don't forget what he did when that uprising tried to wipe us all out, including you, general."

"I know what he did," Berger said. "For his kids, for Gold, for those at Command. I know. And I know that I am sitting here today because Welles warned Marchant that something was going down and my life was at risk. That's why I'm doing this, Harris. We need her for the Zeta, yes, and we need her to protect her kids, yes. But she saved my life once, and I am now returning the favor. Until McKinley is stable, he cannot be alone with them." The general softened his face as he stared at Harris. "This isn't about destroying either of them, Harris. This is about protecting both of our assets so they can help us save everyone when the time comes. See it done."

Carrie sat on a large, flat, man-made rock on the beach, staring out at the ocean. Well, she wasn't really staring at the ocean, she was staring at nothing really. She was staring at the blank haze that was her life right now. All this time she'd been moving toward this one event, the big war, thinking that she was to be a central part of it, and now with this news, she had no idea if she'd even be around to see the end.

She thought of her kids, wondered what would become of them if she wasn't. Or, at the least, if she wasn't mentally able to be there for them. That thought cut her the most. She'd brought them into this world and now there was a chance that she would abandon them in their time of need, that they may have to face the big war on their own without her guidance.

Was she to die young like her own mother did? Were Carrie's kids destined to be motherless like she herself had been?

That turned her mind to McKinley. The thought of telling him this news terrified her. She knew he was going to blame himself, despite the proof stacked against that assumption. Proof that went all the way back to the Darwin mission. She recalled walking down that darkened corridor on the station, following Chet and the sound of Harris's voice. She recalled the movement beside her and the almighty crack at the side of her head, where Logan had hit her. The next thing she remembered was being dragged along the floor by her ankle; the blood running into her eyes…

Then there was the incident in the Hell Town dungeon's control room. The elation of finally getting her signal out, mixed with the vision of Logan's gun to Doc's head. Until then, she hadn't been sure whether Doc was alive or dead, but there he stood before her, pale and sweating as he underwent the transformation to Jumbo. And she knew she had no choice other than to let Chet take her down. Anything to save Doc. And Chet did, he'd knocked her out and she'd woken again in her small prison cell…

Then she was on Mars, free of the UNF, and looking into the secret compartment of Quint's vehicle, who'd agreed to take her to Sharley. She'd looked around at Quint, but he'd hit her hard and she'd awoken in a box, on a spaceship on the way to Meridian…

Then she was in her Centralis apartment, fighting hard against Chet, while Doc fought Logan, both trying to stop Sharley's Jumbos from taking the twins. She recalled, vaguely, Chet pinning her neck against the wall and punching her face, then dragging her away and twisting her neck as though to break it…

Then she was on Eden, trapped in her villa with Drazen, trying to protect Brody from him. Though she'd been faster than Drazen, he'd been much, much stronger. She recalled spitting out her back teeth, seeing them rolling along the floor, and her vision swimming, thinking she was going to die…

Then there was the invasion. She recalled being in Australia and running out of the tunnel exit with McKinley, having reluctantly left her father behind to die. She remembered the explosion tossing them into the air…

Then there was the fight with Sharley at the JEM facility. He'd swung her around into the glass wall and it had cracked. She recalled seeing 499 pairs of eyes staring up at them. He'd slammed her into the wall again and she'd felt the sting of her skull impacting against the surface…

Then there were the three women who'd cornered her in the Hell Town showers. She remembered Jules grabbing her from behind and Carrie crashing her skull back into the woman's face, and they both stumbled in pain before the weighty woman had rammed her back into the wall, cutting the back of her head open…

And then there was the man who had come to kill her at Command. The man who had killed Dr. Morgave. She recalled her attacker slamming his skull into hers, recalled the blood pouring down her forehead… and she'd had headaches ever since.

Headaches that wouldn't quit.

She emerged from her storm of violent memories and stared at the calm ocean, her face wet with tears. Of all the battles she'd seen over the years, was she really surprised she'd ended up like this? She couldn't have expected to escape all that unscathed. There were always wounds, there were always casualties. Despite being Alpha strong, she was still quite human.

But now that the reality was upon her, she hadn't expected it to hurt so much. She needed her mind now more than ever, to connect with the Zeta and gather important intel.

Facing the awful truth, that she might lose her one weapon to aid in this war, to aid her kids, was utterly devastating.

How would she recover from this?

Would she recover? Or was this the beginning of the end?

Harris entered the Fortress and McKinley closed the door behind him.

"When did you last see her?" Harris asked. As soon as McKinley had opened the door he'd asked Harris if he'd seen Welles. Harris, surprised, had shaken his head and told him that he was hoping to find her there.

"I left her with the doctor," McKinley said. "Haven't seen her since. Is she okay?"

Harris looked at him and exhaled heavily. "No. She's not."

McKinley stared back at him, and Harris saw his skin pale a little and guilt fill his eyes. "Wh—what's wrong?"

"Hey, Uncle Saul!" Brody said, entering the living area.

"Hey, champ," Harris smiled at his godson. "How's things?"

"Good. I'm getting my senses done soon." He looked to McKinley. "Did Mom tell you the date, yet?"

"Not yet," McKinley said, darting his eyes to Harris. "Listen, why don't you get Freya and Jesse outside for some target practice."

Brody looked back to Harris. "You wanna see our scores?"

Harris nodded. "Sure do. I'll be out in a minute."

Brody nodded, then called for Freya and Jesse, in the living room, to follow him. Harris and McKinley waited patiently while they vacated the building, then Harris looked back to McKinley. "I saw Roy and Novak out front. Sampson's off shift, then?"

"What's going on?" McKinley said, eyes piercing his.

"Sit down." Harris motioned to the kitchen table.

"What's going on?" McKinley asked again, not moving.

"Sit. *Down*," Harris pointed firmly to a chair, pulling rank.

McKinley exhaled, then reluctantly did so. Harris sat opposite him.

"We have to make some changes," Harris said calmly. "You're not going to like them, but they're necessary. They are necessary for us to move forward, cohesively, to strengthen our defense against the future war."

"What changes?" McKinley asked, eyes still sharp.

"I need you to move into Command with me."

McKinley's hard shell faltered a little. "Why?"

Harris sighed, breathing out calmly, measuredly. "I heard about what happened last night."

McKinley stared at him briefly, before turning his eyes down to the table.

"Relax. I know it was an accident. But it's an accident that *cannot* happen again."

Silence sat for a moment, before McKinley got his mouth to move. "D— did she…tell you?"

"No," Harris said.

"Archie?"

"No," Harris said firmly. "She passed out in front of everyone, McKinley. The new doctor assigned to the Alphas did a thorough check of her. She's… she's not well."

"What do you mean?" McKinley's eyes looked up at his again.

Harris exhaled uncomfortably. "This isn't my news to tell," he said, then paused as his Alpha ears heard footsteps approaching the front door. McKinley's did, too.

"That's her," the major said, standing.

"Sit down," Harris told him. McKinley looked back at him, brow furrowed. "Sit. *Down*," Harris repeated, pointing to his chair.

"What do you think I'm going to do?" McKinley asked accusingly.

"I think you're going to sit the fuck down," Harris said plainly.

McKinley obeyed, though it was clear he wasn't happy about it.

"Relax," Harris said again. "If I thought what happened last night was intentional, you'd be on the fucking floor right now. You're not, because I know you. So, relax."

The door opened and Welles walked in, but she paused upon seeing Harris there. Her eyes darted to McKinley's.

"Hi?" she said questioningly to Harris.

Harris's Alpha eyes could see the red in hers from across the room. She'd been crying. And he didn't blame her, the news she received.

"What's going on?" she asked, stepping closer.

"Everything," Harris said, then pointed at another chair. "Sit down."

"Where're the kids?"

"Outside. Sit down, we don't have long."

Welles moved to take a seat at the head of the table, sitting between Harris and McKinley. McKinley stared at her, eyes trying to read what she hadn't told him yet. Harris saw a purple, gnarly bruise showing through the top of her shirt. Welles noticed and pulled the neck of her shirt together to cover it, and McKinley looked down at the table again in guilt. Or maybe self-loathing.

"I know what happened," Harris said bluntly. "So does General Berger, so does Lieutenant General Marchant. Your AI is forced to report everything to them. So, let's cut the bullshit—"

"It was an accident," Welles blurted.

"I know, Welles," Harris said. "I also know what Dr. Bakshi found. Tell McKinley."

"Tell me what?" McKinley said, eyes fixed on Welles. "What is it?"

Welles exhaled defeatedly. "It wasn't you. It was years of fighting that did this. It's not something you—"

"What?" McKinley demanded. "Someone tell me what the *fuck* is going on!"

Harris fixed him with a firm stare and McKinley eased off.

"What?" McKinley asked more calmly.

A tear rolled down Welles's cheek and she quickly brushed it away. "I have brain damage. It's a condition called CTE. It's from head trauma. My *repeated* head trauma."

McKinley stared at her.

Harris leaned forward on the table. "Berger and Marchant have promised that she will get the best of care, that we're going to try every experimental treatment out there to fight this, to turn it around."

McKinley looked down at the table, his face turning pale again.

"This wasn't you, McKinley," Harris said softly. "What happened last night didn't help things, but it was years of head trauma that did this. Welles may be an Alpha, but she's not invincible. None of us are."

McKinley kept staring at the table. Welles wiped her face.

"So, we've got a problem we need to fix," Harris said calmly. "We gotta try and heal Welles," he said, giving her a sympathetic smile, then he turned his eyes to McKinley. "And we've got to try and heal *you*."

McKinley looked up at him.

"I need you to lead the Alpha units, McKinley, but I can't have you in charge if you're suffering PTSD. We need to heal you."

McKinley sat back in his chair. Harris could tell he was uncomfortable with the spotlight on him.

"It's just stupid dreams," McKinley said. "They'll go with time."

"Or they'll just get worse," Harris said, studying him. "Besides, you know as well as I do now that dreams aren't stupid. They mean something."

McKinley looked back at him. "This isn't those kind of dreams. I don't have that remember? My DNA isn't Zeta enough."

"Maybe not, but I have learned that you don't fuck with dreams, McKinley. They're messages. Messages in bottles floating on the sea of our subconscious."

The silence sat again for a moment.

"So," Harris exhaled again, "you will come and stay at Command for a while with me. We'll work on this PTSD, and we'll work on getting you more in tune with your Alpha-Mech capabilities, while Welles stays here and heals."

"Why can't he stay here with me?" Welles asked.

Harris looked at her. "Because Command can't have another accident like this occur. You are both assets to them and they are protecting both of their assets."

"We are humans first, assets second," Welles said.

"Not to the UNF, you're not," Harris said bluntly. "And quite frankly, I can see their point of view. I need both of you when that war comes."

Welles stared at him. "And if we refuse?"'

"You can't," Harris said. "Do you remember the contract you signed when Jesse was born? If you can't, then I suggest you reread it. It's all in there."

They both stared at him now.

"I tried to but Gold said Andrea couldn't find them on the system anymore."

Harris stared at him a moment. "Well, those contracts had clauses about Alpha soldiers committing violent acts, accidental or otherwise, against their partners, children, or other civilians."

McKinley exhaled and lowered his head into his hand. Welles looked at him and another tear rolled down her cheek.

"I'm sorry to tell you this, McKinley," Harris said softly, "but they've also decided not to remove your kill switch."

Welles looked back at Harris angrily. "Berger promised!"

Harris held his hand up to stop her. "Yes, he did, but then last night happened and he has been forced to reassess things."

"That asshole! We saved his life!"

"Welles!" Harris cut her off. "Believe it or not, he's doing this for *you*. He's doing this to protect you. Where once he couldn't care less about you, he now realizes your worth. You are an asset and he's putting your health above all else."

"Putting my health above all else?" she asked. "What about *my* kill switch? Those nanobots are still inside me."

"I'll speak to him about getting that date to remove yours."

She stared at him, her mind spinning over it all. "What the hell do we tell the kids?"

"You tell them that McKinley's helping Uncle Saul at Command. It's that simple." He looked at McKinley. "This was a one-off incident that no-one needs to know about. Not your kids, not the team, no-one... This doesn't need to be a bad thing, alright? We can get through this. We're *going* to make it through this. This is just another bump on the *very* long road to this goddamn war."

"What does this mean for us connecting to the Zeta?" Welles asked. "We need to get back on that."

"We can't," Harris told her. "At least, *you* can't. Not for a while. Dr. Bakshi strongly recommends you cease. I'll have to try alone."

"This is going to set us back," Welles said. "We spent time establishing me as the female leader of the human race."

Harris nodded. "It *will* set us back. But these are the cards we've been dealt, so now we play with what we have."

He stared at the two for a moment, then stood. "Say your goodbyes. I'll be outside with the kids."

Carrie watched Harris leave, then turned to McKinley, who still had his head in his hands. She reached out and slid her hand over his thigh. He looked up at her.

"Why didn't you tell me?" he asked. "Where did you go before?"

"I needed time to think. To process it... I still don't know how I feel about this."

"What does this mean?" He sat upright and turned to her. "What's going to happen to you? How serious is it?"

Her eyes stung with tears again. "About as serious as it gets." Then she shrugged. "If last night hadn't happened, I would've just continued on until the next knock, or until the symptoms started showing."

"What are the symptoms?"

She shrugged again. "They can vary. Hell, I might've already been showing some but not realized it at the time… I thought everything I'd been through had just hardened me, but maybe it was more than that." She looked at McKinley and smiled sadly. "Killing has become easier for me… Easier to walk away from afterward."

"Killing's never easy," McKinley said quietly. "You always carry that with you. Even for the ones you hated."

Another tear rolled down her cheek. "That's why you have PTSD and why I don't. I have CTE instead and it's stopping me from feeling any sympathy for my enemies."

McKinley's real eye glistened as he stared back at her. "What does this mean for us?" His voice was barely a whisper.

"Nothing!" She shook her head. "It just means you go to Command for a while and help Harris prepare for war, and I… I sit around and hope they let me back into the ring."

"This wasn't supposed to happen," he said quietly, looking down at his boots.

"No. But it has."

He looked back up at her. "I was still asleep. I was dreaming… I dreamed a Zeta, a Priestess, was right in front of me. And then you were there, but… I thought you were a Zeta."

Carrie smiled sadly and nodded, as she ran her hand over her closely-cropped hair. "I probably look like one with this hairdo."

McKinley didn't smile back. "It's not funny. They're right to be alarmed. I could've killed you. If I hadn't been confused, if I hadn't held back…"

Carrie moved to wrap her arms around him. "Let's not think about that," she whispered.

"How can I not?" he asked. "I haven't fought to keep you safe all these years, only to lose you by my own fucking hands."

"You won't," she said. "We're in this together until the end, remember? The *real* end, the war. We'll make it through this. I promise."

He took her in his arms and hugged her tight. She hugged him back as tight as she could, as though forcing herself to believe the words she'd just spoken.

She suddenly remembered the dream she'd once had, of the end, of them all standing on that watchtower; the dream that had confirmed Jesse's existence long before he was ever conceived. Would she ever dream that again? She remembered Harris once saying that fates can change. That for every action there was a reaction, which meant that fates could spiral in different directions.

She wanted to believe the words she'd spoken, she really did, but now she questioned whether she would actually make it to the end, or whether perhaps she would become a ghost, like Doc, living inside Harris's mind.

Harris watched as Brody lined up his shot on the digital target screen, which had been adjusted to appear well back. He folded his arms and waited while Brody took aim and fired his digital weapon. When the results came up, Harris applauded. Brody had scored a bull's-eye.

"That's some great shooting, champ!"

Brody smiled, pleased with himself, and in that moment he was Doc. It made Harris's heart hurt a little to see it. He walked over and hugged his godson.

"I think in time you're going to beat the records of your folks," he told him, ruffling his hair. "And that's saying something."

"I can't wait to wear the Space Duty uniform!" Freya said.

"You still want to be a pilot?" Harris asked her.

She nodded enthusiastically. "I'm going to be the best there is. Better than Uncle Hunter!"

Harris grinned. "Good for you." He turned to Jesse, standing there tossing up a football. "And what about you, kid?"

Jesse shrugged. "I'm going to win the UNFer Bowl."

"He likes to play," Brody told him.

"And I'm good, too," Jesse said.

Freya laughed. "Just 'cause you like to ram people doesn't mean you're any good."

Harris smiled. "You got a little Alpha energy burning inside you, huh?"

Jesse roared and ran at Brody, tackling him to the ground and the two started laughing and wrestling. Freya laughed, too, then launched herself on top of the pile.

Harris saw movement up in the Fortress' floor to ceiling window. Welles stood there. She caught Harris's eye and motioned him back up to the house.

"Alright," he said, grabbing Freya and pulling her off the pile. "Let's get back up to the house. Your father's coming to help me at Command for a while, so you better say goodbye."

Carrie stood back and watched as the children hugged McKinley goodbye, though she noticed his mind was distant. Before he left, he shot her one last tormented look, then hiked his bag over his shoulder and walked out the door.

"I'll be in touch soon," Harris said, then hesitated before adding: "Maybe... maybe try not to dream for a while... give your head a break."

"You know that's not something I have control of," she told him.

Harris thought for a moment, then shrugged. "Maybe we do. Let's try it."

He left and Carrie closed the door.

"When am I getting my senses surgery?" Brody asked her. "Did you get a date?"

Carrie squeezed her eyes shut. "I'm sorry, honey. I got sidetracked at Command today and I—"

"You said you would!"

"I know. I know. I promise I will."

"Why do you keep putting it off? It's not fair!" Brody stormed off to his room.

Freya sighed. "Would you just book it in so we don't have to listen to him anymore," she said, before following her twin up the stairs.

Carrie looked at Jesse. "And you? What's your complaint?"

Jesse looked at her. "Why can't Dad stay here? I want Dad back." When Carrie didn't answer, he stomped after his siblings.

Carrie sighed and rubbed her aching head. "Well, you're stuck with me, kid. Get used to it."

Harris stood inside McKinley's subterranean room at Command. His soldier looked around, clenching his jaw and his fists, agitated, uncomfortable.

"It's just for a while," Harris said.

McKinley nodded.

"Besides," Harris smiled, putting a positive spin on it, "it'll be nice to have a Command roomie. I was starting to get lonely here."

McKinley stared at the single bed in the room, not seeing the positives.

"So," Harris said, "if you need anything, you know where to find me." When there was no response, Harris turned to leave, but then McKinley stopped him.

"You know—" McKinley started.

Harris paused in the doorway and looked at him.

"You know, I mean, *really* know, I would never..." McKinley's voice seemed to cut out. He swallowed, took a moment, then continued. "I would never hurt her."

"I know," Harris said softly. "You forget, McKinley, I was there from the start. I was there the day she first stepped foot on the *Aurora*. I was there when you two first met. And I've been there ever since. I saw you two move from competitors, to allies, to deep friends, to lovers and beyond. I know better than anyone what you two feel for each other, and that's why I'm standing by you. I got your back. This is just temporary. We've been boxed up together many times now and we've always fought our way out, and we will do it again." He smiled reassuringly.

McKinley looked at him, his face lost, his voice soft. "And what if I'm tired of fighting?"

Harris studied him. "If you're tired, then you rest. We all need to rest sometimes."

McKinley nodded, though he did not look convinced. Harris stepped back into the room, walked up to him.

"This is just a setback," Harris said. "We falter, but we get back up because the world needs us to. Didn't you tell me something like that when you came to get me in New Orleans?" McKinley stared at him. "Whatever doesn't break us makes us stronger." Harris stepped forward, pulled him into a hug and slapped his back, then moved away. "And we will be strong motherfuckers after this."

The tension in McKinley's body seemed to ease off a little. He nodded and Harris gently slapped his real arm.

"Go get that rest you need. I'll see you in the morning."

4

Free Will

Harris waited for the call to connect.

"Dad," Ty answered, "what's up?"

"Nothing. I just wanted to say hi. That alright?"

"Yeah. What's happening at Command. I saw the ceremony. Did they apologize for treating you like a criminal?"

"Not in so many words, but I'll take what I can get."

"So, what's the plan? You're helping them now?"

"I've always been helping them, Ty, but now it's in a more... *special* capacity."

"Yeah... So, I've been chatting with Aunt Holly about that."

Harris nodded to himself. "And do you have questions for me?"

"Hell, yeah. How long will we have these Sentinels watching us? When can Sarai and I come see you?"

Harris smiled. "I'll speak to the general. See if we can make it soon."

Ty was quiet a moment. "Sarai needs you, Dad. She's just a kid. Aunt Holly's great, but she needs you. She's hardly seen you since Mom died. That's not right."

"I know," he said quietly, guiltily. "Things have been tough, Ty. Like I said, I'll speak to Command. See if I can move her here on a permanent basis."

"I want to come too."

"You do?" Harris asked, surprised.

"Yeah. I can't think of basketball now. Not when we got fucking aliens coming."

"Language, Ty. It will be a while before they come back. Enjoy the time you have."

"We have to get ready to fight 'em!" Ty said passionately.

Harris paused, an icy-cold feeling sliding down his spine. "You don't need to worry about that for a while, Ty. Alright?" he said firmly. "Enjoy your life, keep sinking those hoops. Make your old man proud, huh?"

"Just let us know when we can come. Alright?"

Harris paused again, feeling an unease swirling in his gut, but he ignored it. "Alright. I'll be in touch."

He hung up the phone, thinking about Ty and the years he'd spent away from him. Ty was an adult now, almost 26 years old. Harris had missed most of his son's childhood while out in space. More guilt smacked at him. He exhaled heavily and lay down on his bed, staring up at the ceiling. He thought of the Zeta, lying strapped down in its bed; thought of the guards escorting McKinley around Command like they did himself; thought of Welles staring down at him from the window of the Fortress; thought of her words about not being able to stop herself dreaming.

He inhaled deeply, then exhaled equally deeply. He had a responsibility now, to not invite Welles into his dreams. At least not for a while, not until they could heal her brain trauma. But how did he do that exactly? His mind turned over, tossing thoughts about. Over the past several years he'd been working to strengthen their connection with some success, so if he could do that, could he turn it the other way? Could he block her out?

There was only one way to find out. He had to sleep and try to stop his subconscious from connecting to hers in his dreams.

Carrie lay in bed staring up at the ceiling. The Fortress was quiet, the kids asleep, her Sentinels outside in the guardhouse. She looked at the empty bed beside her and a deep penetrating sense of loneliness filled her.

McKinley had been taken away from her. So, too, the CTE, possibly, would take her life.

She focused on her brain, trying to get a sense of whether it felt any different. Were there signs she had missed? She still had a headache, but it was mild in comparison to previous ones, thanks to the drugs. But still, had the CTE affected her?

Memories of her fight with Sharley flashed through her mind: being slammed into the glass wall, slamming Sharley in the glass wall, watching Sharley fall to his death. She'd felt nothing at the time. She'd wanted him dead. But was that the CTE? Or was that just the years of torment at his hands dulling any sense of empathy? She recalled truly feeling something only when she'd seen the JEMs staring up at her.

Her sons.

Her 499 sons in the exact image of Jesse.

Except they weren't Jesse. Her son had heart and warmth. The JEMs were cold and sterile. They were little killers, just as Sharley had raised them to be.

She wondered now whether the CTE had made her more like them: cold, merciless.

She cast her mind back to the fight with the women sent by Cavelera to kill her in the showers of Hell Town. She'd felt no empathy for them either. She would've killed them all, given the chance. It was either them or her. What would've happened if Harbourg hadn't come along with those guards?

Tears rolled down her cheeks, but she didn't wipe them away. They weren't tears for her enemies, but tears for herself, for her children.

"Miss Welles," Archie said, voice attuned to a softer tone, *"are you alright?"*

She sighed and wiped the tears.

"No," she said, "I'm not."

"Tell me what is wrong, Miss Welles. I am programmed to analyze and offer my counsel."

Carrie chuckled. "Is there anything you can't do, Archie?"

"If there is, my parameters are not yet aware of it, Miss Welles."

She chuckled again softly, staring at the ceiling with her Alpha eyes, in the dark.

"The only thing I need right now, Archie, is to fix my brain, and I think that's outside your parameters."

"It is, Miss Welles," Archie said. "But I can offer you guidance to ensure you are doing what is best for your brain. My first suggestion, is that you get some sleep, because more than anything, that is what your brain needs in order to heal, to repair."

Carrie's mind turned over. "What if I dream, Archie? Harris doesn't want me to dream."

"I'm afraid I have no control over that, Miss Welles. May I suggest that you simply tell yourself, your subconscious, not to dream. If you implant the thought deeply before you fall asleep, hopefully your subconscious will obey."

"That's just the problem, Archie." She gave a sad smile. "I think the CTE interferes with common sense. I don't think I have control over this anymore."

"Close your eyes, Miss Welles, and try."

Harris was dreaming. He knew it because he was walking along those silvery sands of the Zeta's world. Around him was a circle of darkness and shadows, which he eyed keenly, looking for movement, anything to tell him the Zeta was there. He saw nothing, but suddenly felt another presence strongly.

The hairs on his neck stood on end and he spun around to see Welles standing there.

"What the hell are you doing here?" he asked. "I told you not to dream."

"You think I can control this?" she said, defensively. "If I'm here, you brought me here."

"I went to sleep with the intention of *specifically* not dreaming you here."

"I guess that tactic didn't work, then," she said. "You thought of me as you fell asleep and now here I am."

They heard the Zeta growl in the distance and both spun in the direction of the sound.

"She's here," Harris said.

Welles looked at him. "Because I'm here."

"Welles, you heard what the doctor said. It's too dangerous."

"And so is the war coming our way."

"We have to find another way."

Welles stepped past him, staring ahead through the darkness where the Zeta's growl had come from. "This is the way." She glanced back at him. "I'm supposed to be a part of this. I know it. That's what all these goddamn years of terror and torment have been about. Me, connecting with you, and us connecting with *her.*"

"And if you receive a catastrophic brain injury well before any war comes?" Harris challenged her, eyes piercing hers.

She stared hard at him. "Well, you tell me. You're the one who dreams the future. Am I going to make it to the final war, or is it just my children?"

She looked down at her hands and saw they were old and wrinkled again, like they always were.

"Is that what this means?" She looked back up at him, her eyes shining with tears. "I'm old because my time is running out?"

Harris clenched his jaw. "I'm ending this."

And with that, he woke up.

Carrie waited for the Alpha sensory expert, Dr. Forcaster, to answer her call.

"Second Lieutenant Welles," the doctor greeted her. "How can I help you?"

"I want to book Brody in for his Alpha olfactory and aural surgeries, please."

"Okay," Dr. Forcaster said. "Do you have approval from General Berger?"

"I need approval? He's my son."

"He is your son, but as a First Gen Alpha, any such modifications will need to be approved by the UNF. It was part of your con—"

"Contract." Carrie sighed and shook her head. "These contracts are starting to haunt me."

"I don't think there'll be any problem, lieutenant," Forcaster placated her. "The UNF want their First Gens to be as efficient as possible and as Brody only has the Alpha optical sense, he is therefore behind his First Gen siblings and Colt's children. We just need to follow protocol. I'll complete the necessary request, get your signature, then submit it to the general. Once he approves we're good to go. I assume Brody actually wants the surgeries and won't resist the idea?"

"Trust me, he wants them. He's always wanted them and hates being different from the others, but ever since the invasion, he's been more adamant about getting them."

"He wants to fight." Forcaster's voice smiled over the phone. "The general will be proud. I don't think we'll have any problems pushing this through. What about yourself? Will you be getting the senses done?"

"I can't," Carrie said. "I'm sidelined with… a concussion."

"Fair enough. Leave Brody's surgery with me. I'll get back to you."

Forcaster hung up and Carrie moved over to the floor to ceiling windows of The Fortress and looked out upon the Centralis Command Space Dock. The midday ship to Mars was just taking flight, carrying the latest supplies to the colonies and, of course, for the construction of Station Atlas. Where it once left every two days, it was now a daily occurrence, no doubt a result of the fact that stage one of the Station Atlas build was near completion and stage two was about to commence.

The preparations for war were in full swing. Even her kids were preparing for it. Everyone knew their place, had their role to fulfil and they were working toward it.

Everyone, it seemed, except Carrie.

McKinley stared at his forearms, held out in front of him. He eyed the phoenix tattoo on his left, real arm, seeing the bird rising from the flames of what was once his Jumbo barcode tattoo – though it was partially covered now with the leather wrist cuff that Freya had made for him, which contained the remote for his mech arm. He moved his gaze to his cyber-mech arm, a 'gift' from the UNF after a Priestess Zeta had destroyed his right arm with its heat ray weapon.

"Right," Sidney, his physical rehabilitation coach said. With an athletic build and short gray hair, he looked more like a basketball coach than a UNF scientist. "I want you to try and bring out your laser weapon with your mind. The biological interface means the system will react to your brain waves, and we know this to be true. You've done it before involuntarily, subconsciously, induced by fear when your life was on the line. Now we need to master you controlling it at any time."

McKinley lowered his real arm and held his cyber-mech right arm out straight. He tilted his palm back, bending his wrist at a 90 degree angle to his arm.

"Just relax," Sidney said. "I want you to think of nothing but opening your wrist and bringing out the pistol barrel."

McKinley focused on his arm, pointing aimlessly at the far wall of the shooting range.

Nothing happened.

"Okay," Sidney said, "I'm going to use the remote and remind you how it will work, then I want you to repeat the movement with your mind." He took McKinley's left arm and removed the tiny e-clip pane from his leather wrist cuff and aimed it at McKinley's extended arm. Sure enough, a short, sharp noise sounded, then he heard something move inside his forearm – though he did not feel it. He angled his arm slightly to see an opening at his wrist where the barrel of the pistol protruded. "Okay," Sidney said, "that's all I need to you to try. Once we get you opening it on your own, then we focus on you shooting it. Got it?"

McKinley nodded as Sidney tapped the e-clip, the barrel retracted and the opening closed.

"Go for it," Sidney said.

McKinley held his arm out straight, concentrated, but nothing happened.

"Picture the movement," Sidney said. "Visualize the cavity opening up to reveal the barrel."

McKinley furrowed his brow in effort.

"Just relax," Sidney said.

"Stop telling me to relax," McKinley warned him.

Sidney held up his hands in a peaceful gesture. McKinley looked back at his arm, a light sheen of sweat forming on his forehead as he tried, but nothing happened.

Sidney patiently exhaled acceptance, placing his hands on his hips. "You need to get out of your own head, major," he said. "The only thing stopping your cyber-mech parts from working on request, is you."

McKinley lowered his arm and stared at him. "Yeah, well, I've had a few things on my mind of late."

Sidney nodded. "I'm going to recommend you focus on your brain rehabilitation for now. The physical stuff won't happen until you take care of the psychological stuff and unblock your mind."

"What psychological stuff?" McKinley asked accusingly, wondering how much Sidney knew.

"You're still accepting the change to your body," he said, placatingly. "You suffered immense trauma in the invasion. It will take time to accept the new mech parts of you."

McKinley relaxed a little, sighed, and placed his hands on his hips. Sidney walked up and gave him a friendly pat on his cyber-mech shoulder and handed the remote back.

"We'll get there, major," he said. "And when we do, you will be something else."

Sidney left. McKinley walked over to the shooting range controls. He tapped at the console, looking up his shooting record. He smiled sadly at the memory of how good he once was. He tapped over to another screen and saw a list of rankings. There he was, sitting at number 2 for the current serving soldier record – right behind Welles.

His smile faded as he thought about her, wondering whether the UNF would ever allow him to return home again, or whether they would keep their two precious assets apart to control the weapons they had created.

His smile vanished altogether as he thought about being a weapon, an asset. Then he thought about Welles having lost some of her empathy.

Would that eventually happen to him too, if he became the weapon they wanted him to be?

Harris smiled a "thank you" as he accepted the coffee handed to him over the counter at Coco Joe's, a short walk away from the Command compound. It was as far as he was allowed to go, with his shadows of course.

"Colonel Harris," a familiar voice said. He turned to see the reporter, Miranda Finch, her long, dark hair moving gently in the breeze. "It's good to see you," she smiled warmly. "I didn't think you'd ever come out from behind Command's walls."

Harris studied her curiously. "You've been waiting for me, haven't you?"

"Hold on," she laughed, "I'm not quite *that* desperate."

He sipped his coffee, studying her Southeast Asian features and remembering the time she'd once hit on him for the chance of a story. "I hear you've been requesting an interview with me?"

"So, my messages have been passed on. That's something, at least. I guess you've been ignoring me, then?"

"Tell me, why would I grant Universal Press an interview after the ringer you put me through, guilty without charge and all that?"

She stared at him. "I thought you said last time we met that I'd set you free? That you didn't need to hide anymore?"

He smiled. "You did set me free, but that doesn't mean it didn't hurt. It was a rough ride."

She nodded, accepting the barb. "You'll be pleased to know that I've severed ties with Universal Press. As I told you, the report they aired was not the report I filed. My editor recut it to make it more... *salacious*. I'm currently an independent, though I'm in talks to be the lead reporter for a new outlet on Mars, backed financially by Regan Lotz."

"Regan Lotz is branching into the media?" he asked. "I thought his interests lay in running for the Mars presidency and his Space Mart franchise."

She nodded. "That remains true. He has growing influence on Mars. Now Charles Mortimer has retired and Regan's taken over the All Mart franchise too, he's been quietly building his empire."

"And so he wants to branch into the media." Harris quirked an eyebrow. "Is this to help his next presidential run?"

"Maybe," she smiled.

"The Martians love President Harkowitz. He's going to be hard to beat. Lotz lost the last two runs against him. What makes him think he can do it this time?"

Finch smiled again. "Money, power, and an ally at a rising media outlet on Mars. Besides, sentiment is souring a little for Harkowitz after the invasion. People are questioning how much he knew. His numbers were down in the latest poll."

"What's in it for you?"

She shrugged. "Regan's promised to put me in the driver's seat, which means I get to control what news is released. Besides, I owe him a favor, so..."

"Why do you owe him a favor?"

Miranda smiled. "That's what friends are for, Harris. Now, I owe *you* a favor, so why don't you grant me that interview?"

"Wouldn't that interview be *me* granting *you* a favor and not the other way around?"

"You could view it that way," she said, "or you could see it as my attempt at redemption. My report put a lot of heat on you. Grant me an interview and I will ensure I control the contents of the published version. That will give you a chance to clear the air with the public and allow me a chance to apologize."

Harris stared at her, his mind ticking over. "I assume it will be an exclusive for Regan Lotz's Mars Media?"

She nodded. "Mars Media gets the exclusive. I repay a favor to him and clear the air with you."

"Why are you being so open about the background machinations of this deal?"

"Because..." Her expression was sombre and she swallowed. "I saw those ships invade, Harris. I saw the destruction... I thought I was going to die. I thought we were all going to die." Her face fell further into sadness. "I was so sorry to hear about your wife."

Harris dropped his eyes to the ground, took a moment for the sting to pass.

"We need to work together," Miranda said. "All of us. And... I believe you. I don't know why, but I do."

Harris looked up at her.

"I don't believe you're working against us, conspiring with the enemy," she continued. "I believe you want to help us. I believe you *can* help us. So, I want to do what I can to help you. And the only way I know how is to offer you what I do best: report the truth. It's why I got into this game in the first place. No secrets, no lies, just the truth. No matter how much it hurts."

Harris stared at her, lost for a moment in the sincerity of her dark eyes. He looked away and nodded. "Alright." He looked back at her. "I'll grant you an interview, but only when the time is right."

"And when will the time be right?"

One of his shadows stepped forward and motioned for Harris to start heading back to the Command compound. Finch looked around at the man, then back to Harris.

"Bodyguards?" she asked.

"Something like that," Harris said. "I'll let you know when."

Then he headed back toward Command.

Carrie stood beside Colt as they watched their children running around in the distance enjoying a break from their schooling. Brody, Freya, Jesse, Malik and Alinta were playing football, while Casim kept score on the sidelines.

"I'm sorry, Welles," she said sympathetically, pushing her long braids over her shoulder. "I'm sure Command will find a way to fix it, though. They've got the best medicine and tech here."

Carrie looked at her. "And if they can't?"

"They will. They have to."

"What am I going to do if I can't help Harris with the dream connections? Everything in my life has been leading to this. We can't stop now."

"Harris will figure it out," Colt said. "This isn't the end, Welles, we're just getting started."

"Yeah, everyone else is just getting started and I'm being told to stop."

"Since when have you stopped because someone told you to?" Colt said, resting her hands on her hips. "You're the most stubborn goddamn woman I know."

Carrie glanced at her and flashed a grin.

"You'll fight your way through the mud like you've done countless times before," Colt said.

Carrie's face fell serious again as she looked back to Colt. "If the worst happens—"

"Welles—"

"No, Colt," Carrie cut her off. "If the worst happens, promise me you'll look out for them. My kids."

Colt stared at her.

"Promise me," Carrie said.

Colt shook her head. "I ain't doing that 'cause you're gonna be fine."

Carrie rubbed the back of her neck, watching the kids again for a moment, then looked back to Colt. "What about you? How's everything going?"

"Good. Given everything that's happened, I've told them I'm ready to get back into things. Between the invasion and the uprising, I can't sit on my hands any longer. It's been long enough. It's time I pitched back in."

"Yeah?"

Colt nodded. "I've been working hard, Welles, training with Brown, studying the latest tech. I put a request through the general. He's going to put me to work in the weapons department." She shrugged. "Bombs were always my specialty." She threw a glance at Carrie, saying, "It's time I got back to it," then looked at the children, her mind caught up in a memory. "Sharley is dead now, thanks to you. Harbourg is locked up in Hell Town. The only thing left I have to fear is the Zetas. And I've learned now to face my fears." She looked back at Carrie, her dark-brown eyes Alpha fierce. "It's time I stand up and did my bit, and my strength is bombs and weaponry. So, that's what I'm going to do. Arm you guys to kill those fucks."

Carrie smiled. "Good for you." She held out her fist and Colt knocked it with her own. Carrie looked at the children, her eyes falling on Casim on the sidelines. "How's Casim doing?" she said, referring to Chet's son. "He doesn't seem as physical as the rest."

"Oh, he can be physical when he wants to. The boys fight plenty. But I think he's more about this kind of power," she said, tapping her temple. "He's a smart kid. I don't think we'll see him on the battlefield. I think we'll see him in a control room somewhere."

Carrie nodded, now watching Jesse and Malik wrestling on the ground. "And Malik?" she asked, referring to Logan's son.

"He's the physical one. Always fighting, always running around. I don't think I will be able to stop him from getting out on that battlefield."

Carrie nodded, watching Jesse and Malik still wrestling, and Brody and Freya jogging over to break them up. "And I think Jesse will be there right alongside him."

"If they're not killing each other," Colt chuckled, watching them wrestle and each refusing to give up the ball. Her smile quickly fell away as she realized what she'd said and her eyes darted to Carrie.

Carrie smiled back briefly. "Nah, they'll be friends like their mothers. Not enemies like their fathers. They may fight, but we'll make damn sure they have each other's backs on that battlefield."

Colt nodded. "Brody and Freya? How're they doing?"

"Freya's still keen on flying. That hasn't changed. Brody? I'm not sure about him yet. One day I'll think he's going to be a sharpshooter like me, the next day I see him as a leader, then next day he just wants to fight. But I know that's the Alpha in him. Doc's calmness and patience can only temper that so much. There's still a little of my fire buried deep down inside him." Carrie turned her eyes to watch Colt's youngest, Alinta, her daughter with Brown, running along with the ball under her arm. "What about Alinta?"

Colt shrugged, watching her daughter. "Don't know yet. She's half me, half Brown." She glanced at Carrie as a smile curled her mouth. "I do know one thing, though, she sure holds her own against her older brothers."

"Yeah?" Carrie smiled.

Colt nodded and the two of them turned their eyes back to watch Alinta shrug off a late tackle from Freya and make a touchdown.

McKinley stepped out of the body scanner and looked through the small room's window to Dr. Bakshi, focused on her console in the outer room. She looked up. "Results have come through. You can get dressed now."

McKinley nodded and dressed, then stepped outside the chamber. As he closed the door behind him, he noticed Harris had joined Bakshi.

"Major," Harris nodded to him.

McKinley nodded back, curious.

"Relax," Harris said, "I'm just here for moral support. That, and I'd like to see you in my office."

"For?" McKinley asked.

Harris looked at him. "Strategy. You're my Alpha leader, are you not?"

McKinley relaxed his shoulders. Harris looked at Bakshi.

"When can we expect your assessment report?"

"I hope to have something to you this afternoon," she smiled.

"Good," Harris said then turned to McKinley. "My office?"

McKinley nodded and followed Harris out the door.

Harris took a seat at his desk, while McKinley sat in the guest chair.

"Nice office," McKinley said, looking around. "You're coming up in the world."

"As are you," Harris smiled.

"I don't know about that. I'm effectively a prisoner."

"No, you're not. And neither am I. We are guests of the UNF, that's all. It's temporary. Remember that."

McKinley stared back at Harris, but didn't comment.

"So," Harris said, moving things along, "I think we need to pay another visit to Mars."

"Yeah? Is President Harkowitz still fighting with the UNF?"

"Fighting is a strong word. Let's just say that things are still a little frosty. He resents the UNF not giving him any warning about the Zetas, and he's still pissed the general locked Welles up in Hell Town without his authorization."

McKinley lowered his eyes into his lap.

"In which case," Harris said firmly, keeping his mind on track, "we need to smooth things over. We need Mars' proxy-steel, it's one of the keys to this war. The Martian ore they use to make it is the only mineral that bears any resemblance to what the Zeta ships and weapons are made from. It's our chance to even the playing field with them."

"So, why us?"

"Because we're friendly with Harkowitz. We supplied him with information when the UNF didn't. He trusts us more. Besides, I'm Head of Strategy and Mars is going to be a big fucking part of my strategy. It already is, as it forms the base from which we're building Atlas. I need him as an ally. And given we want you to lead our Alpha forces, I need him to know you, too. I need him to know that he can trust you. So, from this point on, we start paying him regular visits. We're going to break bread with the man until he feels like family."

McKinley nodded. "He's done two terms as president now. What makes you think they'll vote him in for a third?"

Harris stared at him, thinking about Finch's comments on Regan Lotz still making plays for the Mars throne, and especially her comments about sentiment beginning to turn against Harkowitz. "Because at the end of the day, the UNF rules the Space Zone, which includes Mars. If the UNF want Harkowitz gone, they'll make it happen. I know for a fact that Regan Lotz is still trying to land the presidency, and if he's prepared to bend for the UNF, they may just put him in power."

"Isn't that what we want? Someone who will do as the UNF asks?"

"Yes and no," Harris said. "I want a leader with integrity ruling Mars, not someone who will bend for the right amount of cash or benefits. Finn Harkowitz is just like his old man, Gentry. Gentry renewed the people's faith in space colonization after the failure of Inca Station. He was a leader the people trusted, and by all accounts he was a leader who had integrity. I want someone leading Mars who will challenge the status quo if it is required. I want someone who will do the right thing for his people. Lotz, I think, will do what's best for himself. So, I'm backing Harkowitz, because I believe the people will follow him. But it sounds like he might need our support. He's down in the latest polls."

McKinley nodded. "How many terms can he serve before they kick him out?"

"Mars government was established under the amendments of 2035, whereby if the leader is deemed fit and is voted in by the people, they can rule as long as the people want them there. As they say, if it ain't broke, don't fix it. Putting someone new in for the sake of changing things up, isn't always good. If anything, it slows progress down."

McKinley nodded.

"So," Harris said, "as soon as Bakshi gives clearance, you and the *Aurizun* team are giving me a ride to Mars. Got it?"

"Yes, sir."

"I want to do some deep thinking with the team, too. I want each of them to read the ZAEP reports and provide me with their input into their particular fields. Understood?"

McKinley nodded.

"Excellent," Harris said. "It'll be good to see the team again."

A smile curled the corner of McKinley's mouth. "They were looking to set up an Alpha UNFer Bowl with Morrell's and Gold's team."

"Yeah?" Harris sat back in his chair.

"I'll tell Hunter to set it up for when we return from Mars."

Harris nodded. "We'll arrange some special training with all the Alpha units together, make a time of it."

McKinley nodded and Harris smiled. "God, it feels good to be back in control of things."

"I don't feel that way," McKinley said, "but I can see why you do."

"We're all in control of our own destiny, McKinley. The UNF may have strongly encouraged you live here, but make no mistake you have free will. You've been dealt a hand of cards, but how you play those cards, well, that's on you. Take your control back. Work your ass off. Reclaim your life." Harris leaned forward over the table, his body stance reinforcing the conviction in his eyes. "This is your first test as leader of the Alpha soldiers, McKinley. Can you make the right call and fight your way out of this? Or are you going to make the wrong call and fail? The choice is yours. Make the right one."

5

Facing the Future

Harris and McKinley waited in the boardroom for Mars president Finn Harkowitz to arrive.

Harris had gathered the *Aurizun* team and set sail from Earth within 24 hours of his conversation with McKinley. Three days later they arrived at the Mars Docking Station, where Mars' senior UNF soldier, Colonel Samuel Greavy, greeted them and, while the rest of the team took separate transport and headed into Colony Elon for some time off, Greavy escorted Harris and McKinley to the Red House.

As they'd traveled to the Red House, they'd made small talk with Greavy. Harris asked him about the general sentiment among the Mars population since the invasion. The colonel pondered his answer before giving it.

"So-so," he'd said. "A lot of people aren't happy the UNF kept the aliens existence from us."

"Us?" Harris had asked. "Does that include you?"

Again Greavy took a moment to formulate his answer. "Yes. I'm not going to lie. As the lead soldier on Mars, I should've been informed about this."

Harris nodded. He understood how Greavy felt. He probably would've felt the same way in his place. Harris studied the man. Lean but muscled, short graying hair, attentive green eyes that didn't give much away. "Has there been any unrest among civilians?"

Greavy had shook his head. "No."

"How do you know they're unhappy then?"

"Have you seen the latest presidential poll? He's dropped in popularity."

"So, you're basing it just on a poll?"

"No," Greavy said looking him in the eye, a sense of impatience with Harris's questions beginning to rise. "I know Mars. I hear things. And what I hear indicates that people are not pleased."

"Do you envisage this causing any problems?" Harris asked.

Again, Greavy considered his answer. "I'm staying across things. But you don't have to worry because I have my best men guarding him."

"You think he needs guarding?" Harris arched his eyebrow.

"Doesn't every president?"

"Yes, but Mars has always been a little different. It's a lot smaller for one, and most of the population voted Harkowitz in."

"Yeah, well, times change. We're growing. The Mars colonies are no longer like small villages. They're now booming country towns, and in a matter of years I predict they'll become cities. People are arriving every day. There's a lot of work here at the moment between the mines, colony expansions, and the Atlas build. It's a boom planet. At least, it will be soon."

"Do you think it's time Harkowitz got a personal protective detail, like presidents on Earth?"

Greavy sighed. "My men have been handling it. But, yes, it's on the cards."

Harris nodded. "Just say the word, and I'll make it happen."

After they'd arrived at the Red House and had undergone the necessary checks for entry, they were introduced to the president's senior aide, Laurelai Oh, a pleasant and intelligent woman, well-dressed, her dark hair slicked back, who ushered them through to the boardroom to wait for the president.

Harkowitz came soon enough, dressed in a sharp suit as usual. As he entered they stood and the president shook their hands.

"Colonel Harris, Major McKinley," he smiled, as the wrinkles around his eyes appeared. Though Harris saw gray streaking through his dark blond hair, he still found it hard to gauge the man's age. "To what do I owe this pleasure?" His English accent was crisp and refined.

"Just a friendly house call to check how you're doing," Harris said as they all took a seat.

"A house call, you say?" Harkowitz said with a glint in his eyes. "So, this has nothing to do with our hold on the mining and manufacturing of proxy-steel?"

Harris smiled at his no-bullshit approach. "It might have something to do with that."

Harkowitz smiled back. "I see your status within the UNF has improved."

"Yes, Mr. President. It has."

"How quickly things can change." The glint in his eyes turned to burning curiosity. "I heard your team saved the general." He glanced over at McKinley. "You're being hailed as heroes."

"We did our duty," Harris said, then leaned forward and placed his elbows on the table. "But, yes, I'm now Head of Zeta Strategy, and I am here in peace. There comes a time when foolishness is put aside and the needs of the people come to the fore."

"Foolishness?"

"On the part of the UNF," Harris said in a tone of appeasement. "The UNF realizes the error of its previous ways. They should've warned you about the Zetas before they attacked us."

"Yes. They should have."

"We won't make that mistake again. Which is why I'm here. I'd like to arrange a sit down between UNF top brass and all our planetary leaders ahead of the Stage One launch of Station Atlas, and I'd like that meeting to take place here on Mars."

Harkowitz sat back in his chair. "I heard the Atlas launch event was approaching, which I thought was strange as I had not heard anything further, and given many of the attending vessels will need to refuel and recharge on Mars before the journey home… I thought there might've been *some* communication."

"Yes." Harris gave a nod. "That's another reason we are here. I know you're still angry about being left out in the cold, but I assure you, it's going to be warm and cosy moving forward."

"Because you need the proxy-steel that Mars provides." Harkowitz's eyes sparkled intensely.

"I'm not going to lie to you. It's very obvious that, yes, the UNF requires proxy-steel and Mars is the only place that produces it. The ore you've found in the ground here is unlike anything we have back on Earth. The things you do in the manufacturing process to turn that ore into proxy-steel, well, that's something we could replicate on Earth, but we'd still need the Martian ore to begin with. We need proxy-steel for our ships, our stations, our weapons, and possibly our future soldiers."

"Like Major McKinley." Harkowitz's eyes traveled over the major seated beside Harris. McKinley stared back.

"Yes. Like McKinley."

Harkowitz considered them both in silence.

"I'm here to make this right, Mr. President," Harris said. "Now, I gave you some information when you released Welles from Hell Town, but I have more to share. All world leaders, all universal leaders, will have full knowledge moving forward, and where appropriate, you will all have voting rights on our actions. However, I will be recommending that your vote is weighted more than most."

"Because of the proxy-steel." Harkowitz's gaze sharpened.

"Yes," Harris said. "And because Station Atlas will become the primary UNF station linked with Mars, while Station Pegasus is moved elsewhere. We need the planet for many things, but if all else fails, we need to prepare for it to house refugees if Earth is destroyed."

The slightly smug mask upon Harkowitz's face fell away upon Harris's words.

"There is likely going to be a war," Harris said bluntly. "How bad, we don't know yet, but we must prepare for the worst and we need everyone on board to help us. *Everyone.* Now is not the time for division."

Harkowitz's mind continued to turn over.

"Look," Harris said," I know you're pissed at the UNF for withholding information about the Zetas from you, and I don't blame you. But the UNF has kept this quiet for years. Their knowledge goes right back to shortly after Mars was first colonized by the Originals. Well before it was deemed that Mars was big enough to require its own self-governing body, and hence a president."

"That may be so, but why was it deemed necessary for the Moon president to know and not me?"

"Because the Moon president was good friends with a senior member of the UNF who shared information with his good friend that he was not supposed to. That member of the UNF is no longer serving."

"Wilton." Harkowitz nodded. "I see they're referring to the insurrection as the Centralis Uprising and the Command Cleansing, but tell me, who was undertaking the cleansing? Wilton's side or Berger's side?"

"Wilton claims to have nothing to do with the insurrection, as you call it. It was led by the previous Head of Strategy, Colonel Rovine. But to answer your question, Rovine was trying to cleanse Command of me and my team, and the general. However, my team rose up and cleansed Command of Rovine and his allies instead."

"And did your team choose the right side? Was saving the general's life the right thing to do?"

"Absolutely," Harris said confidently.

"Why?" Harkowitz's eyes narrowed attentively.

"Because the general knows that we will help him win the war against the Zetas. He needs us. We are the winning side. Rovine's side would've resulted in everyone being killed."

Harkowitz studied him and McKinley again.

"So, you're here to tell me that I can trust you and that, by extension, I should trust the UNF," Harkowitz said.

"Yes," Harris said plainly.

"And if I don't?"

"You don't trust me?" Harris quirked an eyebrow.

"I don't trust the fact that the general was hunting you down like a criminal, and now you're suddenly best friends."

"The general has seen the light. He has seen that he was mistaken."

"You saved his life and now he trusts you irrevocably?"

"Yes, to a certain extent."

"What does that mean?"

"So long as I don't betray the human race to the Zetas, he trusts me. The second I betray the human race to the Zetas, he will take me out."

"And you call that friendship?"

"It's not friendship. It's war. We are allies. We have a common goal and we need each other to achieve that goal. Just like we need *you* to achieve that goal, too."

"What's in it for Mars?"

Harris let out a small laugh. "Your lives."

"Our lives?"

"Yeah. When the Zetas hit, you're going to want our soldiers to help protect your people."

"I'm preparing a request to establish an independent Mars Colonial Force. I have units here loyal to me."

"They're not enough."

"Then perhaps I'll arm the prisoners of Hell Town to aid me in exchange for their freedom."

"What about the colonists' safety? You would set killers free, rapists and paedophiles free and risk destroying what you've built here, because you're too stubborn to accept an apology?"

"I haven't heard any apology yet."

"I'm apologizing to you now on behalf of the UNF."

"I don't need *your* apology, Colonel Harris. You've done nothing to offend me."

"I speak on behalf of the UNF," he repeated.

Harkowitz leaned across the table. "If you want our proxy-steel, then I want assurances from the general himself that the UNF will not keep anything like this from me again. Like you said, you need Mars."

"And *you* need the UNF."

"I told you, we don't need—"

"I'm not talking about soldiers now," Harris cut him off. "I'm talking about the presidency."

Harkowitz paused briefly, a mixture of confusion and curiosity splashing across his face.

"The people voted you in, Mr. President, but make no mistake that the UNF runs the Space Zone. Right now, the UNF supports your leadership, but at any time they can switch favor to another candidate."

"Such as?"

"Regan Lotz," Harris shrugged. "I hear he's planning to run again and this time he's going to have a media outlet behind him. He's been building quite the empire, amassing his fortune, and he wants your seat badly. With that media outlet behind him he can control what information is released, and he can sway the people."

Harkowitz scoffed. "He's failed the past two times to beat me, what makes you think he can now?"

"He ultimately failed because the UNF would rather you, the son of hero soldier Gentry Harkowitz, run things and not some businessman. But given the latest polls, Lotz might just win it this time around."

"Are you threatening my presidency if I don't agree?"

"No," Harris said honestly, "I'm trying to help you, because I want to see you stay in that chair."

"Why?"

Harris sat back in his seat, staring at Harkowitz, before he shrugged. "I don't know. I guess I like you."

Harkowitz purred with soft laughter. "You want to be friends?"

Harris allowed a smile to slide across his lips. "Why not? We're good friends to have." He motioned to McKinley, who allowed a smile to crack his facade.

Harkowitz studied Harris a moment, his mind turning over. "I *do* trust you, Harris. I do. I just feel my trust with the wider UNF is a little tenuous still."

Harris leaned forward again. "Well, I'm telling you that you can trust me, and by extension you can trust the UNF. I give you my word. I am the Head of Zeta Strategy, and I want to make you a big part of that strategy. I want to work with you, Mr. President. And so too does the UNF. All our lives depend on Mars and its proxy-steel. I want you to be the man in that seat with that power. Not Lotz. And when this is over, you will be the man who helped saved us all."

Silence filled the room as the two stared at each other.

"If we get the general to offer you a personal apology and the assurance you want," McKinley spoke up, "will that resolve this once and for all?"

Harkowitz studied him. "It would help. But it also depends on whether what Colonel Harris is promising, is true. Will you include me in your strategy, let me in on everything that's going on?"

"Yes. And it will start with this next Heads of State meeting ahead of the Atlas launch. Every leader in our universe will be here in the Red House, *your* house, to move forward together. You'll be the host, the star of the show, Mr. President." Harris extended his hand across the table. "I'm giving you my word."

Harkowitz looked at his proffered hand, studied the Alpha barcode tattoo on the inside of his other wrist.

"We are stronger together, Mr. President. Now's not the time to establish an independent Mars Colonial Force. You need to stay united with the UNF, with our Space Duty division. If we work together we stand a good chance at protecting people from the Zetas when they return, regardless of the planet or station where they live. And like I said, when we are victorious, you will be hailed a hero. Just like your father was. Maybe even more."

"I've spent my whole life living in his shadow..." Harkowitz said softly, his eyes glazing over as he became lost in a memory. "No matter what I did, what I achieved, it always came back to him and his legacy..." His eyes sharpened on Harris again. "I'm sick of his shadow, Harris. I want to create my own legacy."

"Help us, and you'll do that."

The silence sat again as the president's mind turned over.

"Alright," he eventually said, "we will host the Heads of State meeting and I will see that Mars complies with your requests." He leaned forward. "And I will hold you to your word, Harris, that Mars will be granted the voting powers you say. I want in. All the way." The Mars president shook Harris's hand.

"You have my word, Mr. President."

Carrie concentrated hard on what Dr. Bakshi was telling her.

"We're working on a cutting edge treatment to see if we can reverse the cell atrophy."

"Atrophy?"

Bakshi nodded. "These darkened regions represent the areas of what we call pathological atrophy. We'll target these areas to see if we can reverse what's happening. We know that the brain can regenerate, however slowly, but it *can* regenerate. The proposed treatment will hopefully speed up the reversal."

"So, I'll be able to get back to work?"

"Let's not get ahead of ourselves," Bakshi said cautiously. "Firstly, we have no guarantees that we will succeed, and even if we do, the last thing we want is for you to take another blow to the head, lieutenant."

"I need to work."

"And in time I'm sure you will. Perhaps they'll find a less physical way for you to contribute."

"But I'm an Alpha. The whole point is for me to be physical."

"That may be so, but your brain is a delicate organ, lieutenant. You cannot take it for granted."

"I don't take it for granted... I need it. More than anything."

"Then, please, heed my instructions. You can still contribute to the UNF, you may just be office bound."

Carrie shook her head. "I need to be on the front lines with my kids."

"You may want this, lieutenant, but your age and brain condition may deem otherwise. You can still help your children in immeasurable ways from a control room, you know. Perhaps even more so."

Carrie sighed and slumped into a chair. "What's this treatment and when can we start it?"

"We're still developing the exact treatment itself. When I have more concrete details, I'll share them with you. We cannot rush these things, but I assure you it's promising."

"So, what do I do until then? Just wait?"

Bakshi nodded. "Rest, lieutenant. The secret to healing, especially the mind, is to rest. You need to relax and avoid stress at all costs."

Carrie burst out laughing. Bakshi looked at her.

"We have aliens coming," Carrie said, "to destroy us."

"Yes, lieutenant, but according to what I've been reading, Colonel Harris estimates we have nearly 14 years to prepare for that. You have time to rest."

Carrie's smile fell away. "It'll take us that long to be ready. It'll take that long for my kids to be ready."

Bakshi studied her with wise eyes and held her tongue. She moved to tap at her datapane. "I'll make contact when I have more information."

Harris drove the Mars Patrol Vehicle lent to them by Greavy and made his way toward the entry of the three massive domes over Colony Elon, stacked like babushka dolls, which controlled the air purification as well as the gravitational forces of the colony. A small, pressurized tunnel system fed vehicles through one dome wall at a time until they entered the central dome where they could drive around freely, and walk around without the need for atmospheric suits. Despite the Mars colonies being built under the puri-grav domes, the civilization was built mostly below ground as a secondary measure. If the worst happened and the domes were destroyed, those beneath the ground could survive.

"Greavy's right," McKinley said studying the colony beneath the domes, "it's starting to look a little jam-packed in there."

Harris nodded. "Yeah. I was looking through a bunch of information the general made available to me, given my new position, and they've been drawing up plans for another four colonies here to tide things over."

"Business is booming."

"Mm-hmm. And they're ramping up the terraforming program, because these domes limit growth. They want to do away with them as soon as possible."

"You think Harkowitz is gonna toe the line with us?" McKinley asked.

"He'd better," Harris said, then smiled. "He'll be fine once his bruised ego recovers from being left out in the cold. As long as we make sure the sun shines on him and keeps him cozy, he'll do what's right."

"He has an ego, though."

"Yes, but so does every man. At least with Harkowitz his ego is about being a hero for the people. Lotz's ego is about being a rich man for himself."

"This talk of an independent Mars Colonial Force is concerning."

"Yeah, but it's understandable. Technically, the UNF started this push for independence. Once they established the Moon, they handed it over for the Moon presidency to run, and they did the same here."

"Yeah, but the Moon doesn't have its own military."

"No, but Mars is going to be a lot bigger than the Moon. I'd say they're almost on par now. Almost. With a large population, they'll need resources to manage that population. I don't think a colonial military force is the answer. Maybe a Martian police force in the interim, while they stay under the larger protective wing of the UNF. Our military has better things to do than break up drunken fights between miners."

McKinley smirked and they sat in silence for a moment as they joined a small queue of MaPVs and MaRz runners waiting to pass through the checkpoints.

"It's nice not to have those Command shadows around us, isn't it?" McKinley said.

Harris nodded. "Oh yeah. Every time I turn around they're there."

"I'm surprised Berger didn't send them up here with us."

"They're just symbolic, you know," Harris told him. "Those human soldiers can't take us Alphas. They're just there to remind us not to fuck with the general, or Command, and to behave with the Zetas. And for you it's Welles." They exchanged an uncomfortable glance. "None of those things are up here on Mars, so we don't need 'em. Besides, I'm sure there're eyes on us somewhere. Don't think there's not."

The silence sat a moment before McKinley broke it. "Wonder where the team are?"

Harris grunted. "We better not find 'em in the Red Dust Saloon, we gotta leave for Atlas soon."

McKinley chuckled.

"What are you laughing for?" Harris said. "They're your team now. You're the one who has to discipline them if they are."

"Damn." McKinley's amusement fell away. "I was hoping to join them."

Harris let out a throaty laugh.

Carrie wandered the subterranean corridors of Command aimlessly, grateful for her special all-access pass. She didn't know why, she just didn't want to go back to The Fortress yet. She thought if she wandered around Command long enough, an idea might form as to how she could stay involved in the war efforts.

She found herself standing outside the cell that Professor Sharley once resided in. She recalled him standing on the other side of that glass, smiling with delight at the news she was pregnant with Jesse and that McKinley was the father. They had, in the end, given Sharley exactly what he'd wanted.

Another glass wall flashed inside her mind then, the one she'd shoved Sharley through when he fell to his death in front of Jesse's clones. She felt a strange ache across her caesarean scar, and walked on. Still lost in her thoughts, her subconscious seemed to be going on some kind of trip down a bad memory lane. She saw the hospital room she'd been staying in when the twins had been stolen. The same room she'd awoken from her coma in, after they'd been returned. She remembered that it had been Evenssen's blood that had saved her. He'd transformed into an Alpha just to save her.

She headed toward the elevator, not sure where to go next. The doors opened and she saw Dr. Serquey standing inside.

"Lieutenant Welles," she greeted her. "I didn't expect to see you here."

"I had an appointment," she smiled, stepping inside.

"Were you going down?" Serquey looked at her quizzically, as she reached out to hold the doors.

Carrie realized she must've pressed down instead of up when she called the elevator. "Oh… sure, why not."

"Only my labs are there."

Carrie looked at her. "How's the Zeta doing?"

"Not as well as I'd hoped. How are you?" Serquey's eyes studied her.

"Not as well as I'd hoped," Carrie said. She thought for a moment. "Do you mind if I visit her? The Zeta?"

"Tess."

Carrie nodded. "Tess."

Serquey looked unsure as she considered the request.

"I'm part of the ZAEP," Carrie said assuredly. "I read your reports. There's no classification here. Besides, I'm the one who's been connecting with her. Or hasn't been, as the case may be. Maybe it'll help if she sees me. Like, really sees me. Awake and in the flesh."

Serquey's mind turned over. "I guess it won't hurt." She closed the elevator doors. "Tess hasn't been the same since recent events and we do need to progress the mind-melding."

Carrie smiled, realizing that Dr. Serquey hadn't been informed of her condition as yet. The elevator quickly descended to the floor below.

Carrie followed Serquey along a white corridor. There was a skeleton crew of staff here and there, all eyeing the visitor curiously. Serquey quickly stopped by her office to leave her coat and bag, pulled on her lab coat, then motioned Carrie to follow her.

Tess's new room was similar to Sharley's old room on the floor above, except perhaps a little more like a hospital room. The one difference: where Sharley had the single glass wall facing the corridor, the Zeta was essentially encased in a glass box placed in the middle of the floor.

As Carrie came into view of Tess, she saw the creature's black eyes, set within its pale-green clammy skin, were turned her way as though Tess was waiting for her. Had Carrie's mere thought of the Zeta alerted it to her presence? Or had Tess sensed her another way?

Serquey seemed to notice too, looking back and forth between the two of them.

"I was thinking about her," Carrie explained. "She must've sensed it."

Tess, in her bed, her one and a half arms strapped down, kept staring at her. Tess looked different from when Carrie had last seen her – doing her best to kill Carrie and Harris. The creature's eyes were curious and hard, but she looked less physically fierce, as though the fight had been taken out of her. In some ways, Carrie understood how she felt.

"She still not eating?" Carrie asked, eyeing the Zeta's thinner, weaker frame.

"No, but we have been doing so intravenously," Serquey said from beside her.

Carrie nodded, her eyes locked on the Zeta. "Can I go inside?"

"I'm afraid not," Serquey said. "Given her state, I do not want to unnecessarily expose her to any germs, you understand. But, if you would like to get closer, please?" She ushered Carrie around the corner of the glass box, which brought her face-on to the creature. Carrie came to a stop, noticing the Zeta had not taken her eyes off her the entire time.

Carrie looked at Serquey. "Can I have a moment alone with her?"

Serquey nodded. "I'll be just over there." She moved away and Carrie stood alone at the glass wall. She looked at the Zeta, her mind turning over. She wondered whether she could try to communicate with the creature awake. After all, in their dreams they communicated in pictures. Could she do that now with the creature? Simply think things and see if the creature picked up on it. Just picturing things wouldn't hurt her brain, would it?

Carrie closed her eyes and took a deep breath. She pictured Tess laying in her bed, took a moment, then opened her eyes again. The creature continued to stare with her black eyes; her pale-green skin shone in the light like a snake's.

Carrie closed her eyes again and took another breath.

She suddenly pictured Tess standing on the other side of the glass, hissing at her angrily.

Carrie flicked her eyes open. The creature stared at her, strapped in her bed.

"Was that my projection or yours?" she whispered.

Tess opened her mouth, tongue flicking out, trying to smell her. She hissed at her. Angry.

"It was you..." Carrie whispered.

Carrie closed her eyes again. She saw Tess standing on the other side of the glass.

"How is this possible?" she whispered.

In her mind, the Zeta opened her mouth again and gave another vicious hiss.

Carrie opened her eyes and felt the room moving. She reached out and placed a hand on the glass to steady herself until the dizziness passed.

"Lieutenant?" Serquey's voice called from behind. "Are you alright?"

"Yeah," Carrie said over her shoulder, then looked back at the Zeta. Tess remained staring at her, but this time she looked curious.

Did Tess detect her dizzy spell? Did she know Carrie's brain was damaged? What would she make of this world's queen, if she was flawed and weakened?

Carrie closed her eyes again, saw them standing nose-to-nose against the glass, and she snarled and hissed viciously back at Tess.

She opened her eyes, hand still pressed against the glass to steady herself and gave a firm look to the Zeta strapped in its bed. "Don't mistake this for weakness," Carrie whispered. "Just like I don't mistake you in that bed for weakness. We are equals."

The Zeta continued to stare at her, mouth open as it gave a long, soft hiss.

Carrie, still dizzy, turned and headed back toward the elevator then, being sure to stick close to the corridor wall for support.

"You're going?" Serquey asked.

"Yeah," Carrie called over her shoulder. "I have something to attend to."

She stepped into the elevator, waited for the doors to close, then slid down to the ground, breathing deeply and waiting for the world to stop turning.

6

Atlas

Harris smiled as he stared out the *Aurizun*'s observation deck window at the vision it beheld.

"She looks sweet as!" Hunter said.

"It sure is shiny," Tikaani nodded.

"She's gonna be big when she's finished," Brown commented.

"She needs to be," Harris said. "Station Atlas is going to be like Command, in charge of all UNF space stations. Tough, agile, and packed with state-of-the-art weaponry."

"UNF Aurizun," a man's voice sounded over their comms. "This is Lieutenant Connolly of Station Atlas. Docking coordinates have been sent to you. Welcome aboard. Over."

"Thank you, Station Atlas," Hunter responded. "It's good to be here. Over."

"Major Gold will greet you outside the quarantine sector," Connolly's voice said. "Over."

"Roger that," Hunter said. "Comms out."

Harris looked to McKinley, whose eyes continued to scan the station outside the window.

"You ready for your inspection, major?" He arched his eyebrows in question.

"Yes, I am," McKinley nodded, "because this is all we got. We don't have time to build another one."

"No, we don't."

*

A little over an hour later, Harris exited quarantine. They'd had their bodies scanned, been pricked with needles, and had all manner of swabs taken and run through machines to clear them of harboring any virus or bacteria that could affect the crew of Atlas, but soon enough the entire *Aurizun* team had been cleared for entry onto the station.

As the doors opened, Harris saw Gold standing there, three senior soldiers by his side. One was Captain Ryker of the UNF *Carcharias*, whom they knew well. The other two – one male, one female – Harris did not recognize. The man was as tall as Gold with a fit physique and short light-brown hair. The woman was Latina and wore her dark hair pulled back in a tight bun. As he drew nearer, he saw their name tags. One was Connolly, the voice he'd heard over the comms, and the other was a Lieutenant Batoya.

Gold smiled and extended his hand to Harris. He returned the gesture, taking a firm hold of Gold's hand and squeezing it tight.

"Good to see you, Major Gold," Harris said.

"And you, Colonel Harris. You know Andy Ryker," Gold hiked his thumb to the captain and Harris shook his hand, "and these are First Lieutenants Connolly and Batoya." He motioned to his accompanying soldiers. "They are my seconds on Atlas and rotate lead duties on the ops deck."

Harris shook both their hands, then turned back to Gold as the rest of the team followed suit with the introductions.

"So, are we ready for the Stage One launch?" Harris quirked an eyebrow.

"Just about," Gold said. "Wanna take a look?"

"Thought you'd never ask!"

Harris's crew proceeded to tour the station over the next three hours, impressed not only with how everything looked, but also by its functionality and adaptability. They toured the orb-like central core, which generated and supplied the station with its power, and served to maintain their gravitational stasis. They toured the station's minor flight decks and inbuilt weapons systems. They toured the soldiers' and officers' quarters, and the expansive operations deck where a crew of 15 manned various consoles. This, Gold told him, would increase to 50 once all three stages of the station were complete.

After the general tour, the *Aurizun* team broke apart to undertake more detailed examinations of their relevant areas. Brown and Steinberg left with the station's engineering lead to inspect the nitty-gritty of the station's mechanical systems. Hunter and Frazer left to further inspect the spacecraft hangar deck and flight systems. Gregson went with the head medic to inspect the med bay facilities. McKinley and Tikaani departed to examine the weaponry more closely and review the weapons planning for the next stages. Yughiarto went to the operations deck to study the comms systems, while Evenssen was tasked with further review of the station's training and general facilities for soldiers. Everyone was expected to provide Harris with a detailed report on their findings.

While the team focused on their areas of expertise, Harris focused on his. Strategy. He followed Gold to the operations deck to look at the data feed from the Deep-Space satellites – of which ten had now been released – where Yughi joined them briefly, before Gold then led Harris to an ops room, which was essentially a boardroom with multiple screens built into the walls and table. Closing the door behind them, the two were left alone.

As they took a seat at the table, Harris noted Gold moved a little stiffly.

"You taking some time to heal from the attack?" he asked.

Gold hesitated in his reply. "Either that, or I'm getting old."

"You're a lot younger than me."

"Forty-three next week."

"Is it the leg or the abdomen still giving you trouble?" Harris wasn't going to let it slide.

Gold stared at him. "Both. Mainly abdomen, though."

"Did I bring you up here too early?"

"No," Gold shook his head, "I'm fine."

"You sure? I wanted you up here leading things, but only once you'd recovered."

"I'm good," Gold said firmly. "I'm happy to be helping you in any way you need, sir."

"Gold, you can drop the 'sir'. It's just you and me in here."

"I know," he said softly.

"So," Harris sat forward, leaning his elbows on the table, "how about you show me your strategy for getting these next two stages online."

Carrie smiled down at Brody as he lay back in the hospital bed.

"You sure you're ready to do this?" she asked him. "It's your last chance to pull out."

Brody shook his head, dismissing the offer. "I wanna do this, Mom. I should've had this done a long time ago."

Carrie ran her hand over his hair and smiled. "When you wake up, I'll be here."

He nodded, then his face fell serious. "They're really coming back, aren't they? The Zetas."

She nodded. "Yeah. They are."

"Because Uncle Saul dreamed it?"

Carrie nodded. "And I did, too."

"I know you dreamed of Decima, but have you dreamed past that? Into the future?"

Carrie pulled out a chair and sat down beside the bed. "I did. Once."

"What happened?"

"We were all standing on a tower somewhere looking down at our army."

"Me too? I was there?"

She nodded. "And Freya and Jesse."

"And Dad?"

"McKinley?"

"What other dad do I have?"

Carrie felt a small tear in her heart at his words. "Well, you have two dads, Brody. You know this. Your biological father may have passed when you were a baby, but don't mistake that for him abandoning you, honey. He died saving you and Freya. He would've stayed if he could."

Brody looked down at his hands, nestled above the bedsheet that covered him. "I know… but I never knew him. I've only known this dad. James."

Carrie felt another tear in her heart. "I know. And you're right in saying that James is your father. Because he is. I know that's confusing."

Brody seemed to mull something over, hesitating before he spoke. "I'm sick of being different," he said quietly.

"Different?"

He nodded. "James is Freya and Jesse's real dad. They each have the senses. I don't have the senses and I don't have my real dad."

"Honey," Carrie said, leaning forward and grabbing his hand. "I don't have the full senses either. Only the eyes, just like you. Because I'm your *real* mother. I carried you, I grew you, I gave birth to you, caesarean or not. And you shared my womb with Freya. She is your twin. Your blood twin. And Jesse shares your mother too. He is your blood sibling. That makes you special. Don't ever feel like you're missing something. You have a family that loves you very much."

He nodded, still looking down at his bedsheet.

"I know," he said quietly.

Carrie ruffled his hair and smiled. Brody looked back at her.

"Malik and Casim don't have their real father either. And their dads are different too. Did you know that?"

Carrie's face fell a little at the mention of Colt's kids and she wondered how much Brody knew, how much Malik and Casim knew. Did Malik know that Brody's father had killed his father? Did Casim know that Jesse and Freya's father had killed his?

"At least I know who my father was, I suppose," Brody said, continuing. "They don't know who theirs are and Sabrina won't tell them."

"Well," Carrie said carefully, "that's not our business, is it? That's their family business." Again she felt a tearing of her heart. How would Brody feel if he knew Malik's father had killed Doc. It wasn't something Carrie or Colt wanted their kids to know. Their kids were friends. They didn't need to know their fathers were enemies.

"Good morning!" Dr. Forcaster said, entering the room and providing Carrie with a welcome distraction. "How's our patient today? Ready to get those olfactory and auditory senses amplified?"

Brody's face lit up. "Yeah!"

"Well, then," Forcaster said, "it's time to take you through to pre-op."

Carrie looked back at Brody and smiled again, running her hand over his hair. "I'll be here when you wake up, alright?"

Brody nodded and Dr. Forcaster and two aides wheeled him away.

Harris gave a deep-bellied laugh as Hunter and Frazer argued over who was the better pilot. The folks of Station Atlas had put on a nice feast for them, and they had washed it down with several glasses of wine and beer. Though they were on station on business, Harris had declared the evening a night of R&R.

And it was the right decision. The *Aurizun* team not only reacquainted themselves with the *Carcharias* team, making plans for their UNFer Bowl, but they also had time to mingle with the key players on the station. In particular, Lieutenants Raleigh Batoya and Dean Connolly.

Despite the laughter and tall tales, and the reminiscing about tight escapes during hard times, Harris sensed Gold was a little distanced from it all. He smiled and laughed with the rest of them, but there was something there behind his eyes that Harris couldn't quite put his finger on. He contemplated whether it was just the stress of getting the station ready for its launch, but he quickly dismissed that as the cause. His gut swirled in a way that told him it was something else. And as he subtly scrutinized Gold across the table, he suddenly saw Sibbie, Etta and his mother, Maeve, appear behind Gold. Their faces showed concern.

Harris's female ancestors stared at him, their eyes telling him there was something he needed to do. Something to do with Gold. He didn't feel it was a warning per se, but he felt it was something that needed tending to.

Harris stood and walked over to Gold, keeping his eyes on his kin standing behind him. As he neared Gold, they vanished. He tapped the station leader on the shoulder.

"Fancy a nightcap somewhere quiet?"

"Er, yeah, sure," Gold said, a little surprised.

He stood carefully and followed Harris out of the room.

Carrie stood at the floor to ceiling windows of the Fortress, staring out upon the Command Space Dock. The midday ship was taking off, its fiery tail burning orange as it thrust through the atmosphere on its way to Mars. She looked down into the enclosed yard below and saw Jesse throwing a football around.

She turned away and moved to check on Brody, who was recovering from his surgeries in his room. When she poked her head through the door, she saw Freya sitting on the floor by his bed, flipping through a reader-pane. Freya looked up and shook her head to confirm that Brody was still sleeping. Carrie smiled and left the twins alone.

"*Miss Welles,*" Archie's voice came over the speakers in the hallway. "*An invitation has arrived.*"

"Oh, yeah? To what?" she asked.

"To the Station Atlas Stage One launch."

She moved to the comms pane in her kitchen and tapped at it to reveal the invitation. It had been a long road. Nine years ago she recalled attending the unveiling of the Station Atlas design, pregnant with Jesse at the time. Finally Stage One was complete.

"Well, at least I get to take part in *something*," she said.

But as the words settled around her, she felt an ache in her head and tears sting her eyes. She'd been on this road with Harris from the start, since that first day she stepped foot on the *Aurora* for the Darwin mission. Though she'd been trained as a sharpshooter, like her father, and was used to waiting for the right moment to do her thing, she refused to believe that her only role in this was to be the mother of the First Gens. She felt it inside her: she was needed, somewhere, somehow. She just needed to figure out what it was.

She sighed and turned away from the window and began down the stairs into the basement. When she stepped inside, she stared at the wall ahead, to the secret door which had allowed her to escape the Fortress after Archie had hacked General Berger's AI, Wilfred. Memories came flashing back of Carrie traveling to Siberia, discovering the JEMs – Jesse's clones – and of course, memories of killing Sharley.

She grabbed a bundle of clothes from the dryer and began folding them, absentmindedly turning over the memories of the JEMs training, of JEM-1 killing JEM-500. Her sons, raised to be killers.

She took the folded clothes and headed back up the stairs to her room to put the clothes away. She felt a slash of pain down her chest as she put McKinley's shirts away, wondering how he was doing, knowing deep down he'd be punishing himself for what had happened.

She opened another drawer to put her own clothes away and paused when she saw the box sitting between neat stacks of shirts. She placed the clothes down and picked up the box. She opened it and stared at the UNF Medal of Honor, the Blue Nova, which had been awarded posthumously to Doc for saving the lives of the First Gens. She traced her fingers over the brass star, eyeing the faint blue shimmer it held.

She put the box away, then moved back to Brody's doorway to watch her son sleeping.

Gold poured Harris a dram of the good stuff and motioned for him to take a seat on the couch in his private, spacious quarters.

"The team are looking good," Gold said, sitting down. "McKinley seems to be doing well."

Harris nodded, sipping his drink as his mind seemed to turn over something. "He still has a way to go." The colonel's eyes sharpened on Gold's. "As do you, I'm sensing. So, tell me, what's on your mind."

Gold paused at Harris's directness. "Nothing. I told you, I'm good," he said, then sipped his drink.

"Gold, I know I'm your superior, but I'm also your friend, am I not?"

"Of course."

"So, what is it? Something's on your mind. Do you have concerns about this station? If you do, you need to tell me."

"No," Gold said reassuringly. "No, the station is a dream."

"You getting homesick? I know it must be hard with Andrea back at Command."

"We're fine," he said, picturing his wife – her bright blue eyes, her long red hair, the curve of her hips. Being away from her was a price he had to pay. "I mean, of course I miss her, but I told you I'm happy to take this post for you."

"I don't want you to take this post for me, under orders, I want you to take this post because you want this post."

Gold put his glass down on the coffee table before them. "Harris, I want this post," he said trying to reassure the colonel with his confidence. "It's all good."

"You miss the *Carcharias*?"

Gold shrugged. "I do, but I like this station gig, too. I mean, where else am I going to get digs this nice on a post, huh?" He gestured to the comfortable, spacious quarters around him, grinning at Harris.

"What is it then?" Harris asked, skipping the joviality and staring at him.

Gold felt uneasy under Harris's piercing gaze. The man could sometimes look at him like he could see right inside him. Though what he could see exactly, Gold wasn't sure. Maybe it was Harris's gift? Maybe he knew something Gold had never spoken to him about? Or maybe Harris knew Gold's own personal future?

Gold grabbed his glass and took another sip, while Harris continued to stare at him. The colonel had the ability to be terrifying. Thankfully, Gold had never seen that side, but he believed it was there underneath. After all, Gold knew what it was like to be an Alpha. He knew what that strength felt like and the confidence it gave a person.

"So," Harris said, "it's not the posting, it's not the *Carcharias*, or Earth, or your wife. Then what is it? I'm here now, Gold, and you can tell me anything. Whatever the problem is, we'll work through it together. We'll find a solution."

Gold exhaled heavily and ran his hand down his face, looking into his glass. Harris wanted something, but Gold wasn't sure what to give him. Where did he start with the things he needed to offload?

He glanced up from his glass to Harris's expectant face. Gold had to give him something.

"You can't find a solution to this," Gold said.

"What?" Harris's eyes were still fixed on his.

Gold exhaled again. He figured Harris would find out soon enough. "I've been diagnosed with a cancer precursor. The survival rate of which isn't great."

"What?" Harris's voice dropped a few octaves as he sat up a little straighter.

"Between the check-ups after the Command Cleansing and being cleared to work up here, they discovered a precursor to the big C."

Harris was a silent a moment, his mind turning over. "Okay, but if it's just a precursor, then you don't have it yet. You can't fight it off before it starts?"

"Usually, yeah, but this is an aggressive pancreatic cancer they haven't managed to cure yet."

"They might before it sets in."

Gold looked at Harris with resolute eyes. "I appreciate your positivity, but I'm needing to face the reality of this."

"How long?"

Gold shrugged. "They're monitoring it. I don't have it yet. I'm good to work now, but…"

"But?" Harris pushed.

Gold couldn't help the concern that crept over his face. "I can't guarantee I will be around when the Zetas hit."

Harris exhaled heavily and sat forward, elbows on knees. He rubbed his hand over his face.

Gold gave a quiet laugh. "Looks like being an Alpha doesn't make you invincible… I can kill a man with my bare hands, but I can't stop cancer from invading my body."

"Fuck," Harris muttered, shaking his head. "First Welles, now you."

"Welles has cancer?" Gold asked, confused. "That's why she collapsed in the ZAEP meeting?"

Harris sat back and looked at him. "No. She's been diagnosed with CTE."

"The brain condition?"

Harris nodded. It was Gold's turn to sit up a little.

"Is that going to affect connecting with the Zeta?"

"Yes. A lot." Harris's mind turned over. "Do they know how you got the cancer? If they only just picked it up, then it's not genetic, or they would've picked it up when you joined the military."

"They don't know how, yet."

"So, it's something new?"

Gold nodded and watched as Harris's mind raced furiously.

"How's the rest of the *Carcharias* team?" Harris asked.

"Fine. I think. Why?"

Harris shrugged. "I was just wondering whether it could be some kind of Zeta radiation or something. You guys battled them in the skies and took some hits from their heat rays." Harris's mind seemed to wander off again.

"As far as I'm aware the rest of the team are fine," Gold said, his own mind turning over, "but now I think about it, they wouldn't have been given the same tests I was before I took this posting. It would've been business as usual, and the usual checks don't look for cancer precursors."

"Have them tested."

"But... what do I tell them?" Gold felt a nervousness shoot through him.

"They don't know about your precursor?" Harris asked.

"No. Neither does Andrea."

Harris stared at him. "You haven't told your wife?"

"I don't have the cancer yet. Just the precursor. I don't want to worry her. Or the team. Right now I'm fine and I want to do my job and help us prepare for this incoming war."

"I appreciate that Gold, but—"

"Harris, I'm fine," he said firmly. "I want to do the job you asked me to do."

The colonel's brow furrowed. "Why do you keep saying it like that? The job I asked you do to... I want to do this for you... like you owe me something. What the fuck, Gold?"

Gold stared at him for a moment. Swallowed. This was definitely not a conversation he wanted to have with Harris right now. Telling him about the cancer precursor was one thing, but the truth about what happened in the invasion? He felt his heart rate shoot up. "I just want to do my job. You're my CO and I'm obeying orders, that's all."

"No, it's something else." Harris sat forward. "Fuck the bullshit. Out with it."

Gold stood from the couch, on edge. "What, being told I'm going to get a terminal cancer isn't enough?"

"Oh, it's enough, but if something else is eating away at you besides that cancer, then you need to spill it. I need you with a clear head up here."

"Harris, it's fine." Gold moved over to his observation window, turning his back to him.

"Gold, I don't have to tell you about my gut do I? How it's *real* good at detecting when something is wrong. And right now? It's telling me something is wrong. With *you*."

Gold kept his back to Harris, but darted a glance to him in the observation window's reflection.

"What is it, Gold?" Harris said, his voice softer.

Gold stared out into the black of space, the orange-brown orb of Mars a marble in the distance. He heard Harris move, felt him come to stand at his side.

"Purge it, Gold. Whatever it is. I'm not leaving until you do."

Gold turned to Harris and saw the man was looking somewhere beside him, as though someone else was standing there. Gold felt the hairs on his arms standing on end. He looked over his shoulder, then looked back at Harris.

"Who's there?" he asked cautiously. "Are you seeing something?"

Harris studied Gold as he contemplated his answer. "My female ancestors. The gift ran strong through them and into me. They're standing beside you. They're letting me know something is going on with you that I need to get to the bottom of."

"Right..." Gold said uneasily, looking over his shoulder again. He knew of Harris's gift, but didn't know much detail about it, other than the basics that McKinley had told him a few months before. Gold didn't know what Harris was exactly, but he knew he was *something*. He knew to believe.

Did Harris already know the truth?

Gold looked back out the window as memories flashed inside his mind. Memories of a savage firefight in the skies over North America.

"*What*, Gold?" Harris said gently.

In his mind's eye, Gold saw the *Carcharias* blow one of the Zeta ships out of the sky, saw it falling away to Earth.

"I..." Gold began, his mouth was suddenly dry, his heartbeat racing.

"What?" Harris said again gently.

Gold turned to Harris, his breathing shallow, his heart racing. "What if I killed your wife?"

Harris pulled his head back, as though Gold just slapped him. "What?"

"We were shooting Zeta ships out of the skies, Harris. We were over North America. The ships fell down to Earth... How do you know that I didn't shoot down the ship that killed your wife?"

"What the *fuck*?!" Harris stepped back from him.

"I can't stop thinking about it. It's killing me, Harris. We were trying to save the world, but..." Words suddenly failed him. They were trapped somewhere deep in his belly, couldn't get anywhere near his throat to speak.

Harris stared at him, breathing hard. His eyes fierce. Alpha hard.

Gold's own Alpha reared in response, but it didn't match the power of Harris's. Gold's guilt made it impotent.

"Why the fuck would you say that?" Harris asked him. "Why would you bring this up?"

"Because..." Gold swallowed again. "I can't stop thinking about it. I told you, it's killing me. You're my friend, Harris. You helped me get out from under Rovine, you brought me into the Alpha program, you put me *here*. I've been fighting by your side for years. And after all of that... what if *I* was responsible for your wife's death?"

The movement was so sudden, Gold's Alpha senses barely detected it. Harris grabbed his shirt in his fist and slammed him back against the observation window, his head smacking against the surface. Harris panted heavily in his face, staring at him with eyes of fire.

"Don't you *ever* say that again. You hear me!"

Gold breathed heavily too now. "But what if—"

"What if?! What if *what*, Gold?" Harris shouted. "What if you *did* shoot down the Zeta ship that crashed into that hospital? What if you did? Is that going to bring her back? Jesus fucking Christ we could all ask ourselves the what ifs! What if I told my wife to *never* to leave the house that day? But I didn't! You think the what ifs are killing you? They are goddamn *annihilating* me!"

Harris pushed him aside and walked away a few steps. Gold panted, staring at him.

"I just..." Gold began. "If I did... if it was my ship that shot it down, the one that landed on the hospital... I'm so damn sorry, Harris... I'm so goddamn sorry..."

Harris moved agitatedly, shaking his arms like he was trying to shrug off Gold's words or maybe stop himself from lashing out.

"Whatever I can do to make it up to you..."

"SHUT THE FUCK UP!" Harris yelled, still agitated and pacing. He seemed to stalk in a circle for a moment, trying to control his breathing, before heading for the door.

"Harris!" Gold called after. "Please! I just—"

Harris spun around, fixing him with cold Alpha eyes. "We don't *ever* talk about this again!"

7

Growth

Harris stood in a room where Gold was frozen in time. He was dreaming, he knew it. He was standing in Gold's quarters and the soldier was about to tell Harris he was responsible for Taya's death. But he was frozen, back turned to Harris as he stared out the observation window into the darkness, oblivious to Harris's kin who surrounded him.

"Why did he tell me that?" Harris asked his ancestors.

"Because," Etta said righteously, clasping her hands together over her plump belly, "he believes it in his soul."

"Was he? Responsible?"

"Does it matter?" Sibbie asked him, her cheeks hollow with age.

"It won't bring her back," Maeve said.

"No," Harris said quietly, "I guess it won't." He scanned the room, frozen in time. "Is she with you? I still haven't seen her."

"She will come to you when you're ready."

"I'm ready," he told them.

"Are you, son?" Maeve smiled sadly at him.

"We'll take care of her," Etta said.

"Until then you must cope alone," Sibbie said.

Harris sighed, knowing it wasn't something he could fight. He nodded at his female kin, picturing Taya standing somewhere behind them out of focus. He thought of Doc then, and suddenly he stepped forward from the shadows.

"The team is falling apart, Saul," Doc said with concern, placing his hands on his hips.

"I thought we were getting stronger," he said, remembering them standing on the Space Dock admiring their new ship *Aurizun*.

"Yes and no," Doc said, ever his sounding board, even in death. "Their loyalty is stronger than it's ever been. That fabric won't break, but it is getting worn with the strain of time. Age is something you can't fight forever."

"You've worked in the shadows for too long, Saul," Sibbie said.

Etta nodded. "You've set your burden free now. You don't have to hide or carry it alone anymore."

"So, why do you?" his mother asked.

Harris considered this. "I don't know," he shrugged. "Habit, I guess."

"If you look far, others will support you like the *Aurizun* team does," Maeve said, smiling as her eyes shone with pride and hopefulness.

"Take the strain off the team, Saul," Doc said. "Share the load and they'll be stronger for it."

"How do I do that?" he asked.

"You'll figure it out, son," Maeve said, as Sibbie and Etta nodded in agreement.

Harris looked back to where Gold stood frozen in time. He thought of Taya's death, how he nearly lost Sarai in the hospital collapse too.

What if Gold and the *Carcharias* had been responsible?

It cut him deeply to think his wife had essentially been killed by friendly fire. After all his struggles to keep Earth safe, that had been his reward.

Despite this deep heartache, he knew that was the price of war.

Everybody leaves with scars. *Everybody*.

He thought of Welles's CTE, thought of McKinley's PTSD, thought of Gold's guilt and his cancer precursor. Then he looked down at his own scarred arms: Zeta claws had left jagged downward lines on his right arm, his left arm had been singed by a heat ray and was left mottled from the medical bacteria that had eaten away his dead flesh.

None of them could turn back time. They could only move forward.

He looked back to Gold again, frozen in time. But as Harris studied him, he saw Gold's eyes were fixed on something out the window, concerned.

Something twinkled in the distance.

Something that was coming toward them.

Harris moved closer to the window, staring at it. Though he couldn't see it clearly, he knew deep down in his gut what he was looking at.

The look on Gold's frozen face confirmed it.

It was a Zeta ship.

Was it heading for Station Atlas?

He suddenly heard an alarm and looked down at Gold's glowing pocket.

Gold suddenly unfroze, oblivious to Harris's presence. He pulled the PDP from his pocket and held it to his ear.

"How many?" he asked quickly, eyes fixed on the ship. "Just one? No other readings? Just one? Is it Zeta? Identify! *Now!*"

Gold swallowed, a sheen of sweat rising on his brow.

"Are you sure it's just one…? Just one Zeta ship? No. No, stand down! *Carcharias* stand down! That's an order, Ryker!" Gold practically pressed his nose to the window. "Be ready, but don't fire unless fired upon. It's only one." Gold's brow furrowed. "I want to know why it's here."

The alarm suddenly grew louder, hurting Harris's ears.

And then he woke up.

Harris moved with his team toward the *Aurizun*'s bay, ready to depart the station and head back to Earth.

"You hungover today, sir?" McKinley asked, eyeing him.

"No. I'm fine."

"You're a little quiet."

"I'm not quiet, I'm contemplative. There's a difference," Harris said, maybe a little too bluntly.

McKinley gave him a thoughtful look, but shrugged it off. As they neared the ship Harris saw Gold standing with Ryker, Connolly and Batoya, ready to see them off. Gold looked a little self-conscious.

Harris walked right up to him.

"A word?" He motioned for Gold to leave the others. The major did so, following Harris along the platform a ways, trying to ensure they were out of Alpha hearing range.

Harris came to a stop and faced him.

"I want you to keep me informed on the station's progress, as well as on the progress of your cancer. As soon as it shows up, I want to know."

"Yes, sir," Gold nodded.

"I'll help you fight it, Gold," Harris said, "and I'll keep you in that chair as long as I can. Understand?"

Gold nodded, giving him a look that was a mix of apology and gratitude. "Thank you, sir. I—"

"What we spoke about last night will never be spoken of again. Are we clear?"

Gold stared at him.

"You don't get to carry the guilt of my wife's death, Gold. You did your duty and sometimes that duty results in collateral damage." Harris felt like he'd been sliced with a knife as he said "collateral damage" so coldly. "For every action there is a reaction and sometimes those reactions are cruel. It may have been your ship, but it may have been another. If you're not careful, that guilt will eat you up before that cancer ever does. Understand?" Harris stepped right up to his face. "My wife's life was my responsibility and mine alone. *I* will bear the weight of her death. Not you. Are we clear?"

Gold fumbled for words, eventually settling on: "Thank you."

"Good," Harris said, wanting to move on. "Now you keep your eyes and ears open out here. I need you in that chair, Gold. I need someone *calm* and *steady*, and not hot-headed to lead on my behalf."

Gold nodded, eyeing Harris curiously, sensing something behind his words, but before more words could be exchanged, Harris turned to board the ship.

Carrie smiled as McKinley walked through the door, followed by Sentinel Sampson.

"Hey," she said, moving to him and wrapping her arms around his neck. He hugged her back and ran his hand over her very short hair.

"It's getting longer."

"Little by little," she nodded, as he looked up the stairs.

"How's Brody doing?"

"Good. Brody!"

Brody, Freya and Jesse came running down the stairs.

"I heard you!" Brody grinned. "From all the way out at the gate talking to Sampson."

"Yeah?" McKinley smiled. "That's good. And the nose?"

"I hate going near the toilet or the rubbish bin. It makes me want to puke."

McKinley chuckled. "Yeah, it takes getting used to."

"How was Atlas?" Freya asked. "Mom got the invite for the launch. Why can't we go too?"

"Because," Carrie said, "I told you, it's a business thing, not a party."

"It's not certified for civilians yet, Frey," McKinley told her.

Freya pouted briefly before perking up again. "I'm top of the First Gen board for the flight simulator!"

"Yeah?" McKinley hugged her. "That's good, Frey."

"I'm first in shooting," Brody said, folding his arms.

"So," Jesse said, "I can run the fastest."

"You can't beat me or Brody yet," Freya said.

"That's because your legs are longer, but I beat all Sabrina's kids."

"Alright, cool it," Carrie said. "You're all going to be great at something, I have no doubt, but it's not a competition."

"Well," McKinley said, "a little competition never hurt anyone."

Carrie considered him. "I guess it was our forte," she said, folding her arms. "How can we expect our kids not to be equally competitive?"

"Yeah, but our competitive streak bordered on something else, though, didn't it." A smile curled the corner of his mouth.

"What?" Jesse asked, looking between them.

"Nothing," Carrie fought a smile. "Go get ready for dinner."

The kids' shoulders slumped, but they moved to the kitchen to get ready. Carrie followed McKinley into the living room, over to the windows. They glanced back to see Sampson standing at the edge of the room.

"Sorry," the Sentinel said, "Command's orders. I gotta stay close."

McKinley turned his eyes away guiltily.

"It's okay, we understand," Carrie told Sampson, then looked back at McKinley. "So, Station Atlas. Tell me all about it."

"How's the head?" he asked, mind still hung up on the previous topic.

"Fine. How's yours?"

He stared at her, glancing over her shoulder to where Sampson was, and further on to where the kids were. "Fine."

"Good. Now, I'm still part of the ZAEP," she said, "so tell me about Atlas."

He sighed with resignation. "It's good, but it's not finished. When it's finished, it'll be great."

"How great? Like, a nice place to visit, great? Or a deadly superstation that will obliterate any Zeta ships that even think about coming close to it, great."

"Hopefully the latter."

McKinley's PDP rang and he answered it.

"Dr. Bakshi?" he answered, eyes flicking to Carrie's. "Yeah, we got back earlier today. I'm just visiting my kids... Yeah, she's here, but you don't need to worry, alright?" He lowered his voice and turned away from Carrie. "I'm just visiting them, what do you think I'm going to d—" He stopped abruptly and listened for a moment. "Why? What's wrong?"

Carrie stiffened, then stepped closer. McKinley turned to look at her again.

"Is it about me or her?" He suddenly pulled the PDP away from his ear and looked at it. "She hung up on me."

"What's going on?" Carrie asked.

McKinley looked at Carrie. "I don't know. Something about test results. She wants to see us both. Now. Harris has been asked to attend too."

"Did she say who it was about?"

McKinley shook his head. "We gotta go. Tell the Sentinels. I'll go say goodbye to the kids."

Harris sat in the boardroom with Dr. Bakshi, General Berger and Lieutenant General Marchant, waiting for Welles and McKinley to arrive.

"You're not going to give me a heads-up what this is about?" Harris asked them.

"We don't know either," Marchant told him.

"I don't want to have to explain this twice," Dr. Bakshi said, as McKinley and Welles finally arrived. "Ah! Here they are."

They quickly took their seats, eyes darting around at the faces at the table.

"What's the problem?" McKinley asked.

"I'm not entirely sure it's a problem as yet," Bakshi said, "but it is certainly worth a discussion and further examination."

"What is?" the general said.

Bakshi brought up a pristine holographic brain scan on the projectors in the middle of the table. The brain seemed to hover midair, transparent in form, though it showed the organ in intricate detail.

"This is Major McKinley's brain," she said, as McKinley stiffened, uncomfortable. She tapped the tablet before her. "You will see here..." A small, darker section suddenly glowed green. "This dark section is abnormal."

"Abnormal?" McKinley said nervously.

"Well," Bakshi said, holding up her hand to placate him, "abnormal for normal human beings, however, not, it seems, for some among the *Aurizun* team."

"What do you mean?" Harris said, leaning forward, fully engaged.

She tapped at the tablet and two more brains appeared, one either side of McKinley's, hovering over the center of the table. "This is Lieutenant Welles's brain, and this is Colonel Harris's brain." She pointed to each. "You will see similar dark sections, but they are much more pronounced in the latter two."

"I've got CTE?" Harris blurted.

"No," Bakshi said, reducing the other two brain scans and leaving only Welles's. "Here and here," she tapped at the tablet and other sections of Welles's brain glowed red. "These are caused by the CTE. The green section," she said, "that is a different area." She locked eyes with Harris. "And it is one that doesn't exist in other humans."

They stared at her, stunned.

"What do you mean, it doesn't exist?" the General asked, brow furrowed in concern.

"I mean," Bakshi said, "this area has developed over time, since Lieutenant Welles first joined the UNF. Look," Bakshi brought up another clear brain scan. "This was Lieutenant Welles's brain scan when she first joined the UNF. You'll note it is clear of both the CTE and this other abnormal area. And this," she brought up a third scan, "is from a scan taken after she was rescued from the Hell Town dungeon." Harris noted a small dark patch showing in the brain, in the same area as the green section of the other brain. "And this," Bakshi brought up a fourth scan, "is from when she was brought back from Eden. This scan shows the green glowing area larger and more dense. It also shows the beginnings of her CTE."

"What does this mean?" Welles found her voice. "What is it?"

"Something that has grown at a similar rate to Colonel Harris'," Bakshi said, bringing up another two brain images. "Though his is far more pronounced. As we can see from your first scan, colonel, to your latest scan."

Harris stared at the dense green glowing section of his brain. He studied it carefully. It wasn't just a shadow, there was something underneath. Something bulbous.

"What's underneath? Is it a cancer?" He thought of Gold as he said this.

"No," Bakshi said with certainty. "This, colonel, is a new area of the brain, never seen before in humankind."

"How can that be?" he asked.

"We thought we knew every section of the human brain, of the human body, but every now and then we discover something new, something hidden within that we never knew existed."

"So, what the hell is it?" Berger asked bluntly.

"I'm still trying to work that out," Bakshi said, "but I believe we are witnessing evolution in progress. Albeit at a rapid pace." She smiled. "This appears to be a redundant part of the brain, a node that's been dormant for generations, possibly millennia. Over time it receded due to lack of use. And for some reason it's been stimulated and is coming back to life."

"But it's only in them?" Marchant asked.

Bakshi nodded. "I need to widen my study area, of course, but, yes, this dormant node has remerged in their brains and grown at a significant rate. Knowing what I know now, I can only assume it must be linked with their

Zeta DNA and the," she looked to Harris, "*gift*, they have awakened and have been nurturing."

"But what about McKinley?" Marchant asked. "You said it was in his brain, too, but his DNA showed far less of a match to the Zeta markings as the other two."

"Yes," Bakshi agreed, "he showed minimal trace of any match to the Zeta DNA, but it would seem, regardless, that this node has been awakened in him too."

"The fuck?" McKinley's words fell out of his mouth before he could consider his audience. Berger shot him a glance.

"How is that possible?" Welles asked. "I mean, I get it being in our brains," she motioned to Harris. "We've been trying to grow the connection between us and we've been working with the Zeta, so I can see that maybe this node has been stimulated. But McKinley hasn't been involved in any of that."

"No, he hasn't," Bakshi conceded. "And I do not know why this has suddenly awakened in him now."

"Maybe him listening to us talking about it all the time," Harris proffered, shrugging. "The power of suggestion and all that. Maybe it's realized itself in him."

"Possibly," Bakshi said. "Suggestive thought can be very powerful. Studies have shown that the mind can be persuaded to believe many things, which can then herald physical responses. This could be a placebo effect, but I cannot say this for sure."

"If that were true it would be present in the rest of the team," Marchant said. "Hell, it should be growing in me too."

"It can't be..." Berger said with uncertainty, "sexually transmitted or something can it? Like a virus?"

Carrie and McKinley looked at him.

"I certainly didn't give it to Welles that way," Harris said plainly.

"We can rule such theories out during our studies," Bakshi informed Berger.

"What about the heat ray?" Harris said. "Both McKinley and I got hit with one. Could it be some kind of radiation that stimulated it?"

"But I never got hit with it," Welles said. "And you and I had our growth before Decima."

Silence sat in the room for a moment.

"What part of the brain does it live in, this node?" Harris asked.

"The part that involves the deep subconscious," Dr. Bakshi said.

Harris exchanged a look with Welles.

"What if Tess awakened it in us?" Welles said, staring at the floating brains. "Triggered it somehow. Like picking up a weak signal and fine-tuning things until the exact wave was locked on."

"I don't like the sound of that," Berger said, fixing his eyes on Harris, who held his hand up to stop him continuing.

"McKinley hasn't connected with the Zeta," Harris said, "so it rules Tess out."

"No, but both of yours have grown significantly since connecting with it," Berger said.

"And with each other," Harris said. "Each one of Welles's scans aligns with the trajectory of our connection."

"Yes," Bakshi said, "and you must remember the two of you were growing this node before the Zeta came along. It's grown exponentially since you connected with her, however." Bakshi sighed. "There is much work to be done to get to the bottom of this. I will need your compliance with further tests."

McKinley hung his head back. "More tests…"

"We need to get to the bottom of this, major," Marchant said.

McKinley looked at him, becoming serious as his mind rolled over something. He looked over at Bakshi.

"Does this mean it's not PTSD?" he asked her. "My…" He paused and looked at Harris. "My dreams."

"Fuck…" Harris stared back at McKinley, feeling the shock wash over him. "Dreams."

"No," Welles said, looking between them. "No way…. They were nightmares, weren't they?"

McKinley shrugged a little nervously. "I got no idea."

"I wouldn't rule out PTSD just yet, major. You've been through quite a lot."

Harris looked back to Bakshi. "Does anyone else in the team have this node?"

Bakshi nodded. "Yes."

"I thought you said it was only them?" Berger said, motioning to Harris, Welles and McKinley.

"Apologies, when I said 'them' I meant the *Aurizun* team. We'll need to obtain updated scans, but I believe the node has begun development in some. And they align with those who have higher levels of the Zeta DNA."

Harris's mind raced to recall the results he was once told. "Yughiarto had the next highest match after Welles."

"That's correct," Bakshi said. "His last scan was taken after he returned from Australia, and in the node area I detected a dark patch developing, which indicates a thickening of the tissue and the possible beginnings of the reemergence of this node. It was still early in its development, but it has begun in him."

Harris's mind flashed over the events in Australia. He saw himself and Welles trying to connect to the Zeta ship, while Yughi assisted by leading them in a meditation to set their minds free.

Harris nodded to himself in acceptance. They must've triggered something when they underwent that exercise.

"Who else?" Marchant asked.

"Corporal Colt and Sergeant Evenssen have shown slight progression, but not to the same extent. I believe the node area has turned a darker shade, but I cannot say with any certainty until I take new scans and study them further."

"Yughiarto, Colt and Evenssen," Harris thought aloud.

Berger stood. "Bring them in for testing, but let's keep this quiet for now. Test the whole team, including the *Carcharias* team and Morrell's unit, too, under the guise of Alpha checks. Anyone who has spent time with Harris and Welles and who knows about this… *gift*. I want to see each one of their brains. If this node is growing in our soldiers, I need to know *who*, I need to know what it means, and what the hell we should do about it."

Carrie and McKinley walked along the windowless subterranean corridor of Command toward his quarters. His newly allotted guards, that Harris referred to as 'shadows', followed.

"This is it," he said, stopping by a door and swiping his pass over the control panel to open it. The door slid back and they stepped inside, while the two soldiers stopped by the door. McKinley eyed them, then moved over and sat on his bed.

"They don't even give you a room with a view?" she asked, trying to lighten the mood, as she stepped further into his featureless room.

McKinley shot her a glance. "Nope. It seems I've spent most of my life in one cell or another."

She sat down on the bed beside him, reached out and slid her hand onto his real hand. He looked down at their hands, then squeezed hers.

"So..." McKinley said, looking at his mech hand, flexing it. Carrie was still amazed by how real it looked.

"So..." she said.

McKinley sighed. "I can't believe this, you know?"

"Believe what?"

"First I gotta deal with the Jumbo virus and hiding in the shadows, then I gotta deal with the Alpha units and the UNF suddenly embracing us, then I gotta deal with being an Alpha-Mech, and now I gotta deal with possibly being like you and Harris."

She gave him a sympathetic smile and squeezed his hand. "We need to wait and see what Doctor Bakshi uncovers from her further studies. We shouldn't rule out PTSD just yet. You were having nightmares, I'm sure of it."

McKinley looked down at her hand holding his and he pulled away. The silence sat for a moment as he stared down at his feet. Carrie watched him, her mind ticking over.

"Tell me about your dream?" she said gently.

McKinley looked at her. "Which one?"

"The night you... the night I flew across the room."

McKinley glanced at the guards on the door.

"McKinley," she said, voiced lowered, "if you do have what we have, you have to start getting used to talking about your dreams. Who knows what information it could give us."

He thought for a moment then exhaled heavily. "I don't think I was dreaming the future. I think I was dreaming the past."

"So, tell me," she persisted. "Tell me what you dreamed? I remember you said something about thinking I was a Zeta."

"It started as a bright white light. It's always a bright white light... It's blinding."

"You think it's from the Zeta's heat ray?"

McKinley nodded. "Either that or maybe the light that filled the sky when the *Barbican* jumped back to earth. That happened right before the Zeta hit me. One minute Harris and I were celebrating that the *Barbican* was back to help us, the next... half my body was on fucking fire."

His body seemed to shudder involuntarily, and his real hand rubbed his mech arm.

Carrie nodded, clasping his knee. "And that's all you dream? The bright white light?"

McKinley stared off at nothing. "No," he said. "There's the light, then the pain, then when the light fades, there's a Zeta standing right there, looking at me." He turned his face to hers. "That night... I thought you were the Zeta." He ran his hand over her hair. "You looked like one when I was half asleep."

Carrie let a smile curl her mouth. "Thanks for the compliment."

He smiled back. "I didn't mean it like that."

Carrie let his words sink in. "I wonder what that means?"

McKinley studied her curiously.

"You said I looked like a Zeta?" she said. "A Priestess, I take it?"

McKinley nodded. "It was only for a split second."

"Maybe," she said, "but we need to consider things if you're having a dream like me and Harris. We need to know what it means. Is the bright white light important? Or is it you thinking I'm a Zeta?"

McKinley looked away as her words sunk in. "I don't know," he said quietly.

"Like it or not, you have to remember your dreams from this point on," she said, standing. "Whether PTSD or a node, we gotta analyze them."

He looked back at her. "I still don't understand how this can happen to me. I'm not like you two."

"You are now. Well, like, maybe elementary school level. Consider me and Harris as college students in this." She gave him a cheeky smile.

They stared at each other for a moment, before Carrie leaned down, slid her hand over his real cheek and kissed him. He kissed her back and for a moment all their problems disappeared. She pulled away.

"Let yourself dream tonight," she said. "And so will I."

Harris lay in bed and couldn't sleep for all the things crowding his mind. It had been some time since he'd felt anxiety like this. Having key information at his fingertips but not yet able to grasp it. Worse still, was the uncertainty. Just when he thought they'd made their way through the mud, having survived the Command Cleansing, now suddenly things were being thrown into disarray again.

Gold was on his mind and the confession he'd made about Taya and about his cancer precursor. Was Gold going to be fighting alongside him when the war came, or would Harris lose him before then? Did they need to be worried about the radiation effects of the Zeta weapons? Were they all at risk of cancer from exposure?

And McKinley. Harris couldn't fathom McKinley being a part of this. He'd always known McKinley would be a key player, being an Alpha-Mech, and with Harris appointing him to lead Earth's armies. But to have the dreams too? The gift? Was it even a gift? Or was this just evolution? The Zetas had created humans. Perhaps not exactly, but they fertilized Earth and humans were the result. So, if humans carried traces of the Zeta's original DNA, he shouldn't be surprised their Thought Technology, their Thought *Biology*, was suddenly being triggered to regrow given contact between the two races.

But McKinley?

Then there was Welles. She'd always been a key to this war in one way or another. Their connection had sparked the regrowth in Harris. She, unknowingly, had triggered it in him and started him on this journey. Then she gave birth to the First Gens, which ultimately led to the creation of the JEMs. Harris didn't know how yet, but he knew the JEMs would play a part in the war, too. The First Gens as well. Then Welles had been so critical to connecting with their captured Zeta. Harris may have been the vessel carrying her there, but the Zeta paid attention to her and they had worked to establish Welles as Earth's leader. But now she had CTE, and every connection she made could be her last. Harris couldn't let that happen. The First Gens needed their mother to guide them. McKinley needed Welles to be his rock. Harris could not do either of those things in her place. Not to the same extent.

But he knew Welles enough, to know that she would not be satisfied with just being mother or wife. Welles had been coming into her own playing Earth's leader, and he knew how stubborn and defiant she could be. He knew she was not going to take a back seat. Even if her life was at risk.

He sat up and threw his sheets back, placing his feet on the floor. He took the glass of water by his bed and drank, realizing how thirsty he was.

As he stared at the water, a memory suddenly surfaced of him talking with his sister Holly about their ancestors. The male aberrations, like himself, who had saved the lives of folks whose children went on to do key things in the future war. One saved a woman from drowning, and her child went on to devise the "Bellator Fortis" program that Sharley built upon, creating the Jumbo/Alpha soldiers. One saved a boy from fire, and his child went on to accidentally discover the first Zeta signal. Harris had deduced with Holly, at the time, that the link could be elemental – one was saved from water, one from fire. If this was so, then Harris was aligned with earth and air. Earth Duty and Space Duty. He was Welles's "Guardian", had needed to protect her on Earth and in space, because, like those saved by his male ancestors, Welles had given birth to those who would play key roles in the future war: the First Gens. And the JEMs. Those who would be soldiers in the future war, no doubt across both Earth Duty and Space Duty.

Did the First Gens or JEMs have the nodes too? Would they develop in time? What exactly did these nodes mean?

He looked at the clock. It was near midnight. He couldn't sit still. He couldn't wait for Dr. Bakshi to give him more answers. He had to find some of his own.

He picked up his PDP and called Yughi.

"Sir?" Yughi answered, brushing off sleep.

"Yughi," Harris said, "we're taking a trip tomorrow. Back to the Zeta ship near the Carlsbad Caverns. We're going to try to connect with it. I want you to be ready by 0600. Got it?"

"Yes, sir."

"Good." Harris hung up and dialed Hunter.

"Yeah," Hunter said, sounding half asleep.

"Hunter, it's me," he said. "We're taking a small party out to the Zeta ship near the Carlsbad Caverns tomorrow at 0600. I need you to get me a small aircraft to take us there. Understand?"

"Yes, sir," he said sounding more awake now. "What's up?"

"I'll tell you tomorrow. Just be ready."

"Alright."

Harris hung up and proceeded to call Dr. Ross, and put the archaeologist on standby too.

By now his body was surging with adrenaline, and his gut was telling him this was the right thing to do. As if in support, his female ancestors appeared, standing before him. They stared at him with strong gazes, nodding as they did.

8

Connectivity

Carrie watched as Brody stood in the yard of The Fortress, blindfolded. Her son stood quiet and still, his nostrils flaring every now and then as tried to pick up Freya and Jesse's scents on the wind.

Jesse giggled.

"Ssshhh!" Freya scolded him.

"He's testing the new ears too, Jesse," Carrie said. "Don't forget that. You need to stay silent and downwind. Stalking your prey is about learning to deceive all their senses, not just one. Change positions."

Freya and Jesse changed their positions as stealthily as their Alpha muscles enabled. They were effectively playing a game of Marco Polo. It was actually a good exercise for the three children, Carrie thought. While Brody got to know his new sense of smell and hearing capabilities, Freya and Jesse were learning how to move around without being detected. And who knew, in the war to come, just how useful these skills would be.

Their Sentinel, Novak, watched on, amused. Carrie felt a little guilty that he spent so much of his time guarding her children while his own sons grew up without him back in Slovenia. Still, that was the job, she guessed.

While the children moved around the yard carefully, her mind began to drift, imagining her grown children playing cat and mouse on a battlefield with Zeta pursuers. And soon enough, her mind turned to

McKinley and the dream he had told her about. The one where he had mistaken her for a Zeta.

Carrie had dreamed last night, and it had been one full of memories. She wondered whether McKinley or Harris had dreamed the same dream, because the memories had involved all three of them. At first, they were stalking down the corridors of the Darwin, aiming to get power back to the *Aurora*... Next, she was on the mats facing off against McKinley before the Pegasus mission, while Harris barked instructions from the sidelines... Then, not long before they went to Eden, she was sitting at the table in her old apartment with them. They had just told McKinley about Harris's gift and she'd said: *It's like we're back on Darwin, isn't it? The three of us caught up in all this, needing to stick together and do what needs to be done...* Next, she was in Australia, leaning through the window of the crumpled PV, placing her hand on Harris's cheek, telling him that she was going to get him out of there. She looked at the motionless burned body beside him and realized it was McKinley... Then suddenly she was in the *Aurora*'s pod, kneeling between Harris and McKinley while Gregson tried to shock McKinley's heart – except, Carrie, talking to Harris and distracted, forgot to let go of McKinley and the shock surged through her and into Harris before passing back through her again.

She remembered gasping in her dream, and that was when she had woken up. She'd sat up in bed panting and sweating, before a gnarly headache had set in and she'd closed her eyes again.

"Ow!" Jesse called out. Carrie was pulled from her reverie. Brody had caught his younger brother. Carrie smiled.

"Well done! Okay, you sit out now, Jesse. Let's see if Brody can catch his sister."

"No chance," Freya said, hands on hips, as Brody smiled at the challenge, and Jesse moved to stand by Carrie's side to watch.

Harris walked along the sloping, sandy pathway behind Dr. Ross, while Yughiarto and Hunter trailed them. They'd left Frazer behind to guard their small ship.

Harris wasn't sure if what he planned to do today would work, so he didn't want too many spectators standing around bored, messing with his mindfulness. He needed Yughi, of course, to help aid his connection to the ship, and Dr. Ross was an expert on the 'artefact', but Hunter was here purely for observation as an independent party. He wanted someone watching without preconceived thoughts. Besides, as the *Aurizun*'s chief pilot, Harris wanted him to witness the Zeta vessel in action if it came to that. As Harris thought about it, he was kicking himself that he hadn't invited Lieutenant Colberge to join them, given that Avilov was touting him as a Zeta ship savant.

As Harris traversed the long illuminated tunnel toward the buried Zeta ship, he felt the hairs on his arms stand on end. It had been a while since he'd been here and so much had happened since then. So much with his gift, so much with his connection to Welles, and of course his new connection to the captured Zeta.

Tess. He reminded himself that was what Dr. Serquey requested they call the creature. They had to stop dehumanizing her, or dezetafying her, as the case may be, to connect with the creature and help bring her back from the dark hole she was currently in. Harris was prepared to try anything if it meant getting the Zeta to communicate with them again.

They finally arrived at the entrance to the Zeta ship and stepped inside the round chamber that was one of the three flight decks. The chamber consisted of pearly-gray walls and little else. The only feature was the console lip that jutted out about 30 centimeters; positioned halfway up the wall, it ran the circumference of the room. Minus the two doorways, of course – the one onto the ship from outside, and the one into the corridor to the rest of the ship.

He stepped up to the lip, which although it hit his lower chest, would probably only reach the waist of the tall Priestess creatures. Yughi moved up beside him while Hunter and Ross stood back, observing.

"It's just like the one in Australia," Yughi said, looking around.

Harris nodded. "Yeah. But it's smaller than the one in Egypt."

"The one you call the mothership?" Yughi asked. He'd only ever toured the one in Western Australia before.

"Is it a mothership, though?" Hunter asked. "A mothership indicates smaller ships dock on it, and the Egypt one isn't that big, is it?"

"You're right," Ross said thoughtfully. "We should be careful with our terminology. It is likely just a larger ship in their fleet. Aside from the fact that it had six flight decks as opposed to this ship's three, the other main differential is the iconography. Whether it was simply artwork on the larger ship, or whether a Zeta, perhaps dying, captured their experiences here on Earth for others, we don't know."

"Have we found out what killed them yet?" Yughi asked.

"Not yet," Ross told them. "I'm being kept abreast of the analysis on the recent Zeta and HH-warrior bodies brought into command. They've been making comparisons with the skull fragments previously found, dated some 500-700 thousand years ago, where the DNA is not quite human. But essentially they need more bodies to study. Ideally, the bodies of the Zetas who belonged to these ships and never returned to them. We've never found the bodies. Only their ships."

Harris nodded in thought, recalling the first briefing Marchant had ever given him, McKinley, and Welles, on the Zetas, which included information on the skull fragments found. "I recall Marchant mentioning something about a coin and an idol found with the skull fragments?"

"Yes," Ross nodded, "and a gold chain. Knowing what we do now, we believe the warrior featured on the coin is indeed one of the Homo heidelbergensis warriors. The idol we're still working on, but my intuition tells me this may be a likeness to the Alma Mater. The chain, however, is still a complete mystery."

"So, you're saying these beings, the Zetas, were a lot like us if they used coins and worshiped idols?" Yughiarto said.

"Quite," Ross said. "And it's easy to deduce as we believe them to be our ancestors; advanced beings who came to Earth and fertilized it with vertebrates, then visited again over time to check on our progress. Perhaps they brought these items as gifts. Perhaps they taught the early humans how to make tools."

"But they came back and enslaved the HH," Hunter said. "Weren't they just breeding vertebrates to use for slaves? Why would they help them?"

"Slaves need tools to work for their masters," Harris said.

"If the Zetas exist," Ross said, "it's not absurd to think there are other beings out there too. Other beings they could trade with. Perhaps that is where the coins came in. Or perhaps they bartered with each other; each race of Zeta may have ruled their own part of the universe. We don't know.

There are many assumptions and little facts. The sooner we can connect with Tess, or a ship like this, we may get answers as to what happened and why these ships remain here buried."

Harris nodded, then took a deep breath in and exhaled slowly as he looked down to the console lip in front of him. He placed his hand upon the soft, gray, squishy skin-like material that matched the walls. Beneath his hand, the console glowed blue. He looked to Yughi.

"Are you ready?"

Yughi gave a nod. "Okay. Close your eyes."

Harris contemplated whether he should tell Yughi about the possible developing node in his brain before they began. Would the knowledge trigger Yughi's to grow a little bit faster? Possibly. But it could also throw Yughi off what he had to do today, tie his mind up with other thoughts, and Harris couldn't risk that. He would tell him another time.

That said, another thought occurred to him. That of Gold's cancer precursor, and how he got that cancer. Were they being exposed to radiation every time they awakened these ships?

He made a mental note to check with Ross and Colberge on that in private. Right now, though, he had to move forward. Consequences be damned.

Harris placed his other hand on the console as well, and closed his eyes.

"Breathe in..." Yughi said calmly. "Breathe out..."

For minutes they just breathed, while Hunter and Ross seemed to hold theirs.

"Picture yourself as one with the ship," Yughi finally said, his voice still calm and soothing. "Picture your hands sinking into the console... disappearing right inside. To control it, you must be one with it. Breathe in... Breathe out... You are open to receive the ship... You're calm. You are not threatening to it. You want a connection..."

After a few minutes, Harris couldn't help but take a peek at the console. It was still glowing blue, but no more than when he had started.

"Shit," he muttered.

Yughi looked at him.

"It's not working," Harris said. "Is it me?"

"We're doing everything we did last time," Yughi said.

"Maybe the ship in Australia was different somehow," Hunter suggested.

"I don't know about the ship, but I know I am," Harris said, turning to look at him. "Since Australia I've been connecting regularly with a Priestess. My own personal Thought Technology is stronger."

"You mean biology," Ross said. "The Thought Technology applies to the ship. Its biological interface is what connects to the Zetas, through their Thought *Biology*."

"Well, my Thought Biology has grown through the roof since Australia," Harris said. "So, why is it shutting me out?"

"Maybe we need other Zeta ships to awaken it first like last time?" Yughi mused.

Harris looked at him. "Or the difference is Welles."

"Quite possibly," Dr. Ross said. "Don't forget, colonel, we are dealing with a female dominant race. If it let you in last time, it may have been because of Welles."

Hunter grunted as he rested his hands on his hips. "It doesn't like your Y chromosomes, fellas. We need more Xs."

"We don't have any," Harris sighed. "Not with Welles's brain in a fragile state."

"What's wrong with her brain?" Hunter asked.

"I wondered why she didn't come with us," Yughi added.

Harris figured they'd find out soon enough. "She's been diagnosed with CTE. Know what that is?"

"Rugby players get, it," Hunter said, concerned.

"You get enough knocks on the head, anyone can get it," Harris said. "And Welles has had her fair share, and by Jumbos, too."

"Shit," Hunter said. "She going to be okay?"

"We're doing everything we can, but I'm trying to keep her away from the mind-melding for a while."

"This leaves us in a pickle then, doesn't it?" Ross said. "We need a female to get us into the ship. I don't suppose you know any others?"

Harris shook his head, then paused as a thought occurred to him.

"You do?" the archaeologist asked.

"Who?" Hunter asked.

"No-one," Harris said, wiping Sarai from his mind. She was still a child, he couldn't use her. He struggled to think of a replacement, though.

Colt?

Her node was too undeveloped. There had to be another answer.

He headed for the exit. "Let's head back to Command."

Carrie watched as Novak ushered Harris and McKinley into the Fortress, then left again.

"Hey," she said. "What's up?"

"We've got a problem and we need a solution," Harris said.

"What problem?" she asked.

He sat down at her kitchen table. "I went out to the Zeta ship in New Mexico. Yughi and I tried to connect with it, but it wouldn't let me in."

"Wait," Carrie shook her head trying to take his words in. "You tried to connect with a Zeta ship? Why didn't you call me?"

"Welles," Harris said, "you know why."

She sighed and sat down opposite him, as McKinley took a seat also.

"How did Yughi take the news of his budding node?" she asked.

"I haven't told him yet. Maybe I should have. Maybe that would've helped." He rubbed the back of his neck. "Oh, who am I kidding? This is a female dominant race. We need a female."

"I'm right here," Carrie said.

"You have CTE. I can't use you. We need someone else."

"There is no-one else."

Harris averted his eyes. Carrie detected his usually confident exterior appeared anxious. Nervous.

She looked at him, searching for the reason. "You know someone. Who?"

"No-one," he said, shaking his head and averting his gaze.

Carrie stared at him, wondered why he was being so guarded. Then her breath caught as a realization hit. Her hand shot up to cover her mouth.

"What?" McKinley said, looking between the two. "Who?"

"Sarai," Carrie said softly, knowing the girl shared her father's gift. Carrie recalled when she collected Sarai after Taya was killed, Sarai had told her that she'd dreamed Carrie would come, and that her dad had told her to believe in her dreams.

"No!" Harris said adamantly. "She's just a kid, Welles. We *cannot* use her. I am not throwing her into the ring with Tess or one of those ships."

"Then you have to let me do it," she said, sitting back and folding her arms.

Harris's Alpha eyes pierced hers. Carrie unfolded her arms and sat forward again.

"If not me, then we have no choice but to use Sarai," Carrie said. "With her ancestry, she's going to be much stronger than me. If we start her now, by the time they come, her node will be—"

"No!" Harris said.

"Hey, I get you don't want her involved in this war, but we're all in this, like it or not. You think I want my kids involved? Jesse's her age."

"I know, Welles, but I just lost her mother," he said quietly, through gritted teeth.

Carrie's shoulders softened.

"Look," McKinley interrupted, "if this node thing is growing in my brain and maybe Yughi's, then what's to say it's not growing in others? There could be another female out there who could help us."

"*I* want to help," Carrie said firmly.

"We need to figure out how this thing started in me," McKinley said, ignoring her. "We figure that out, then we've won the war. What if we can awaken this in others?"

Harris looked at him intently. Carrie did too.

"Did either of you dream last night?" she asked them.

They both nodded.

"Tell me," she said.

McKinley shrugged. "Just the bright light again."

"Was I there?" Carrie asked. "The Zeta?"

He shook his head. "Just the bright light, then I felt my arm burning… then I dreamed I woke up and the burning was inside my head."

Carrie studied him a moment. "You dreamed about your node…" She turned to Harris. "You?"

"I couldn't sleep much," Harris said. "When I did, I just kept rehashing things that've already happened in our past."

"Memories? With just the three of us, right?" Carrie asked. Harris nodded. "Me too," she said. "We were on the Darwin, then we were training, then I found you two in the PV, then we were on the *Aurora* pod and …" she paused and looked at McKinley, "and Gregson was shocking your heart."

Harris nodded, and they both spoke at once: "The shock went right through me," Carrie said. While Harris said to McKinley: "Doc was leaning over you."

"What?" they both said, staring at each other.

"You said Doc was leaning over…" she pointed to McKinley, "McKinley?"

Harris nodded. "My memory is a little hazy as you can imagine, but I remember opening my eyes and seeing Doc there, leaning over McKinley… He was telling him to stay where he was." He looked at McKinley, recalling the details. "Doc said if you crossed over he'd beat your ass back."

Carrie's eyes stung with tears. She looked at McKinley, whose face had flushed pale. She realized it couldn't be easy hearing them talk of a time when he was technically dead, but it looked like he was touched by Doc's words.

"What about you?" Harris said. "You said something about the shock?"

Carrie nodded and wiped her eyes. "I was holding your hand, telling you to hold on, to stay with me. I was saying that to both of you. I forgot I was still holding onto McKinley's thigh. Gregson yelled "clear" and the shock ran right through me from one hand to the next and back again… Like it… went through McKinley, into me, then into you," she said to Harris, "then back… *again*…" She barely got the last word out as she stared dumbstruck at Harris.

"What?" he asked, darting his eyes to his scarred arms where gooseflesh was spreading across his skin.

"Could…" Carrie was fighting to get her brain to work. "Could that be how…?" She looked back at McKinley.

"How what?" Harris asked.

Carrie stared from one to the other then reached out and grabbed Harris's hand. The familiar vibration of static electricity flowed through them. She dropped his hand, then picked up McKinley's real hand. She felt nothing. She slumped and let go.

"You think the surge of current that ran through the three of us is what kickstarted McKinley's node?" Harris said, realizing what she was getting at.

Carrie shrugged, though was unsure. "Why not? Our brains are effectively a power hub for our bodies. This whole connection thing involves some kind of static electricity thing, right? What if, after that current ran through you, it took something back with it into McKinley. Something that awoke the node inside his subconscious? Triggered it to grow."

Harris sat back staring at her, his mind turning over.

"If that were true," McKinley said, "then we could awaken it in others."

The silence fell thick around them, as they each held their breath, didn't even blink.

"Shit," Carrie said, her eyes alight with possibility.

"There's one small problem, McKinley," Harris said. "You were technically dead at the time. If that's the only way to awaken it in other people, we'd have to kill them first."

Another thought hit Carrie like a tidal wave and her breath caught again. They looked back to her waiting for an explanation. She stared at Harris.

"You can talk to the dead..." she breathed. "Right? That's your thing. Doc. Your ancestors."

Harris nodded, his face paling now. "Sometimes the old *Aurora* crew visit me too... Sometimes others..."

"McKinley was dead when that current ran through us. I remember now," she nodded. "It was after that Gregson finally got his heart restarted. Gregson was shocked. He didn't expect that to happen."

"What are you saying?" McKinley's brow furrowed.

"I don't know exactly," Carrie said. "I just know that Harris can talk to the dead, in his dreams, in his subconscious state. At the time Harris was fading in and out of consciousness." She motioned to Harris like an exhibit. "He said he saw Doc there at the time. That means he was connected to the dead... at that time." She looked back at McKinley, tears brimming her eyes. "You were technically dead at the time," she whispered. "I don't know how or why, but I think there was something about the state you were both in, and I think when that current ran through us, it got you back, but I think when it got you back, there was some link to Harris's subconscious that's triggered yours. Your node." She threw her hands up in the air. "I... I don't know how..." She shook her head. "But I know I believe."

Again the silence sat as they each considered the ramifications.

"Wait," McKinley said, "how does this explain Yughi?"

"He had a greater match to the Zeta markings," Harris said, thinking things over as he spoke. "The redundant node was there to begin with. And he believes. He's always believed in the power of the mind. That's why he's always been so heavily involved in meditation." Harris studied McKinley. "You… I think you were an accident. An… aberration."

They sat silent and still for a moment.

"That aside," McKinley said, trying to shake off the information, "how I got this… node… this doesn't help us figure out who else can help us. What I'm hearing is that you either have the presence of the node because of the Zeta DNA, or you don't. And unless we're going to kill people and try and shock them back through you two, it ain't going to happen."

Carrie slumped. "No, I guess not."

"So, really," McKinley said, looking at Harris, "by some freak accident, you cursed me to this dream life."

"It's not a curse, McKinley," Harris said. "This gift could save fucking lives. I know that now. It's a blessing. You can use it. Besides," he said, running his hand over his buzz cut, "I don't believe in accidents anymore. I believe in fate."

"You just called me an accident. An aberration."

"Yeah, I did, 'cause I'm one too. The gift runs through the women in my family line. My sister should've got it, not me. I'm an aberration, just like you. And I know now, it's not an accident. It's fate."

"It was fate that McKinley lived," Carrie said, mind turning over. "That's why Doc was pushing him back. The stars aligned and he was revived through the two of us." She looked at McKinley. "It may not be your fate to have the gift. It was just your fate to live, and the gift was an accidental extra."

Harris shrugged and nodded, conceding it could be true.

"But *my* fate," Carrie said, "is that you need to use me to connect with the Zetas and their ships. I'm all you've got if you don't want to use Sarai."

Harris looked down for a moment, thinking something over, before looking up into Carrie's eyes.

"We are not alone," he said. "I know of one other. And if they exist, there will be others. We just need to find them."

"What?" Carrie said, confusion setting in.

Harris nodded to himself and stood.

"Fate, Welles. I think this happened for a reason. You no longer being physically capable of helping me connect with the Zeta, I think has forced our hand. It's time we put the call out and find others like us."

"You know someone besides Sarai?" McKinley said. "Who?"

Harris looked at him, then glanced away. "I won't speak their name yet, but I will soon. First, I need to clear a path with Berger and Marchant. When it's safe I will bring them in, and then we'll find others."

Carrie stood too. "But wait. What about me? What do I do?"

"I still need you, Welles," Harris told her. "I can't do this without you, don't worry. But we need help. Time is running out and we have much work to do." He motioned McKinley to the door then looked back at Carrie. "I'll be in touch."

Harris swept out the door into the night air. McKinley hesitated. He reached out and squeezed her shoulder.

"We'll figure this out," he said, sensing her heartbreak. "It's early days."

He kissed her and left. She moved to stand in the doorway, watching as they passed through the guard gate and into their waiting vehicle.

She closed the door and moved to the windows overlooking the space dock. She felt numb.

They'd made some major breakthroughs today, breakthroughs that were encouraging in terms of their defense in the oncoming war. But despite that, she felt less sure as to where her path lay.

Harris took a seat in the guest chair beside Marchant, opposite Berger's desk.

"You said you wanted an important strategy discussion?" Berger asked.

Harris nodded, thinking things through one last time, knowing he needed to be careful about how he did this.

"You need to grant me permission to do a live interview with Miranda Finch."

"What?" Marchant said. "Why?"

"This whole thing with McKinley, and Yughiarto, it's got me thinking. There are more people out there like me and we need to bring them in to assist us."

"What do you mean, there're more like you?" Berger said.

"I know that I am not alone in my gift," Harris said, looking Berger in the eyes. "And I strongly believe there are many more like me out there."

"More who can connect with Zetas?" Berger asked, eyes narrowed.

"Maybe," Harris shrugged. "I know there are others who can dream the future or feel things strongly like my See'er and Sense'er ancestors. We need them. If they have this gift, I believe we will find they match highly with the Zeta DNA, and if they have those markers, I believe they can help us connect to that Zeta, and to their ships, and I believe with all my heart they can help us win the war."

The silence sat as both Berger and Marchant stared at him.

"How do you know this?" Berger asked.

"I know of one person who can dream the future. And I know a child who can too."

"A child?" Marchant asked.

He stared at them both with firm eyes. "My daughter, Sarai, has the gift. The other person, I will pick up and bring in, but I need you to understand that they fall under my protection. No harm will come to either."

"Who is this person?" Berger asked. "We need to bring them in immediately so we can watch them. Same with any others. If this is true, Harris, we need to round them all up."

"Round them up? No," Harris said firmly, "you're not getting this, general. We do not round them up like they are cattle or criminals. We ask them to come in. We ask them to volunteer to assist us. But we must assure them that no harm will come to them. All of them, every single one of them with this gift, will fall under my protection."

"How many do you think there are?" Marchant asked.

"I don't know. That's why I need to do the interview with Finch. I will tell her all about my gift and I will implore any others like me to come forward. If they have the gift, they will know my call for help is coming and the ones who matter will feel the call to respond to me."

Berger sighed and sat back in his seat. "This is a huge risk, Harris. We risk destabilizing faith in our military forces if we put out a call like that.

We'll draw every phony psychic out from under their rocks around the globe. We'll be a laughingstock. We're still rebuilding the faith we lost after the invasion, then Finch's report on you, and now the rumors surrounding the Command Cleansing. Stability is what the people need now, not… not this."

"What if we start with Sarai and this person you know?" Marchant asked Harris, seeking compromise. Harris could sense that Marchant believed. Believed in Harris, at least.

"No-one goes near my daughter, understand?" Harris said firmly. "I'm telling you this because I swore I would be open and honest with you. No-one deals with her but me. And I don't want her involved yet, she's too young."

"Understood," Marchant appeased him. "What about this other person? Who are they?"

"And how do you know whether they'll be any good to us?" Berger asked.

Harris thought once more about the right words to say.

"He may know a network of people like him. We can start there."

"He?" Berger asked. "You told us it's stronger in the women."

"Yes, but like me, he is an aberration."

"And he's legit? You know for a fact he has a gift?" Berger asked.

"Yes, he has the gift. But as I said, he falls under my protection. Do you understand?"

"Why so protective?" Berger asked, eyes narrowed again.

"He… may have a criminal record that we'll need to overlook."

"What?" Berger asked.

"I suspect he has a criminal record," Harris said. "I can bring him in to assist us, but in exchange, we may need to see that criminal record erased."

"In exchange?" Berger said, leaning forward. "We have a war coming, Harris. If this man is gifted like you say, then he should want to do this to save his own skin, if not the world's, not clear his record."

"Why should he help us?" Harris arched his eyebrow. "If we're going to treat him like a criminal?"

"I just told you why."

"How about we check his record first?" Marchant stepped in. "What are we talking, Harris? Murder? I'm not so sure we can erase that."

"I don't think murder will be on there. At least I hope it's not. But... he runs in a gang, so..."

"A gangbanger?" Berger exclaimed. "You want us to roll out the red carpet for gangbanger?"

Harris took a calming breath. "He can dream the future. Right now, if you won't let me interview with Finch and call others in, he's all we got. We need to explore this further."

"We need a female," Berger said firmly.

"We do. But let's get him in and find out what he knows. Trust me, general. This guy had books on ancestral lines. I need him. I need to tap into his knowledge."

"Give me a name and I'll consider it."

"Give me your assurance he won't be harmed."

Berger stared at Harris and he stared right back, unflinching.

"Welles is down," Harris said. "I think the ignition of McKinley's node might have been a fluke. This guy is what we have right now."

"Why do you believe McKinley's node was a fluke?"

"I'm about to visit Dr. Bakshi and explain my theory, but I don't think this node is going to just start growing in anyone. It will only develop naturally in those with a high instance of Zeta DNA markings. What happened with McKinley, it was like the stars aligning; a once in a millennia kind of thing. We can't recreate the circumstances to trigger others. It just won't happen."

"What circumstances?" Berger asked firmly.

Harris sighed. "I think McKinley's node was triggered when he was technically dead, right before Gregson brought him back. Welles and I were there, physically connected with him and I was communing in a semi-conscious state with Doc."

The two men stared at him.

"Lieutenant Walker?" Berger asked him. "The *deceased* Lieutenant Walker."

Harris stared back. "Yes. And we can't go killing people and bringing them back to life while Welles and I connect to them, hoping we can kickstart that node."

"No," Marchant said after a moment, "we can't."

The silence lingered as each man thought things through.

"Alright," Marchant spoke for the general. "Bring this guy in and we'll take it from there. We'll keep this classified for now. If it turns out legit, then we'll consider your request to go wide and find others."

Berger looked at Marchant.

"What can it hurt checking out this one guy?" Marchant said.

"General, you made me Head of Strategy," Harris said, "and I believe these people will help us in the war. The Zetas are big on their Thought Technology and Thought Biology. We gotta fight fire with fire. If we can communicate with each other on the battlefield though our minds, or intercept Zeta thoughts, *imagine* what an advantage that would give us? These people are key to that. We must explore the possibilities."

Berger considered things for a moment, rubbing his fingers along his jaw.

"Alright. But before I approve this, I want a name. Now."

Harris shrugged. "I don't know his full name but I know where to find him."

"His name," Berger said firmly.

Harris stared at him. "DaJuan."

9

Contact

Gold walked hurriedly onto the Operations Deck, straight to Batoya.

"What is it?" he asked.

She looked at him, the shock present in her eyes. "It's one of the Deep-Star satellites, sir. It's picked one up."

"One what?" he asked, though he knew the answer.

"A Zeta ship."

Gold stared at her moment in pause.

"When?" he asked. "How long for? Which direction was it headed?" He moved closer to her to get a good look at the data flowing on her screen.

"According to this data, not long. But it did slow to examine and circle the satellite, then went on its way."

"Which direction?"

Batoya looked him in the eye. "Based on its trajectory… it's headed our way."

Gold stared at her, as his heartbeat kicked up in his chest.

"How many? Was it alone?" he asked, keeping his voice calm, as every eye on that Ops Deck was focused on them.

"It seems to be just the one, sir."

"Just one?" His brow furrowed. "Are you sure?"

Batoya nodded, bringing up the relevant data as the screen highlighted her pale-brown skin. "There," she pointed, bringing up footage from the satellite. "Only one ship was captured on the camera and only one estimated from the matter displacement gauge."

Gold watched the footage of the obsidian-black, triangular prism-like ship, as it blinked into existence before the satellite, circled it, then blinked out again.

"It jumped?" he asked. "Or cloaked itself?"

Batoya looked back at the footage again. "Based on the matter displacement, I'd say it cloaked, sir."

"It could be here at any moment," Sergeant Samara Abioye said worriedly from her console a few feet away.

"Stay calm," Gold said, looking up through the observation window into the dark beyond.

"What do we do, sir?" Batoya asked, her usually confident manner betrayed by concern.

Gold continued to stare out the observation window, breathing hard.

"Sir?" Batoya asked.

Gold looked back at her. "Weapons on standby. Get Colonel Harris on comms. Find out what other ships are close by, but *don't* alert them yet."

"Yes, sir," Batoya turned back to her console and got to work shouting orders, and soon the observation deck was a hive of activity.

"The *Barbican* isn't airborne yet, is it?" Abioye asked.

Batoya shook her head. "Their relaunch is two weeks out."

"What if this is another attack?" another specialist asked.

"Stay calm," Gold said firmly. "The displacement data confirms it's only one ship, and we'll have the Atlas AI confirm this." He gave Batoya a nod to do so, and she nodded back.

Gold turned and swiftly made his way to his office. If he was worried he wouldn't get to see any war, his fears had been misplaced. God knows what omen this Zeta ship heralded.

But it was only one.

Why was it coming alone? What did that mean?

Marchant entered Harris's office.

"Are we clear to pick up DaJuan?" Harris asked. Through Harris's information and the Command AI's access to New Orleans criminal records, they'd identified the mysterious DaJuan Joeseph Hines.

Marchant gave him a concerned look. "Are you sure about him?"

"Positive."

"He's got quite a list of felonies against his name, Harris. Black market weapons and tech seem to be his specialty."

"I knew he wasn't squeaky clean. Any murder?"

"No."

"Rape or sexual assault?"

"No."

"Then we can work with him. When can I leave?"

Harris's intercom buzzed. He answered it. "Yeah?"

"Sir," a Command operator's voice sounded, "I have an urgent transmission from Major Gold on Station Atlas."

Harris locked eyes with Marchant. "Put him through."

Harris angled his comms screen as Marchant stepped closer to view it. Gold appeared, his eyes looking at something off-screen.

"Gold," Harris said, "what's wrong?"

Gold looked at the camera. "Colonel, a Deep-Star satellite has made contact with a Zeta ship. We believe it's headed our way."

Harris sat forward, exchanging another look with Marchant. "When?"

"Just now. Our readings confirm it's just one ship, Atlas AI has confirmed, so this isn't an attack. At least, I think it isn't. What do you want us to do?"

Harris's mind raced. "If it approaches Station Atlas or Mars, you try and keep it there. Do not fire unless fired upon. Understand?"

Gold nodded. "What do you want us to do with it?"

"Just hold it. I'm on my way back to you right now." Harris ended the comms and stood, looking at Marchant. "DaJuan will have to wait. The UNF doesn't touch him while I'm gone."

Harris's leg shook with anxiety. He was eager to leave Earth, but had to first make a very important transmission.

"Colonel Harris?" President Harkowitz answered, looking a little disheveled.

"Mr. President, I have some important news."

"I figured, given you demanded I be woken. What is it?"

"There is a *single* Zeta ship on approach to your vicinity."

"What?" he said, suddenly wide awake.

"I need you to remain calm, sir. I am telling you this because I gave you my word I would. But rest assured, there is only *one* ship. Our new Deep-Star system established this, our Atlas AI confirmed this, and the Command AIs have also now confirmed the diagnosis. I am on my way to you now. If the ship approaches Mars or Atlas, we plan to try and communicate with it. By all means get your military ready, but I do not believe you will need to use it. I request, sir, that you do *not* take any action without my knowledge or authority. Do I have your compliance?"

"I thank you for the warning, Harris, but I don't need your authority to protect my planet and its people."

"No, you don't, sir, but that military of yours ultimately belongs to the UNF and we hold the authority regardless of your relationship with the senior Martian soldiers. I'm upholding my end of the bargain and I will continue to do so, all I ask is that you trust me to make the right calls when the time is right. Are we understood, Mr. President?"

Harkowitz seemed to be rolling around the options in his mind.

Harris stared into the screen. "I will not put Martian lives at risk, sir. It's one Zeta ship, not a fleet. If communication fails, Station Atlas or my ships will destroy it."

"Alright," Harkowitz said, "but I want regular updates, Harris. If I feel the silence is growing a little too long, I will do what I need to."

"Understood."

Harris ended the transmission and strode out the door.

Carrie paced as she waited for her AI to respond. She'd received a message from McKinley letting her know that the *Aurizun* was leaving asap for Atlas.

She'd asked why, but he hadn't responded. She didn't think he was ignoring her, nor did she think he was obeying orders by not responding. She sensed he was just too damn busy getting the crew together to leave.

So, she sought answers from Archie instead.

"I'm part of the ZAEP, Archie, there're no restrictions for me."

"The ZAEP have not been notified of this."

"Archie, where is McKinley headed. Tell me!"

"To Station Atlas. He informed you of this."

"But why? Why the urgency?" She stopped pacing as she looked out on the Space Dock, her mind racing over possibilities. One rang true to her. "Are the Zetas back? That's why they're in a hurry?"

Her AI was silent.

"Archie, goddammit, tell me! I command you."

"Yes, Miss Welles. A Zeta ship was detected on approach to the vicinity of Mars and Station Atlas."

Carrie sucked in her breath, then turned and raced toward her bedroom.

Harris marched quickly along the Command Space Dock with the *Aurizun* crew in tow, headed for their ship. The team had gathered swiftly, their focus razor sharp, keen to get to Atlas fast.

He heard running footsteps from behind, as did the others, and they turned to see Welles sprinting toward them with a kitbag over her shoulder.

"What the fuck are you doing?" Harris asked, stopping to face her, then looked at McKinley. "You told her?"

"He just said the *Aurizun* was heading off planet," she puffed reaching them. "Archie told me why."

"Doesn't matter," Harris said. "You're on medical leave. Go back."

"It's a fucking Zeta, sir," she said firmly. "You need me there."

She walked past him toward the ship's entry.

"Are you fucking kidding me?" Harris said with disbelief.

McKinley's mind turned over. "She's right," he said, looking at Harris. "We might need her. And technically, it's my ship now, so..." McKinley looked to his crew. "What are we waiting for! Load up!"

Harris glared at him as the soldiers moved aboard.

McKinley shrugged back. "You gave me the ship, sir. It's my job to lead the Alpha soldiers."

"You're willing to put her life at risk?" Harris asked.

"No," McKinley said, bluntly. "If it looks like it's a risk, I'll pull the plug. Until then, we keep her around. Even if it's just a matter of her being physically close to you to help you project, or whatever it is you do. We gotta play it by ear. But she's no good to you back here on Earth. We gotta go."

Then he turned and disappeared inside.

President Harkowitz sat at the boardroom table with Colonel Greavy and the two Martian senators who were effectively colony mayors: Charlie Butten representing Brahe, and Senator Edgar Pope representing Elon. They were having what was akin to a crisis meeting, as Harkowitz filled them in on news of the approaching Zeta ship.

"They'll be three days!" Pope said, the boardroom lights shining off his balding head. "We can't wait for them if it shows."

Harkowitz raised his hand to interject. "It's three days to Mars, but closer to two and a half to Atlas. The UNF have it covered. It's one *small* Zeta ship, not an invasion."

"Those small ships destroyed many of our battleships last time," Butten scoffed beneath his bushy mustache, agreeing with Pope. "You forget about their heat rays! The damage that one small ship could do."

"And what if there are more Zetas on the way?" Pope asked. "Last time they hit Earth, maybe now they want to hit us and test our defences."

"Atlas has some pretty sophisticated weaponry," Harkowitz said calmly, "and it also has the *Carcharias* as a dedicated warship. There are other UNF vessels they can call in also."

"And we can scramble smaller fighters from the MDS to cover the colonies if needed," Greavy said.

"If needed?" Pope said, exasperated.

"I understand your concern, gentlemen," Harkowitz said. "Don't get me wrong I, too, am concerned, and I've told the UNF that if I feel we need to make a move, we will. I will *not* risk Martian lives."

Pope sat back in his chair. "How many more of these things are out there? This could soon become a daily occurrence."

"I wish I knew," Harkowitz said.

"Well perhaps, as president, you should be demanding more information from the UNF," Butten said firmly, his eyes hard.

Harkowitz stared back at him. "I have an open line with the UNF, hence them contacting me to give us this warning. They know little themselves."

"Do they?" Pope asked. "Or are they just telling you that?"

Harkowitz stared at Pope. "I have it under control."

Pope stood. "We're the ones who have to answer to the Martian people in our colonies, Finn."

"You think I don't have to answer to them? I'm the damn president."

"Then do your job and stop kowtowing to the UNF," Butten said, standing and storming out, with Pope following.

Harkowitz sighed and looked at Colonel Greavy.

"I'll get my soldiers and ships on standby," Greavy said, as he stood.

"On *standby*," Harkowitz affirmed. "Don't send the fighters over the colonies until I say so."

Greavy stared at him a moment, then gave a nod and left.

Gold hit the comms panel beside his bed.

"Yes?" he said, shaking off the sleep. He hadn't slept long, hard as it was to shut his mind off, but not knowing how long it would be until the Zeta ship arrived – that is, if it even did arrive – he knew sleep was the smartest option while he waited.

"*It's hit our radar, sir,*" First Lieutenant Connolly, the night shift's ops lead, said urgently.

"On my way!"

Gold threw the sheets back, grabbed the clothes he'd readied by his bed and was out the door within 45 seconds.

He strode quickly along the corridor headed for the ops core at the center of the station. Through the strip of observation windows either side of the corridor, he could see the silver orb of Station Atlas's core glinting in the starlight. Gold felt his gut pull tight. They'd come so far, were about to launch Stage One, and it could all be destroyed within a matter of minutes. He couldn't allow that to happen. Not on his watch.

"How far?" he called out, as he entered the ops deck.

"Right now, it's about 100 klicks," Connolly said, "but it seems to have stopped."

"Did it cruise up to us," Gold said reaching him, "or did it jump there?"

"It's hard to say for sure, sir, but we think it jumped."

"When it appeared," Second Lieutenant Lennard Khatri, radar specialist said, "it just blinked onto the screen. It didn't appear to cruise in."

"It could've been cloaked," Abioye said.

"But now it's stopped and made itself visible," Gold said, eyes narrowed in analysis, staring at the blinking icon that was the Zeta ship on the radar screen.

"What would you like us to do, sir?" Connolly asked.

"Nothing," Gold said.

"Nothing?" Connolly asked in surprise.

"Raise the shields, keep the weapons on standby but disengaged."

"Yes, sir," Connolly said, turning and passing on the order.

"We're still sure it's a solo ship?" Gold asked.

"Yes, sir," Abioye said. "Matter displacement matches that detected by the Deep-Star satellite. The station AI concurs, sir."

Gold nodded. "Good."

"So, we just wait and watch, sir?" Khatri asked.

"Yes," Gold said. "Colonel Harris is on his way. We need to hold it here until then, keep it away from Mars."

"Colonel Harris is days away. How do we do that?" Connolly asked. "What if it jumps?"

"Well," Gold said, "if we don't come across as a threat, maybe it'll stick around. Either way, we can't let it approach Mars or head to Earth. We need to keep its attention fixed on us."

Harkowitz sat with Laurelai preparing media statements based on possible outcomes of the potential Zeta contact. Greavy burst through the door.

"I have an update, sir," he said.

"What is it?" Harkowitz asked.

"The Zeta's appeared on the Atlas radar."

"What's it doing?" Harkowitz asked quickly.

"Nothing. It's just sitting there so far."

"Harris hasn't contacted me."

"He left Earth a short while ago, he's probably been busy with departure."

Harkowitz sat back in his chair. "They won't arrive in time."

"Sir, Atlas have confirmed it's only one ship. The *Carcharias* is alongside Atlas, on standby, but there are other ships I can call in, and my fighters can provide air support to the colonies, like I said."

"So, what do you advise?" Harkowitz asked him.

Greavy thought about things. "Say the word, I'll scramble my force. It'll give a strong defensive show to the Zeta ship."

Harkowitz thought things through as Laurelai stared at him, awaiting his answer. He felt an intensity stifle the room as a potential life and death decision was being made. In fact, as he thought about it, this was the most important decision he'd ever had to make in his presidency.

"No," he eventually said. "Harris wants to try and communicate with it. I'll wait for him to make contact."

"Are you sure, sir?" Laurelai asked. "We need to show decisive action."

"We are showing decisive action. Until that thing attacks, we have no need to defend."

Gold's eyes were fixed to the radar. The Zeta ship was now circling the station, albeit at a distance.

"It's looking for a way in through our shields," Connolly said, attention glued to the screens before him.

"Not necessarily," Gold said. "It might just be checking us out. Distance?"

"Still 100 klicks, sir," Khatri said.

"Outside our weapon's range," Gold thought aloud.

"*The* Carcharias *is ready to head out when you say so, major,*" Ryker's voice sounded over the comms.

"Thank you, *Carcharias.* Wait for my order."

"We're just going to sit here and let it circle us like a shark, sir?" Connolly asked, his eyes intense.

"Relax, Connolly," Gold said. "It's one ship."

"It still has a heat ray that could cut us up, sir. I saw what those rays did in the invasion."

Gold looked at him. "So did I. I was in the skies with them. The *Carcharias* took hits from that weapon. I saw them destroy our ships."

"And my brother's ship was one of them," Connolly said, jaw clenched. "I say we blow this one out of the skies."

"You will obey my command or I will stand you down," Gold said. He didn't raise his voice, but it was Alpha hard, sounding more like Morrell's or Harris's than his own. He noticed the crew eyeing both him and Connolly warily. Everyone on station knew that Gold and the *Carcharias* crew were Alphas. They didn't fully understand what that meant, but they knew enough to know they shouldn't push things with them.

"It's on its third rotation now," Abioye said, breaking the silence.

"Everyone stay calm," Gold said, looking around at them all. "Weapons stay cold."

He eyed Connolly, who was staring at the screen before him, jaw clenching, hands fidgeting.

Harris's words echoed through Gold's mind. Words of cool heads prevailing. He had to keep everyone calm.

Carrie watched as Harris checked in with Gold via transmission from the flight deck.

"We're en route," Harris told him, "but you know we're still a good two days away. You think you can hold its interest that long?"

"I don't know. Right now it's circling us. I'm betting it'll get sick of that soon."

"It's a good sign that it hasn't fired on you."

"Maybe," Gold shrugged, "but we're a lot bigger than its ship. So is the *Carcharias*. Maybe it's just being cautious."

"We need to try and make contact with it," Carrie said to Harris.

"How, Welles? We've never met this Zeta before."

Carrie thought for a moment. "Well, I'd never met our Zeta before I dreamed with you, either." She looked into the screen at Gold. "Can you transmit your images of the ship to us? We'll try focusing on that. See if we can make contact."

Gold looked to Harris. "Sir?"

Harris nodded. "It might work. Do it."

Gold nodded and ended the comms. Harris looked to Welles.

"Are you sure you're up for this?"

"Yeah," she nodded. "I've been resting since the incident, and I was doing just fine with the mind-melding before you pulled the plug on me. I can handle a headache."

Harris glanced around the *Aurizun* crew on its flight deck.

"Yughi come with us. Gregson, you too. I want you on standby in case Welles needs it. The rest of you, focus on getting us to Atlas as fast as you can."

"Yes, sir!" they called.

Harris and Welles sat in the *Aurizun*'s training facility, eyes closed and cross-legged on the mats, with only Yughi and Gregson for company. They had tried to lay down and sleep, but both were too wired to do that, so Harris had another idea. Projection.

What they were doing now, with Yughi's help, was get themselves into a more relaxed state of being. One with no tension or constraint.

"Heartbeats at rest levels," Gregson said quietly. He'd hooked them up to a wireless device to track their heartbeats and brainwaves.

"Alright, Welles," Harris said. "I want you to project some kind of comms to the Zeta ship. Describe it to me so I can visualize it as well."

"Okay, I'm picturing us standing at the Atlas observation window. We're staring out at the Zeta ship."

"Good. I'm picturing it. Let's both try to project that *into* the Zeta ship."

"Projecting the image."

"Done," he said.

"Now I'm picturing us standing on the Zeta's flight deck. It's empty."

"Projecting that…"

"Now the Zeta is there. The Priestess is angry."

"I see it…"

"Wait… She's in a hospital bed… her arm is missing…"

"Fuck," Harris opened his eyes. "That's Tess, not the one at Atlas."

"Shit," she said, opening her eyes too. "Did we just connect with *our* Zeta?"

"From out here?" Gregson said.

"If you did, that's powerful projection," Yughi said.

"Wait," Harris said, "did Tess see what we saw? Did it see the Zeta ship off Atlas?"

"Fuck…" Carrie said, eyes popping wide. "Did we just tell Tess that help is on the way?"

"How do we even know it's a Priestess on that ship?" Yughi questioned. "There are five species of them, right?"

"More importantly," Gregson said, "if you two novices could connect with Tess from here, then what's to say Tess isn't connecting with the Atlas Zeta right now?"

"It's too far away, surely?" Yughi said.

"I don't know," Harris said. "Thought Technology and Biology is their thing. I'd say there's a real good chance we just told our enemy it has a friend in the vicinity."

"We need to sleep," Welles said. "We need to access our deep subconscious and stay down there for a longer period."

"We tried Welles, we can't sleep."

She looked to Gregson. "You need to dope us. Not too much, just enough to get us to sleep."

"Welles," Harris said, "I'm Head of Strategy. I cannot allow myself to be doped up. If Gold contacts me with a development, I need to respond."

"That's what McKinley's for," she said. "He'll handle things. If it gets urgent, Gregson gives us an upper to wake us up."

Gregson looked at her. "You think I'm a drug dealer on a street corner, Welles?"

She smiled. "We know you have the good stuff. Don't try to hide it."

Gregson held his hands out innocently.

"Damn it," Harris said, mind turning over. "Alright, but you be ready to wake me up if needed." He pointed firmly at the medic.

"Cross my heart," Gregson replied.

"And not too much or we won't dream at all."

McKinley sat in his chair on the sleek flight deck of the *Aurizun*, watching the feeds carefully. On one screen, footage rolled from Station Atlas's cameras. On another, the feed from the med bay where Harris and Welles slept, having been given a little something from Gregson to help them on their way.

McKinley had already split the team into two rotating shifts, which meant right now Frazer, Brown, Yughi and Evenssen were sleeping, while Hunter, Steinberg and Tikaani remained awake with him and Gregson. McKinley planned to split his time between the rosters to ensure face time with each of the crew. Though he wouldn't start that until Harris awoke.

According to reports, the Zeta ship had now stopped circling Atlas and simply hovered in the distance, some 100 klicks from the station. For some reason, it would not come any closer. Having inspected the weapons system when he'd visited, McKinley knew that the Stage One Atlas facility only had short-range weapons currently operational and the range was 100 klicks. How the hell the Zeta knew that, was a mystery to everyone.

Movement on the med bay feed caught McKinley's eye and he saw that Welles was beginning to twitch.

"Is she dreaming?" he spoke into his desk mic, which fed directly into Gregson's earpiece to ensure the patients weren't awakened.

Gregson stepped closer to Welles, studied her a moment, then looked up at the med bay camera and nodded.

"I wonder if that's why the Zeta ship has stopped circling?" Hunter said, following their interaction. "Maybe it's focusing on their communication."

"Maybe," McKinley said returning his eyes to the Zeta ship. "Maybe."

Carrie walked along a darkened corridor. It reminded her of a recurring dream she'd had many years ago that she experienced after the Darwin mission. In the dream she had been walking down a darkened corridor until Chet's face had suddenly appeared in circle of light. However, this time the darkness was lightening into a pearly-gray shade that she recognized as the interior of a Zeta ship. She reached out and touched the soft, squishy skin-like walls, a blue glow beneath her fingertips.

Suddenly, a face hit a beam of light up ahead and it stopped her in her tracks.

It wasn't Chet's face.

It wasn't even a Priestess face.

It wasn't a face she recognized at all.

"The Alma Mater," Harris's voice sounded with contained surprise.

She turned and saw him standing beside her.

"We're doing it," Harris said, "we're connecting with the Zeta. It's let us in."

Carrie looked back to the rounded face with its broad cowlike nose.

"Let's sit down," Harris said. "Slowly. Let's show it we are not a threat."

"But what if it's a threat to us?"

"If it was a threat, we'd know it by now. It hasn't fired on Atlas. My gut's telling me… my gut's telling me this one is different… Sit."

Carefully, with clear movements, almost as though in a trancelike interpretive dance, they made their way down to the floor and sat cross-legged.

The Zeta did not move.

"What do we do now?" Carrie asked Harris.

Before he could answer she heard her words played back to her: *What do we do now?*

"It's trying to communicate," Harris said.

"We *really* need a language translator for these guys. I mean, *girls*."

"Yes, we do."

Suddenly, they saw images of a war. It took Carrie a moment to focus and understand what was going on, but she recognized it as the events of Decima. She saw Zeta ships being attacked and falling out of the skies.

Harris nodded slowly to the Zeta, then an image flashed inside Carrie's eyes of the *Aurora* blowing up, then of other UNF ships falling out of the skies. Then she recognized the hospital crash site. Then she saw Harris holding Taya's body.

Her vision returned. The Zeta stared at them. *Did Harris project that?*

Next, Carrie saw Tess, held prisoner in her bed, growling at them.

"Oh, shit," Harris whispered. "They've been talking."

"Have they been talking? Or is Tess here too?" Carrie asked.

Tess hissed at them.

"She's here," Harris said. "This is a four-way conversation."

Carrie closed her eyes and projected an image of Tess injuring Morrell during the uprising, then trying to kill Harris while he was still strapped to his bed.

Tess projected back an image of Morrell cutting off her arm during the invasion.

Harris projected then, and Carrie saw the burned and charred bodies of Morrell's men, killed by the heat weapon strapped to Tess's arm.

The images stopped and they stared at each other again.

"Fuck, I wish I knew their word for peace," Harris muttered. "How do I show peace?"

Carrie lowered her head and squeezed her eyes shut. She projected an image of the Alma Mater sitting before them, cross-legged; of them all smiling. Then she pictured the images of war, and raised her hand wiping them away. When they were gone, she showed a green field, blue skies, the sun shining, flowers moving in the gentle breeze, butterflies dancing among them.

"Welles," Harris said carefully.

She opened her eyes and saw the Alma Mater standing right before them, nostrils flaring, eyes piercing. Carrie's heart thumped against her ribcage.

Slowly, the Zeta got down to the floor and sat with them.

Harris projected an image of the *Aurizun*, making its way to Station Atlas; showed Harris and Carrie aboard, making their way to the Zeta ship.

"We're coming," he told it. "Don't leave."

The Alma Mater stared at him, then at her.

Carrie projected herself standing on one of the Zeta's flight decks, with Harris beside her. Though observation windows did not exist on the Zeta ships, Carrie pictured one, and she showed the Alma Mater, through the window, Station Atlas in the distance. She showed the *Aurizun* docking at Atlas, showed a smaller ship bringing the Alma Mater aboard Atlas. Then she showed the creature an image of them standing in a room on Atlas together.

A growl in the distance made her open her eyes. Tess still lay in her bed and she clearly did not like Carrie's proposal.

Suddenly the language Harris once spoke of, the bright lines and dots, began flashing back and forth between the two Zetas. It looked angry to Carrie, but she had no idea what the foreign text said.

The Alma Mater turned back to Carrie and stared at her.

Carrie bowed slowly, in a sign of respect. At least, she hoped the creature would take it as one.

The Alma Mater continued to stare at her. The silence sat.

Then, the Alma Mater slowly bowed back.

The Alma Mater turned her eyes to Harris, eyed him over, then stood and vanished, along with Tess.

Carrie and Harris sat in silence for a moment just staring into the dark where the Zetas had vanished. When they did not return, she looked at Harris.

"Oh my god… I think that worked."

Harris nodded. "Now we just need her to hold by Atlas for the next couple of days until we arrive."

"We'll connect with her every day," Carrie said. "We'll show her our flight path, let her know we're getting closer."

Harris nodded again. "And hope no-one else ruins our plans."

10

Relations

Gold watched the Mars Media news feed, saw the reports of a Zeta ship circling Atlas, then lowered his head.

"*Fuck*," he hissed. It had been approximately 28 hours since the ship appeared, but there was no reason for the media to have found out without a leak. He looked up at the faces on the ops deck, wondering if any of his crew had been responsible for the leak, or whether it had come from Command, or maybe Mars forces.

"Incoming transmission from Lieutenant General Marchant, sir," Batoya said.

Gold nodded and moved to his office for the call.

"Yes, sir," he answered, eyeing Marchant on the screen before him.

"How the fuck did this get out?" Marchant asked.

"I don't know, sir, but I'm going to find out."

"Panic is starting to rise. People think we're going to war again."

"You need to calm them, sir. Harris and Welles are still a day and a half away."

"Jesus Christ!" Marchant said, ending the comms.

Gold sat there a moment, then initiated another transmission, this time to Harris.

"If you're calling me about the news channels," Harris answered, "I've already had Berger chewing out my ass." He looked to be in his quarters. "Was it one of your crew?"

"I'm looking into it," Gold said. "In the meantime, I wanted your permission to contact Miranda Finch. We go back a ways. I hear she's working for Mars Media now, and I'm hoping she can assist us in imploring people to calm down."

"Let me call her," Harris said. "If nothing else, I might be able to trade with her."

"Trade with her? For what?"

"My time. An interview. Leave it with me."

"Alright," Gold said. "How're things going with the Zeta?"

"So far, so good. Don't worry, we'll keep things good on that end. I'm not worried about the Alma Mater. I'm worried about irrational humans right now."

"Okay. Update me when you can, sir."

The transmission ended. Gold headed back to the ops deck. He saw Connolly and Batoya doing a handover. Before Batoya turned to leave the ops deck, Gold subtly motioned her over.

She moved to stand by his desk, as he typed into his console:

>>> Find out who leaked the news of the Zeta ship. Was it one of us? <<<

Batoya read the screen, then gave him the most subtle of glances and a nod.

Satisfied, Gold deleted the message, and returned his eyes to the Zeta footage.

Harris waited for the transmission to connect. President Harkowitz appeared and he looked unimpressed.

"Did you leak this to the press?" Harris asked.

Harkowitz stared at him. "No, I did not. You think I'm going to allow a leak and not do an official press conference to announce something like this? To let my people know I have things under control."

"Alright. Was it any of your people?"

"I can't say for sure, but I'll look into it."

"Let me know what you come up with," Harris said. "I'll do the same. We need cohesion and cooperation, Mr. President. Without unity we are nothing."

Harris ended the comms, took a moment to steady his breath, then made another transmission to Miranda Finch. When she appeared onscreen she looked genuinely surprised, then her eyes sharpened in concentration.

"Colonel Harris?" she said, tucking a long strand of dark hair behind her ear, as though wanting to ensure she heard what he had to say clearly.

"You can guess why I'm calling, Miss Finch."

"I told you, it's Miranda. And if you mean the news of the Zeta ship circling Station Atlas, then, yes."

"Who leaked the news to you?"

"No-one leaked the news to me."

"Mars Media aired the story."

"Yes, and the reporter was Kellan van Pelt. He's young and hungry."

"Well, I need a favor from you," Harris said.

"You need a favor from me?"

"Yes. I think you owe me one, don't you?"

Silence was her reply.

"I'll take that as your agreement," he said. "I need Mars Media to appeal for calm. Yes, a Zeta ship has made contact with Atlas, but so far it is friendly in nature and there is only one alien ship. Our specialized satellite system Deep-Star has confirmed this and both the Atlas and Command AIs support this. There is nothing to fear. I am personally on my way to Atlas as part of an envoy of peace. Between our military on Atlas and that of the *Carcharias* and *Aurizun* crews, we have this handled. I need you to reassure the public of this."

"You can understand our fear, colonel, after what happened," she said.

"Yes, I can, Miranda. I lost my wife in that invasion. I think I understand better than most."

"I—I'm sorry… I didn't mean—"

"Will you do this for me?"

She stared at him, searching for something in his eyes.

"I have given you an exclusive," Harris told her. "And I will grant you that exclusive interview soon, if you do this for me."

"Alright," she said, eyes sparkling with intrigue. "Deal."

"Thank you," Harris said. "I'll be in touch."

As soon as he ended the comms with Finch another comms came through. It was Harkowitz again.

"Mr. President."

"Harris, I'm looking into the leak, but something else has come to my attention that you should be aware of."

"What's that?"

"A series of civilian craft have departed the Mars Docking Station and are apparently heading for Atlas. It would seem some local miners fancy themselves as vigilantes. They're gunning for the Zeta ship."

"Shit..." Harris breathed. "You gotta stop them. Make contact. Presidential orders or something. Demand they stop."

"And if they don't?"

Harris gave him a hardened look. "The UNF will be forced to stop them."

Harkowitz's eyes narrowed. "You would kill human civilians before stopping that Zeta ship?"

"I don't plan on killing civilians, but if they threaten the peace I am trying to broker, or attack that Zeta ship unprovoked, then I will do what needs to be done. Please contact them, Mr. President."

Harkowitz analyzed him a moment, then nodded. "I'll do what I can."

Gold ran his hand through his hair.

"Yeah, we see them, alright," he said.

"I'm hoping the president will talk sense into them," Harris said, "but if he fails, it's on you to stop them. We've told the Zeta we are coming in peace. If it comes under attack... We *must* preserve the Zeta and its ship. Understand?"

Gold nodded. "Roger that."

"And Gold? Now the media has its eyes on you, you need to tread carefully. We need those civilian ships turned back peacefully."

Gold exhaled as though to steady himself. "Understood, sir."

He ended the transmission, then pulled the comms mic to his lips. "Carcharias, I have a job for you."

"*Yes, sir,*" Ryker responded. "*Go ahead.*"

"We've got four civilian ships headed our way from Mars. I need you to send them back. Understand?" said Gold.

"*When you say send them back...?*"

"Block their passage and turn them around. They are not to approach Atlas or the Zeta ship. They are apparently armed and on some vigilante justice mission. If they do not turn around, if they attempt to fire upon the Zeta ship, you have permission to scare them. If scaring them doesn't work, you have permission to disable them, but we must try to preserve life. Confirm?"

"*Affirmative, sir.*"

"You think you're enough or do you need back-up?"

"*We're your biggest ship in these parts, major,*" Ryker said. "*We'll have to be enough.*"

"Stay sharp, Ryker. Keep it cool."

"*Roger that.*"

He ended the comms.

"I see them," Connolly said. "Four bogeys inbound."

"How long until they're in range?" Gold looked down at the radar and saw the blips on the edge of the screen.

"At that speed, I'd say three hours," he replied.

Lieutenant General Marchant sat in his office keeping one eye on the feed from Atlas and one eye on the Earth news feeds. Harris had reported that he'd spoken with the reporter Finch, and Marchant was keen to see her next move. Marchant had also expressed his disappointment at learning that Welles was on the *Aurizun* and communicating with the Zeta. Harris assured him he was watching her carefully, and that she was bunking with Tikaani, not McKinley, and that the *Aurizun* team would act as his shadows.

A knock on the door broke his attention.

"Come in," he said. The door opened and Major Morrell entered, looking as mean as he always did, though perhaps slightly older, perhaps weaker in some way. He'd always had a strong physical presence – whether that was due to the fact he was once classified with the UNF's highest threat level as a soldier, or not, Marchant didn't know – but something had been missing from the soldier since Tess nearly killed him. He wasn't quite the same man as before. Had he lost his edge?

"You called me, sir?" he said.

Marchant nodded and motioned to the screens. "Have you seen the news?"

Morrell nodded. "Can Gold handle things?"

"For now he is," Marchant said. "Harris and the *Aurizun* crew are en route, but a problem has arisen in that a small group of vigilantes from Mars and are on their way to kill the Zeta."

Morrell stared back, but offered no comment.

"I can see in your eyes that you're on the vigilantes side, but we need that Zeta alive. Harris tells me it's an Alma Mater, not a Priestess. We need her."

"How does he know that?" Morrell asked.

Marchant shot him a look to say "you know how". Morrell nodded to himself.

"So why did you call me, sir?" Morrell asked.

"Because if Harris is successful, I would like him to bring the Alma Mater back here to Earth. And if we have vigilantes on Mars, we will have vigilantes here. I need you to stay sharp and ensure that Command, the Space Dock and the Sea Dock are not compromised. Understand?"

"Yes, sir," Morrell said.

"The trouble didn't end with the Command Cleansing, Morrell. Just our trouble *inside* the UNF ended. But Command is a small place. We must assume there is a greater number of unfriendlies out there in the civilian population who want the Zetas dead, and who will despise us for protecting them while we try to learn from them."

Again Morrell said nothing, but Marchant saw his mind turning over.

"You nearly died because of the unfriendlies we had in-house," Marchant told him. "Tess attacked you, yes, but make no mistake, it was the human unfriendlies that caused that to happen. You could die by the hands of the unfriendlies outside. You've always been vocal, always spoke your mind on things. I hope now you've seen what we're trying to do, and how valuable those Zetas are to us, you will remain vocal and share that with your troops. Harris and Welles are learning a lot from them. Information is power. If we do not harness that power we will lose the war if it proceeds and they come in great numbers. Tell me you understand this?"

Morrell considered things for a moment. "I do, sir. But I won't pretend to have any love for those creatures. That captured Zeta killed my men, and it nearly killed me in the Cleansing, but I do know it only happened because we were betrayed from within. I hate the Zetas, but if I am one thing, sir, I am loyal and I will not tolerate betrayal."

"So you will do your duty and keep Centralis safe from any further uprising, and you will ensure your soldiers follow your lead?"

"Yes, sir. You have my loyalty and that of my soldiers. As do my Alpha brothers in Harris, McKinley and Gold."

"Good," Marchant said. "Dismissed."

Morrell gave a single nod, took one glance at the Atlas feed, then left.

Miranda Finch stood with the Command building and Space Dock visible in the background as she stared into the camera.

"I have spoken directly with Colonel Harris and he assures me that reports of another invasion are false. He confirms that a *single* Zeta ship has made contact with Station Atlas, but reassures us it is only *one* Zeta ship and this has been confirmed by the new tracking systems established by the UNF, as well as the highly advanced UNF AIs." She glanced at the datapane in her hand. "Colonel Harris is en route to Station Atlas as we speak and is just over 24 hours from arrival. His plan is to communicate with the Zeta and attempt to broker peace. As such, he implores everyone to remain calm and insists that we are not under threat. I repeat, he insists we are *not* under threat and he asks that everyone remain calm. I now have an open line with the colonel and I will continue to provide updates as they happen. This is Miranda Finch, for Mars Media."

"And we're clear!" her camera operator, Julie, said, lowering the camera.

Miranda's phone immediately rang with an off-Earth transmission call. It was Regan Lotz.

"Regan," she answered, holding the screen up to view his face, "what's up?"

"I've received word that a series of civilian ships are en route to Atlas. They're gunning for the Zeta. President Harkowitz tried to talk them down, but failed. Go back live and announce that."

"Shit," Finch said, motioning for Julie to not pack up. "When did this happen?"

"They're hours out from the station. This could turn into a major incident. I need you to emphasize Harkowitz's failings."

"You want me to *what*?"

"Report the truth, Miranda. Harkowitz failed to stop those vigilantes."

Miranda's mind processed his words. "You want me to damage him to improve your chances in the next election?"

"You're simply reporting the truth."

"Am I?" she said, feeling torn. She'd promised Harris she would instill calm in the people. Would this be stoking the fires again?

"This proves Harkowitz is losing the faith of the people," Lotz said. "It's business. He's past his prime and it's time for a new leader on Mars."

"All this proves is that a band of extremists are out for blood. God himself probably couldn't talk sense into them."

"Go back live, *now*."

"Where are you getting these tips from?" she asked. "Who's leaking this information to you."

"That's irrelevant. Remember who you work for, Miranda. We had a deal."

"Yeah, and that deal was to establish your media outlet with my face, a *known* face, a known name. I owed you a favor, and that favor was repaid. I told you when I accepted the offer that I wouldn't work for a muckraking news outlet again. I would report facts only."

"These *are* the facts and this is an exclusive, Miranda. So, get on air and do your job!"

Regan Lotz hung up on her.

"What is it?" Julie asked, sensing the tension from the conversation.

Miranda glanced around at the Command building as her conversation with Harris replayed in her mind. She looked up into the gray sky, as though seeing Mars and Station Atlas. She pictured Gold and wondered how he was handling things up there. Then she pictured Regan Lotz, and sighed in resignation. She turned back to Julie.

"We need to go live again. Right now."

"Right now?" Julie's eyes popped and she swung the camera back up.

Miranda took a deep breath and stared into the camera.

Fuck Regan Lotz, she thought.

She wasn't going to cause more damage to Harris, or Gold, for that matter. This time, she was going to be their ally.

Regan Lotz watched Miranda's report fixedly.

"We've just had reports that a number of civilian ships have left Mars and are headed toward Station Atlas. It is believed they are armed and dangerous. The Mars president himself has requested people remain calm, showing that universal leaders support Colonel Harris and what he is trying to achieve in brokering peace. Once again, a number of civilian ships have left Mars and are headed toward Station Atlas, and are believed to be armed and dangerous, as tensions mount in this *very* delicate situation. More updates as they become available. This is Miranda Finch for Mars Media."

Regan stared at the screen coolly as a commercial came on. He clenched his teeth and made a transmission call.

"What the hell was that?" he said as she appeared on his screen.

"The truth," Finch replied.

"You want to report the truth and be impartial? Why didn't you tell the truth that Harkowitz failed? Because he's pals with Harris? That's what this is all about, right. Why the sleazing up to Harris?"

There was silence for a moment before she answered: "Because he has more integrity than you."

"What does Harris have over you and Harkowitz?" he questioned.

"Nothing," she replied. "That why I like him. What you get is what you see. And favors are optional. Not demanded."

Regan laughed. "Go work for him, then. You're fired."

"Too late," she responded, "because I already quit. Didn't you see my news report? That was my resignation letter."

"Just know you never repaid your debt," he said.

Finch hung up on him.

Regan threw his phone down and swung his chair around to stare out at the hazy-brown horizon of Mars. He mulled things over before swinging back to his desk and contacting his assistant.

"Get me Kellan."

Gold watched the screens carefully as the radar blip that was the *Carcharias* made its way toward the Mars civilian fleet. He moved his eyes further afield to look at the opposite side of the station, where the Zeta blip remained stationary, just outside of the station's weapons range.

"*Mars civilian fleet,*" Ryker's voice sounded over the comms, "*this is the UNF* Carcharias. *Identify yourselves.*"

Silence sounded over the ops deck, until Batoya broke it; Gold had called her back early, wanting all hands on deck as the tension rose.

"We've identified the four ships from the MDS logs," she told Gold. "We have the *Yorke*, the *Alexi*, the *Fayden Rah* and the *Maiden Glint*."

"Mars civilian fleet," Ryker said again, "identify yourselves."

Eventually an answer came from the ship identified on Gold's screen as the *Yorke*.

"We're just a coalition of concerned Mars citizens," a male voice said that Gold guessed belonged to someone in his 40s or 50s. "We thought maybe the military on Atlas needed a hand, given that Zeta ship is still flying about."

"Thank you for your offer of assistance, mate," Ryker said with his amicable Aussie accent. "However, Atlas military have things under control."

"Do you?" the male voice said. "Why is that ship still flying around? It could blow Atlas up at any time."

"Sir," Ryker said politely, "that Zeta ship has been here for almost two days and no act of aggression has occurred. Please turn around and head back to Mars and let us handle this."

"That's just it, you're not handling shit!"

"Sir, I repeat, please turn your ships around and head back to Mars."

"Get out of our way," another, younger, voice sounded. "If you don't have the balls to take care of this, we will."

Sergeant Abioye looked to Gold. "That came from the *Alexi*."

Gold nodded, then spoke into his comms. "Mars coalition, this is Major Gold of Station Atlas. You are ordered to return to Mars immediately."

"*You have no authority over us!*" the younger voice on the *Alexi* sounded.

"President Harkowitz does and he has requested that you turn around," Gold said.

"He's a coward just like you!" the older voice said from the Yorke. "You let one of them live, there will be more. We exterminate them until they learn to leave our solar system alone!"

"We have this handled," Gold said firmly. "I ask you again, turn your ships around. *Now.*"

"*Make us,*" the younger voice said.

Silence filled the ops deck.

Gold spoke into his mic again, this time on a secure channel.

"Ryker, raise weapons."

"Yes, sir."

"Weapons online," Batoya reported.

Connolly stared at Gold intensely.

"What you gonna do?" the older Yorke voice said. "Shoot your own civilians?"

"There are greater things at stake here," Gold said on the public channel, "than your need for revenge. Now, for the last time, turn your ships around."

"The *Alexi* just brought their weapons online!" Batoya reported.

"*Lower your weapons,* Alexi," Ryker said firmly but coolly.

"Shit," Connolly said, urgently, "the Zeta's heat ray is coming online!"

Gold's stomach leaped into his throat.

"It's self-defense," Gold said, then clicked on his comms again. "Stand down, *Alexi*! I repeat, stand down!"

"That Zeta's firing up its ray!" the Yorke man said.

"Because you're firing up yours!" Gold said. "Stand down!"

"We gotta turn weapons on the Zeta ship!" Connolly said, looking at Gold.

"No," Gold said.

"What?!" Connolly said, exasperated.

Gold looked at him. "I said, *no!*"

"It's going to fire on us!" Connolly said. "We can't just sit here!"

"I repeat, *Alexi*, stand down!" Gold barked into his comms, as Connolly stared at him.

"Fire up Atlas weapons!" Connolly turned and ordered the ops deck.

"What are you doing?" Gold barked. "I said no! Get off the ops deck!" Gold pointed him away. "Batoya has control."

"It's going to fire on us!" Connolly argued angrily.

"Its ray is on because *every* other ship in the vicinity has their weapons on!" Gold said heatedly. "Now stand down!"

"All four civilian ships have their weapons online!" Batoya called out.

"Yorke! Alexi! Fayden Rah! Maiden Glint!" Gold said quickly, firmly. "Stand down your weapons now or we will be forced to fire!"

"That Zeta is going to fire!" the Yorke man barked.

"Alexi on the move!" Lieutenant Khatri called out.

"Carcharias! Warning shot!" Gold ordered.

The *Carcharias* did so, shooting across the *Alexi*'s bow.

"Zeta heat ray is online!" Connolly barked. "It'll fire any moment!"

"I said *stand down*, Connolly!" Gold barked back.

"You're putting our lives at risk!" Connolly said, marching up to Gold. "*You* stand down, sir!"

"Alexi has fired on Carcharias!" Batoya called.

Gold whipped his eyes back to the screen to see the *Alexi*'s fire bounce off Carcharias's shield.

"Sir?" Ryker asked. "Permission to disable the Alexi."

"Another warning shot, Ryker," Gold responded on the secure channel.

"Yes, sir."

Connolly pulled a small laser pistol and thrust it in Gold's face. Gasps sounded as the ops deck fell silent.

"I am relieving you of command, sir," he said. "Stand down."

Gold stared at the pistol, then at Batoya who watched on with wide eyes.

"Continue," Gold said calmly to Batoya. She nodded and looked back to her screens. Gold looked at the rest of the crew on the deck. "All of you, continue."

"Sir," Connolly said, "I won't ask you again. That Zeta ship will fire any second! Our lives are in danger!"

Gold stood calmly, hands in the air. "Will it? If it was going to fire on us it would've done so by now."

"Carcharias has fired another warning shot!" Batoya called. "The Alexi continues to approach."

"Move!" Connolly said, motioning Gold away from his desk. "Now!"

Gold saw sweat on Connolly's brow.

"Connolly," Gold said, "you need to remain calm. One false move and we have a major incident on our hands."

"Alexi has fired on the Carcharias again!" Batoya called.

Gold darted his eyes to the screens to see the fire bounce off the shields again.

"Zeta ray targeting!" Khatri called.

"Prepare to fire on the Zeta ship!" Connolly called.

"What's it targeting?" Gold said.

"Prepare to fire!" Connolly shouted.

"WHAT'S IT TARGETING?" Gold yelled.

"US!" Connolly yelled back.

"NO!" Batoya shouted. "It's targeting Alexi!"

"What?" Connolly said, looking at her. "Fire! FIRE NOW!"

Gold saw his opportunity. He smacked the gun aside with his left hand and threw a mean right hook that connected with Connolly's cheekbone. The lieutenant saw at the last moment and tried to defend, but Gold was too fast and too Alpha strong to stop. In an instant, Connolly was unconscious on the floor, while the ops deck looked on in shock.

"Sir!" Ryker called. "The Zeta's going to fire. Orders, sir?"

Gold leaped back to his desk. "Fire on the Alexi. Disable the ship!"

"*Yes, sir!*" Ryker replied.

Within seconds the sky was alight with electromagnetic pulse fire, as the *Carcharias* fired a volley of shots at the much smaller *Alexi*'s shields, and within seconds of that, the other three ships in the Mars coalition fleet began emitting laser fire on *Carcharias*.

"Atlas!" Gold called to the ops deck. "Weapons on the fleet, now!"

"You want us to fire on *them*?" Abioye asked, surprised.

"Yes! Defend the Carcharias!"

"Weapons on the Mars fleet!" Batoya called, sweating with adrenaline.

"What about the Zeta ship, sir?" Khatri asked.

Gold flicked his eyes to the screen showing the Zeta ship. He saw the red ray alight and primed to fire. "It's just ready to defend itself," he said. "It won't fire if we don't fire."

"How do you know that, sir?" Abioye asked. "They fired without prejudice during the invasion."

"They did," he nodded, "but so far this one hasn't. This one is different. Do *not* fire upon it unless fired upon. Now fire upon those that *do* fire upon us! Start with warning shots."

"Yes, sir," Abioye said and turned back to her desk.

A volley of fire shot forth from Atlas's weapons, racing over and under the ships firing upon the *Carcharias*. The *Alexi*'s shield lit up then disappeared as the Carcharias's pulse fire disabled it. Within moments, the *Fayden Rah* turned around and sped back toward Mars.

"The Fayden Rah is running!" Khatri yelled.

"Advise ground troops to meet them," Gold said, casting a glance to Connolly, who still lay on the floor unconscious.

The *Carcharias* continued to emit pulse fire upon the *Alexi*, first disabling its small weapons, then its flight systems until it was a limp duck, while Atlas continued to fire warning shots at the other two ships. As soon as the *Alexi* was disabled, the other two ships turned and fled as well.

"Remaining two are running!" Batoya called, a slight smile of relief on her face.

"Alert ground troops," Gold said. "What's the Zeta doing?"

"Just sitting there, sir," Abioye said.

"Weapons?" Gold asked.

"Still hot, sir."

"Alright, the *Alexi* threat has been taken out. Lower our weapons."

"While it still has its weapons on?" Abioye asked.

"Yes," Gold said. "It is smaller than us and outnumbered if need be. Lower weapons and it will follow suit."

"You heard Major Gold," Batoya said. "Lower weapons!"

Gold flicked to the secure comms channel. "Carcharias, seek Alexi's surrender. Assume hostile until then. Do not board until I say."

"*Roger that,*" Ryker said.

"Atlas weapons offline," Batoya reported.

Gold flicked his eyes back to the screen showing the Zeta ship.

It hovered there, red heat ray glowing beneath the ship.

Gold's chest rose and fell heavily with anticipation.

Had he made the right decision? Or had he doomed them all?

The seconds passed painfully slowly, as he stared at that red glow promising death and destruction.

Finally, the red glow began to dim.

"Zeta heat ray offline!" Batoya called with a toothy smile.

Gold nodded to himself, then exhaled in relief, leaning on his console.

The crew broke into applause and cheers of relief. He looked around at them, as they stared back waiting for the next order.

Gold looked down to the still unconscious Connolly.

"Someone cuff Connolly and place him in the brig. He is relieved of any command on Atlas."

11

Course Correction

Harris listened intently as Gold updated him on events.

"Good work," he nodded. "Lock up the crew of the *Alexi*. See if they'll talk. We need to find out if it was just these four ships or whether there's a wider group of supporters. If the Command Cleansing taught us anything, it's that we need to stamp this shit out quickly, or it will fester."

"Yes, sir."

"What are you going to do about Connolly?" Harris asked.

"Well, right now he's in the brig. I'm sending him home. I can't keep him here. He pulled a gun on me."

"Agreed. But you need to manage the fallout. If we just throw him out, he'll likely turn bitter and that will have ramifications for us all. We don't want that. We can't have that. We need every soldier we can get. Let's not push him to the other side."

"He's already bitter. His brother died on the *Llangollen* during Decima. That's why he was so trigger-happy to kill the Zeta. He wanted revenge."

Harris nodded, his mind turning over. "And he won't be the only soldier, either. We need to stamp that out, Gold. Try talking to him. I know he pulled a gun on you, tried to overthrow you, but what's important is that he didn't succeed and the rest of the crew had your back."

"That I know of."

"Well, even if some were on the fence, hopefully watching how quickly you took Connolly out might make them think twice about fucking with an Alpha CO in future."

Gold gave a small smile. "Maybe. I think I'm going to sleep with one eye open though."

"You do that," Harris said. "We'll be there in less than a day to relieve you. Keep the *Carcharias* crew close."

"Roger that."

"Stay safe," Harris said and ended the comms.

Harris sighed and stood. He exited McKinley's office, which he'd commandeered, and headed for the flight deck. As he entered, McKinley looked around.

"Is it under control?" the major asked.

Harris nodded. "For now. But it came fucking close. The good news is, that Zeta was only looking to defend itself. It lit up, but it didn't fire. It kept its cool, which is what I want the UNF to do." He looked to Frazer at the controls. "How much longer?"

"We've got her at full speed. We're looking at 21 hours until arrival."

Harris nodded, then turned to see Welles enter with a pot of coffee.

"We okay?" she asked him.

"Yeah, but put that coffee down. We better check in with the Zeta and make sure shit is cool."

She nodded and handed the pot to McKinley. Harris turned back to Frazer.

"Wake Gregson and get him to meet us in the med bay."

"Aye, sir."

Harkowitz sat in the boardroom with Laurelai, as Greavy and Senators Pope and Butten appeared onscreen from different locations.

"The UNF fired on civilians, protecting that Zeta ship!" Pope effused. "We *cannot* be seen to support this, Finn!"

"He's right," Butten said, "this is a *very* bad look."

"Those civilians fired first, correct, Colonel Greavy?" Harkowitz asked.

Greavy cleared his throat. "No, sir. The *Carcharias* was the first to bring their weapons online and the first to fire, albeit a warning shot across their bow."

"Warning shot! There you go," Harkowitz said. "The first targeted direct hits came from the civilian ships, though, yes?"

"I'm still to receive an official report, but yes, that is my understanding."

"It doesn't matter," Pope said. "We're firing upon our *own* civilians!"

"I've prepared my statement," Finn said, "and I'll be going live to present it as soon as I speak to Colonel Harris."

"Why do you need his authority to speak with your people?" Butten asked.

Harkowitz stared at him. "Because rash decisions only cause more chaos. We must be thoughtful and timely with how we respond, and present a united front."

"I'm curious about this change in your attitude," Pope said, eyes narrowed in accusation. "Not that long ago you were espousing the desire to break from the UNF and establish an independent Mars Colonial Force. What happened? Why are you suddenly in their pocket?"

"I'm not in anyone's pocket," Harkowitz said firmly. "The UNF have reached out peacefully to me and offered to improve their communication, which so far they have done. Right now, I'm prepared to work with them."

"So, the Mars corps is off the table?" Butten asked. "When were you going to tell us that?"

Harkowitz took a steady breath to retain his composure. "The Mars force is simply put to the side for the moment, while I analyze UNF offerings. So far, Colonel Harris has stayed true to his word."

"Well, you need to stay true to your word to *us*," Pope said.

"Agreed," Butten said. "You leave us out in the cold, Finn, you'll start to find Mars incredibly frosty."

"Agreed," Pope echoed. "I want to see your statement before you issue it. For now, I have constituents to go and pacify."

Pope ended the transmission.

"I'll expect the same," Butten said, before his screen went dark.

"Keep me apprised," Harkowitz said to Greavy, who gave a nod and disappeared also.

Harkowitz sighed and looked over to Laurelai. "Shall we go over it one more time?"

She stared at him. "This is a major incident, sir. We need to tread very carefully."

"I'm fully aware of that."

"I'm not just talking about the polls, sir. Losing a few points is something we can come back from. I'm talking about serious dissent. Those civilians, *your* civilians, ignored your pleas to turn around and head back to Mars."

"Well, that's why we need to respond quickly and assure my people that everything will be okay and we have everything under control."

Carrie sat cross-legged on the Zeta's flight deck, waiting. Harris sat beside her, glancing around suspiciously.

"What is it?" Carrie asked.

"We're not alone," he said quietly.

As though in response, Tess growled. They both turned to see her strapped down in her bed, hissing at them.

"Oh, it's you," Carrie said coldly.

"Welles, we need to make friends with her."

"Do we?" she said. "I like the new Zeta better."

"We need to practice what we preach. We need everyone on the same page. If we turn both these Zetas to peace, they can pass the message to the rest of them and we can avoid a war."

Carrie looked at him. "Do you really believe that, though? We dreamed of the eve of the great war before. We're going to war, I feel it. It's coming."

"Fates can change. And even if the path doesn't change, we might still be able to smooth out the edges and minimize the scale of it."

She stared back, nodding. "You never dreamed of this, did you? The Alma Mater coming?"

"I dreamed of a Zeta ship coming but I didn't take it as a warning that a Zeta was coming, and certainly not an Alma Mater. I thought the dream was about me keeping Gold at Atlas." He sighed. "I guess given Decima and my injuries, Taya's death, you in Hell Town, being prisoner of the UNF, trying to communicate with Tess, the uprising... I don't know, my mind's been focused on other things. I'm not as in touch with my 'future' dreams as I once was. I need to carve out time and keep my mind open wide to the possibilities of the future, not just focused on what's in front of me. Which I have been. I've been too focused on the present and closing myself off to everything else."

A chill ran down Carrie's arms.

They both suddenly looked straight ahead to see the Alma Mater there, half in shadow. How long had it been there? Could it understand them?

"Bow in greeting, your majesty," Harris said quietly to Carrie, "and I will follow."

Carrie gave a slow bow and Harris followed. The Alma Mater stared back.

"I'll project the offenders in the brig," Carrie said. Harris gave a nod.

She closed her eyes and pictured the civilians standing in a cell, then she gently pushed the image toward the standing Zeta.

"Let me try," Harris said. Carrie nodded. They closed their eyes and she saw footage of the firefight, with an emphasis of the Zeta ship being protected by Atlas and the *Carcharias*, all aiming their fire away from the ship.

Tess growled.

The Alma Mater turned toward her fellow Zeta in study. Bright lines and dots filled the space between them. Carrie and Harris remained silent and watched.

The Alma Mater turned back to them. She had a concentrated look upon her face and a sheen of sweat across her brow.

An image shot into Carrie's mind of a planet with silver sand. She saw many humanoid Zetas standing around in gray robes. There were the Alma Maters, and others the UNF called Zisis, Amphibia and Salacia. Zisis, the mother of birds: they stood with feathery wings tucked around their bodies like a shawl. Amphibia, the mother of amphibians: they stood with their hairless skin, bulging black eyes and rounded bellies. Salacia, named after Neptune's queen: they stood lean with strong limbs and wet, scaly-like skin.

And they all stared at Carrie and Harris with intensity and curiosity.

"Oh, my god," Carrie breathed. "Are we on a conference call to Zeta Archelois or something?"

Harris threw her a glance before his attention was stolen by images of the standoff at Atlas again.

"She's explaining to them what happened," he said.

When the images ended, Carrie stared at the Zetas before her, studying them carefully. Tess growled from her hospital bed. Carrie looked at her, then back to the other Zetas again as a thought occurred to her.

"Where are the other Priestesses?" she asked Harris. "I see all the Zetas except them."

Harris was quiet as his eyes jumped from Zeta to Zeta. "You're right. They're not present."

More bright lines and dot exploded in their vision. They both squinted at the brightness and flashes. It was frenetic and disorienting as though several Zetas communicated at once.

Carrie suddenly began to feel dizzy.

"Oh, shit…" she said. "I'm going to faint."

"What?" Harris said. "How can you faint when you're asleep?"

"They can't see me weak. Pull out. Pull out!"

*

"Welles?" she heard Gregson's voice. "Welles? Wake up."

She felt a tapping on her cheek, then smelled something rotten. She groaned and rolled her face away.

"Come on, Welles," Gregson said. "That's it. Come back to me."

She heard another groan. *Harris?* She opened her eyes to see Gregson standing over her bed, watching the heart monitor beside her.

"What happened?" she slurred.

"She alright?" Harris was suddenly standing beside Gregson, rubbing his face awake.

Gregson nodded, still studying the monitor beside her. "Yeah," he said. "Her BP just suddenly crashed and her neural waves went haywire, but they've stabilized again." Gregson looked at Harris. "What happened in there?"

Harris rubbed his face again and sighed. "I don't really know, but I think we just met the rest of the Zeta family."

"You did?" Yughi asked, moving up to them. "Were they happy to see you?"

"Jury's out on that," Harris said, "but we did notice one thing."

"What?" Yughi asked.

"There were no Priestesses with them. Just the other four Zetas and their kin."

"What does that mean?" Gregson asked.

"I don't know," Harris said, "but I'd like to find out."

Carrie moved to sit up.

"Whoa!" Gregson said, taking her arms. "Take it easy, Welles."

The room spun a little for Carrie.

"Lay back down," Gregson said, studying her monitor again.

She took deep breaths as her eyes rolled around the room. "Why did this dream affect me so much?"

The room was silent for a moment, before Harris broke it.

"Because we weren't dealing with just one Zeta, Welles. There was a whole heap of them, and that's a lot of Thought Biology to deal with." He looked around and rubbed his forehead. "Even I'm feeling it and I don't have CTE. Our human brains aren't built for mass communication like theirs is."

Carrie looked at him. "The Alma Mater was sweating. I don't think it was easy for her either."

"No, probably not," Harris said. "She would've been carrying us to connect with them, and if they were in Zeta Archelois, that's a hell of a distance to carry a subconscious. We sure as shit didn't do that on our own."

Carrie swallowed, waiting for the last of her dizziness to pass. "We're not strong enough to handle them in big numbers or over great distances."

Harris stared at her. "Apparently not." He looked away from her, his mind consumed by something, as he then headed for the door.

Gregson handed Carrie some water. "Drink this."

Carrie took it and sipped, trying to ignore the deep ache throbbing in her skull.

Gold walked along the corridor, on his way to the brig, when Lieutenant Batoya called his name from behind. He stopped and turned to her.

"Lieutenant," he gave her a nod.

"Can I have a moment, sir?"

"What is it?" he said.

"I checked the logs for the leak," she said quietly, stepping up to him. "It didn't come from us, sir."

"You sure? It wasn't Connolly?"

"No, sir. There were no transmissions on file and I also had the station AI check for unregulated offline or scrubbed transmissions. There were none, sir. Station Atlas was not the source of the leak."

"Okay. Thanks."

Batoya gave a nod. "You're going to see Connolly?"

"Yeah," Gold said, "he and I need to have a little talk."

He turned to walk away but stopped and turned back to her.

"Batoya?"

"Yes, sir?"

"Thank you for your support back there. I appreciate it. It's good to know I can rely on you."

"No problems, sir." She smiled and walked away.

Miranda Finch waited as the transmission connected. Harris soon appeared.

"Colonel," she said, "thanks for taking my call. Do you have any comment about the firefight off Atlas?"

He stared at her a moment. "Not at this time."

"We have to act on this," Miranda told him. "If you stay quiet on the truth, that's when the lies will spread."

Harris contemplated her words. "This is true, but I'm still getting to the bottom of what happened. I'll have an official statement soon."

"You want me to instill calm in the public sphere," she said, "so help me do that. What happened out there? Don't let your enemies get the first word."

Harris took a moment, then took a breath and sighed deeply in resignation. "Civilians tried to take matters into their own hands and almost caused a major incident that could have assured us of another war in short order. However, UNF forces subdued the offenders and, therefore, strengthened our chance of securing peace with the Zetas."

She nodded, scribbling down notes. "What's the next step?"

"Well, I am now half a day away from Atlas. I will commence peace talks when I arrive. All offenders have been arrested and are currently answering the UNF's questions. I will give you more when I have it."

She nodded again. "Okay. Thank you." She went to end the transmission, but Harris stopped her.

"Miranda," he said, "one thing. Off the record."

Her eyes lit up. "Sure. What is it?"

"Who's leaking these stories to Mars Media? We've confirmed it wasn't anyone on Station Atlas, or anyone else within the UNF."

"I don't know," she said.

"Can you ask that reporter, Kellan van Pelt?" Harris asked, eyes fixed on hers.

She shrugged. "I'll try, but Mars Media is no longer an ally of mine."

"You just started with them." Harris quirked an eyebrow.

"We parted ways. Lotz didn't like my reports being so supportive of you and President Harkowitz."

"I'm sorry to hear that."

"Don't be. I'm not. Leave it with me and I'll see what I can find out."

He gave a nod. "Thank you."

"Colonel?" she said, as a sudden thought occurred to her.

"Yes?"

"I'm thinking in order to continue our new arrangement, our alliance, I'll need new comms gear. The kind supplied by the UNF and encrypted as such. I'm currently using Mars Media gear, and I've just realized I can't guarantee that we're not being listened to."

"What are you going to do if you no longer have a media studio behind you?"

"I'll start my damn own," she said. "It's about time I did. I know an independent station that can air my reports until I have my own setup. The World News Network. My contacts there are friendly."

Harris gave a nod. "I'll have new gear sent to you."

"Thank you."

"If you uncover anything, please let me know."

"I will," she said.

Harris gave a single nod and ended the comms.

Miranda sighed and turned away from the screen. She walked over to stare out the windows of her Centralis apartment, then she looked back to her Mars Media gear and scowled.

She grabbed the gear, opened her window, and dropped them down to the pavement below, watching them smash to pieces.

"Fuck you, Mars Media."

Harris waited for the transmission to connect. Within moments, President Harkowitz stared at him.

"Colonel," he said, "I'm glad the standoff is over."

"As am I, sir," Harris said, "but we still have a problem."

"What's that?"

"Are we on a secure transmission?"

"All my transmissions are secure."

"Alright. We've confirmed the leak to the media did not come from within the UNF. The only other party who knew about it was your office."

Harkowitz stared at him. "That's a hell of an accusation."

"It's the truth, sir," Harris said. "And if it wasn't you, I'd be very worried."

"If it wasn't me?"

"Was it you?"

"No. It was not."

"Then you have a problem on your hands. Someone in your office is feeding the media information. You need to find them and remove them, sir. I promised I would tell you everything, but I cannot tell you anything if you have a mole who is gonna run to the press every time something happens. Neutralize them, then we can talk."

"Now wait a minute," Harkowitz seethed. "My people are loyal."

"Are they?" Harris asked.

"They've been with me for years."

"That may be so, sir, but loyalties can change with time. Who, on your side, is not happy you're working with me to secure peace. Who wants war?"

"No-one *wants* war, Harris."

"Maybe not, but who wants you out of that chair? Who wants to control the proxy-steel? Who stands to benefit from the money to be made from it?"

Harkowitz stared at him. "There are many investors in the Mercandez company, but I'm sure they would prefer their money not be paid for in human lives."

"Don't be so sure," Harris said. "But, alright. Who, then, thinks it's time for you to step aside for a new president, say, Regan Lotz?"

Harkowitz's brow furrowed.

Harris shrugged. "I told you, word is he's planning on running against you again. He's grown in power, Mr. President. He built his own fortune, then married into the Khalid fortune, now he's established Mars Media. If you're not careful he will have a stranglehold on you before you know it. Whoever is leaking information to him, is helping him take you down from within."

Harkowitz stared back at Harris as his mind turned over.

"Just be careful who you trust," Harris warned. "I gotta go."

Marchant knocked on the door of General Berger's office and was quickly ushered through.

"They saw all the Zeta races?" Berger cut to the chase, pointing at the report on his screen.

Marchant nodded. "Yes, but it was too much for the two of them to handle. Harris reiterated the need to bring in this DaJuan and others like him."

"Do we have intel on this guy's whereabouts yet?"

"No, we can't find any trace of him. He's in hiding."

"So, we can't bring him in?"

Marchant shook his head. "Not until Harris tells us where to find him."

"Well, how hard can it be? Based on his criminal record, all his offenses were in the New Orleans jurisdiction. We send troops there and shake some trees until we find him."

"Sir," Marchant held up his hand, "if we go storming in there, Harris will be pissed. We gotta wait for him to bring this guy in."

"Harris is the one saying they can't do this on their own, and he's off-Earth."

"I know, and as soon as he returns he'll bring this guy in, but for now, we have to wait."

Berger stared at him. "You know we can find him. It's just a matter of twisting a few arms for the right information."

Marchant nodded. "I know. But I'm asking you to wait."

A knock at the door sounded, and they both looked around as it opened and Morrell entered.

"Sorry to interrupt," Morrell said, then looked at Marchant. "I was told I could find you here."

"What is it?" Marchant asked.

Morrell motioned to the window. "Take a look outside."

Berger turned in his chair and Marchant moved to stand beside the general. Below at the gates of Centralis, a small crowd was gathered.

"Concerned civilians," Morrell said, locking eyes with Marchant. "I'm told more are gathering in cities on mainland US and around the world."

"Shit," Marchant said, looking back to the crowd.

"Elevate our security status," Berger told Morrell. "Spread word to our Earth Duty units stationed around the globe. We don't have time for this shit."

"How long until Harris reaches Atlas?" Morrell asked.

Marchant checked his watch. "He'll be there in about eight hours."

Morrell nodded. "Let's hope he can get some answers to calm this lot down or we'll have a problem on our hands if he brings that Zeta back."

"We won't have a problem if you do your job," Berger told Morrell.

Morrell took the hint, gave him a nod, and left.

Carrie sat on her bed in the med bay, staring at Harris and Gregson.

"I'll be fine. We'll just go in, tell it we're on the ship that's about to arrive, then we pull out."

"We don't need two of us for that," Harris said. "I'll go in alone."

"But I'm the leader."

"So," Harris shrugged, "I'm the messenger."

McKinley entered the med bay then.

"ETA is five hours," he said. "You gonna tell that Zeta not to burn us as we approach?"

"Yeah," Harris rubbed his neck, "I'm about to give it a try."

"*We* are about to," Carrie said.

"Gregson, what are her vitals?"

Gregson rested his hands on his hips. "Her BP is still a little low. Neural patterns still a little erratic."

"Then the answer is, no," Harris said, climbing onto his bed.

Carrie exhaled her disappointment, then locked eyes with McKinley. "What about him?" she said turning to Harris.

"Me?" McKinley said, straightening. "No," he shook his head.

Harris looked at him curiously.

"Any dreams I've had have been completely involuntary and accidental. No!" McKinley said firmly. "Besides, I'm watching my ship." He turned and walked out of the med bay.

"He's right," Harris said. "I'll do better on my own than trying to hold his hand in there. Gregson? Give me a dose, then wake me up."

"Alright," Gregson said, stepping forward and picking up a needle he'd prepared.

Gold stood outside Connolly's cell in the Atlas brig. Never did he think the first person to grace these confines would be one of his own soldiers.

There was little to the cell other than three gray walls and a proxy-steel row of bars facing into the brig proper. The cell sat beside four others – one of several small brigs located throughout the station. Inside each was a simple pullout bed, a basin, and a curtained latrine, but that was it. They were not designed for comfort.

The disgraced lieutenant had looked at him briefly, long enough for Gold to see the nasty bruise and swelling on his face, before Connolly had dropped his eyes to the floor.

"How's the head?" Gold asked, taking a soft approach.

Connolly glanced up, then back to the floor. "You hit hard."

Gold shrugged. "Well, I'm sorry about that, but you did pull a gun on me."

Connolly's eyes remained on the floor.

"A lot of people died in the invasion, Connolly," Gold said gently, "and a lot of people are hurting, but going renegade and being bloodthirsty for revenge is not the answer. Cool and calculated moves are what's going to help us win a war."

Connolly looked up, his eyes accusatory beneath the bruises. "You were going to shoot down civilians to protect that alien. That is not the UNF I signed up for."

"We were never going to shoot down civilians, only disable their ships."

"The *Carcharias* could've destroyed that ship with one stray firing."

"Yes, it could. But cool heads prevailed. I said if warning shots did not stop them, then the *Carcharias* needed to do what it had to, to protect my soldiers's lives, but they had to preserve civilian life. Those civilians fired direct hits at our ship first, Connolly. They gave no fucks about killing our soldiers to get to that alien. Are you saying you condone civilians taking the lives of soldiers? Where is the humanity in that? *Our* human lives were worthless compared to their need for revenge on the alien that, by the way, had nothing to do with the invasion. It's a different Zeta altogether, and that Zeta has not fired upon us. Do you not think we should try to communicate with it to understand what it wants? Why this one *hasn't* fired upon us? To try and make peace? Or are you just so thirsty for revenge that you would prefer a full-blown war to satisfy your need? Shoot first and ask questions later. That's not a military I want to be a part of, Connolly. I will fight if I have to, *no* question, but if there's a chance for peace, I will take that every time."

Connolly kept looking at the ground, now rocking his body a little, agitated. Gold sensed that it wasn't anger, but pure emotion at what had taken place and how Gold's words stung him now.

"You were one of my ops deck leads, Connolly. You were given that job because the UNF saw real potential in you. You did a good job up until this incident. I still see potential in you."

Connolly looked up at this.

"You're hurting from your brother's death, I get that," Gold said. "You need some realignment. Did you ever get any counselling?"

Connolly shook his head and cast his eyes down. "I was stationed on Mars then. We were untouched."

Gold nodded. "I'm going to give you some time off. You go back to Earth, you get some counselling and you grieve your brother's death. Then, if you choose to wear the uniform again, and your mind aligns with our principles *and* our orders..." Gold paused, to highlight "orders", until Connolly looked him in the eyes again. When he did, Gold continued. "Then we can talk about you coming back here."

"You'd have me back?" Connolly asked, confused. "I pulled a gun on you."

"And I knocked you out before you could think of using it," Gold said firmly, unable to stop the Alpha from flowing through his eyes, before he softened them again. "But I understand why, and I believe in forgiveness and redemption."

"Why?" Connolly asked. "Why do you believe in forgiveness and redemption?"

"Because," Gold said, "I am not perfect. I, myself, have had to be forgiven for things." He stuffed his hands in his pockets as he continued to stare at Connolly. "But if you *ever* pull a gun on me again..." He didn't finish the sentence. He didn't need to.

Connolly eyed him briefly, then averted his gaze, perhaps a little terrified, before nodding an acceptance.

"I'll put you on the next flight out," Gold said. He went to leave, then paused and looked back at the bruised lieutenant. "Just make sure you get that counselling, Connolly. Alright? If you've given up on the uniform, so be it. Just get that counselling and right your mind. I didn't know your brother, but I'm sure he wouldn't want you to go down this path."

And with that, Gold walked away, leaving his words hanging thickly in the air of Connolly's cell.

12

Disorientation

Mars president, Finn Harkowitz, exited his office, straightening his suit jacket. He'd been drowning in his thoughts and needed to clear his head. He closed the door and saw Laurelai approaching.

"Shall we proceed with the press conference, sir?" she asked expectantly. She had always been detail oriented and career-driven, and that's what he liked about her. Whatever he asked, she would get it done. She was top-notch at strategy and PR, and had always helped him read the future. But just how career-driven was she? Enough to help oust him if she thought he was done?

"Er, no," he said, "not yet. I'm just going to take a walk and clear my head."

"We need to move on that soon, sir. Are the UNF delaying you?"

"No. No, not at all," he said. "I just want to be sure of what I'm going to say before I say it. I'll be back soon."

He smiled politely, then went on his way. Despite the small number of staff in the Red House, despite the number of constituents on Mars who had voted for him, he suddenly felt very isolated. Was Harris right? Was someone trying to take him down from the inside?

He made his way to the lookout balcony on the Red House roof. He needed some space to consider his options. As he reached the roof, he saw four UNF soldiers on watch at various intervals. They each gave him a curious nod, then returned their eyes to the Red House grounds encased in the domes. Dressed in their blue and silver Space Duty uniforms, they stood out from the burnt-orange Martian landscape that surrounded them.

They were Space Duty soldiers, but his mind turned over his recent plans to change them to Martian soldiers. He'd thought these soldiers didn't belong to space, they belonged to Mars, and if he were to evoke their true loyalty, they needed to feel a sense of place, of belonging. Making them soldiers of Mars would do that. But strangely enough, right now, he felt a sense of relief they were still Space Duty soldiers, effectively under Harris's command.

Unless, of course, this talk of a mole inside the Red House was just a UNF ploy to ensure any plans for a colonial force were squashed. Making Finn worry about enemies in his midst was a surefire way to do that, to make him think he needed UNF support. But would Harris do that to him? Would Harris lie? Could Finn really trust a man working for a powerful military organization that wanted his Martian ore?

He sighed and moved to the lookout railing that held views over Colony Elon some 20 kilometers in the distance. He studied the large domes and the top stories of the buildings that poked out of the ground. He'd been the only president they'd known all these years. He cared about this planet and its people and that was why he kept being elected. Thanks to a bill endorsed by the UNF, he would be eligible for re-election for a third term, and he had been confident that it would happen. But now? Had the people grown tired of him? Had he become too confident, too complacent, while Regan Lotz amassed power behind the scenes ready for another run at the presidency? He was amicable with Lotz on the surface. They ran into each other frequently, whenever an event was held on Mars, so they were both smart enough keep things civil. But having beat him twice before, had Finn made the grave mistake of letting his guard down?

Had he been a fool?

He looked up into the sky, turning around as though trying to spot Station Atlas. Of course he couldn't, it was too far away for the human eye. The only station visible from Mars, and only at night, was Station Pegasus.

One of his earlier conversations with Harris circled his mind, about the UNF control of space and Mars, and how he was only president because the UNF wanted him to be president. It made Finn question just what he was president of: a mineral-rich planet with a minimal civilian population, a high-tech prison in Hell Town, and a strong military presence backed by not one but two stations circling just off the planet.

Minerals, miners, military, and inmates: they were his core constituents. He'd been fighting hard to shift public perception of Mars away from its Wild West image and had made some inroads, but was he fighting a losing battle? Was he fighting the inevitable? Were his dreams of turning Mars into a flourishing civilian planet, a pipe dream? If the Zetas came back and war ensued, the military needed Mars's proxy-steel. Was the Mars president destined to be a mere puppet to safeguard things for the UNF?

Was that such a bad thing? Isn't that what politics was all about? He couldn't fight the framework that held him in place, but he could still use his position to do what he felt was right. And what he thought was right, was him presiding as president for as long as he could, because he cared for Mars and wanted it to be something greater than the Wild West. He wanted it to be a new frontier of hope. If Regan Lotz became president he would care only about profits and power, which was not something Finn's father would've stood for, and certainly not something Finn would stand for. If he had to be the UNF's puppet to ensure Mars was kept from the clutches of Lotz, then so be it. He could still hope for a better Mars.

He heard footsteps and turned around to see Colonel Greavy approach.

"Sir," Greavy said, eyeing him curiously, "everything alright?"

Finn nodded. "Yes, just felt like stepping outside," he said, then smiled. "As outside as one can be under a dome on Mars. And you, Sam?"

"Fine. I heard you spoke with Harris, then went for a walk." He scanned the view of Elon, then looked back at him. "Something on your mind?"

Finn studied his longtime friend and ally. Sam had been by his side for many years, helping Finn to oversee Mars and its burgeoning growth. Sam had always been the voice of reason and caution, particularly when it came to the earlier tense standoff with the UNF. After all, Sam was caught in a difficult position between the two. He was both loyal to Mars and loyal to the UNF. But if push came to shove and he had to choose, which one would he choose? Sam had always cautioned against playing hardball with the UNF, had always taken the view that an independent Mars force could never withstand the might of the rest of the UNF. Had Finn's talk of independence pushed him too far? Had he tested his loyalties one time too many? Could Sam, his longtime friend and ally, be the one to undermine him? To try and oust him?

"Nothing," Finn smiled assuredly. "Just thinking about what's happening up at Atlas. Have the perpetrators talked yet?"

"Not yet," Greavy told him. "Nothing useful, anyway, I'm told. Just complaints about how we should've taken action against that Zeta ship." Greavy looked like he was going to say something further but he paused.

"What is it?" Finn asked him.

Greavy looked at his feet as he clasped his hands behind his back. "They're questioning our loyalty to Martian civilians. They're pissed we put the life of that Zeta over our own constituents."

Finn turned around to face him. "Those constituents fired upon a UNF vessel. Did they really think the UNF would look the other way? They started it, the UNF ended it."

"That may be so, but this is a problem, Finn. They see the Zetas as our enemies and we're protecting them."

"The Zetas *are* our enemies," Finn said sharply. "Make no mistake of that. But I trust Colonel Harris and what he is trying to do. If at any time we lose our faith in him or the UNF... we deal with that when it happens." Finn studied the colonel before him a moment. "Aren't you pleased I'm supporting the UNF now? Listening to what they say. Not playing hardball."

"What's changed?" Greavy asked, eyes narrowed as he waited for the response.

"I saw the error in my ways," Finn said lightly. "You're right, we do need them. It would be foolish to close doors on our allies."

Greavy nodded as he considered his response. "These vigilantes, they're not the only ones speaking out against you."

Finn studied him. "Who else?"

"I'm hearing things from my soldiers in the colonies. They're hearing things."

"Let people talk," Harkowitz waved them off. "They're allowed to have opinions."

"Sir," Greavy stepped up to him, "I questioned whether or not to tell you this, but I think you need to know."

"Know what?"

"We've been receiving death threats, sir. Against you."

Finn stared at him, scanning his friend's eyes for the truth. "How many?"

"Ten so far."

"Over what period of time?"

"Since the invasion."

Harkowitz nodded. "Who's been sending them?"

"We haven't been able to identify all of them yet. Some have been using an encrypted system. I've been trying to deal with this in-house, but…"

"But?" Finn asked.

"I think we need to take it seriously," Greavy told him, then looked out over the horizon. "Mars is growing by the day and my attention is being pulled in different directions, as is my soldiers'. I think it's time you have a dedicated protective service like those on Earth."

"You think they're serious, these threats?" Finn asked him.

"After what these vigilantes did, yes. Besides, like I told you, my soldiers hear things. They've heard rumors of a group that's formed. One that seeks an independent Mars."

Finn studied him. "I've heard whispers too. It's only natural that other political parties would develop eventually. People suggest to me all the time that Mars should be independent, and I reply that I am seriously considering it. Perhaps I shouldn't have done so."

"This goes beyond what you've heard about a new political party potentially headed up by Regan Lotz. I'm hearing talk of an underground group that's forming, one that's not scared to bear arms, who are prepared to *ensure* Mars has independence."

"Are you talking about a terrorist group?"

Greavy gave a single nod.

"Why are you just telling me this?" Finn asked.

"Because I was hoping it was just talk, but after these vigilantes, I'm not so sure."

Finn nodded absently, his mind turning things over. "Tell me, Sam, do your soldiers ever talk to the media?"

Greavy looked at him, surprised by the question, perhaps offended, even a little suspicious.

"Not to my knowledge," he said.

Finn gave a reassuring smile. "Well, thank you for telling me." He patted Sam's shoulder, then began to move away.

"Where are you going?"

Finn smiled at him again. "To do a media conference to reassure the people of Mars there is nothing to fear. Sounds like it's overdue."

Finn continued, heading for the elevator. As he stepped inside, he glanced around to Greavy and saw that he remained standing, hands clasped behind his back, staring out at the Martian landscape.

Finn couldn't help wonder, then, whether some of Sam's soldiers were sympathetic to this independent Mars group?

As the elevator doors closed, two other faces popped into his mind: Senators Pope and Butten. Could they have been the leak? Did they think it was time for Finn to relinquish his seat?

A cold sensation settled in his stomach. The truth was, he wasn't sure who he could trust anymore.

Harris watched intently as the *Aurizun* approached Station Atlas. In the distance, visible on radar, was the single Zeta ship, just hovering.

"Authority codes accepted," Hunter said, "proceeding with docking at the station."

"Status on the Zeta ship?" McKinley asked.

"It's there," Frazer answered, "but weapons are offline."

McKinley looked to Harris. "Looks like the projections worked."

Harris nodded. "She knows we're not a threat." He looked to where Welles sat beside Tikaani. "How're you feeling?"

Welles looked at him. "Good as new. I'm fine."

He turned his eyes to Gregson and arched his eyebrow in question.

"Her vitals have returned to normal," he confirmed. "I guess maybe you just need to request a little one-on-one time with the Zeta and ask her to keep her friends and family out of it."

Harris grunted. "Easier said than done."

"The Zeta's one thing," Evenssen said. "What about these vigilantes? And I'm not talking about the Mars civilians. Gold's ops lead pulled a gun on him."

"We need to keep our eyes sharp," McKinley said. "Gold handled the fucker, but there could be more. If someone pulls a gun on me, they'll be sleeping for a looong time."

"Damn straight," Brown said.

"Alright," Harris said, "prepare to board."

Carrie followed the *Aurizun* crew onto Atlas. They'd been cleared through quarantine and were walking the corridors of the station proper, following a sergeant sent by Gold to escort them to the ops deck. They found Gold deep in conversation with a woman Carrie was soon introduced to as Lieutenant Batoya.

"Thank for handling things for us," Harris said to Gold. "You did good."

Gold smiled and Carrie noted he looked tired. Or at least, like he had a ton on his mind.

"Glad to have you here," Gold told Harris. "Where do you want to start?"

"Well, we let the Zeta know we were arriving, but I think we need to let her know that we're aboard and want to meet face-to-face."

"And how do you do that?" Gold asked, as Batoya watched on attentively.

"We'll need your med bay. Gregson will give us something to relax us, then we take a nap. Something you should probably do," Harris smirked as he studied Gold. "You look tired."

Gold smirked back. "Yeah, well, it's been a time, that's for sure."

"Well, you can rest under our watch," Harris gave his arm a friendly slap. "We better start."

"Sure thing," Gold said. "This way."

*

Carrie stood at the end of a darkened corridor alone. It often took Harris a little longer to start dreaming as he wouldn't let Gregson give him too much of the drug to ease him into sleep, and so it delayed his larger body succumbing to it.

Harris stepped up beside her. "Anything?"

"No, I've just been standing here waiting for you."

"Alright, let's move on."

"And hope it's only her here this time," Carrie said as they began to walk.

Soon enough the black walls turned pearly-gray. They came to a round door that slid across and found themselves on one of the Zeta's flight decks. They were alone.

Harris moved to the center of the room, placed his hands on his hips and waited patiently. Carrie slowly moved around the periphery of the room, running her fingers along the console lip and watching the electric blue light shining beneath the tips. She always found it mesmerizing.

"Welles," Harris said firmly, but calmly.

She turned around to see the Alma Mater standing in the other doorway – the one that led further into the Zeta ship. Harris moved slowly down to sit on the floor. Carrie saw the Alma Mater's eyes were watching her fingertips, alight with the blue of the console. She pulled her hand away, then moved slowly to sit beside Harris.

"So, where do we start?" Carrie asked, but before Harris could answer an image projected in her mind. An image of the civilian Martian ship firing upon the *Carcharias*.

"She has questions," Harris said, studying the Zeta.

"You wanna answer?" Carrie asked.

Harris nodded and closed his eyes. Carrie did, too, and she saw images from Decima, of UNF ships being blown from the skies. Then, she saw the Martian ships targeting the Alma Mater's ship. Then, she saw a soldier pulling a gun on Gold and the major knocking him out. Then she saw the *Carcharias* firing back on the civilian ships and disabling them.

Carrie and Harris opened their eyes to see the Zeta staring at them. This time, however, Tess was there, growling like she did.

"Some of our kind don't want you here, but we will protect you," Harris said. "We mean you no harm."

Suddenly an image burst into Carrie's mind. It was chaotic and she felt dizzy for a moment as she tried to fixate on what was happening. She saw a battle. She saw all the different Zetas fighting: the Priestess kind, the Alma Mater, the Zisis, Salacia, the Amphibia. Then she saw a mass of ships leaving the planet with silver sand. Then there was nothing, but blackness.

She groaned and opened her eyes again. "What does that mean?"

Harris considered things a moment before answering. "I think she's trying to tell us they've had their own civil war."

"Who won?"

"I don't know."

Tess growled, and suddenly they saw an Alma Mater get its head cut off.

Carrie looked from Tess to the Alma Mater. The Alma Mater stared at Tess, then looked back at them. Another image flashed inside their minds, this time of a Homo heidelbergensis – one of their captured HH warriors. It was naked. Next, an Alma Mater stood beside it. It too was naked. It was male.

Carrie's mouth fell open. "So they do have men…"

Then the Alma Mater cut off the head of its male equivalent.

Then a male Priestess had its head cut off. Then a male Zisis, then a male Salacia, then a male Amphibia.

"They really don't like men, do they?" Harris said quietly.

"You better let me do the talking from here on in," Carrie said. She closed her eyes and projected an image of her holding Harris's hand. Then of her holding McKinley's hand. Then she pictured them smiling. Then she pictured the male Alma Mater getting its head cut off, trying to frame it as a question.

"Why do you kill your men?" she asked the creature.

The Alma Mater stared at her a moment, before another barrage of images shot into her mind. She saw anger, she saw violence, she saw oppression… and it was all at the hands of the male creatures against the females. She saw arguing, crowds gathering, saw the civil war. The females rose up in fierce battle. She saw victory, then saw the male Zetas marched onto ships that left the silver sand planet. Then she saw the new female rulers sitting in some kind of hall of power.

The images ended and Carrie stared at the Zeta, her head beginning to throb with a deep ache.

"They rose up and banished their men," she said, feeling sweat on her brow.

Another image projected inside her mind. It was fast, it was aggressive, and she was sure it came from Tess this time. She saw the HH on Earth being marched onto ships.

Carrie cleared her vision and turned to stare at the Priestess.

"You got rid of your males, so you took ours and oppressed them."

Suddenly another image burst into her mind. This time she saw a group of Zetas talking – bright lines and dots filling the air, along with that strange cacophony of humming, buzzing and clicks she'd heard before on early radio recordings played to them by Marchant – then it seemed to grow heated. The Priestess at the gathering stormed off. The Amphibia followed. The Alma Mater, Zisis and Salacia remained. Next, Carrie saw a fleet leaving Zeta Archelois. A Priestess fleet. Next, she saw a fleet return, saw Priestesses marching their HH slaves off and showcasing them to the others. Next, she saw a female Zisis demonstrating what looked to be some kind of in vitro fertilization. She saw baby Zetas growing in the womb. She saw more arguing, more division. She saw the number of HH slaves growing, saw more arguing, more division, crowds gathering. She saw the Priestesses and Amphibians invading some strange planet with their HH, saw them decimate the population of alien creatures, saw them establish a base. Then she saw the Alma Mater before her, standing on her silver soil, watching all that the Priestesses and Amphibians did. Zisis stood beside her, looking out upon the destruction, while Salacia stood close by, her eyes on the ground. Then she saw a fleet of the Priestess ships heading toward Earth.

Then Tess, still strapped in her bed, growled at Carrie and Harris, and suddenly all the Zetas were there staring at her and Harris again, and a sharp pain seared through Carrie's brain like a knife.

She cried out.

The Alma Mater stepped toward her, eyes fixed with intensity.

And everything went black.

Harris woke suddenly to yelling. Drenched in sweat, he looked dizzily over at Welles. Gregson was leaning over her, shouting.

"Welles! Wake up!" he said, as the Atlas's chief medical officer tore open a cupboard beside her bed, pulled out defibrillator paddles, and handed them to Gregson.

Harris shook his head, trying to throw off the drugs in his system, and sat up. He looked to Welles's monitor and saw it was erratic, then flatlining.

"The fuck?" he said, getting out of bed, as Gregson prepped the defibrillator.

Just as Gregson was about to shock her, her heart suddenly started beating again.

Gregson, eyes wide and panting, was glued to the monitor. They both watched as her heart began to beat in a normal pattern of peaks and troughs.

"What about her brain?" Gregson mumbled to himself, eyes now fixed to another monitor, which was still showing a flatline.

Harris moved closer and took hold of Welles's hand.

"Welles? Wake up!" He felt the faint vibration of static electricity through her skin. Then her neural wave monitor began to show signs of activity.

Noise down the corridor caught his attention; the sound of thumping footsteps. He turned to see McKinley race through the door.

"Is she alive?"

Harris nodded. "She's back. She's back."

McKinley moved up beside him as Gold appeared in the doorway, watching on curiously. Gregson moved to the other side of Welles's bed and began shining a light in her eyes.

"What the fuck happened?" McKinley asked.

"I don't know," Harris said. "I think she overloaded or something."

"She can't keep doing this," Gregson said firmly to Harris, as he snapped an oxygen mask over her face. "We'll kill her."

Harris looked at Welles. Her vitals monitor looked fine, but she was still unconscious. McKinley took her hand off Harris and held it in his own, his real own.

"Carrie?" He caressed her hair. "Carrie, wake up."

Harris stepped back. He still felt a little faint himself. He turned around and leaned on his bed to catch his breath. As he did, he locked eyes with Gold in the doorway.

"Did you set up a meet with the Zeta at least?" Gold asked gently.

Harris shook his head. "No. We didn't get that far."

Gold exhaled, looking down at the floor as he rubbed his neck. "How long do you think we can keep it here?"

"I don't know," Harris said, "but I know we need help. We have to put out the call."

"A call for what?" Gold asked.

"Help," Harris said, standing again. "Help from people like me."

Carrie groaned and rolled over onto her side.

"What's wrong?" Gregson said urgently. "Explain it to me."

"The room's spinning," she said closing her eyes again. "Make it stop."

"Okay. Hold on." She heard him rummaging around and asking the Atlas chief med officer where something was. Carrie breathed hard, trying to fight the urge to vomit.

"Oh god… make it stop," she said between breaths.

She felt the stab of a needle in her arm.

"I just gave you an anti-nausea shot," Gregson told her. "Give it a few minutes to kick in."

Carrie continued to lay on her side, eyes closed, breathing through the sickness. The minutes passed and she felt the nausea recede like an ebbing tide. When she felt it was safe, she opened her eyes again. The room was no longer spinning, but it was bright and she squinted. When her vision adjusted, she laid eyes on McKinley, who sat by her bed, his blue eyes fixed intently on hers.

"You can't do that again," he said. "I'm banning you."

She managed a faint smile. "Even if our world depends on it?"

"Your heart went haywire, Carrie," he said, not seeing the humor. "Your fucking brain waves were flat."

The smile slipped from her face. "They were?"

He nodded.

"You scared the shit out of us," Gregson said, his face concerned.

"I did?" she said, feeling it was safe to roll onto her back. Gregson nodded.

"I don't give a fuck about the world," McKinley said, standing. "You can't do that again. We'll find another way."

He leaned down and kissed her forehead, then stormed out of the room.

Harris sat in the Atlas boardroom with Gold and McKinley, on transmission with Berger and Marchant, debriefing them.

"But she'll recover?" Marchant asked.

"Yes," Harris said.

"And she won't be doing that again," McKinley said firmly. "Not until you fix her brain."

"Agreed," Harris said. "But, moving forward I can't guarantee the Alma Mater won't try to reach her when she sleeps. We've established contact between the two. The Alma Mater might take offense if Welles suddenly won't speak with her."

"We need to find a way around that," McKinley said.

"We do," Harris agreed, then turned back to the screens. "That's why I need to bring in DaJuan and put out a call to others."

"We need to be careful there, Harris," Berger said. "There's civil unrest building across the space quadrants. Word's out about how the Atlas standoff played out and some people aren't happy we protected the Zeta. We need to let things cool first. If we now go and put out a call for people like you, there could be a further descent into chaos."

"That is why I need to grant Miranda Finch a no-holds-barred interview. I need to explain what it is I do with the Zetas and the information I have gathered from doing so. I need to be open and honest and transparent. They will have nothing to fear."

"There will still be some who fear, Harris, because they don't understand it," Berger said. "You will never win the support of 100 percent of the people. That's just the way it goes. Even if you manage to sway 99 percent, that one percent can still create a lot of damage and chaos that will affect the other 99 percent."

Harris sighed. "That may be so, sir, but we have to try something and we need to move fast. You made me Head of Strategy, so let me do my job. We bring DaJuan in, start there. Then I do the interview with Finch and we see what that shakes out of the tree. Agreed?"

"Agreed," McKinley said quickly and firmly.

Harris looked at him, then turned his eyes to Gold. "Thoughts, major?"

Gold took a moment before exhaling heavily. "I trust your instincts," he said. "You were right about the Zeta, protecting it. It hasn't made any move to fire upon us and I believe this means we have a chance to engage with it and learn from it, and maybe even negotiate peace. If your last… *conversation…* is anything to go by, it looks like they had their own civil war, right? Which means that, although this Alma Mater is potentially friendly to us, there are other Zetas out there who may not be. Which means war could still be headed our way." Gold shrugged. "As you say, information is power. If war is coming, I want to know my enemy's weaknesses. And if the only way to get that information is by doing this dream thing with the Alma Mater, then we need to do this dream thing. If Welles can't do it and if you alone are not enough, then we need to bring others in. Time's a wasting."

Harris looked back to the screen and his superiors. "Gentlemen?"

"I agree, Welles is off the table," Marchant said. "I think we need to move cautiously, but we do need to move. That Zeta won't hang around forever waiting for someone to speak with."

"General?" Harris moved his eyes to the UNF leader.

Berger considered things a moment. "I still have my concerns and reservations. I don't consent to the interview with Finch, but I agree to bringing in this DaJuan and starting there. I would've had him here already, but you wouldn't let us."

Harris gave a sharp nod. "Thank you, sir. I'll try to engage once more with the Zeta, alone," he shot McKinley a look, "then we'll depart for Earth and see if we can convince the Zeta to follow us."

"And if it doesn't?" Marchant asked.

"Then, I'll have to bring DaJuan here. But I'm hoping it might like a tour of Earth. If nothing else, I'm sure it believes information is power too."

"You're going to expose our defenses to the Zeta race?" Berger asked.

"Hey, I'm not giving it our nuclear codes," Harris said. "I'm just going to bring it to Earth, maybe point out a few trees and mountains. That's all."

"It already knows our capability anyway," McKinley said. "It's seen the images from Decima. It knows our ships and our firepower. At least, what it was back then. We need to keep our improvements, since, under wraps."

"Agreed," Marchant said. "Proceed."

Mars president, Finn Harkowitz, logged into the transmission eagerly.

"Colonel Harris," he greeted his caller.

"Mr. President," Harris nodded. "You requested an update. Are you confident this is a secure channel?"

"Yes. One fit for a president. Go ahead."

"Alright. As you know, I'm on Station Atlas and we have been communicating with the Zeta. We are making progress, somewhat slowly. I am looking to invite the creature to Earth to work further on our communication. As I assured you, this creature has made no aggressive moves toward us, so there is no threat. If that remains, peace is an option."

"What have you learned from it so far?"

"I'm still sorting through what she has communicated to me, but I believe theirs is a race that has suffered a civil war of some kind. I can't comment any further on that yet, as it would be pure speculation, sir, and I'd like to provide you with cold hard facts."

"May I ask exactly how you are communicating with it?"

"It's hard to explain, sir."

"I obviously know the high-level detail, that it's something to do with dreams, but I would like to know more."

"I understand, sir, but it's not something fitting for a transmission, despite how encrypted this may be. Let's just say it has to do with the subconscious and what we're calling Thought Technology and Thought Biology. That's all I can say for now, but I vow to explain things better in due course."

Finn studied him a moment, before conceding with a nod.

"Did you have any luck looking into the source of the leak?" Harris asked, changing subject.

"Nothing confirmed, but I have my suspicions. In fact, that is where you may be able to help me, Harris."

"Yeah? And how's that?"

"Until I'm sure of who I can trust, I can't ask any of my staffers to investigate this. I need an outside person."

"Who do you suspect?"

"Well," Finn sighed, "I suspect many, but the first one you can help me clear is Colonel Greavy."

"He's your top soldier on Mars. You sure about that?"

"I want to be wrong, Harris, but I need to know if he or any of his soldiers are passing on the information. Are you able to look at what links he has, particularly with Regan Lotz? Also, I'm hearing whispers there has been an armed group forming here, one hoping for an independent Mars. They might be linked with this vigilante group."

Harris thought this over. "If Colonel Greavy is involved, he's pretty high up in the Space Duty division. How can you trust my guys won't tip him off to the investigation, or he be alerted somehow?"

Finn considered this. "How do you suggest I find this out if I can't use my people or your people?"

"You said you needed an outside source. That's exactly what you need. An outside source. Someone who is not part of the Mars political halls of power, but close enough to it, and someone who is not part of the UNF, but who may have lines to investigate both without raising suspicion."

"You sound like you know someone."

Harris nodded. "Miranda Finch."

"Finch? The reporter? Are you kidding? She dated Lotz for some years."

"She did, but it ended and it grows less friendly by the day. I think she could work."

"I'm not comfortable involving a reporter in my business, Harris."

"I understand that, but I think we can trust her to keep this on the quiet."

"Why?"

"I believe I have her allegiance. Leave it with me," Harris said. "In the meantime, please continue to keep the Martian people calm and keep your ear to the ground on whether more insurrections are planned. The UNF will be protecting this Zeta from harm, but we do so in order to protect ourselves from other Zetas. It's imperative that message comes across."

Finn nodded. "I just gave a press conference to that effect. I'll continue to do my best, but the sooner we weed out the leak, the better my chances will be."

"Understood."

13

Eyes on the Prize

Harris stood by Welles's bed, looking at Gregson.

"You need to knock her out so she doesn't enter my dream."

"Will she accept your invitation?" Welles asked him. "You're not our leader."

"I will speak on behalf of our leader," he told her. "Besides, I've been thinking. They must be able to detect the gift is stronger in me. They must know my gift is propping up yours. Don't get me wrong, given what they've gone through, it's important we show men and women have an alliance on our planet, but having one or two conversations with me alone, shouldn't hurt. I just represent myself as your top soldier, speaking on your behalf." Welles didn't respond but he could see her mind ticking over. He looked to Gregson. "Knock her out. Once she's out, you can dose me up."

Gregson nodded and prepped a needle.

"You know you're not going to be able to keep knocking me out, Harris," Welles said. "The drugs themselves won't do my brain any good and you risk turning me into an addict."

"I risk turning *both* of you into addicts," Gregson said with concern.

"We're working on replacing you, Welles," Harris said. "It's just until the Zeta learns to listen to a new face or two."

Gregson swabbed her arm and injected Welles.

"Maybe you could project me there," she said, as she began to blink. "Trick it into thinking I'm with…"

Harris watched her eyes close. He looked up at Gregson.

"That's not a bad idea, you know," he thought aloud to the medic.

"Can you do that?" Gregson asked. "Without drawing her into your dream state?"

"I'm going to try."

"What if it somehow brings her into it?" Gregson asked. "It's a risk after last time."

"Well, did you dope her up good?" he asked, studying Welles's sleeping face.

"I think so, but I still don't really understand this whole Thought Technology, Biology, thing."

"The higher level of drugs dampens her subconscious activity. Blocks it out," Harris said. "It worked in the past when we were at Command, but there's only one way to find out."

He climbed onto the pod-bed beside hers, lay down on his back, and held his arm out. "Stick me."

Harris opened his eyes and saw the Alma Mater standing before him. He was cross-legged on the floor of the Zeta flight deck.

He pictured Welles sitting beside him. The Alma Mater glanced at the projection, then back at him. He bowed, trying to show submission and servitude, trying to convey that he was speaking on behalf of Welles. The Alma Mater continued to stare at him.

He projected an image of the *Aurizun* headed back toward Earth; pictured the Zeta ship following, under UNF escort. He projected them leaving their ships on the Centralis Space Dock and heading toward the Command building.

Tess growled then, appearing in her bed as she tugged on her restraints. Harris eyed the Priestess, then projected standing outside her cell in Command with the Alma Mater standing beside him – looking *into* the cell at its sister Zeta.

Tess hissed.

Suddenly images flashed inside his head of the Atlas standoff, then of Decima, of Zeta ships blown apart. Harris looked to the Alma Mater standing before him, then projected images of the *Carcharias* firing upon the insurrectionists, defending her. Then he pictured Earth Duty troops on Centralis providing protection for the creature.

The Alma Mater stared at him, her mind thoughtful.

Harris projected extending his hand and holding onto the Alma Mater's hairy, hoof-like hand, then he projected the word "peace", left it floating in the air.

"That's my language," he told it. "Just like your lines and dots, that's mine. That word is peace. It means we work together. We do not fight."

The Alma Mater stared back at him but projected nothing.

"Peace," he said, then projected the Earth symbol for peace – the circle intersected by three lines, three pieces of a pie. Maybe the Zeta would understand a symbol easier than a word? "The lines in that circle," he told her, picturing it in his mind and pointing to it, "are semaphore signals, visual signals, for the letters N and D. They stand for Nuclear Disarmament. They mean no war. They mean peace."

The Alma Mater stared at the symbol, then at him, then turned away. He watched as it pressed its hoof-like hands against its flight deck console.

Harris's breath caught at what he was witnessing, watching exactly how the Zeta used its ship. The console lip turned bright blue and the hoof-like hands sank deep within it. The Zeta's eyes stared off into nothing for several minutes, before it retracted its hoof-like hands, the blue light faded, and it turned back to him.

His projected image, the one of the *Aurizun* leading the Zeta ship back to Earth, flashed inside his mind, as did the one of them walking toward the Command building surrounded by many Earth Duty soldiers.

Then the Alma Mater slowly bowed to him.

Harris stared back, mouth agape. "Is that a yes? You'll come?"

The Zeta's eyes moved to the empty space beside Harris. He realized he'd stopped projecting Welles sitting beside him and projected it again. The Zeta's eyes moved back to his.

He gave a bow, and then slowly, the Zeta bowed back.

Carrie made her way to the *Aurizun*'s flight deck, shaking off the last of her doping. As she entered, she saw Hunter and Frazer at the helm, preparing for departure from Atlas. Hunter glanced around at her.

"Welles! You're awake. 'Bout time you stopped sleeping on the job," he grinned. "How you going?"

"I'm looking forward to getting back to Earth. I hear the Zeta's going to follow us?"

"Yeah, apparently. We'll soon find out."

She nodded. "Are we going to be enough firepower to protect it?"

"Gold's giving us the *Carcharias*," Frazer said. "We'll have more escorts once we near Earth."

"Well, that's something," she said.

"Relax, Welles," Hunter said, as McKinley entered the flight deck. "That pissy colonial rebel contingent can't match UNF firepower. If more come, we'll handle it."

"Yes, we will," McKinley said, moving to his seat.

Carrie sat down next to him. He turned his face to hers and the overhead lights made the proxy-steel plate along the right side of his skull shine. He seemed to be studying her head, too, and she felt it ache.

"Here's to securing peace," she said, trying to shift his attention.

McKinley looked unconvinced, and the truth was Carrie shared the feeling. She turned to the observation window as the *Aurizun* departed Atlas.

Harris sat on the *Aurizun*'s flight deck, watching as two UNF Space Duty ships, the *Benevolent* and the *Windsor* approached to escort them to Earth. They were just a few hours from Earth now, and in the journey so far, there had been no incidents. No incidents of violence or aggression, that is. There had been one single ship that had followed them from Mars. It kept its distance, made no attempt to make contact, but it followed.

Soon enough reports hit the media that the *Aurizun* and the Zeta ship had left Atlas and were heading toward Earth. Whoever was on this mystery ship was reporting on their movements. Harris had been in regular contact with Finch. Firstly, to ask her about looking into Colonel Greavy and his soldiers, then secondly, to see what she could find out about this mysterious ship, which they'd managed to identify as the *Golden Orb*.

"On paper it belongs to the Mercandez Company, the proxy-steel magnates," Finch had reported. "Lotz is on the Mercandez board. He's a significant shareholder."

"So, it's essentially a Mars Media vessel then," Harris said.

"Of course," she said. "My guess is that Kellan van Pelt is aboard."

"So, who is this reporter exactly?"

"He's a rising star in journalism with a ferocious appetite for stories that get hits. He's ambitious and I sensed he was pissed that Lotz initially made me the Mars Media star. Now I'm gone, he's going to stop at nothing to make his mark and Lotz will support him in that endeavor."

"Did you ask him about the leaks?"

She'd nodded. "He's not answering my calls. I suspect Lotz has told everyone in Mars Media to cut me off."

Harris nodded. "I guess that means you're in the firing line as much as us now."

"Don't worry," she smiled, "I can handle myself. I've been doing this long enough, I don't scare that easy anymore."

"Good," he smiled back.

"So, about that other matter. Greavy and his soldiers," she'd said. "I've asked around. It's difficult to find anything incriminating because everyone knows everyone on Mars. I can't find anyone who's actually seen Greavy ever meet up with Lotz or Kellan, or anyone from Mars Media, but they would've crossed paths at events before, for sure. Greavy and Lotz are also both members of the Mars Golf Range."

"Interesting," Harris said. He'd never been there himself, as the underground golf range was a new addition to the outskirts of Elon, and even then it only contained a driving range and mini-golf course – something to tide the residents over until the fully domed, surface level golf course was completed. Still, it could be a way to innocently cross paths without drawing attention.

"I could call in some favors to see if they both attended at the same time, but I feel like that's going to raise a red flag if we don't know who we can trust. Most of the board of the Mercandez Company, the owners of the

Golden Orb, are also members of the new club. A lot of people will be. It's circumstantial at best."

"I see," Harris nodded. "Well, keep digging, but put your feelers out carefully. See what else you can find out without putting a target on your back. Keep me posted."

"Will do," she said, then smiled. "You know you owe me a big favor after all this."

"And you'll get it," he smiled back. "The interview. Ain't nothing going to be bigger than that."

The conversation rolled through his mind as he watched the two UNF ships move into formation either side of the Zeta ship, while the *Aurizun* continued to lead and the *Carcharias* took the rear.

And all the while, the *Golden Orb* floated in the distance, watching.

Carrie and the *Aurizun* team disembarked the ship, watching as the Zeta ship descended, hovering a moment as though in hesitation, before finally touching down on the tarmac.

Major Morrell greeted them with at least a hundred soldiers spread out around the Space Dock ready for any trouble. But it would be hard to find. The surrounding walls kept civilian eyes away, and as the UNF had enacted safety protocols and closed the entire facility for the occasion, the soldiers were the only ones present on the otherwise deserted Space Dock.

Despite that, they still had eyes on them from the skies as the *Golden Orb* floated in the distance, outside the no-fly zone.

"We should erect a cover for the ship," Carrie said to Harris, glancing back at the Command building. "Run it back to the building to stop those prying eyes."

"Yeah, but we don't have time for that now."

McKinley shook hands with Morrell, as Carrie and Harris watched on.

"Any trouble?" McKinley asked Morrell.

"Not in here," he said, "but we got some visitors outside the Command gates, who aren't happy about our guest. They're not all bad, though. A few of 'em actually welcome our new overlords." Morrell cracked a smile.

McKinley looked back at him, not seeing the humor.

"Relax," Morrell said. "They're peace-loving hippies and the last of our worries. It's the rest we gotta watch out for. There's bound to be one or two cowboys in the crowd who think they know better."

"Well, it's your job to ensure they don't do anything stupid," Harris said firmly. "We got a lot of shit to do, Morrell, and we do *not* have time for what's going on outside."

"I understand that," Morrell said, "and my soldiers are taking care of it." He looked over to the Zeta ship. "You going to escort it inside?" Though the Zeta ship was on the tarmac now, no move had been made for the Alma Mater to exit.

They turned their faces as the *Carcharias* landed, a wave of heat and space dock spice rolling past them.

"Yeah," Harris said. "We'll handle that with the *Carcharias*."

"Does it know it has to go through quarantine?" Morrell asked.

Harris nodded. "I tried the best I could to convey that before we landed. I'll personally go through quarantine alongside it, so it knows what is being done to her is also being done to me."

"You'll be pals in no time," Morrell said.

Harris gave him a plain look. "That's the plan, Morrell. Ever heard that saying, 'Keep your friends close and your enemies closer'?"

"Speaking of enemies," Carrie said, looking into the skies as the *Golden Orb* circled the perimeter. "What are we going to do about that spying ship?"

"It doesn't have clearance to land here," McKinley said. "It'll have to land over on the Commercial Dock once that's reopened."

"There's not a whole lot we can do about it," Harris said. "Free speech and all. But I would like to ask them some questions." He looked back at Morrell. "Have the Commercial Dock keep them in a holding pattern over there for a while. Later, when they land, would you like to do the honors?"

"I'd love to," Morrell smiled.

Harris smiled back. "Don't hurt them, Morrell. Friendly, now."

"Friendly's my middle name," he said devoid of a smile.

"Alright," McKinley said, "let's get this Zeta inside before some idiot lines it up for target practice."

Harris nodded. "*Aurizun* team! Come with me. Tell the *Carcharias* to meet us."

McKinley nodded and got on his PDP to relay instructions to Ryker.

The *Aurizun* team moved toward the Zeta ship and the *Carcharias* team soon followed. Harris instructed the teams to surround the ship, but face away from it, scanning the perimeter for threats. All except Carrie, Harris and McKinley who faced the ship.

"Alright, my queen," Harris said, tongue-in-cheek, "let's go meet our visiting royalty."

Carrie looked down at her basic UNF fatigues. "It's a shame we couldn't put our official uniforms on, huh?"

Harris shrugged. "It's not what you wear, it's the attitude with which you wear it."

Carrie smiled. "Shall I strut?"

Harris quirked an eyebrow at her. "Do what you will, your majesty."

A door slid back on the Zeta ship and they watched with bated breath for the Alma Mater to show its face. Carrie wondered whether it would look like it did in their dreams, or whether the alien in her dreams had just been an avatar of the real Alma Mater.

It wasn't an avatar.

As the Alma Mater appeared in the ship's open doorway, staring out at them, she looked as they'd dreamed she had. She wore a plain gray robe of floor length, draped material. Broad, stocky, a cowlike face with a broad nose; her appendages were covered in a hairy hide; her hands and feet hoof-like; the nails thick and a yellow-brown in color. It looked like some genetic experiment, a mash-up of several mammalian creatures. But Carrie guessed the truth was that humans were the genetic experiment, not the Zeta.

"Alright," Harris said, "let's go meet her."

Carrie nodded, took a deep breath, then she turned to McKinley and slapped him on the ass, grabbing it tight.

He looked at her like she was crazy. *WTF?*

Carrie smiled. "Just making sure she knows you're mine. You know, in case they're planning to take you as breeding stock."

McKinley shook his head as a smile curled his lips, and Carrie walked away.

Carrie and Harris came to a stop a few meters away from the open door.

"Stay behind me," Carrie told Harris. "You're my slave, remember?"

"No, I am your royal guard. There's a difference."

"Either way, it's time for the chicks to talk."

Harris shot her a plain look. "Watch your brain," he said quietly, as he dropped back a couple of steps.

Carrie eyed the Alma Mater in the doorway.

"Welcome to Earth," she said. "You do not need to be afraid. We mean you no harm."

She closed her eyes and projected an image of the Zeta leaving its ship and walking alongside Carrie. Then she projected an image of the soldiers around the Space Dock, facing their weapons away from the Zeta, ready to defend it.

The Zeta took a moment, then stepped out of the doorway. Carrie stepped aside and swept her arm forward. The Zeta stared at Harris and he bowed and stepped aside also.

The Alma Mater moved forward cautiously. The Zeta was a good head taller than Carrie, who now turned and moved alongside the Zeta, keeping to the Alma Mater's cautious pace, while Harris fell in on the Zeta's other side.

The Alma Mater looked at both of them again, before her eyes fixed on McKinley, obviously detecting his differences to the rest of the human soldiers surrounding them.

"Don't get any ideas," Carrie said, through a smile to the Zeta, "he's spoken for."

McKinley turned and led the way to Command, hand on his weapon, as the *Aurizun* soldiers formed a guard around them, and the *Carcharias* soldiers took the rear.

Morrell watched them carefully as they passed, and he too followed with a unit of his men until they made it inside the walls of Command.

Harris, having been scanned, stepped through the Tube and looked back at the Alma Mater who had paused.

"What's it doing?" Morrell asked from behind the creature, as McKinley and Welles gathered around.

"Just be patient," Harris said. "I gotta keep projecting to her, to let it know it's safe."

He closed his eyes and showed the Alma Mater what the machine did. He opened his eyes and the creature stared at him. Harris motioned gently with his hands for the creature to follow him.

The Alma Mater studied the machine carefully, her nostrils flaring as she sniffed the air. Then, tentatively, she stepped forward. One hoof-like foot stepped on the plate. Harris closed his eyes and projected the doors of the Tube closing. The creature projected back an image of Tess strapped down in its bed, then an image of the Alma Mater strapped down appeared. Harris shook his head. He projected back an image of the Alma Mater walking out of the Tube and down the corridor by Harris's side.

The Alma Mater stared at him a moment, her eyes piercing his with a warning. Or maybe a promise of what she would do if he lied to her. Then she stepped inside the Tube. Harris looked over to the operator and gave a nod.

The Tube's cylindrical door closed and Harris saw the flashes of light emanating as the machine scanned the creature.

As it did, Harris had a sudden, panicked thought.

An alarm sounded loudly, red lights flashed, and an automated voice blared.

"*Warning! Foreign body detected. Warning!*"

"Oh, shit!" Harris hissed, realizing their error. Of course, the Zeta's whole body was foreign – not just the possibility of any bacteria or virus it carried.

"*Advise response protocol,*" the automated voice said, as the red lights continued to flash and the alarm sounded. "*Contain or destroy?*"

Harris looked at the operator. "Shut it down! Shut it down. Now!"

The Alma Mater called out then, and it sounded like a melange of a mooing groan, a pig's squeal, and monkey's scream. He heard her hoofed hands and feet banging violently on the inside of the Tube, fighting to get out.

Morrell raised his weapon at the Tube, ready, and McKinley raised his too.

"Get her out of there!" Carrie yelled.

"SHUT IT DOWN NOW!" Harris yelled at the operator. "NOW!"

The operator's hands quickly darted around the console, shutting down the Tube, as the Alma Mater continued to violently rock the device, making an awful racket as she tried to get out. Morrell moved around, ready to face the creature as it exited, while the *Aurizun* team spread out too.

"Don't you fucking shoot it!" Harris warned them. "Lower your weapons!"

Morrell looked at him. "It's pissed, Harris!"

"I don't care, lower your weapons. Now!"

McKinley holstered his pistol just as the Tube doors opened.

The Alma Mater moved faster than Harris expected her to.

She shot out of the Tube, lightning fast, and barreled into Harris, knocking him on his back, then racing off.

Someone fired a shot.

"DROP YOUR FUCKING WEAPONS!" Harris roared, rolling over and springing to his feet. "McKinley! Welles! With me. Shed your fucking weapons!"

Harris raced after the Alma Mater, darting a glance over his shoulder to see McKinley shed his weapons as he and Welles ran after them.

He heard a scream up ahead and followed it, muttering to himself. "No, no, no, no. Don't hurt anyone. Don't hurt anyone."

"I'm projecting!" Welles yelled, stopping and closing her eyes.

Harris rounded a corner to an elevator bank where the Alma Mater was cornered, and a Command worker ran away. Harris held his hands out peacefully.

"I'm sorry. I'm sorry. I fucked up. I'm so sorry. We're not going to hurt you."

The Alma Mater was still angry, nostrils flaring, grunting and breathing heavily as she paced back and forth agitatedly, looking like a wounded bull about to charge.

Harris moved forward slowly. "We're not going to hurt you."

The Alma Mater looked over his shoulder and Harris saw that Welles had caught up. She carefully moved to Harris's side, then got down to her knees, sitting back on her heels. Harris did the same. Welles closed her eyes and projected.

"Careful with your brain, Welles," Harris said as he closed his eyes to join her.

He saw the three of them sitting down together, peacefully, calmly. He opened his eyes and saw the Alma Mater staring at McKinley.

"Get down on your knees," Harris whispered to him.

"You sure we want to submit like that?" he asked. "I thought we wanted to be equals."

"She's scared, McKinley. We need her to know we're not a threat."

McKinley relented and got down on his knees.

"What's going on?" they heard Morrell whisper loudly from around the corner.

"Stay the fuck back!" Harris whispered back. "Send anyone with weapons the *fuck* back. I see a weapon I'll take your uniform, understand!"

"Do as he says," McKinley said firmly, leaning back and looking around the corner.

Harris heard the scuttle of feet moving away.

The Alma Mater did too, looking in the direction of the fading footsteps.

"I'm sorry," Harris said calmly. "We're not going to hurt you. Let's start again."

An image pierced his mind sharply. Tess in her bed, hissing angrily. Then he saw the Alma Mater strapped down in a bed.

"The Priestess is fucking us over," Welles said.

Harris closed his eyes and projected an image of him unstrapping the Alma Mater from its bed. He helped it out, then looked back at Tess still strapped in her bed, before ushering the Alma Mater from the room. He opened his eyes again.

"You're different," he said to the Alma Mater. "You're not like Tess. You want peace. I can feel it. So do we."

Welles carefully got to her feet, in slow obvious movements. She stood a moment staring at the Alma Mater, then stepped slowly, carefully toward her. The Alma Mater watched her carefully, her muscles tensed, her nostrils flaring. Welles stood before her, shorter and half the width of the creature. They stared at each other, before Welles held out her hand to it, palm upward.

The Alma Mater looked down at her proffered hand.

"We came from you, didn't we," Welles said gently. "Your kind. You are the mother of mammals. You know this, or you sense this. I can feel it. You know, somehow, we are your kin. Your grandchildren of hundreds of thousands of years of evolution. You don't wish to destroy us like the Priestess. And we don't want to destroy you. We don't want war and I sense you don't either. Let us talk peace."

Welles closed her eyes. Harris did too. An image filled his mind of the Alma Mater placing its hoof-like hand on Welles's palm.

He opened his eyes again. The Alma Mater stared at Welles, and seemed calmer now.

And as he watched, he saw the image in his mind, happen in the flesh.

Welles gasped in pain and pulled her hand back, as the two stared at each other curiously.

"What?" McKinley asked quickly.

"A spark?" Harris asked.

Welles nodded, rubbing her hand. "Goddamn, she's strong."

Carrie looked through the mirrored glass at the Alma Mater in the room on the other side of the wall. It squatted before a table of various types of food and drink, prepared by Dr. Serquey, sniffing everything. McKinley stood by the creature's open door. They felt she might panic if they enclosed it again, and wanted only McKinley guarding it – someone the creature didn't yet see as a threat. He remained unarmed but, of course, Harris knew the weapons his body carried. Even though McKinley couldn't use most of them properly yet, if worst came to worst, his proxy-steel bones would handle the creature better than human bones.

"She's a fascinating creature," Dr. Serquey said. "So different to Tess, yet I sense similarities."

Gregson entered their observation room and handed Carrie some headache tablets. She smiled a thank you and swallowed them.

"You alright?" Harris asked, studying her.

She nodded and changed the subject. "We're getting better at projecting while awake."

"We are," Harris nodded, rubbing his neck, "but it's tiring, and I can't imagine how taxing it is for you."

She shrugged, not wanting to make a big deal of it. "I'm okay."

"We're not going to be able to provide coverage, the two of us alone. We can't physically be open to receive messages 24-7. If she gets talkative, that's a lot of projection and your brain won't handle it."

Carrie shrugged. "If it's just her, I'll be fine. If she brings her friends into it, maybe not."

"Even Tess butting in, weighs us down," Harris said. "That's two different entities pushing into our mind, not to mention the two of us being connected. That's three at any one time in your brain. Tess ain't going to butt out of our conversations. She's going to want to hear everything."

"Unless you drug her," Gregson said.

"No," Dr. Serquey said, "I'd prefer it if you didn't. She's too fragile. Besides, we need her lucid. There has never been a better time to learn from this race than to watch the two of them interact."

"She's right," Harris said. "Besides, if we drug Tess, that may affect the trust the Alma Mater puts in us."

"And speaking of trust and treating them as equals," Dr. Serquey said, "I'm glad you're now referring to Tess by her name. We need to do the same for the Alma Mater. Let's start as we mean to continue. What shall we call her?"

"Alma?" Harris shrugged.

"Yes, but that's like calling one of us human. Let's use a derivative like Tess being from Priestess. How about… Ally? Or Martha?"

"She looks more like a Martha to me," Carrie said. "Plus, it's close to mother, and she's the Mother of Mammals."

"Done," Dr. Serquey nodded. "Her name is Martha."

"Martha…" Carrie repeated as she stared at the Zeta. She looked at Harris. "My hand still feels funny from when she touched me. Like, it's still aching and tingling a little."

Harris nodded in thought, while Dr. Serquey looked fascinated.

"We must study this sensation," she said. "We must understand how this relates to their mind connections."

Marchant entered the room then, wearing a face mask. Harris studied him curiously.

"We don't know what bacteria or viruses this creature may be carrying," he explained on seeing Harris's look. "Anyone who has been in contact must go into quarantine until we're satisfied they're healthy."

"I found nothing on Tess for us to be worried about," Dr. Serquey said. "I believe we'll find the same with this one. If anyone should be afraid, its them. Dr. Ross believes something on this Earth made them sick and caused them to flee last time."

"And we still need to find out what that was," Marchant said, as Carrie moved closer to the window in study.

"Even if it was something as simple as a human cold virus," Dr. Serquey said, "it wouldn't be a fast solution in the event of war."

"No, but if it wipes them out eventually," he said, "then it's just a matter of holding out. That tactic has been used in past altercations effectively."

Carrie looked at him. "That tactic was used horrifically in the past. I've heard the stories about the diseased blankets given to the Native Americans under the guise of peace."

Marchant shrugged. "Granted, that wasn't a great event in human history, but if those Zetas invade are you saying you wouldn't use that tactic to ensure your survival?"

"To defend against an invading force, perhaps," Carrie said. "But I abhor an invading force using it to take what's not theirs."

"Welles," Harris interrupted, "you need to rest. It's been a long day. I'll take first shift and I'm hoping DaJuan can take the next one."

"He'll be here soon?" Marchant asked.

Harris nodded. "I've arranged for his collection. I need Martha to get to know him and trust him, so he can relieve Welles from all duties."

"Harris," Marchant said, "I don't think we should trust him with our intergalactic relations just yet. By all means bring him in, but I cannot authorize him to deal with the Alma Mater on our behalf."

"I'm not bringing him to negotiate for me. I'm bringing him to babysit her for us. If she needs or wants something, hopefully she can communicate that to him. I will personally handle the negotiations."

"How do you know he will be able to do what you and Welles can do with the Zetas?" Dr. Serquey asked.

"I don't." Harris sighed. "But I know some of his gifts align with mine, so I'm hoping the projection will too. I just need him to be open and able to receive and pass messages."

"I'm the leader," Carrie said, folding her arms. "She'll want to talk with me."

"I'm authorized to speak on your behalf," Harris said firmly. "You heard McKinley, Welles. You're banned from the dream connections, and you shouldn't even be doing the projections during your waking hours. It's still affecting you. That's what the headache tablets are for, right? We're only allowing it because we have no other choice, but as soon as DaJuan gets here, that changes."

Carrie sighed. She wanted to fight this turn of events, wanted to take part given the gravity of the situation, but her headache weakened her resolve. She sighed and looked to Marchant. "He's right. Someone needs to be able to check in with the Zetas regularly and Harris can't do it alone. Tess will be talking to Martha and we need to know what lies she may tell." She looked to Harris, as a thought occurred to her. "I forgot to tell you. I visited Tess the other day. We had words. Well, *projection*."

"You what?" Harris turned to her.

"She's definitely not friendly," Carrie said, "but if we can win Martha over, we may be able to correct the course of our relationship with Tess. Either way, we can't let our guard down. Someone must be available, on call, and ready to attune themselves to any messages."

"That's going to take a lot of energy," Dr Serquey said, "being in a constant state of concentration and openness."

Harris shrugged. "We don't necessarily have to be constantly open, but we do have to make regular visits to both Zetas and see if they want to pass on any messages to us."

Carrie nodded.

"So, go rest," Harris said firmly. "I'll have DaJuan here in a matter of hours. Then we need to find more like us."

"Ones that we trust," Carrie said, locking eyes with Harris, before they turned back to see Martha finally begin to pick at the food.

14

Widen the Scope

Finn Harkowitz studied the screen showing footage of the Red House gates. A group of protestors had gathered, angry at the Atlas incident and angry the Zeta was still alive.

He sighed and looked at Greavy, who had notified him. "It's their right to protest. We can't stop them. They'll leave when their atmospheric suits run out of air."

"They're setting up camp in their MaPVs. They're using the solar and wind panels to recharge the recycling units in their suits. I don't think they're planning on leaving anytime soon."

"We'll ride it out. All the attention will be on Earth now."

"My soldiers are hearing a lot of dissent in the colonies. The tide is turning, Finn."

"So, we'll turn it back."

"You received more death threats."

Harkowitz stared at him. "Why are you trying to block my path? You once rolled with whatever happened, now everywhere I turn, you're forming a roadblock."

"Because it's my job to protect you," he said, "and I'm getting sick of you not listening to me, or taking the threats seriously."

Harkowitz stared at him, trying to gauge whether he was genuine. He wanted to believe he was, but until he knew who was undermining him with the leaks he couldn't trust anyone.

"I'm sorry, sir," Greavy said, glancing at his feet, "but until we can find out who is behind the threats, we need to be careful."

"Surely the UNF AIs can trace and unencrypt the sources?" Harkowitz asked.

"I'm being told they can't, sir. So, you must listen to my advice."

"I appreciate your concern, Sam."

"Good," Greavy said firmly, "because your new personal detail starts today. They're outside."

Harkowitz watched, surprised, as Greavy moved to the door, opened it and ushered two men inside.

"Mr. President, please meet Sentinels Beach and Aston. They will be your new detail covering you during your working hours, while my soldiers will continue to guard you while you sleep."

Beach and Aston lined up before Finn's desk. Beach, dark-haired, looked to be in his 40s, experienced and calm. Aston, light-haired, looked to be in his late-30s and confident. Both looked fit and alert.

"Mr. President," Beach said, "it's an honor to serve you."

Aston gave a sharp nod in agreement. "Agreed, sir."

"Beach will take the day shift," Greavy told him, "while Aston will take mid-afternoon onward until you sleep."

"Thank you, Sentinels," Harkowitz said, knowing Greavy wasn't giving him a choice in the matter. "I look forward to working with you."

Harris waited at the rear, private entrance to Command, watching as the black unmarked vehicle with tinted windows pulled up before him. A moment passed before the door opened, and the tall, lean, figure of DaJuan exited the vehicle, eyeing his surroundings suspiciously, as his long bright-blue dreadlocks swung around his torso. Dressed in dark cargo trousers and a black T-shirt emblazoned with the words "I believe", his eyes soon fell on Harris. DaJuan smiled, flashing his three gold teeth, and moved toward him.

"It's good to see you," Harris smiled back, extending his hand.

"Brother!" DaJuan said with his Jamaican-inflected accent, as his grin grew broader. He slapped Harris's hand and clasped it in a solid grip. A static zap passed between them, and they locked eyes, before DaJuan continued to survey his surroundings.

"They treat you alright?" Harris asked, motioning to the plainclothes soldiers arranged by Morrell.

"They did," DaJuan nodded, acknowledging the guards, then looking back at Harris. "But I knew they would."

Harris studied DaJuan's eyes: one a natural green, the other a dark tech-enabled contact lens, upon which Harris's Alpha eyes could see minute text scrolling.

"You dreamed it?" Harris asked curiously.

"No, man," DaJuan said. "I trusted you wouldn't fuck me over." He said it firmly, but friendly, reminding Harris that DaJuan was a leader in his own right, and not a weak man. He would make a firm ally, so long as he was treated right.

"I am a man of my word," Harris said.

"So," DaJuan said, "you brought me 'ere for a reason. What makes this time so right?"

"You been watching the news?"

DaJuan nodded, eyes narrowed.

"We need help connecting with our new friends," Harris said. "There are two of us who can do it, but Welles is struggling with CTE, so I need more brains on deck."

"You want me to connect with your alien? I've barely connected with you, man."

Harris nodded. "I know. We have a lot of work to do. And we can't do it alone. I'm preparing to cast the net wide and find more like us. I figured you might know a good fishing spot or two." Harris quirked his eyebrow.

DaJuan studied him a moment, then nodded. "Yeah, I know a few."

"Good," Harris said, then motioned him toward the doors of Command, where his shadows stood. "We'd better get you settled into your new quarters."

"I'm staying 'ere?" DaJuan pointed to the building.

"There's a small hotel attached," Harris said. "We'll put you there."

"Five-star, I hope."

Harris grinned. "This won't be a holiday, DaJuan. And I'm going to need to relieve you of all your tech."

"Say what?"

"Everything inside those doors is classified, I'm afraid." He motioned a guard forward, who held out his hand. DaJuan looked at him.

"You can trust me, DaJuan," Harris said. "You'll get it back, in time."

DaJuan looked at Harris intently, then eventually began to empty his pockets. He removed his contact lens and a hearing device, which he placed in a small container from his pocket.

"That it?" Harris asked. "They don't play here. I need everything."

DaJuan smiled, then removed a pair of sunglasses and some other small devices and handed them over to the guard.

"Thank you," Harris said, then ushered him inside toward the quarantine channels.

Carrie stared across the boardroom table at DaJuan. He sat, quiet and contemplative, no doubt soaking in the briefing he'd just received: information on the Zetas and their five different factions, their ships, the Thought Technology and Biology, the history of their visitations and their captured signals, the two Zeta specimens being kept at Command, and what Carrie and Harris had been able to achieve in communicating with them through their dreams and projections.

"It's a lot to take in," Carrie said to him.

DaJuan looked at her. He said nothing aloud, but his face said *No shit.* He turned to Harris. "So you want me to help you with the two Zetas?"

"Yes," Harris said. "One of us needs to be 'on call' to check on them regularly, in case they want to communicate. With three of us, that's eight-hour shifts. But we need to remove Welles from that rotation as soon as possible."

Carrie went to speak, but Harris cut her off.

"No, Welles. End of discussion."

Marchant entered the room and Harris made the introductions. Marchant extended his hand to DaJuan.

"Thank you for coming in to assist us," he said, eyeing him carefully, taking in his long blue dreadlocks.

DaJuan nodded cautiously, as he shook his hand.

"I believe you may know others that can help us?" Marchant asked.

DaJuan shrugged. "Maybe. I need to see exactly what you need from me first. When can I meet the Zetas?"

"Right now," Harris said, standing.

Carrie watched as DaJuan approached the glass cell Tess was being kept in. The Zeta's eyes were already fixed and waiting for them, waiting for Carrie. Even Harris and DaJuan noticed that, although Tess glanced at them, she mostly stared at Carrie.

"She doesn't seem to like you," DaJuan said.

Carrie shrugged. "Fear, respect, it's all the same thing."

"Is it?" Harris quirked an eyebrow.

The Priestess's eyes moved to fixate on DaJuan next. She hissed quietly, her tongue tasting the air.

"She's curious. I wonder if she senses something about you," Harris said, as the creature turned her eyes to him now. "When I came across one in the field, I felt it. They know. They discern those of us who are different. They must sense an open channel in our brain or something."

Carrie nodded. "We need to check the size of his node."

DaJuan looked at her. "The size of my *what*, now?"

Carrie smirked, and motioned between her and Harris. "Nodes have developed in our brains. They've grown due to our connection with each other and with the Zetas. They think maybe this node was always there, but recent happenings have reinvigorated, or awakened, it. Saved this dormant node from extinction. We think there'll be one in your brain, too."

"No, shit." DaJuan stepped closer to the glass, staring at Tess. "So, when you communicate, you just picture something and they pick up on it?"

"Yeah," Harris said, "but I think we need to ease you into her life. I think tonight we try to dream you there. She's seen you here now, awake, but I think the next step is for her to see you in the dreamscape. If she meets you in the dreamscape with us, she'll truly know you're one of us. I mean, someone on our level of trust. Someone who can represent humanity."

DaJuan's eyebrows rose in surprise. "I'm speaking on behalf of the human race?"

"No," Carrie said firmly, looking at him, "you'd just be a messenger, speaking on behalf of *me*, the one they know to be the leader of the human race."

DaJuan studied her a moment, then flashed his gold-tooth smile. "You do radiate some boss-bitch energy."

Carrie flashed a smile back. "Thank you."

DaJuan looked back at the Zeta. "So this one is the unfriendly and the other is friendly?"

"Something like that," Harris said, "but our relationship with both is tenuous at best. The Alma Mater – Martha – barreled me down easily. She could turn on us in an instant. We need to strengthen ties with both."

"Well, then," DaJuan said, "I'd better meet the other one. Then the three of us better practice this projection thing."

McKinley entered his room at Command, ready for some shut-eye. He'd spent the past few hours getting Martha used to Tikaani and Steinberg, so they could take the next shifts protecting her. It wasn't feasible that he be the only soldier she trusted. Just like Harris and Welles were feeling the strain of being the only ones to communicate with her, the *Aurizun* team would need assistance with her protection at some point.

A message chimed on his PDP and he opened his portal. It was a message from Dr. Bakshi. He opened it and saw it was an appointment for him to see the psych. Both Harris and Marchant had been copied in, no doubt to apply pressure, or perhaps as a reminder of why he was forced to stay here at Command and not with Welles and the kids. The arrival of Martha had delayed him meeting with the psych, and the truth was he wasn't sure he had time for it now, either, with all that was going on.

He sighed and tossed his PDP aside as he lay on the bed. He stared at the ceiling in his little "cell". He didn't want to be here, but he didn't want to speak with the psych either. In fact, the thought terrified him. Who knows what they'd unearth once they started digging through his damaged mind. Would it keep him from Welles and the kids longer? That thought alone filled him with angst.

Harris stood in the observation room alongside DaJuan and Welles, looking through the one-way mirror. Inside, Martha stood with Dr. Serquey undergoing minor, non-invasive tests. The door to her room was open, she was still a guest, and Tikaani and Steinberg stood outside the door.

Harris changed the mirror's setting and lit up the room to show Martha them standing there. Her eyes scanned Harris and Welles through the window, then they fixed on DaJuan.

"As you can see," Harris said, "Martha is very different to Tess." He looked at DaJuan to see him staring blankly at Martha.

"DaJuan?" Harris said, noticing his vague stare.

DaJuan suddenly took a step back and shook his head. "Whoa!"

"What?" Harris asked.

"What happened?" Welles asked.

DaJuan shook his head again. "I think she just projected."

"She did?" Welles asked. "I didn't feel anything."

"Neither did I," Harris said. "What did she project?"

"I don't know," DaJuan said. "I saw stars. I think I saw the HH you showed me. I saw time passing."

"She was giving you a message?" Welles asked. "Already?"

"No," DaJuan said, brow furrowed as he stared at Martha like he was trying to solve a puzzle. "I think it was the other way around. I think she was trying to pull information from me. From my mind."

"Why *you*?" Welles asked.

Harris considered this. "Maybe it's because DaJuan is more attuned to his gift then we are. I mean, we're getting attuned to it, but we have to work to fully open it up. DaJuan's been open to his gift for a long time, his mind is permanently open."

"I've been open my whole life, man," DaJuan said, looking at Harris. "My mother raised me from birth to accept who I was."

"Yeah," Harris nodded. "Mine didn't. She tried to keep it from me."

"It was non-existent in my family," Welles said.

"Was it?" DaJuan asked. "From what I know about my research into the See'ers and Sense'ers, it seems we all have some kind of family history. Maybe you need to look further into yours."

Welles stared at him, her face unsettled but curious.

"I'll help you," DaJuan said. "Ancestral lines are my specialty."

Harris looked at Welles. "You should do that. He has a point, Welles. There's got to be a reason it's strong in you."

"There is," she said. "I gave birth to the First Gens. It was your job to help me keep them safe because they'll be needed in the future war. Our connection arose out of necessity. That's why you're an aberration."

"It doesn't arise out of nowhere, woman," DaJuan said. "It's in your blood. Somewhere, somehow, it's in your blood." He thought about this for a moment. "Just like you're talking about these nodes coming to life. It's already there within you."

Harris exchanged another look with Welles.

"By the way," DaJuan said, "what's a First Gen?"

"That's another briefing," Harris said.

He looked back to the window and flinched to see Martha standing right up to the glass. He hadn't even noticed her move there.

She slowly, carefully, placed a hoof-like hand up against the glass. DaJuan looked at it, then moved forward slowly and placed his hand against the glass, in line with hers.

"She likes you," Harris said, a sense of peace rolling over him. "A lot."

DaJuan pulled his hand away and tapped his temple. "Because my doorway is open wide. She wants to come inside."

"Then let her," Harris said. "Fancy a nap?"

DaJuan nodded and Harris pointed a finger at Welles.

"You watch only."

*

Harris walked along a darkened corridor, waiting patiently for DaJuan to join him. It seemed to be taking a while and Harris was wondering whether the gang leader was suffering from a little performance anxiety.

Harris turned to his left to see him suddenly standing there. DaJuan gave his gold-toothed smile.

"Well, this is good," Harris said, as relief washed over him. "If I knew it would be this easy to have you join me in my dreams, I would've brought you in earlier."

"Ah, there is a time for everything, man," DaJuan shrugged. "You brought me in now, because the time is right. Tess wasn't speaking to you, this new one is, and Welles can't help you no more. Besides, I can help you clear the doorways in your mind, help you to harness your gift, but I won't be much help with your war."

"Yes, you will," Harris said, studying him carefully as another feeling of peace rolled over him. "You're doing it right now. This is helping us with the war."

As if on cue, his female ancestors appeared.

DaJuan turned his face to them. "And who is this?"

"You can see them?" Harris asked, surprised.

His female ancestors nodded slowly, calmly. He looked back at DaJuan.

"They're my kin," Harris said, "from the other side."

DaJuan glanced at Harris then looked back at his ancestors in awe. "You can commune with the dead? This is *big*, man."

"Is it?" Harris asked.

DaJuan nodded. "Very few can do that."

"You must be one of them if you're seeing them too," Harris said.

DaJuan shook his head. "I've dreamed things, man, and I've felt guided before, but I've never communed with the dead." He looked back at Harris. "I'm open to receiving all spirits, but if I'm seeing and talking to them now, it's because of *you*."

Harris turned back to his female kin. "Do you have a message?"

Welles suddenly appeared to Harris's right. For a moment he was livid she was there, but then he realized it was just a projection from his kin.

"She must stay out of things now," Etta said.

"It's too much for her," Sibbie nodded.

Maeve agreed. "She must be preserved."

The vision of Welles faded, and Harris nodded.

DaJuan looked at Harris. "Do you think the Zeta will come with me 'ere?"

Harris thought for a moment. "I've communicated alone without Welles before, so... hopefully."

They waited for several moments in silence, but Martha didn't show. Harris looked back at his kin. "Will the Zeta come with *you* here?"

Sibbie smiled. "They will only see us if you let them see us. Just like he can see us now." She motioned to DaJuan.

"Why can't the Zetas see you without my help?" Harris asked. "They're stronger than us both."

Etta looked at him with eyes that made the remaining hairs on his scarred arms suddenly stand on end. Somehow, Harris got her meaning.

"Because they've passed," DaJuan voiced his thoughts.

Sibbie and Maeve nodded.

"The Zetas don't commune with their dead?" Harris asked.

They shook their heads, he felt a breeze across his face, and they were gone.

"They don't commune with their dead," Harris thought aloud, staring at the empty space left by his kin.

DaJuan looked at Harris in surprise. "That's why you're special, man."

Harris stared at him, waiting for him to elaborate.

DaJuan shook his head, long blue dreadlocks knocking together. "I wondered why you came to me. This is *big*, man. You can talk to the other side, few can do that, but you can also talk to the Zetas."

"But what does that mean?" Harris asked. "There has to be a reason for it. Why don't the Zetas, with their powerful Thought Biology, commune with the dead?"

DaJuan shrugged. "You're the aberration that had to happen. You're in the military, you can talk to the dead, and you can talk to the Zetas. The aberration wasn't a mistake, a thing of accident or chance. It was fated, man."

Harris stared at him as his mind turned over quickly. "And you're the aberration that was destined to help me understand this."

DaJuan nodded.

"Dad!" a voice sounded. Harris turned his face to the darkness. The hairs on his arms were standing on end again. "Dad!"

"Sarai?" he stepped forward.

Suddenly his daughter appeared. She beamed a smile of relief, ran to him and hugged him. He caught her and hugged her back.

"Dad! I'm here!" she said excitedly.

"No! You shouldn't be here, Sarai. You gotta go." He took her shoulders and shook her. "Wake up."

"But Dad?" she frowned.

"Wake up! *Now!*"

Sarai vanished.

"Why'd you do that?" DaJuan asked.

"She's too young."

"She's strong to be doing that at her age," DaJuan said. "Don't shut her out, man."

"She's too young," Harris said firmly.

"So, you're going to do to her what your mother did to you?" DaJuan asked. "How's that going to help us win the war? She's female, and she's strong. We're gonna need all hands, man."

Harris stared around at the darkness. Deep in his heart he knew DaJuan was right, but his brain was refusing to acknowledge it. He sighed. "Martha's not coming. Maybe we should go?"

DaJuan nodded, eyes still showing disagreement with the Sarai topic, but he turned and vanished.

Harris stood there alone in the darkness. He glanced around one more time, wondering why Martha hadn't shown.

In the distance, Tess hissed.

Martha suddenly stepped forward from the shadows, staring at Harris with her face tilted in thought.

Had the Zetas been watching all along?

Had they seen Sarai?

Martha stared at him a moment more, before the shadows enveloped her once again.

Carrie stood in the Command hospital, her mind turning over all that Harris and DaJuan had just told her.

"But what could it be?" she asked Harris. "Do your kin know how we can beat them? If so, why don't they just tell you?"

"I don't think they do," Harris said.

"But Sibbie dreams the future, right?"

"When she was alive, yes. But who knows, maybe when I dream of them they're not actually contacting me, but it's my subconscious speaking through a visual projection of them, trying to reach my conscious thoughts? I fought the gift for so long, I never listened to my inner voice, but when it came down to it, for some reason I always listened to *them*. But maybe it was just my intuition all along speaking as though it were them?"

"Spirits can only guide," DaJuan said. "They cannot control our fate. That responsibility lies with us. We must have our own agency. They cannot have it for us."

"Yes, but if the lives of the entire human race are at stake?" Carrie countered. "If they could see the future, they'd have to warn us, surely."

DaJuan shrugged. "Not their problem. It's ours." He turned to Harris. "We're the ones living in this realm and we can dream the future. I dreamed a wounded black soldier would turn up and need my help, and I felt *strongly* that I had to aid him. That soldier was you. And now here we are. Our spirits guide us through dreams, but we are the ones in control of our destiny in the waking world. I could've chosen to not help you, man. But I listened to what my dreams were telling me. And so here I am. Our spirit-guides, however they show themselves to us, are the wind that blows through our lives, but it is up to us to adjust the sails to get where we need to go. I dream the future, but my dreams are intermittent. They are not my core strength. I don't believe that is why we were drawn to each other. I understand the gift better than you. *That* is why I am here. To guide *you*. You dream the future, Harris, stronger than I. And you're not just a See'er but a Sense'er too. What's your intuition telling you about the dream we just had? Speak the truth, man."

Harris looked thoughtful for a moment. His eyes narrowed as he studied DaJuan. Hesitation ran across his face, then a resignation washed over him. His shoulders slumped.

"I think you need to meet my daughter," Harris said softly.

"Sarai?" DaJuan said.

Harris nodded. "The gift is strong with her. Stronger than it ever was in me. She dreams a lot. She's just a child, but if it's strong in her now, then..."

"She will be powerful in the future," DaJuan nodded.

Harris's Alpha ears heard urgent footsteps and he turned to the doorway to see McKinley eventually march in.

"I thought I said she wasn't supposed to do this again?" he demanded.

"I didn't," Carrie held her hand up to calm him.

"She just watched us," Harris said.

"It's a risk her even being around this, isn't it?" McKinley asked, eyes still flaming blue fire.

"McKinley," Carrie said, "I'm just on standby to ensure DaJuan transitions okay."

"And if your brain overloads?" McKinley asked. "It fucking flatlined on the ship when you did this dream thing last time!"

McKinley's shadows appeared at the door making their presence known. Guilt flashed over him and he eased off a little.

"I know," Carrie said, stepping up to him and placing her hands on his chest calmly. "And I haven't done the dream thing since. The projections while I'm awake have been okay. Nothing more than a headache."

"That stuff has to stop, too. DaJuan's here now."

"McKinley—"

"What happens when you suffer a catastrophic brain injury?" McKinley stared at her. "What do I tell the kids?"

Carrie looked at him. No words came to her mouth.

"He's right," DaJuan said quietly, then looked at Harris. "She needs to stay away. Your kin told us as much."

"They what?" Carrie asked, stepping back from McKinley and darting her eyes between Harris and DaJuan.

"They said you can't take part any longer," Harris said. "That you needed to be preserved."

"*Preserved*? For what?" Carrie asked.

"I don't know," Harris said. "But if they're telling me you gotta stay away, we gotta listen."

"Even the dead can see the sense that you can't," McKinley told her.

Carrie looked at him and her shoulders slumped.

"Look, Welles," Harris said, "I know you want to help. We'll find something else for you to do. In the meantime, we're going to bring in Sarai to see what she can do."

"You're really bringing her in?" Carrie asked.

"She's young," DaJuan said, "but she has potential. Imagine how strong she will be if we start training her now."

Harris looked at McKinley. "So, you can calm down, alright? Anyway, what are you doing here? I thought you were sleeping."

"I tried to, but I kept receiving updates from everyone," McKinley said.

"What's up?" Harris asked.

"Numbers outside the Command gates have grown. I've had reports of the same on Mars, so I put a call in to Colonel Greavy. He's had to put Sentinels on the president, alongside his soldiers."

"Why?" Harris asked.

"Turns out he's been receiving death threats."

"How serious?" Harris asked.

"Serious enough for Greavy to put extra security on him."

"Shit," Harris said. "Did Morell manage to speak with the folks on the *Golden Orb*?"

"Nope," McKinley said. "They circled for a bit, then left. Intel says they refueled at a private property on the mainland, belonging to one of the board members of Mercandez. They've been there ever since."

"Rich people funding conspiracy theorists," Harris said flatly, rubbing his neck.

"There's a lot going on," McKinley said. "We're starting to wear thin."

Harris sighed. "I know. I'll go see if I can get clearance from the general for that interview with Finch."

"And you better bring your daughter in asap," DaJuan said.

*

Carrie sat in the back of the vehicle as it slowly made its way through the Command gates. The crowds of people pressed against the vehicle trying to look through the tinted windows at her.

She saw signs that read: 'US or THEM!' and 'ILLEGAL ALIENS!' and 'REVENGE OVER COWARDICE!'. She sighed, though she was unsurprised. She understood their anger over what had happened. She felt it deep within her soul. She'd lost her father in the invasion, almost lost McKinley. They'd lost Murphy, and Harris had lost Taya. But despite it all, if she and Harris could broker peace and avoid anyone else having to go through that, she would see it through.

A hand slapped across the window, fingers spread wide, startling her. She saw the face attached to that hand, and paused.

She recognized the peroxide-blond hair and darkly painted lips of Roxy Harbourg, daughter of Original soldier Clint Harbourg, aka the Greenback. Roxy stared through the windows at Carrie with unfriendly eyes, but as the vehicle found a gap in the crowd it surged forward and she was gone.

Carrie tried to look through the rear window to find her again, but she'd disappeared in the crowd.

What was Roxy Harbourg doing there?

15

Diversions

General Berger stood at his window looking out on the ocean, his mind turning over. He had a lot to process.

A knock at the door sounded.

"Come in." He turned to see Marchant enter as expected.

"You wanted to see me?"

Berger nodded, motioned for Marchant to sit, as he did the same. "Harris has put in another request to do the interview."

Marchant nodded. "It might alleviate the crowds outside."

"Or make it worse. What if he screws it up, or she stabs him in the back again. She hung him out last time."

Marchant shrugged. "Apparently she's claiming her editor recut the piece. Harris seems to think she's an ally now."

"And if she's not?"

Marchant considered this. "I think we need to trust Harris's gut instincts and foresight on this. If it was a mistake, I think he'd sense it or something."

"Things are already unstable. It will destabilize things further." Berger leaned back in his chair, mind turning over. "What do you make of the death threats against Harkowitz?"

Marchant shrugged. "He's a president. It's par for the course."

"We can't afford to have him vacate that chair just yet. Who knows if the next president will be as amenable to us."

Marchant shrugged. "If they're not, then we flex our muscles a little. They'll soon learn to be amenable."

"The people like him. Well, they used to... his father is still regarded as a hero." Berger stared at Marchant. "UNF sentiment is at a low point. It will look very bad for us if Harkowitz is attacked. We need to ensure he stays safe."

Marchant mulled this over. "I was speaking to Harris on that. The leak about the Zeta ship, and what happened with the insurgents, was likely from a source inside the Red House."

Berger studied him. "Does Harkowitz know this?"

"Yes. Harris has someone looking into it."

"He needs to clean his house," Berger said firmly. "This is a problem we don't need with everything else going on."

"I agree. There's the crowd outside our gates and across mainland posts. Tensions are rising on Mars. McKinley's still not undertaking psych treatment, and Welles is having trouble stepping away from the mind-melding and projection, which puts her at risk of a serious brain injury."

"We need to use her until this DaJuan is ingratiated with the Zetas."

"McKinley told us in no uncertain terms he's banned her from anymore sessions."

"It's not his call."

"He's the head of the Alpha soldiers now, technically h—"

"And I am the head of the entire UNF." Berger stared at him. "Our universe could be at stake."

Marchant raised his hand peaceably. "If we break her brain, she's no good to us. We need to shelve her until the medical staff can fix the problem."

Berger considered this, then relented. "So, put her on light duties. I thought that's what we were doing."

"We were but then the Zeta appeared. We need to give her something more solid to do. You know what she's like. If she feels that we're pushing her down, she'll resist."

"She's a soldier. It's her job to take orders," the general said.

"She also has CTE and we can't be sure she won't do things that have repercussions."

"So, we just let her dictate to us what she can and can't do?"

"No, I'm saying we give her something meaty to do. Something that makes her feel like she's contributing. Something that takes her focus away from connecting with the Zetas until her brain has been repaired."

"Such as?"

"I don't know," Marchant said. "Her forte was weapons. Let's put her with the team studying the heat ray or something."

Berger's mind ticked over. "That keeps her around Command, near the Zetas. If you want to keep her away from the mind-melding, I think we should *physically* keep her away from them, and from McKinley, to stabilize him."

"Like where?"

Berger's eyes narrowed as an idea struck him. "What if we send her to Harkowitz as a gift."

"A gift?"

"A goodwill gesture. We send our best sharpshooter to help guard him."

"What about the First Gens?" Marchant asked.

Berger shrugged. "They go with her. They've never been into space before. Maybe it's time they grow accustomed to it."

"And we keep McKinley based here?"

"For the most part. But definitely for the next while. We need him and the *Aurizun* team to help protect the Zetas."

"What about Welles's treatment?"

"We'll send Dr. Bakshi to Mars if they come up with a treatment plan they think will work, but right now they haven't got one."

Marchant considered the strategy. "It could pay to have one of our inner circle on Mars, watching things."

"Yes," Berger said, clearly teasing the strategy out in his mind. "Harris divides his time between Command and the JEMs, supported by Morrell's team here. McKinley, when he's not guarding the Zetas, splits his time across our universal bases with the *Aurizun* team. We've got Gold manning Station Atlas with the *Carcharias* team, while Welles would stick close to the president on Mars. We'll have eyes and ears across all the main pockets."

Marchant nodded. "It's not a bad plan."

"No, it's not. See it done."

Marchant nodded and stood.

"One more thing," Berger said. "If we're sending the First Gens to Mars for a while, it's time they're given their AISs."

"At 11 and nine? That's a bit young, don't you think?"

"We won't chip the kids just yet," Berger said. "We'll wait until they've finished growing to do that, but until then, they should have their dedicated AIs close. Their training, their *serious* training, starts here. Harris informs me he's bringing his daughter in, so we start on the next generation, now."

Marchant nodded.

"Ensure Archie goes with Welles to Mars," Berger said, "to keep an eye on her. They'll each have their personal Artificial Intelligence System with them at all times, and at all times their AISs will be linked here, to Command."

Marchant nodded. "Understood. I'll let Harris know the plan."

Harris stood with his shadows in Command's quarantine, waiting for Tyson and Sarai to arrive. He'd sent Hunter and Frazer in a private jet to collect them.

"She's been telling me you were going to call," Holly, his sister, had told him over the phone when he'd rang. "She kept saying, 'Dad needs me'."

Though Harris still felt torn about inflicting something like this on his daughter so young, at the same time, he knew it could help ensure her survival if he helped develop her gift now. He hadn't prepared Taya properly and she was dead. He couldn't make the same mistake with his kids.

"I do," he'd told Holly. "And I've spent too long away from her. It's time I find out who my daughter is, and she finds out about her father."

"Ty's going to escort her," Holly told him. "He wants to see you, too. Like, really see you. For the first time in a long time he wants to be with you."

"Yeah, I'm not sure it's for the right reasons, though," Harris said quietly.

Holly was silent a moment. "He talks a lot of revenge for what the Zetas did to Taya."

Harris had nodded to himself at the time. "Don't we all. That's why I want to keep him away from Command. We're not going to win a war, seething with revenge."

"That's exactly why I think it's a good idea he spends time with you. He's not listening to me. He's a grown adult now. He has his own ideas, but I think if anyone is going to get through to him, it's you."

"Yeah, I don't know about that. Like you said, he's almost 26. He's his own man now. I'll try."

"Try hard, Saul. You're his father, he needs your steady hand."

The conversation circled his mind, like so many others at the moment. He'd had a call from Marchant earlier, where he was informed of plans to send Welles to Mars to keep an eye on the president. Harris had mulled over the information and he had to agree it was a good idea. Firstly, it would indeed keep her away from the Zeta mind-melding, which was critical for her health. Secondly, if Mars was at risk of destabilizing, then they needed someone they could trust to ensure it didn't. It made sense.

He'd broken the news to McKinley but, surprisingly, he'd taken the news well. McKinley realized whatever kept her away from the mind-melding had to be a good thing for her, despite the distance it would put between them. Harris had assured him it was a short-term measure until Mars was stable. Now he just had to tell Welles.

"Dad!" Sarai's voice sounded in the distance, pulling him from his thoughts. He looked up to see her racing toward him. He smiled at her, held out his arms and she jumped into them. He lifted her up and swung her around.

"Hey, baby!" he said, hugging her tight before putting her on the ground again and examining her. She'd grown and was as tall as his waist now. Even the fact she was calling him "Dad" now and not "Daddy" proved just how quickly she was growing and how fast time was passing. He grinned at her, then looked up to see Ty walking over with their cases in hand. Followed by their Sentinels.

Harris stepped toward his son, who stood taller than him. Which was saying something because Harris was 6'2. "All that basketball's been stretching out your body, I see."

Ty laughed. "Nah, you just shrinking with age, old man." He held his hand out to slap Harris's.

Harris stared at it. "What? No hug for your old man?"

Harris caught him around the neck and pulled his son into a hug. Ty laughed again, but went with it, squeezing him hard. Harris chuckled at the bear hug Ty gave him. "You may be taller, but don't forget I'm Alpha," Harris said with an arch of his eyebrow.

Ty pulled away. "Yeah, I want more detail on that."

"You'll get it," Harris said, caressing Sarai's head.

"When?" Ty asked.

"Not here," Harris said, glancing about. "Come on, let's go."

Carrie, sitting in the Fortress, stared down the comms screen at Harris.

"Mars!"

"We need someone we can trust to watch over President Harkowitz."

"What about the Zetas? Sarai will need a woman's support—"

"Sarai is my daughter, Welles," Harris said. "I got it covered."

"I'm the leader, the Zeta at least needs to see me handing over to Sarai."

"Is this the CTE talking? Why don't you realize the seriousness of your condition?"

"I do, but I also realize the seriousness of the war that might come our way."

"The answer's no, lieutenant. You go where I post you, or you will hand in your uniform."

"You need me here, sir."

"We need you *alive*, not dead. Your husband, the leader of all Alpha soldiers, has agreed to this."

"He did?" Carrie asked, hurt that McKinley hadn't mentioned it.

"Look, this decision has only just been made and it isn't permanent. It's temporary until we're sure the threat against Harkowitz has been nullified. And the top brass think it'll be good for the First Gens to start exploring things off Earth. Regardless, it's not up for discussion. You leave the day after tomorrow."

Harris hung up the comms.

Carrie sighed. "Mars? I don't want to live on Mars. They're trying to take me out of the picture."

"It's simply a reallocation of resources, Miss Welles," Archie said. "Situations arise from time to time that require the redeployment of soldiers. You've been very lucky to have been based primarily in Centralis these past years."

"But the Zetas are *here*, not Mars!"

"That may be, Miss Welles, but I think you underestimate the importance of the Mars colonies. We need the proxy-steel. Stability on Mars is imperative right now. You're being asked to play an important role."

Carrie moved to the windows overlooking the Space Dock, surveying the scene. Things were much quieter than normal, as security measures had been tightened due to the presence of the second Zeta.

"The Carcharias is currently here on Earth, and Major Gold is stationed on Atlas," Archie said, "which means the nearest Alpha soldier is several hours away from Harkowitz should an emergency arise. It makes sense for the UNF to station an Alpha soldier by his side."

"And we'd be there too," Roy, her Sentinel said, from behind.

Carrie turned to him. "You heard?"

He nodded. "Lieutenant General Marchant just gave me the orders."

She studied him, sensing something was wrong. "What is it?"

Roy seemed to think for a moment, caressing the reddy-brown mustache over his lip, now streaked with silver. He looked her in the eye.

"I've been thinking about retirement," he told her.

"Oh," Carrie said. It wasn't exactly surprising. He'd been with them for 10 years, after all.

"I wasn't planning on it just yet," Roy said, "but going to Mars…"

"Has brought the decision forward," Carrie finished his sentence.

"The kids are growing fast," Roy said. "They're not going to need us much longer. Besides, Marchant told me about the personal AIs the UNF is bestowing on them."

Carrie nodded. She hadn't had time to get her head around that yet.

"Novak and Sampson are overdue for promotion. They're both keen for the Mars posting."

Carrie nodded. "Will you be replaced?"

Roy shrugged. "Honestly, between you and the kids all being Alphas… You'd probably be the ones protecting us," he gave a smile.

Carrie smiled back. She stepped forward and hugged Roy. "I liked having you and Sampson around. It felt like I had a piece of Australia with me."

Roy nodded as she stepped back. "And Sampson will remain with you." He smiled. "But it's your turn to play guard to Harkowitz now. Novak and Sampson will see the kids through the next couple of years, then they'll move to other postings. Time marches on whether we like it or not."

"It sure does," Carrie said.

"I'll inform Command," Roy said, then turned and left the Fortress.

"I'll start preparing a list of what you must pack, Miss Welles," Archie said.

Carrie looked through the window, saw the midday ship to Mars being loaded. She felt a sting of emotion. Time was certainly moving on. The world was changing, and she was starting to struggle to keep up with it. She knew she was never going to live forever, but it still hurt to think that the sands of time were now working against her.

She'd never felt more lost.

And now they were sending her further away into space.

Harris entered the boardroom at Command with Sarai by his side. He'd left Ty at their Command quarters to unpack and settle in. He'd wanted his kids to live at his apartment outside the Command complex, but until he knew how the tension outside the walls would play out, they were safer inside Command with him.

Waiting for them in the boardroom were Welles, McKinley and DaJuan, along with Marchant. Sarai was a little shy at first, clinging to his side, but she brightened up when she saw Welles.

"Hey, Sarai," Welles smiled at her. "My god, you've *grown!*"

"Take a seat." Harris pulled a chair out for Sarai. Harris motioned to Welles. "You know Carrie and James," he said, as McKinley gave her a friendly nod. "And this here is my boss, Lieutenant General Marchant."

"Hello, Sarai, it's nice to meet you," Marchant said. "Thank you for coming in to help your dad."

Sarai nodded back at him.

"And this here," Harris said, motioning across the table to the last person to be introduced, "is—"

"DaJuan," Sarai finished his sentence.

The room stilled.

DaJuan gave a gold-toothed smile. "My reputation precedes me."

"You were in that dream with Dad," Sarai told DaJuan. "I remember your blue dreadlocks and gold teeth."

DaJuan chuckled at this.

Harris stared at his daughter. "I never told you his name."

"I've dreamed of him before," Sarai said.

"You have?" DaJuan asked, intrigued.

She nodded. "You were helping me and Dad open our minds."

The room sat in silence for a moment. Harris locked eyes with Welles, then Marchant.

"Yes, he will be," Harris said.

"What else have you dreamed, Sarai?" Marchant asked casually.

Sarai looked at him, unsure.

"It's okay," Harris said, squeezing her hand gently, "you can tell him."

Sarai thought for a moment. "I dreamed we were in a school." She looked at Harris. "A school for people like us."

"Like us?" Harris arched his eyebrow.

Sarai nodded. "See'ers like us. And Sense'ers like Great-grandma Etta."

Harris and DaJuan exchanged a look.

"How many people were in this school?" Marchant asked curiously.

"Not many. There were more of us, but this class was special. They were really good with their minds."

Harris exchanged more glances with Welles, McKinley and DaJuan.

"Did you recognize anyone in this class?" Harris asked.

Sarai thought for a moment, then shook her head. "Their faces were blurry. But one had long bright-orange hair. A girl."

"How young?" Harris asked.

Sarai shrugged. "I think she was a teenager."

The silence sat again, as their minds turned over.

"Is this thing stronger in children?" Marchant asked Harris. "Are we gonna have to rely on kids for this?"

"No," DaJuan said confidently. "It's something that develops over time. Theoretically speaking, the older generations will be stronger, but if a child is strong, then she has the potential to be an immensely strong adult."

Harris nodded to himself and looked at Marchant. "We need to put a call out. There're more of us out there."

"The general wants us to hold off until things cool down outside."

"We're wasting time," Harris said.

"We're walking a fine line, Harris," Marchant replied firmly. "Let's try walking that line with DaJuan and Sarai, and when we're confident things won't fall over, then we try to run that line."

Harris inhaled and pushed down his frustration as DaJuan locked calm eyes with his, then turned to Harris's daughter.

"Sarai," DaJuan said, "what do you say we see what your mind can do?"

Carrie walked with the others toward the room where DaJuan was going to test Sarai. She tugged McKinley to fall back alongside her as the others went ahead.

"You agreed to my Mars posting?" she asked him.

McKinley glanced at her and nodded, but kept walking.

"It's indefinite," she said. "Me and the kids."

"It's short-term," he said. "Besides, are you really surprised? They want to keep you away from the Zetas, and away from me." He threw her another glance, locking eyes.

"Is that all you have to say about it?"

McKinley took a deep breath in, and rubbed his forehead. "I'm not happy about it, but we gotta go where they post us. Besides, Harris wants me visiting Mars and Harkowitz more regularly, so it might not be as bad as we think. I'll be up there soon enough."

She studied him. "So long as it's them pushing us apart and not you pushing me away."

McKinley shot her a masked look, but walked on in silence. She could see he was tired. She decided to drop it.

Harris ushered Sarai through to a small room with beanbags and children's toys. Being nine, Sarai ignored the toys and moved straight to a pile of books in the corner.

DaJuan moved to enter the room but Harris caught his arm and stopped him. The gang leader looked at him.

"I know I don't have to say this to you, DaJuan, but I'm going to, just so it's clear. I love my daughter with all my heart and I would do anything to protect her. If you hurt her in any way… I will fuck you up."

DaJuan stared back at Harris for a moment. Harris let his Alpha rear to the surface and permeate his eyes.

"I may be a gangbanger, man, but I don't fuck with kids."

"Good. We're on the same page."

Carrie, Harris and McKinley stood in an observation room watching while DaJuan and Sarai sat on beanbags in the room next door. They both had their eyes closed, trying to connect with each other.

"When are you going to introduce the Zetas to each other?" Carrie asked. "Like, in the flesh?"

Harris shrugged. "Soon. But we already know they're communicating. They've been together in our dreams many times. Just because they haven't seen each other physically means shit."

"Leaving you with the two Zetas is dangerous." Carrie folded her arms across her chest, exhaling with frustration. "Sending me to Mars to watch over President Harkowitz when he's already had his security boosted, it doesn't make sense. I should be a part of this, *here*," she motioned to DaJuan and Sarai. "I can still observe and assist in ways that don't require my brain to connect."

"If Harkowitz is under threat, then he needs one of us up there, making sure that threat isn't realized," Harris said.

"Politics isn't my forte. I can't stop a political assassination," Carrie said.

"No, but you can stop a physical one," Harris said.

"You really think it will escalate to that?" Carrie asked Harris.

Harris shrugged. "I don't know. What I do know is that sentiment has been turning against him and there are forces trying to remove him from power. I need someone up there we can trust. Someone Harkowitz can trust. You think this is a shit posting but it's actually a critical one, Welles. Besides, politics goes hand in hand with this job. The faster you learn it, the better a leader you'll be."

"What about my kids? Taking them out of school here and sending them to Mars. Won't that set them back?"

"Their education won't suffer. They'll get the best at the Red House."

Carrie looked back at Harris. "What?"

Harris smiled. "Marchant told me you'll be residing in the Red House. We want you as close to Harkowitz as you can get."

Carrie's surprised eyes moved past Harris to lock onto McKinley's.

"The folks on Mars are going to get to know us real well," Harris said, "and they will come to understand that we have Harkowitz's back, and any move against him, is a move against the UNF."

*

Carrie laid out the three small boxes on the kitchen bench. Each box was smooth and black, and embossed with their names and the UNF logo: the winged horse, Pegasus, rearing over the Space Duty and Earth Duty shields.

"What are they?" Freya asked, as Brody and Jesse crowded around.

"These are a gift from the UNF," she said carefully. "Open them."

Each child took the box with their name on it, and opened them to see a plain silver wristband, half an inch in thickness.

"A bracelet?" Jesse furrowed his brow.

"No," Carrie said. "It's your own personal AI in the form of a wristband."

The children stared at her, stunned.

"Place it on your left wrist," Archie told them. "You must wear it at all times. It will monitor your health. It will answer any questions you have. It can relay messages if you find yourself in trouble. It is like—"

"You, Archie?" Freya asked.

"Yes, Freya. They are like me."

They each took their allocated wristband and put it on, studying how it looked.

"Each has a UNF codename that you will refer to it by, just like your mother refers to me as Archie."

"What's mine?" Freya asked excitedly.

"Freya, your AI is called Ruby. Brody, yours is Pearl. Jesse, yours is Jade."

"Is this to bribe us into going to Mars?" Brody asked.

"There's no bribing about it, honey," Carrie said. "Orders are orders and we have to go. The UNF just think it's time you have your own personal AIs. You're getting older and they'll be phasing out the Sentinel protection eventually."

"They're not coming to Mars?" Freya asked.

"Roy won't be, no, but Novak and Sampson will."

The First Gens contemplated this news.

"What about Archie?" Freya asked. "He's not coming with us?"

Carrie smiled. "He will be. Archie's *my* personal AI."

"Where's your wristband?" Jesse asked.

"I don't have a wristband," Carrie told them, picking up her metal box and opening it to show them the discs she took to Australia during Decima. The children looked at the two round discs, each about four centimeters in diameter, etched with a five-pointed star in the center.

"They're earrings?" Freya asked.

Carrie shook her head and picked one of the discs up. The top side was slightly curved like a shield, while the underside was a shallow cavity where several coils of miniature bio-mechanical wires sat.

"These suckers," Carrie pointed to the wires, dig into my neck behind my ear to read my biometrics, listen to my speech and hear what I hear." She tapped the wires and they wriggled about like a living organism.

"Ewww," Freya scrunched her face. "Gross."

"Mine's an older model," Carrie said. "Count yourselves lucky you only have a wristband."

"When do we have to go?" Brody asked.

"We leave on the midday ship tomorrow."

"I don't want to go to Mars," Jesse said moodily, pushing his box away and folding his arms, a flicker of McKinley about him.

"I know, honey, but it's just for a little bit. President Harkowitz needs us."

"I can't wait to go!" Freya beamed. "We're finally going into space! I'm going to pack!" She ran up the stairs.

Carrie looked to Brody. "What about you? How do you feel about it?"

Brody thought a moment, then shrugged. "It'll be cool, I guess." He followed his twin up the stairs.

Carrie looked back at Jesse, who stood with his arms folded and a scowl on his face. She pulled him in to a hug. "I know you want to stay here, but it's just for a bit, honey." She took his shoulders and moved him back to look into his blue-gray eyes, so much like her own father's. "I need you to accept this, Jesse, because we need to protect the president."

Harris walked along the silvery sands of Zeta Archelois in his mind. He thought maybe this would make Martha more comfortable, to have a piece of home. He was alone, opting for some one-on-one time with Martha to get her to respect his communications, without Welles present.

He found an open space and sat down, crossing his legs, waiting patiently. The seconds ticked by. After a moment, he heard Tess growl low in the distance.

"I'm not here for you," Harris said calmly.

As if on cue, Martha stepped forward from the shadows, staring at him. He gave her a bow in greeting. She did not return the bow, just stood there and stared.

He closed his eyes and pictured his forehead pressed against Martha's, trying to convey a peaceful connection. He projected the image toward her.

Martha stared another moment, before she reached down with hoofed hands and scooped some of the silver sand, then let it pour down to the ground like a silvery waterfall. Then she clenched her hoof-like hands and viciously threw the remaining sand at Harris.

It whipped him in the eyes like tiny shards of glass and he groaned, blinking rapidly as tears began to fall down his cheeks. Suddenly, a series of vicious projections burst into his mind. He saw war between the various factions of Zetas. He saw fighting, blood spilling, bodies falling to the ground and laying strewn about, maimed. He saw fires, large fires, and Zeta bodies being thrown atop. He saw the ashes scattered into a large body of water, an ocean of some kind. He saw the silver sand washing ashore. He saw Zetas praying or something, sifting the silver sand and tossing it to the wind.

And he realized, then, what the silver sand was.

It was the ashes of dead Zetas.

He opened his eyes and stared at Martha. Tess growled low in the darkness. Harris quickly vanished the silver sand from his mind.

"I'm so sorry," he bowed. "I didn't know. I meant no disrespect."

Martha projected the silver sand back.

Harris was confused.

Martha stepped forward, grabbed another handful of sand and let it flow back down to the ground.

Suddenly Harris saw images from the invasion, of Zeta ships being shot down. He heard Zeta cries in the form of projected images of terror, of explosions, of aircraft crashing. He saw Martha again, flowing the silver sand to the ground. Then he saw himself carry Taya's dead body, laying her down. Saw her vanishing into sand. Saw himself scooping up the sand and releasing it back to the ground like Martha.

He looked back at Martha, sandy tears still rolling down his cheeks, but for a different reason now. Thoughts of Taya. Martha stared at him curiously, tiling her head. Suddenly she was right in front of his face, burning with fascination.

An image of Welles flashed into his mind. Then of DaJuan.

Then of Sarai.

Harris's breath caught.

Martha pulled back, still curious.

Suddenly, Sarai was standing by Martha's side.

"Sarai, no!" Harris barked. "Not yet! Go! Leave!"

Martha brayed at him and stomped her foot, kicking sand at him.

"I'm sorry," Harris flinched, realizing his mistake – being male and yelling at a female, would not sit well with the Zetas.

Martha turned to Sarai calmly, and Sarai turned to the Alma Mater.

"It's okay, Dad," Sarai said, barely above a whisper. "I don't think she means us harm."

Tess growled again in the distance, louder this time.

"Maybe not," Harris said, motioning to the darkness, "but *she* does." He looked back at his daughter. "Wake up," he said calmly but firmly. "Now, Sarai!"

16

New Chapters

Carrie stood on the dock with her three children and McKinley, while his shadows hung back, giving them privacy. Her link to Archie was contained in the discs she wore against her skin, behind her ears. It still grossed her out to put them on, feeling the tickle of movement as the discs slid into position, tucking themselves behind her ear like hermit crabs, then the sharp spike that ran through her like a dozen pins had been thrust through her skin. She wasn't looking forward to putting them on and taking them off throughout her stay.

The kids were nervously excited about the adventure that lay before them, but Carrie and McKinley felt different. There was an air of sadness, of the truth, suffocating them. The UNF was keeping them separated, and what better way to do that than on different planets.

"Hey, Ruby," Freya spoke into her wristband, "provide stats on the *Red Dawn*."

"*Yes, Miss Freya,*" Ruby answered in a female, English accent, then proceeded to spout all kinds of facts about the ship that would take them to Mars, while Freya wandered along the concourse toward it.

"Why are our AIs British?" Brody asked Carrie.

"Because their posh accents sound more knowledgeable and calm than American ones."

"Is that right?" McKinley said.

Carrie smiled. "Hey, look, I'm Australian. My accent is too laid-back, and yours is too... assured."

"Assured?" he said, raising an eyebrow.

"What accent do we have?" Jesse asked.

"Mixed," Carrie said, stroking his hair, "You say your Rs like an American, but I catch plenty of Aussie words and twangs every now and then."

McKinley smiled. "Told you the kids would be American."

"And I told you they would know their Australian heritage."

"Hey, Pearl?" Brody spoke into his wristband. "Who's the better shot out of Mom and Dad?"

Carrie grinned at McKinley.

"Your mother, Carrie Welles, was a much greater shot than your father Daniel Walker."

Everyone's smile fell away.

"No, I mean James McKinley, stupid!" Brody said with an angry furrowed brow.

"Brody—" Carrie began, but Pearl's answer cut her off.

"I apologise, Brody. Your mother is still the better shot out of the two soldiers."

Brody looked at them, but the fun was gone. He grabbed his bag and followed Freya.

"Well, what can I say, AIs can't lie," Carrie said, trying to lighten the moment, and grinning at McKinley whose eyes were on Brody walking away.

"Hey, Jade," Jesse said into his wristband, "who has the worst farts out of me, Brody and Freya?"

"I'm sorry, Jesse," Jade responded. "I don't have any data on that to answer your question."

"You need to start a file on that, Jade," Jesse said, laughing and running after Brody to tell him what he just asked Jade about.

Carrie watched them, then turned to McKinley. She sighed. "Brody seems to hate Doc and I don't know why."

"He doesn't hate him," McKinley said. "He hates that his real father's not around and that makes him different. I felt the same way when my father died."

"I've been wanting to give Doc's Blue Nova to Brody, but I can't give it to him while he's like this."

"Give it time," McKinley said.

She moved to him and hugged him. "I'm sorry. I know it's not easy for you when I talk about him."

McKinley hugged her back. "I feel different about it now."

Carrie pulled back. "You do?"

McKinley nodded. "Hearing Harris say that Doc was there urging me to stay alive… I don't know… It was good to hear that. Doc would've known. About us. And he wanted me to stay."

Carrie looked into McKinley's blue eyes, always finding it fascinating how closely they matched, though her Alpha eyes could tell which eye was real – which eye was the window to his soul.

McKinley's face suddenly fell. "He might change his mind in hindsight, though," he said, running his hand over her short hair, around the spot where her skull had hit the wall.

"It was an accident," Carrie stared into his eyes, "a one-off."

"A one-off that's sending you and the kids far away from me."

"They're sending me away because of the Zetas," she said, then sighed. "Like you said, orders are orders. Besides, I've been thinking about what Harris said, about politics being intertwined with leadership. If I can't be involved with the Zeta comms moving forward, then maybe I'll find my path out there. Maybe this was meant to happen. I can't deny that if there's one thing I've learnt these past years, it's that although it doesn't make sense at the time, the path always becomes clear eventually. When Doc died, I was devastated, but that opened the pathway to *you*, which opened the pathway to Jesse." She paused. "Which opened the pathway to JEMs…"

McKinley's brow furrowed as though a ghost from the past had been raised from the dead.

Carrie shook off images of the JEMs, the little killing machines. "But everything has led us here, and is leading us to where we need to be. I mean, what were the chances that I got put on the Darwin mission with Harris? We know Sharley selected me, and we believe Sharley knew about Harris's ancestors…" She paused as another thought occurred to her. "You think Sharley had the Zeta DNA? The node?"

McKinley shrugged. "They weren't testing for it back then."

Carrie's mind turned over. "Not the node, no, but before I went to Siberia, he told me he studied the Zeta DNA on the skulls they found, told me he discovered the Zeta DNA markers in my and Harris's blood. Have Harris check on the node. I want to know if Sharley was one of us. Maybe there was more to his plan than we realized. Maybe that's why he was so obsessed with us."

"Mom! Hurry up!" Freya called. "We'll be late!"

Carrie looked around at her. "You going to say goodbye to your father?"

The kids raced back, hugging McKinley roughly all at once, but his proxy-steel infused bones barely felt it. They raced back toward the ship again, as Carrie kissed McKinley, pressing her body against his.

"I look forward to your visits to Mars," she purred.

She turned to walk away, just as McKinley slapped her on the ass.

She paused and looked back at him. He grinned.

Harris looked across the desk to Marchant.

"I hear you, sir. We're preparing Sarai, but she's not ready to be brought into this in a full-time capacity."

"And I hear you, Harris, but it seems Sarai has brought herself into this, and I'm not sure anything you say can stop it now. If Martha has connected with her…"

Harris sighed. "I just want her to get used to connecting with people first before dealing with the Zetas."

"Harris, you forget what kids are like," Marchant said. "I got three of my own, and grandkids now, too, so I know. Kids are like sponges. They learn so much faster than we adults do. They are more adaptable and flexible and courageous than we are. Now, yes, they need to be tempered with the right education, information, common sense, and restraint, but I think you're discounting how fast Sarai is going to pick this up. I know you came to this late in life, but *your* journey, your experience, is not *her* journey or her experience. I know you're scared for her, but I think you need to roll with it. We're not going to allow anything to happen to her. If it looks like things are turning bad, you yank her out like you've been doing. It's that simple."

Harris sighed in resignation.

"You keep working on Martha," Marchant said. "DaJuan spends time with Sarai imparting his knowledge to her. We go from there. One day at a time."

Harris took a moment, then nodded acceptance.

"So, what's your next step?" Marchant asked, moving things along.

Harris nodded, thinking. He had a lot to catch up on and to get things back on track. "I'd like Dr. Ross and Colberge to confirm whether they've detected any radiation from the Zeta ships that could be of risk to our soldiers."

Marchant nodded. "I know radiation is something they've been testing, I'll have them report."

"Good," Harris said. "Our priority is to clear up what's going on outside, so I can do the interview with Miranda Finch. There will come a time soon when I will need to grant her that interview, whether the general approves it or not."

"Step carefully, Harris. There's only so much I can protect you from."

"I'm doing this to protect all of us."

"You won't protect anyone if the general feels the need to trigger your kill switch."

They stared at each other.

"I'm your ally, Harris," Marchant said. "Remember that."

Harris took a moment to temper his emotions. "About that. Speaking of kill switches, Welles was supposed to have hers removed by now. Let's lock that in."

Marchant gave a nod. "I'll speak with Dr. Bakshi."

Dr. Arielle Serquey pulled her lab coat on as she made her way toward the Zeta rooms, for her latest inspection. As she neared, she paused at what she saw.

Martha stood outside Tess's cell, with the soldiers Hunter and Evenssen standing close by, watching the creatures intently, weapons at their sides.

"What happened?" Arielle said quietly, moving cautiously.

The soldier, Hunter, glanced over at her. "They're having some kind of conversation." He looked at Evenssen. "Call Harris."

"No," Arielle said. Hunter looked at her. "Let them interact with privacy."

"And if they're planning an escape?" Hunter asked her.

"Do they look like they're planning an escape?" she said, coming to stand by Hunter's side. "I've been watching them. They may both be Zetas, but they are not friends. I don't even think they are allies. They have commonality in their race, but I'm not so sure their ideologies are aligned."

"Still," Hunter said, "we need a mind-melder up here." He gave a nod to Evenssen who clicked his comms on.

Tess hissed viciously at Martha.

"Wait," Arielle said, holding her hand out to Evenssen.

They watched as Martha huffed a mooing grunt through her nostrils. Tess clearly turned her eyes to Hunter, then Evenssen, and hissed again viciously, pulling on her restraints.

Martha turned around to look at them. To eye Hunter's tranq gun, then Evenssen's. Martha seemed to pause a moment, then moved slowly up to Evenssen.

"Take it easy," Hunter said carefully to the other soldier, as he subtly placed his hand on the grip of his tranq gun.

Martha stopped right in front of Evenssen and began to sniff him. Taller than the blond soldier, her nostrils traced across his forehead. Evenssen held still, remaining calm, though Dr. Serquey saw him swallow thickly.

Martha finished her examination and pulled back, eyes fixed on his. The silence sat as they stared at each other. After a moment, Evenssen stepped back from her, startled.

"What is it?" Hunter said.

Evenssen studied Martha, shocked, curious. "I... I think she just tried to mind-meld with me."

"What did she say?" Arielle stepped forward.

"She didn't say anything," Evenssen said. "I... I just saw memories of my life flash through my mind. Like she was searching for information. Like she wanted to know who I was."

"She was pulling images from you," Arielle said. "What did she see?"

Evenssen shook his head, confused, still staring at Martha standing before him. "Just stuff from my past. But Harris was there. The memory from when I joined the *Aurora*."

Arielle smiled at a realization. She'd read the report from Dr. Bakshi about the neural nodes she had discovered in some of the *Aurizun* team. Arielle had been informed, because it was something they'd wanted her to investigate with the Zetas. Previous scans on Tess clearly showed the presence of this node, large as a grape in the Zeta. Arielle had not yet managed to give Martha the required scan to view the internal structures of her brain. Studying the Zeta and the soldier now, she wondered whether Martha could sense it in him. Or perhaps sense the Zeta in his DNA, however few those markings may be.

Evenssen noticed her smile. "What is it?"

Arielle contained her smile. It wasn't her job to tell Harris's soldiers about the nodes. "I think Martha likes you. She's made a connection. Roll with it."

"I thought it was only Harris and Welles who could talk to them?" Hunter said.

"Maybe they can talk to all of us. Go with it," she nodded to Evenssen.

Evenssen looked at Martha. He slowly, carefully, held his hand out to her. Martha looked down at it, then raised her hoof-like hand to his. Evenssen allowed a smile to cross his face as he looked at Martha.

But when Tess hissed viciously again, his smile fell away, and so, too, did Martha's hand before they could connect.

McKinley knocked on Harris's office door.

"Come in," Harris's voice called back.

McKinley entered to see Harris reading through something on one of his screens. He glanced over at his visitor.

"Welles and the kids take off alright?" Harris asked.

"Yeah," McKinley said, taking a guest chair opposite his desk. Harris kept reading for a bit, then looked back at him.

"Everything alright?"

"Yeah," McKinley said, though his mind was caught up elsewhere – predominantly on his conversation with Carrie about Sharley, their history. She'd sparked a curiosity in him. It was infectious.

Harris sat back in his chair. "Speak your mind, McKinley."

McKinley scratched the stubble across the left side of his face. It was the only place a beard would grow after the Zeta's heat ray. "I was talking to Welles before she left. She raised something. Wanted me to ask you to look into it."

"And that is?"

"Sharley," McKinley said. "She wondered whether him choosing her for the Darwin mission was just purely on her record, her shooting. She said he knew about your ancestors, suspected your gift."

Harris nodded. "He did suspect. He said things to me that suggested he had to know about it."

"Welles wonders whether Sharley had the Zeta DNA markings. Maybe even the node. She wants to know whether he was one of you."

Harris stared at him, mind turning over. "Sharley's dead. What does it change if he was?"

McKinley shrugged. "I don't know. Sharley did a whole bunch of research on us. Apparently he told Welles that he knew about the Zeta markers you both had. You think he knew about the nodes too?"

"He couldn't have. Dr. Bakshi only just discovered the nodes."

McKinley shrugged again. "Doesn't mean Sharley didn't have one though. Maybe he had some kind of gift too. He took the original program, what was it called? Something Latin."

"Bellator Fortis."

"Bellator Fortis," McKinley nodded. "He took that, turned it into the Jumbo program, which became the Alpha program, which branched out into the First Gen program, the JEM program, the Alpha-Mech program... I don't know. What if something specifically led Sharley to do that and target us?"

"Well, it's a possibility, I guess," Harris said, "but Sharley was also obsessive and deranged. He's dead now, I think we need to bury him. Psychologically. They're *our* programs now."

McKinley nodded. "Just something to consider, I guess." He shook it off. "How're things going with Martha?"

"So-so," Harris said, rubbing his face. "Welles ever tell you about the silver sands we saw in our dreams?"

McKinley nodded.

"Turns out it's the ashes of their dead."

"That's a lot of dead."

"They've been around a lot longer than we have. Maybe even seen more wars, too."

"You think there's a civil war happening now between the Alma Maters and the Priestesses?"

"Possibly." Harris sat forward. "The other Zeta races might be involved too, and then there're the males. God knows where they are now or whose side they're on."

"What I don't understand is how the females were oppressed for so long, then suddenly turned the tables on the males," McKinley said.

Harris shrugged. "They banded together, I guess." He sighed and motioned to McKinley's forehead. "How're your sessions going?"

McKinley shrugged, averted his eyes. "I haven't had one yet."

"I know," Harris said directly. "The general tells me that you better have a session soon or he's going to pull you out."

"Pull me out?" McKinley asked. "He needs me."

"You should've got help a long time ago, when your father was murdered. Someone should've stepped in when your mother couldn't handle things."

"I've survived," McKinley said glancing down to where his hands sat clasped in his lap.

"I say this, McKinley, as someone whose father was killed when I was a child. Luckily for me, though my mother struggled, I had a grandmother and great-grandmother who stepped in to support her. And me. Regardless, I still had to step up to the plate like you and take care of things well before I should have had to." McKinley looked back up as Harris's voice softened. "Your mother had mental health problems. My older brother had addiction problems. We did what we did to keep ourselves afloat, but that doesn't make it right, and it doesn't mean we can't realign things now that should've been realigned a long time ago." Harris relaxed and leaned back. "You've been to hell and back your whole life. You're a tough motherfucker, McKinley. Many would not be sitting here today before me, but you are."

McKinley shrugged. "Not sure I'd still be here if it weren't for you and Welles. And the kids." McKinley gave a soft laugh. "Kids... Can you believe I'm saying that? Never thought I'd like being a dad."

Harris gave a throaty laugh. "The McKinley on the Darwin mission certainly wouldn't believe it. But I guess that shows the effect Welles had on us both. She changed the direction of both our lives."

McKinley nodded to himself and glanced down into his lap, as his conversation with Carrie floated around his mind again. He looked at Harris. "Speaking of kids... what's the latest with the JEMs?"

Harris's smile fell away. He glanced back at his screen. "Funny you should mention that. I was just reading the latest update from Siberia Nine. He's telling me I'm overdue for another visit. They need to see their leader apparently." Harris studied McKinley for a moment, eyes narrowed in thought. "Do you want to come with me?"

"To see the JEMs?" he asked, surprised.

Harris nodded, still in thoughtful mode.

"Is that a good idea?"

"For you or for them?"

McKinley thought for a moment. "Both."

"Well, for them it's good. Because if I were to die, you were programmed as their next leader. I think they should meet you and see that you are my second in command."

"And for me?"

"I see the curiosity in your eyes. You've never met them. Welles has. I warn you, it won't be easy. Seeing Jesse like that. I mean, they're not Jesse, but they sure look like him. Well, not exactly. They're a cold, sterile version of him. It's hard to look at them... but you're going to have to face them sometime. I guess it depends if you're ready for it, mentally, with everything else you've got going on. Or whether, like Welles, this could give *you* a catastrophic brain injury."

McKinley's mind turned over the idea, before he looked back at Harris resolutely. "If I'm going to lead the Alpha soldiers, the JEMs are part of that. I need to see what their capabilities are. Whether it hurts or not. We need to rip the band-aid off."

Harris nodded in thought, still studying McKinley. "Alright. I'll book it in."

McKinley stood from his chair. "And Sharley?"

Harris sighed, turning that over in his mind too. "I'll see what medical information we have on file."

Harris's PDP rang. He answered it.

"Colonel Harris," Dr. Serquey's voice sounded. "I witnessed an interesting exchange between the Zetas. I've just sent you the video file."

He exchanged a look with McKinley, waved at him to stay, then brought up the video file.

Carrie walked toward the observation window in the Mars shuttle, the children at her sides, while their Sentinel, Novak, stayed nearby. Sampson was off shift, sleeping.

"It's so beautiful up here!" Freya gasped. They saw the curvature of the Earth as they left it behind for the starry backdrop of space. Carrie experienced a sudden flashback to the time of her first space journey, the Darwin mission. She'd been just as in awe as Freya was now.

"It sure is," Carrie smiled. "What do you think, boys?"

"I wanna go back," Jesse said quickly.

"We'll be back soon enough," Carrie assured him. "Enjoy the adventure."

Carrie looked to Brody who was silent in contemplation. "What about you, kiddo?"

Brody looked at her, his face serious and so much like Doc's. "We need to protect it."

Carrie's smile fell away. "We do."

An older man moved to stand beside Brody, looking out at the view. Carrie noticed Brody's nostrils flaring. He looked at the man, brow furrowed.

"It's illegal to smoke on the ship," Brody told the man.

The man looked at him, then at Carrie, then turned back to Brody. "My last smoke was on Earth, kid. I suggest you get your facts straight before making assumptions."

"It's illegal on Centralis too."

"I didn't smoke on Centralis, I smoked back on the mainland where it *is* still legal!" The man threw Carrie a hard glance, then turned and walked away.

Brody looked at Carrie. "I could smell it on him!"

"Honey, I'm sure you did," she lowered her voice, "but you've got Alpha senses now. You're going to pick up subtle traces of things that normal humans can't. What you need to learn, what you *all* need to learn," she looked at Freya and Jesse, too, "is to keep that sensory information to yourself. It's rude to call someone out for things like smoking, or even farts, Jesse."

The kids grinned.

"I'm serious. If you want to be a soldier one day," Carrie said, "those senses can be a weapon. Take in the information, the sights, the smells, the sounds, and store it away until you need it. You ever heard that saying 'play your cards close to your chest'? That's what you need to do." The kids stared back at her, really listening to what she had to say. "So, you smelled tobacco on that guy. If, later, there's a smoke alarm on board this ship and they're looking for a culprit, you could possibly have information to find the person responsible."

"But aren't we meant to stop people from doing bad things *before* they happen?" Brody asked.

"We are, but only if that's possible to do. Now, you can't follow that guy around the ship for three days, to see if he's going to have a smoke and inadvertently set off an alarm. That's not possible. But, say you smelled him smoking from afar, then, with your Alpha eyes, saw he was about to do something that could cause a fire, *then* you should stop him. Understand?"

"A smart soldier is also a spy," Freya smiled.

Carrie smiled back. "In a way. That's why you're practicing your stealth. It's important we remain vigilant and stay in the background, but when we need to, we step forward and do what we can."

Brody nodded, then looked back to the Earth's curvature. "He also smelled of booze."

Carrie threw her arm around Brody and squeezed him in tight. She smelled neither of those things on that man with her human nose, which meant Brody's new Alpha senses were working just fine.

Harris sat at the small table in his living quarters with Tyson and Sarai, eating a Command cooked dinner of roast chicken and vegetables. He was tired. Given what had happened between Martha and Evenssen, he'd had to brief Marchant and Berger, noting he would need to update the team soon. Given they were Alphas, they were used to regular physical check-ups, but now the nodes were a factor, it wasn't something Harris should keep quiet much longer, plus he should share the data on the Zeta DNA. Many of the team had low Zeta profiles and no showing of nodes so it wouldn't really affect them, but for those who had, the news would obviously be a shock, and possibly a concern, to them. Harris would need to reassure them that he was in the same boat, and that the node wasn't going to be a problem, but hopefully instead a blessing.

"Why can't I join school with Carrie's kids?" Sarai asked.

"Because they've gone to Mars for a bit," Harris told her.

"Well, what about Sabrina's kids?"

"They're Alphas, honey. They go to a special school."

"But you're an Alpha and I'm your kid?"

"Yes, but you're not an Alpha, honey."

"I don't want to school alone," she said glumly.

Harris sighed, studying her. "I'll speak to Marchant and see if you can join some of the academic classes of Colt's kids."

Sarai smiled and it was like the sun coming out from behind the clouds. It also reminded him a lot of Taya. And that made his heart hurt.

Sibbie, Etta and Maeve appeared behind Sarai then. Harris studied them wondering whether they were showing approval or warning. He felt no trepidation about them; it was approval.

"I miss Mom," Sarai said, smile melting away and the clouds reappearing.

"We all do," Ty said. "But don't worry, we're going to get the assholes who took her from us."

"Ty," Harris said softly.

"What?"

"What did you get up to today?" Harris changed the subject.

"Applied for some jobs, signed up for a local basketball team."

"Yeah?" Harris asked, curious.

Ty nodded.

They ate in silence for a moment, as Harris's mind ticked over.

"I'm happy you're here, Ty, but it's not too late to go back to the mainland and keep your spot on the state team."

"I told you, no," Ty said. They stared at each other. "If those Zetas come back, Dad, there'll be no basketball."

"If there's a war, and I say *if*, it's years away, Ty. You should enjoy the tim—"

"I told you, I can't think of playing now," Ty cut him off. "If we annihilate them, I'll go back to playing ball then."

Harris continued to eat, trying hard to contain his misgivings.

"That's why I signed up to join Earth Duty," Ty told him, scooping a forkful of dinner into his mouth.

"You, what?" Harris said.

"How?" Sarai asked. "You're supposed to do a term with the US military first."

Ty nodded. "And I will. But on the application, you can select which paths you wish to take. I ticked Earth Duty. Once I do my stint for the US, all going well, they'll select me for Earth Duty. I'm fit, I'm fast, why wouldn't they? Besides, with *you* as my dad, they'd have to."

Harris continued to stare at him.

"What? You're in the military, Dad. You're an Alpha, and you're leading all the Alpha soldiers. Don't tell me I can't do this."

Harris felt the hairs on the back of his neck stand on end. There was something about Ty, the way he stared back, the look in his eye, the tone of his voice. It was like seeing the ghost of his brother, Terence.

And suddenly there he was. Standing behind Ty. His dead brother folded his arms defiantly like he did, a smile of pride in his eyes at Ty standing up to Harris. There wasn't malicious intent from Terence. There never had been. He'd just been an addict who blamed the world for his problems, instead of trying to overcome them. He never liked being told what to do, never liked his younger military brother dishing orders to him, or having his life more together than him.

And that's what worried him about Ty.

There was a glimmer of Terence in him, a glimmer of that defiance. In the right circumstances, his rebelliousness could be a good thing, but it could also become a very bad thing. He had to make sure it didn't overcome his son like it had his brother.

His female ancestors looked at Terence, then they all disappeared from Harris's mind.

"Okay," Harris said calmly, not wanting to fight, or push Ty away.

"Okay?" Ty asked surprised. "You're okay with me doing it?"

Harris stared back at his son, careful to keep his face soft, his voice gentle and calm. "I was fighting, so you didn't have to. I was fighting because I wanted to protect you, because I love you… But I understand why you want to do this, and I can't protect my children from what might come, while others put theirs on the line to save us."

Tyson and Sarai stared back at him. Harris felt a chill wash over him as he pictured Ty on a chaotic battlefield of Zetas and HH, saw Sarai going toe-to-toe in a Zeta's mind.

"We're all in this together," Harris said with seriousness, "and together we can keep each other safe." He reached out and clasped his big hands over Ty's and Sarai's. They squeezed his hands back.

"Damn straight," Ty nodded, then grinned.

It was then Harris noticed the slight tingling sensation, the vibration coming from Sarai's hand. It was faint, but it was there.

"Oh! That reminds me!" Sarai said, leaving the table and moving to her bag. She pulled out a photo and handed it to Harris. He looked at it and saw it was a copy of the photo from the fridge in his Centralis apartment; a childhood photo of him and Holly sitting on the porch steps with Sibbie and Etta, their eyes piercing through time, while Terence stood in the background. "Aunt Holly gave me her photo. I think you should have it up while you're here."

Harris studied it, then looked at his daughter. "Thank you, honey."

Carrie stared at Dr. Bakshi on her monitor.

"And dreams?" Bakshi asked.

"No," Carrie said. "Whatever drugs you've given me are knocking me out every night."

"Good. When you arrive on Mars you will transfer to the care of the president's physician, who will be on hand if needed."

"Are you any closer to coming up with a fix for my brain?"

"Not yet, we're looking at several treatments and advancing those we think are promising. We're getting closer, but cannot rush the process."

"Patience never was my strong suit," Carrie said.

"It's going to have to be now. Your brain is too delicate to take chances."

Carrie sighed and nodded in acceptance. "Can you at least give me an idea of what treatments you're looking at?"

"Well..." Dr. Bakshi looked a little hesitant. "I've been made aware of your kill switch."

"Yeah, the one that's supposed to be removed, but hasn't been yet."

"And it may not be."

"What?" Carrie's Alpha anger reared up.

"Lieutenant," Dr. Bakshi said, holding her hand up to calm her, "the nanobots injected into you might actually save you."

"How?" Carrie asked.

"We're investigating how we might reprogram them to help fix your brain. The nanobots were designed to attack your organs and cells, but with some reengineering, they might be able to help us rebuild your brain from the inside."

"How?" Carrie asked again, feeling her Alpha slide back down.

"Like I said, we're still investigating things."

"Is this for real? Or is this just a lie to force me to keep the kill switch because I can communicate with the Zetas? Be honest, doctor."

Dr. Bakshi smiled gently. "I don't know much about the circumstances of your kill switch, lieutenant, so I cannot comment on that. But I know that these nanobots may provide a real opportunity to heal you. That's all I can say for now, and it may take some time for us to work out the details. Until then you must rest and avoid stress."

Carrie laughed. "If only!"

"I shall continue to monitor her, Dr. Bakshi," Archie spoke from the discs against her neck. "I will ensure she takes care of herself."

"Thank you, Archie," she said. "Enjoy the rest of your journey, first lieutenant."

"Goodbye, Dr. Bakshi."

Carrie ended the transmission. She removed the discs with a wince of pain, placing them on the bedside table in a special cleansing solution.

"*Goodnight, Miss Welles,*" Archie said from the discs.

Carrie stared at them. "Can I just carry those discs around, Archie? Do I really need to put them in all the time?"

"If I am to read your biometrics, yes."

Carrie sighed. She lay down in bed, ready for another night of dreamless sleep, wondering whether the Zetas were noticing her absence.

Harris sat in his bedroom, staring at the small purple book in his hands, titled *Notes for the Bequeathed*. He'd kept it close in his possessions, and every now and then he opened it and flicked through the pages. With gold gilded edges, worn with time, he carefully turned the hard cover over to stare at the list of names hand-scrawled on the inside. The ones at the top had been written some time ago and were faded with time. The bottom of the list, contained his direct family line:

Etta Mae Washington
Sibbylla Clarese Jones
Maeve Jacinta Jackson
Saul Fabian Harris

He paused a moment, thinking, then found a pen and added one more name to the list:

Sarai Sibbylla Harris

He thumbed through the pages to add her name to those scrawled in the margins of the section titled 'See'ers'. He then flipped through to the section titled 'Sense'ers' and added hers there, too. Then, finally, he flipped to the section titled 'Connectors', where his name was listed beneath that of his ancestors, Bryant Todd and Charles Washington, the other aberrations. And once again, he reread the text:

'Connectors are a rarity, bestowed with a gift formed from the two strongest: the See'ers and the Sense'ers. They take up aspects of both gifts, and like all gifts they will vary from being to being, as each bequeathed adapts the gift to their own personal traits. Connectors are often referred to as Guardians. This gift of Guardianship, is only inherent in the male.'

He sighed and put the book aside, making a mental note to share it with DaJuan in the morning.

17

Machinations

Dr. Arielle Serquey watched the monitor carefully. Tess lay strapped in her bed, hissing in her sleep. Arielle double-checked the monitor to ensure it was recording, then looked back at Tess again.

She'd noted a distinct change since Martha had been brought to Command. Tess's disposition had become more lively. She wasn't sure whether it was hope and the thought of an alliance that buoyed Tess, or perhaps a burning curiosity as to what Martha was doing here and why she wasn't being strapped down or imprisoned.

But that was something Arielle was looking to fix. They couldn't keep Tess bound like a prisoner for much longer. She'd considered every scenario and knew that further medical tests would be difficult if Tess were unrestrained, but the only way to gain her compliance might be to allow her freedom. After all, they were trying to seek peace with the Zeta, and this could not be achieved while Tess was strapped to her bed and imprisoned in her cell.

She turned her eyes to a second monitor showing Martha, who lay on a mattress on the floor. The Alma Mater had pulled the mattress from the bed and made a nest of sorts in the corner of the room with the sheets and rugs. Martha was naturally on edge, being in a foreign land, but so far had contained any aggression. Though Arielle didn't doubt for a second that

Martha would unleash if she felt threatened again – like she had done in the Tube incident.

The exchange between her and Evenssen had been fascinating. Why had she been so fixated on him and not Hunter? The only explanation had to be the presence of a node and Zeta markings in his DNA. Harris had taken note of the exchange and shared it with both Marchant and Berger. What their next steps were to be, she didn't know.

Using a hand-held scanning paddle, she'd tried to scan Martha's brain as best she could to detect the node. The scan was rough, as the Zeta did not stay still, but it was enough for Arielle to see the large dark node clear as day. In fact, it looked larger than Tess's. But what did this mean? Martha's node was larger because she was older? Or because she was a higher rank in the Zeta pecking order? Did this mean Martha was more powerful than Tess? She was considering knocking both Zetas out to take even more detailed scans, but worried about eroding trust. For now, the slightly blurry scan would have to do.

A loud mooing bray, as though in objection, sounded from Martha, while Tess hissed again. Arielle darted her eyes between the screens, studying the two. She was in no doubt that the two were connecting and having a heated discussion.

Her burning question at this point, was whether Harris had joined them and could tell her what it was about.

Harris was dreaming again, walking along a darkened space. There was no silver sand, but, instead, black sand. He saw the flicker of flames ignite in the distance, smelled smoke. He looked back down at the black dirt and wondered whether it was the embers and ashes of whatever the flames were burning up ahead.

He heard a ship zoom overhead, saw the flash of a heat ray from another, saw a massive explosion and parts of the ship shatter and fall toward him. He threw his arms up to protect himself and tried to take cover near a blackened, destroyed building. There was silence for a moment before he heard hissing, and an aggrieved braying in the distance.

He came out from the cover of the destroyed building and saw he was covered in black ash. He shook his head and arms to dust it off.

"Dad?" Sarai asked. He looked to his left and saw her taking cover in more rubble nearby. He went to admonish her, but bit his tongue. The Zetas were here somewhere and he didn't want them to see disorder, or tension, on the human side.

"Stay calm," Harris said firmly but quietly. "Don't show them weakness. Show them confidence."

Sarai came out from beneath the rubble, straightening up. Harris suddenly thought of the rubble she'd once been buried beneath with her dead mother. His heart tore in that moment, but he swallowed the pain.

He studied his nine-year-old daughter as she approached him, saw how young and fragile she was, but also how time was beginning to pull her toward adulthood. He felt a hint of regret for not having Welles here with him. Maybe Welles was right, she needed a motherly figure around.

Martha stepped out from some rubble up ahead. She didn't look as calm or regal as she usually did.

"What's going on?" Harris asked her.

The Alma Mater raised her hoofed hands and with one swift movement, waved him off violently.

Harris's body went flying to the side, crashing into the burned structure beside which he stood.

"Dad!" Sarai yelled, then disappeared.

Harris watched as Martha walked toward him.

"Dad!" Sarai said.

Harris flicked his eyes open and saw Sarai standing over him. He was in his bed, in his Command quarters, drenched in sweat.

"Are you okay?" Sarai asked.

Harris, panting with shock, nodded. Sarai hugged him and he hugged her back.

He wasn't sure what that dream was about, or why Martha was angry, but what he did know was that Martha had shown him just how powerful the Zeta's mind really was.

DaJuan sat surrounded by three screens. Each was enacting searches on the ancestry of each of the *Aurizun* team, and on the recent addition of a Professor Raymond Sharley, who Harris had informed DaJuan had been found to have Zeta DNA markers in his blood. The man was deceased, and Harris didn't seem too sad about that, but regardless, they wanted to know about the guy, so DaJuan would deliver.

Ancestry searches were a lot easier for DaJuan since he'd established his own programs and search engines to find the data he needed, through the right channels and through some hacked channels. If there was a record to be found, he would find it. But records only went so far. The rest he had to do on instinct.

Sometimes he would stare at family trees or photos for hours, willing the ghosts of the past to guide him. He'd never really thought about it before, but knowing what he did about Harris, he was in awe that the man could converse with the dead. DaJuan had been open to this way of life since he was born, but that did not make him stronger than Harris. Though DaJuan had traced both their ancestries to sisters in Africa, reconfirmed through the familial book Harris had given him called *Notes for the Bequeathed*, that did not mean the See'ers they were today would hold the same power. There was more involved than that. It was a lot like the Zeta markers. Much depended on the breeding stock throughout the ages as to whether the Zeta markers had been bred out or remained strong. DaJuan was strong, but he felt, just by looking at Harris, that the soldier was much stronger. Stronger than Harris even knew he was. There was something about him, an aura, a vibration; invisible but present. DaJuan could almost feel the untapped potential flowing through Harris's veins. A potential that had grown immensely since DaJuan had seen him last.

Of all the *Aurizun* team he'd searched so far, Yughiarto stood out as having a semblance of lineage. It was there, but nowhere near as strong as Harris. The biggest puzzle for DaJuan, of all the crew, was Carrie Welles. She was clearly strong to have been connecting with Harris and the Zetas, despite how much Harris's gift may have been carrying her. Yet, he found her lineage somewhat weak. She came from generation upon generation of white Australians, until, eventually, he found a link back to Ireland, and from there to the Vikings. That discovery had made DaJuan chuckle. He'd traced McKinley's family back through Scotland and then to the Vikings also. DaJuan thought it somewhat poetic that these two of Viking blood, had found each other centuries later.

Still, something was scratching at DaJuan's psyche. Something telling him that he didn't have the whole story. The trace on Welles so far had followed her father's side.

Now, DaJuan thought, it was time to trace her mother.

Harris walked the corridor of Command with McKinley, having summoned the Alpha-Mech to join him.

"We're heading out to see the JEMs," he'd told McKinley earlier when he'd called him.

"We are?" McKinley had said, a little surprised at the short notice.

"Yes. Like you said, we gotta rip the band-aid off sometime."

"Alright," McKinley had answered.

"Change your clothes, though," Harris told him. "We can't wear anything identifying us as UNF."

They walked the corridor now in civilian clothing, on their way to catch the ride that Hunter had organized.

"Colonel Harris," a woman's voice called from behind. Harris and McKinley turned to see Dr. Serquey approaching. "Do you have a moment?"

Harris checked his watch. "A moment. We're about to fly out."

"I noticed some unusual behavior between the Zetas last night. They were connecting. It seemed lively. Did you join them?"

"I did, but they threw me out."

"Threw you out?" McKinley asked.

Harris nodded. "Martha threw me out with her mind. It... actually kinda hurt in the dream. Their minds are way more powerful than we're giving them credit for. I think they've been holding back, hiding their true strength."

"From what I can gather, Martha's node is *much* larger than Tess'." Serquey showed concern. "What if Tess is trying to turn Martha against us?"

"We can't let that happen," Harris said.

"No, and I have a suggestion."

"Which is?" Harris asked.

"I propose we release Tess from her restraints."

"What?" Harris straightened. "I'm not sure that's a good idea."

"I am," Serquey said resolutely. "If we want to make Tess more amenable like Martha, we need to treat them the same. We need to stop treating Tess like a prisoner and more like a potential ally. As they say, you catch more flies with honey than you do with vinegar."

"If you release her, you won't be able to get physically near her again. She almost killed Morrell."

"Yes, we'll need to gas her into submission if that's the case, but I strongly believe that we can no longer keep her restrained. She must be free to move about her cell like Martha. It's the only way. Do I have your approval to proceed?"

Harris considered it for a moment. "Alright. Try it. But put extra guards on the cell and have the gas ready to deploy."

"Thank you," Serquey said, then turned and quickly moved off in the opposite direction.

"You sure about that?" McKinley asked.

Harris looked at him. "If we're not getting results, then we need to change tactics. We need to get on Tess's good side again. And we need to stop her from turning Martha against us."

They continued toward the Commercial Dock where Hunter and Frazer were meeting them for their journey to the JEM facility in Siberia.

"So, I looked into Sharley's blood like Welles asked," Harris said.

"Yeah? And?"

"He had the Zeta markings. I've got DaJuan looking into his ancestry and that of the whole team." Harris cracked a smile. "He gave me his initial findings this morning. Turns out you, Welles, Steinberg and Evenssen trace back to the Vikings."

McKinley smirked. "Yeah, Mom always told me that's where the traces of red in my beard came from."

"Yughi and Tikaani trace back to the Mongols. Me, Brown and Colt naturally hail from various African lines."

"And Hunter?"

"He was a mix of European and South American. DaJuan's still working on things to give a more definitive answer, but you know what this tracing of ancestral lines got me thinking about?"

"What?"

"The buried Zeta ships we've found so far. Where were they?"

McKinley thought for a moment, then looked back at Harris. "Spread throughout the globe."

"Yeah, in isolated areas, each landscape different, but I feel like each is pointing to areas of ancient civilizations. Think about it. Egypt, China, Mexico, Peru, Australia."

"And the Carlsbad Caverns?"

"Native Americans," he shrugged. "Ancient Egyptians. Ancient China. The Aztecs. The Incas," he glanced at McKinley as they continued walking. "The Australian Aboriginal is believed to be one of the oldest peoples on Earth."

"So, what does it mean?" McKinley asked, confused.

"I don't really know yet, but it's got me wondering if there's a link between the ancient cultures of Earth, the Zetas' past visits, the Zeta markings in our blood, and those who are strongest with the gift."

"You think if we look hard enough we'll find more Zeta ships in Viking territory and down in Africa?"

Harris shrugged. "I don't know, but we need to investigate every possibility. I've asked Dr. Ross to focus on the areas of our most ancient cultures, and to focus on similar landscapes to the other found ships – mountains, caves, bodies of water." A thought struck Harris. "I dreamed there was water on Zeta Archelois. The Zetas poured their dead's ashes into it. It created the silver sand. They must like the water."

"It would be so much easier if the Zetas could just tell us all this."

Harris grunted a laugh. "Tell me about it. What I really need is to find a See'er or Sense'er who is also a language expert. Now *that* would be great."

"We should boost Yughi's node. He knows a lot of languages."

"He knows about five or so," Harris said, "but not the Zeta language."

"Well, they've mastered wearable electronic translators for humans," McKinley said, referring to devices that humans could wear in the vicinity of their voice boxes that automatically translated the words spoken. "We need to get them happening for the Zeta language ASAP."

"Easier said than done."

——————— ★ ★ ★ ———————

Carrie stared out the observation window at the orange-brown marble that was Mars. They'd been travelling for two days and had now switched from Earth time to Martian time.

"So, that's our home for the next while, huh?" Brody thought aloud.

"Jade said there's not much there," Jesse said.

"It's still in its infancy, but it's growing by the day," Carrie said.

"Is that Atlas?" Freya asked, pointing to a glint of light in the near distance.

"No, that's Station Pegasus," Carrie said. "I lived there for a time, you know?" She smiled at the memories of the early days of her relationship with Doc, of dancing at the Nectar Bar, endless days in her apartment and bedroom with him. But her smile soon faded as other memories poured in. Namely, Chet and Logan taking Doc, McKinley, and herself, prisoner; being held in the secret lair beneath Hell Town; forcing Doc and McKinley to become Jumbos. How their lives were never the same again.

"What's wrong?" Brody asked.

"Nothing," Carrie said, "I just got lost in a memory."

"We might get stationed on Pegasus one day," Freya said to Brody. "It's the military outpost for Mars."

"*Atlas will be taking over that role, Freya,*" Archie spoke from Carrie's discs.

"Oh, yeah," Freya said, looking at Carrie. "What will happen to Pegasus once Atlas is certified?"

"Pegasus will still be a base," Carrie said. "They'll assign it different duties and move its position elsewhere. It'll probably still be off Mars, just on the opposite side to Atlas."

"So they can scramble fighters quickly depending on which is closer to the action?" Freya asked.

Carrie nodded and smiled. "That's it, honey."

"See," Freya turned to Brody, "we *could* be stationed on Pegasus one day."

Brody rolled his eyes. "You wanna go to Pegasus, you do that. I'm going to Atlas because it'll have the latest tech and weaponry."

Freya thought for a moment. "Good point."

"I hate to break it to you, kids," Carrie said, "but generally you go where the military sends you. You rarely get a choice, hence why we're being sent to Mars now."

"But we're First Gens," Jesse said. "We're not like the rest."

"No, you're not like the rest. This much is true."

"Where will they send us?" Freya asked.

Carrie shrugged. "I don't know yet, but I do know that Alphas were built for physical fighting. I suspect when the times comes you'll be planetside somewhere, not in space."

"Good," Jesse said.

Freya's face fell. "But I want to fly ships."

Carrie rubbed Freya's back. "Someone's gotta fly the troops around to where they're needed."

"Yeah," Freya reassured herself, "like Uncle Hunter. He's an Alpha *and* a pilot."

"Colonel Harris wants all Space Duty pilots to be Alphas," Carrie said. "They need our quick reflexes."

"They should keep us near Earth," Jesse said. "That's our home. That's what we need to protect."

"The Moon and Mars are also our homes, too, though," Carrie said. "And our stations. We need to protect them all."

"I guess it'll be good to see Mars, then," Brody said in contemplation, staring out at the planet growing before them. "If we have to protect it, we should get to know it."

Carrie smiled at him, agreeing with his sentiment, then turned her eyes back to the orange-brown orb and wondered just what she would need to protect President Harkowitz from.

Harris stepped down from the small spacecraft that Hunter and Frazer had flown in stealth mode to Siberia. It was the kind of ship that shot into the atmosphere, rode the Earth's curvature, then dove back down to Earth, making the trip a matter of a couple of hours, compared to the longer time a commercial Earth aircraft would take.

The air was cool and the ground rather green, and the surrounding trees, fresh from spring, were budding all kinds of bushy leaves. McKinley climbed down beside him and they surveyed the JEM facility. Berger had granted them leave without the need for their 'shadows' due to the highly sensitive nature of the facility. This was the first time Harris had seen the building from the outside. The last time he'd visited he'd had a bag over his head. The facility looked like a small ramshackle building on the surface, clearly to disguise what lay underneath.

"This is it?" McKinley asked, confused.

"This is the entrance," Harris said. "The facility lies below ground." Harris looked back to his pilots. "Stay here."

Hunter gave a nod, and Harris and McKinley made their way to the entrance. When they reached the door a familiar face greeted them. Tall, ginger and pale, the man gave a nod.

"Colonel Harris," he said, then moved his eyes to McKinley.

"Siberia Nine," Harris said, "this is Major McKinley."

"Yes," Siberia Nine said, "the father-source."

McKinley stared back at Siberia Nine. He'd been quiet and tense the whole trip there, as Harris had explained everything he knew about the JEMs, the line of command, how they were to act as leaders, and how the JEMs, despite being seven years old, were not normal children. He told McKinley how it was important they stay cold and emotionally unavailable in front of the JEMs. Harris was going to stick close to McKinley during this visit, and more importantly, afterward when everything he would see here today would sink in and he'd have to process it all.

"Yes," Harris said plainly to Siberia Nine, "the father-source and second in command of the JEMs, ahead of Jesse Ethan McKinley himself. Shall we?"

Siberia Nine motioned them through to an elevator where they descended to the sub-levels. All the while Siberia Nine stared at McKinley, fascinated. McKinley noticed and turned to stare back.

"I'm sorry if I stare," Siberia Nine bowed slightly. "It's just that I've seen your picture on our wall for almost 10 years now. It's an honor to finally meet you. Especially now you've been upgraded to an Alpha-Mech."

McKinley's jaw clenched and unclenched in response.

"I would love to see a demonstration of what you can do," Siberia Nine continued. "It could generate new ideas for the JEM training."

"I'm not a puppet who performs on request," McKinley said directly.

"Yes," Siberia Nine gave a subservient nod. "My apologies."

"How are the JEMs doing?" Harris steered the conversation in another direction, as they stepped out of the elevator and began walking along a corridor toward what Harris expected would be the control room overlooking the JEM warehouse.

"They are faster and stronger since you last saw them," Siberia Nine said.

"And how have they been handling the death of Sharley and JEM-500?"

"If anything, they are stronger of mind. Sharley was a scientist and he carried and sculpted them with his knowledge, but he had taken things as far as he could. What they need now is a military leader to take them through the next phase. We have become even more regimented and as a result they have become more like soldiers. The death of JEM-500 taught them that they are not unbreakable and they must strive harder to become so."

"But the First Gens are still human," McKinley finally spoke. "They are not immortal."

"No, but they've been taught not to be afraid of death their whole life. And they know about you, their father-source, being an Alpha-Mech. A soldier who faced death and returned to life. They know that dismemberment does not mean the end. They know they can continue to serve the UNF until their last breath."

McKinley locked eyes with Harris.

"It is as it has to be," Harris said firmly, holding his look. He looked back at Siberia Nine. "Let's begin."

They entered the small control room, where a balding, spectacled man sat at a console. The observation window was tinted black so they could not yet see onto the training floor below. Siberia Nine closed the door behind them and motioned to the man sitting at the console.

"This is Siberia Seven," he said. The man gave a nod to Harris and McKinley. Harris nodded back.

"Are we to announce Major McKinley to the JEMs?" Siberia Nine asked Harris.

Harris thought for a moment. "Yeah. Let's do a formal introduction like you did with me. He won't say anything, though. I am their leader, but they need to see that he is the second in command. They've met their mother-source, it's time they meet their father-source."

"Agreed. It will reaffirm the chain of command and their allegiance if they see their living gods."

"Living gods?" McKinley's brow furrowed.

"Just roll with it," Harris said, then looked back to Siberia Nine. "What you said about reaffirming their allegiance, have you detected any cracks?"

"No," Siberia Nine said, "but it has been a long time between visits. Sharley would show his face at least once a month."

"I've been largely bound to Command for the past while, but I will endeavor to visit more regularly moving forward. And if not me, McKinley will."

Siberia Nine nodded, then looked to McKinley. "If you stand back over there until we call you." He pointed to the corner of the room, out of sight of the window. Harris nodded for McKinley to do it, as Harris stepped closer to the window.

"Are there words I am to speak like last time?"

"When I say so, we should reaffirm their vow to you." He tapped a screen before Harris and the words appeared for Harris to read. Siberia Nine motioned for Siberia Seven to begin, and the man's hands darted around the console. They heard an alarm blaring in the warehouse and an automated voice calling: *Prepare for inspection!* After a few moments the blackened observation window lightened until Harris saw through clearly. Before him, 499 JEMs stood to attention in perfectly straight rows, eyes staring at the wall ahead of them.

Harris stepped right up to the window and examined them. It had been a few months since he'd seen them and the changes were clearly visible. They looked slightly taller, their faces slightly harder, and the musculature along their arms clearly noticeable. They did not look like children, but little men.

They looked less like Jesse than they had before. Though Jesse Ethan McKinley was older than them by two and a half, almost three years, it was now the JEMs who looked older than their original. Or maybe it was just that they looked harder.

"Attention, soldiers!" Siberia Nine said firmly into the microphone. "Prepare for inspection by your leader, Colonel Harris."

Four hundred and ninety-nine pairs of eyes looked up and zeroed in on Harris. They saluted him. He noticed how they all stood a little taller, eager to impress.

"Go ahead," Siberia Nine said to Harris.

Harris clasped his hands behind his back and made a show of running his eyes over each line of JEMs.

"JEMs," Harris said coldly, darting his eyes to his projected speech on the nearby screen. "I am your leader. You will obey my command. If you do not... you will die... I am your god," he said, noticing McKinley staring at him, clearly feeling much the same way as Harris did when he'd first heard the words. "I am your master and your commander. You will obey only me. Do you understand?"

"JEM-1, what say you?" Siberia Nine said.

"Yes, sir, commander!"

McKinley turned his eyes to the observation window, which he could not yet see through.

"And the rest of you?" Siberia Nine said.

"Yes, sir!" hundreds of voices, akin to Jesse's, shouted.

Harris saw through his Alpha periphery that McKinley's chest had begun rising and falling with more anxious vigor.

"And when I am not around," Harris continued coldly, "you will obey your second in command, Major McKinley... Your father-source."

"Soldiers?" Siberia Nine prompted them.

"Yes, sir!"

"Would you like to meet him?" Harris asked. "Your father-source?"

"Yes, sir!" they shouted, the tenor of their voice rising slightly with excitement.

Harris let the silence sit a moment as he cast his eyes over them again. "Very well... Major McKinley, step forward."

McKinley moved out from the shadows to stand by Harris's side. Harris's Alpha ears could hear McKinley's heartbeat thumping from where he stood, heard him swallow deeply as his eyes took in the sight of his sons, all 499 of them, smelled a spike in sweat and pheromones oozing from his skin.

The JEMs below fixed their eyes on him and cast crisp salutes.

Siberia Nine played that overwhelming music, the Eastern European choir and orchestral music, while spotlights lit up the images of Harris and McKinley along the wall and the JEMs turned to salute to them.

"Jesus fucking Christ," McKinley breathed.

"Hold it," Harris said firmly, under his breath.

The music finished and the JEMs turned back to view them up high in the control room.

"Prepare for closer inspection," Siberia Nine told the JEMs. "The colonel and the major will walk among you."

The window turned black again.

"Audio off," Siberia Seven confirmed.

Harris looked at McKinley who was still staring at the black window.

"Take a minute, but that's all you got," Harris said to him. "We gotta walk among them and allow them to impress us with what they can do."

McKinley didn't answer, didn't move.

Harris motioned for the Siberia officers to leave the room. They did.

"McKinley, I know it's hard, but you gotta shake it off."

McKinley turned his face to him. "I got 500 fucking kids out there… It's a lot to take in."

"It's 499, and yeah, I know, but we can't change that fact. They're here, they're alive, and they're being trained to be killers who will help us if and when the Zetas hit Earth again."

McKinley looked back at the blackened window, then down at his feet, rubbing his forehead agitatedly. "How the fuck am I going to look Jesse in the eye again after this?"

"Easy," Harris said, "because once you meet these JEMs you'll realize they aren't a damn thing like him. Not up here," he pointed to his temple. "Jesse has heart and soul. These JEMs don't."

McKinley looked back at him. "That's supposed to make me feel better?"

"Jesse is your boy. The JEMs aren't. They just share his DNA." Harris moved to the door. "Come on. Let's get this over with. Band-aid, remember?"

Harris approached the door leading to the main warehouse floor. Siberia Nine walked alongside, while McKinley walked behind, lost in his own thoughts.

"I have matters to discuss with you after your inspection," Siberia Nine said, casting Harris a meaningful glance.

"Is this about your place in the food chain?" Harris arched an eyebrow.

"No," Siberia Nine said earnestly, "this is about those who are watching the facility."

"Who's watching the facility?"

Siberia Nine studied him a moment as though trying to read whether Harris was testing him. "That is why I insisted you pay us another visit. We have matters to discuss." They reached the door. "After your inspection, we will talk."

Harris nodded and looked back at McKinley. "Remember, cold and emotionless. Do *not* show weakness. You are *not* their father. You're simply a DNA donor."

McKinley gave a small nod and Harris stepped through to the warehouse floor.

The JEMs stood in straight lines, facing them, now side on to the observation window. Harris couldn't help but marvel at the distance Sharley had fallen when Welles had thrown him through that window. His eyes quickly sought the spot on the concrete floor below, where the man had finally died. He glanced at McKinley and saw him eyeing the same spot, as though reading his mind. Harris paused a moment to wonder if McKinley's mind had actually been in synch with his, or whether it was simply because Welles would've told him the story so his mind and gaze instinctively went there.

Their eyes soon returned to the JEMs before them.

"Salute your leaders!" JEM-1 called out, and the JEMs saluted them again.

"At ease," Harris said, moving to stand before them. He cast his eyes over them as McKinley stood to his left and Siberia Nine to his right. At eye level, under the strong lights, the definition in their arms was something else. So, too, was the cold, emotionless look in their eyes. Harris noted, in particular, the way JEM-1 stared at McKinley. Though still cold and emotionless, Harris detected a spark of curiosity lurking beneath.

"Is there something you would like to say, JEM-1?" Harris asked.

JEM-1 stepped forward. "Sir! It is an honor to stand before you, and to meet the father-source, sir!" he called out in soldier mode.

Harris moved closer to JEM-1 and McKinley followed.

"Would you like a fighting display, sir?" JEM-1 asked.

Harris hesitated a moment. "Yes, I would. But I don't wish for a display that ends in death. Are we clear?"

"Yes, sir!" JEM-1 said. "May I fight you, sir?"

A smile tried to slide across Harris's lips but he fought it down. "You want to fight a grown Alpha man twice your size, JEM-1? Is that wise?"

"If we are to get better, stronger, then we must fight those stronger than ourselves. I can beat my brothers. I need my next target, sir."

Harris glanced at Siberia Nine, arching his eyebrow in question.

"JEM-1 is our best fighter, colonel. As firstborn, Professor Sharley designated him unit leader of the JEMs, something which has come to him naturally."

Harris looked back at JEM-1 with cold eyes. "You are not ready for me yet."

JEM-1 gave a nod. "And the father-source, sir?"

Harris glanced at McKinley, who stared at JEM-1, clearly working hard to keep any emotion off his face. Harris stepped closer to JEM-1. "If you are not ready for an adult Alpha, you are most certainly not ready for an adult Alpha-Mech. Know your place JEM-1, and know your capabilities. Your time will come to fight those greater than you, but that time is not now."

JEM-1 nodded again. "Yes, sir. I hope to one day show you how strong a fighter I am, whether against Alpha or Zeta."

"I look forward to it," Harris said, then turned to Siberia Nine. "Let's begin the demonstration, shall we?"

Siberia Nine started barking instructions as Harris cast his eyes across the JEMs.

But then suddenly something caught his eye.

There, in the background, below the control room window, a familiar face stared back at him and gave an eerie, prideful smile.

Sharley...

Harris's face fell flat.

"Colonel?" McKinley's voice sounded. "Colonel?" he said firmly as he nudged Harris's shoulder.

Harris looked back at him. "What?"

He saw everyone was staring at him, assembled in groups, ready to begin the demonstration.

Harris glanced back to the spot beneath the control room window again, but Sharley was gone.

18

Spies on the Prize

Carrie looked out of the Mars Patrol Vehicle's window as they approached the Red House. They'd just passed Colony Elon and the children were excited, first by their ride in a MaPV from the Mars Docking Station, then by pointing out the Martian landmarks that Carrie had made them learn on their journey, their AIs proving to be useful teachers.

"It's more brown than red. Why do they call it the red planet?" Brody had asked.

"It looks like the desert heart of Australia if you ask me," Sampson said, "just not as bright or colorful."

"Elon looks small," Jesse had noted. "Isn't it the biggest colony here?"

"It looks small because the majority of the buildings are below ground," Novak said.

"Whoa!" Freya gasped. "Is that the Red House?"

"Sure is," Carrie had said, looking at the spacious compound before them, covered by its own purification and gravitational domes. Two stories high and built from local Martian stone, it was almost camouflaged by the orange-brown dirt surrounding it. That said, the external landscaping beneath the domes looked very much like a desert oasis.

"That's where we're staying?" Jesse's eyes popped.

"I can't believe we're staying with a president," Brody said.

Carrie had smiled at their enthusiasm and awe. She started thinking that maybe this stay on Mars might be good for their development after all.

"Who are those people outside?" Freya asked as they approached the outer gate.

Carrie looked carefully and spotted a small crowd in atmospheric suits and several MaPVs parked along the dome walls.

"Protestors," the driver told them.

"What are they protesting?" Brody asked.

"They're not happy about the Atlas incident or the UNF protecting the Zeta."

"But they're trying to make peace?" Freya said.

The driver shrugged back at her, as the car slowly made its way up to the gate, through the people.

A few hands banged on the vehicle and signs were pressed against the window: "US or THEM!", "SHOW NO MERCY!", "TO LET THAT ZETA LIVE WHILE MY SON DIED IS A DISGRACE!", "HARKOWITZ IS NO LONGER FOR THE PEOPLE!", "FREE THE COURAGEOUS FEW WHO TRIED TO SAVE US!".

Carrie noticed the children had drawn quiet and moved away from the windows. The UNF soldiers, expecting them, quickly opened the gates so they could continue through.

"They're really mad," Freya said, looking through the back window at the protestors.

"That's why Mom's here," Brody said.

"Things will calm down soon," Carrie said, wanting to reassure them, though deep inside, she felt concerned.

Dr. Arielle Serquey stood outside Tess's glass cell, a small remote in her hand, ready to release the Zeta's restraints.

She'd placed a rat in a container inside the cell, ready for Tess's next meal, and had run a series of medical checks, and taken biological samples, unsure as to when she would next be able to do so. Even if they had to gas Tess out every time they needed to run tests or clean her cell, it was a better option than leaving her permanently restrained. Her arm stump had long healed and Tess needed to get back to as normal a life as she could.

She made eye contact with the soldiers on duty outside the cell: Brown, Steinberg and Tikaani. Martha appeared at the door to her cell, perhaps sensing that something was about to happen.

Arielle gave her a smile of reassurance, then turned back to Tess and pressed the remote. They heard the restraints retracting and watched as Tess realized she was being released.

Martha moved up to the cell's glass wall.

With the restraints gone and her arm and stump free, Tess stared at Arielle and the soldiers, tongue whipping around as though seeking danger or a trap. After sensing none, however, she sat up, then slid off her bed.

She was shaky at first, having been lying down for so long. She leaned on the bed with her good arm, then sat down again, still darting her eyes from person to person outside the glass walls.

"Give her time," Arielle told them. "Once she's stable on her feet she will become more active."

"And no doubt look for a way out," the soldier called Tikaani said.

"That's why we're here," Brown said.

"We're here to keep an eye on Martha," Steinberg said. "Now our attention is divided."

"Tess cannot break free from that cell," Arielle assured them. "I've also taken the precaution of increasing your numbers from two to three. I believe that will be more than sufficient."

"Let's hope," Brown said.

Carrie, having undergone all the required security checks, including a small delay while they double-checked the clearance for their AIs to be present, entered the grand entrance of the Red House, where smooth circular walls curved upward, while a proxy-steel staircase curved underground. Overhead a chandelier hung, while along the smooth walls, expensive paintings and photographs dotted the walls.

A well-dressed young woman with dark hair pulled back, approached. Everything about her looked efficient. Her outfit was detailed but not overdone, her make-up the same. She carried a datapane and extended her hand.

"Hello, lieutenant, I'm Laurelai Oh, senior aide to the president. How was your journey?"

"Great, thank you." Carrie shook the proffered hand.

Laurelai turned as President Harkowitz emerged from a side room, shadowed by a tall, athletic man with dark hair, wearing a dark suit.

"First Lieutenant Welles-McKinley," Laurelai said, "President Harkowitz, and his guard, Sentinel Beach."

Carrie extended her hand to the Mars president.

"Mr. President," she said, eyeing his crisp blue suit and giving a quick nod to his Sentinel.

"It's nice to finally meet you," he smiled as he shook her hand. "I recall seeing you at the Atlas design launch, but we never spoke. I've heard so much about you."

"Thank you for securing my release from Hell Town, sir."

"You have Harris to thank for that. And your husband," he said, turning to her children. "And you must be Brody, Freya and Jesse?"

"Yep," Freya said, as her brothers nodded.

"And our Sentinels, Novak Skoda and Sampson Warra," Carrie motioned to the two men.

Harkowitz gave them a nod and turned back to the children. "Is there anyone you recognize in the photographs on the wall?"

The kids looked stumped and moved over to inspect them. Carrie followed and picked him out immediately. The photo was of a group of Space Duty soldiers sharing a celebratory toast in a modest habitat. Outside their hab windows was nothing but dark reddy-brown soil. She'd seen it countless times growing up, just like the similar celebratory image taken on the Moon.

"Grandpa!" Jesse pointed to the photo Carrie stared at. Brody and Freya crowded around him to see.

"Well spotted!" Harkowitz said. "Your grandfather was one of the Originals who helped first colonize Mars. That photo was taken on Day One of occupation."

Jesse looked on with pride before his face fell. He looked back at Harkowitz. "Grandpa died in the invasion."

"He held off the Zetas so we could escape," Freya added.

"Yes, I'm sorry." Harkowitz's face softened. "He died a hero."

Carrie squeezed Jesse and Freya's shoulders.

"It is therefore my honor to have Colonel Welles's descendants here," Harkowitz said. "Please make yourself comfortable. Laurelai will help settle you in."

"Then we should talk, if convenient, Mr. President," Carrie said, eyeing him.

He stared back at her and gave a nod. "Yes, we should. Laurelai will bring you through to the boardroom when you're ready."

The president returned to the room he'd emerged from, while Laurelai motioned Carrie toward the staircase.

Carrie moved for the steps and began to descend, but when she looked back to check everyone was following, she noticed Brody was still staring at the photo of his grandfather.

"Honey," she called to him, "come on or you'll get lost."

Dr. Arielle Serquey watched as Tess, now steady on her feet, began to pace her cell. She'd sniffed at the rat, but was disinterested, her attention more attuned to what was happening outside the cell.

Martha remained at the cell's glass wall, and Tess eyed her in the same way she eyed the soldiers, warily. For the most part, though, they had both been calm and nothing alarming had taken place.

A shift changeover with the soldiers, meant that the soldier, Brown, had left and the soldier, Yughiarto, had subbed in. As soon as he'd arrived, Martha's eyes were upon him, studying him in a similar way to how she'd affixed herself to Evenssen. The one difference this time, Arielle noted, was the soldier, Yughiarto, was not as surprised or concerned as Evenssen had been. In fact, it was the soldier who had moved slowly, carefully, up to Martha and stared at her, as though wanting to communicate with her.

Arielle sat quietly at her desk and watched them, ensuring her camera was recording. All the while, Steinberg and Tikaani held back, switching their attention between the two Zetas, ready for anything.

Carrie walked around their Red House apartment. It was stately yet homely, with three bedrooms and a generous living space. Laurelai had told her it was one of three such apartments, normally used by visiting dignitaries. Carrie had settled her things into one room, while the kids settled into another room furnished with three single beds, and Novak and Sampson took the third.

Though they were underground, a screen on the wall showed them the above-ground view outside which, past the desert oasis garden, through the domes, was miles of nothing but orange-brown soil and rocks, a slight dusty haze, and in the very distance, she could just make out the sparkle of aircraft descending to land at the Mars Docking Station.

She glanced around the apartment again, listening to the kids as they giggled excitedly and unpacked in their room. The apartment had everything they'd need and they would be very comfortable.

As much as she hated to admit it, maybe being forced away from the Zetas might actually do her some good and help her clear her mind. To remove herself from being at the heart of the action and the detail; to give her space to see the bigger picture.

Still, Carrie reminded herself why she was really here. This wasn't a holiday. She was here because the president had received death threats and Command needed to know whether those threats were real, or just members of the public venting with no intention of follow-through.

She looked back at the monitor view, to the slight haze covering the planet for as far as she could see. It was symbolic, she thought. Mars was still considered the Wild West and things operated differently here. She had to clear that haze from her eyes, as quickly as possible, to ensure that whoever was making death threats against the president – if they were in earnest – did not succeed.

Harris and McKinley followed Siberia Nine to a meeting room to debrief. Harris was still processing everything he'd just witnessed. Not only had the JEMs grown in stature and muscle, but their fighting skills were… vicious to say the least. By the time they had finished their demonstration, bruises were swelling, and blood was being spat out. He felt that pool of dread and abhorrence curdle in his stomach, and could see it all over McKinley's face.

Harris had kept needing to nudge McKinley, reminding him to hide his emotions as he watched his sons brutally fight each other. McKinley occasionally flinched as though wanting to step in and stop it. After JEM-40 stepped up to the major, gave a bloody smile, and said, "I see myself in you, sir," and McKinley had been unable to respond, Harris had known it was time to end the demonstration.

Harris wondered, now, whether bringing McKinley to see them had been such a good idea, considering everything else going on in his life at the moment. McKinley was supposed to be working through his stressors and here was Harris adding to them.

They entered the meeting room and Siberia Nine closed the door.

"So, you said something about someone watching the facility?" Harris asked him, cutting to the chase.

"Yes," Siberia Nine nodded, tapping at a console and bringing up security footage. Harris saw a series of still shots of vehicles in the distance, a man with binoculars, and a drone flying overhead.

"Who are thinking?" Harris asked Siberia Nine.

"So, it's not you? The UNF?" he asked. "I wondered whether perhaps the UNF was keeping a close eye on me after Sharley's departure."

Harris shook his head. "Not to my knowledge. Let me check."

He stepped away, made a call to Marchant, then sent him the images. Several minutes passed before Marchant confirmed it wasn't the UNF.

"If it's not us, then who is it?" Harris asked Siberia Nine.

Siberia Nine shrugged. "It must be the Russian government."

"But Sharley obviously set up an alliance in order for you to be here?"

"Yes, but Sharley is dead now. I've had no contact with them myself, but perhaps they've been trying to contact Sharley directly and wondering where he is."

"So, without Sharley around, the alliance is under threat?" McKinley finally spoke.

"Shit," Harris exhaled, closing his eyes briefly. "We do not need this right now."

"If the UNF want to keep this facility operational," Siberia Nine said, "then you'll need to reaffirm this alliance with the Russians. *Or*, move us to UNF soil. And me with it."

"Trying get out of Russia, Siberia Nine?" Harris quirked an eyebrow.

"I go where the JEMs go," he replied, his face a mask.

Harris's mind turned over. "Fuck… We *really* do not need this now."

"Can the UNF reach out to the Russians and arrange a deal to stay?" Siberia Nine asked.

Harris sighed. "They could try, but I'm not sure the UNF is going to want to admit they have knowledge of what's happening here. And if Sharley's out of the picture, I don't think the Russians will want to deal with the UNF. A scientist paying good cash for space to run black ops experiments is one thing, but the UNF?" Harris shook his head. "There's peace between Russia and the UNF, but that peace is tenuous at times. I don't like it. We need to move the JEMs somewhere safe where we have full control."

"How are you going to get 499 JEMs out without someone noticing?" McKinley asked.

"I don't know, but we're going to have to do it quickly. We're obviously on borrowed time. Whatever private path Sharley had cleared with the Russians, that path is about to close. They won't want to deal with the UNF." Harris stood and looked at Siberia Nine. "Prepare to evacuate, but do it quietly and carefully. As soon as plans are in place, I'll let you know." He looked to McKinley. "We gotta go."

They exited the facility and started walking hurriedly to where Hunter and Frazer awaited in their jet.

"Where are we going to put them?" McKinley asked.

"I don't know. The UNF will have a bunker somewhere we can use. But if we don't move fast and the Russians take control of that facility, we'll lose the JEMs."

McKinley nodded, his face paling slightly.

"How are you doing anyway?" Harris asked. "I know it was tough today."

"Yeah," McKinley said, but was otherwise lost for words.

"I'm sorry, man. But you had to see it some time."

McKinley nodded, then glanced at Harris. "What about you?"

"What about me?" Harris asked.

"You seemed to wig out yourself at one point. Before they started their demonstration."

An image flashed in Harris's mind of Sharley standing there smiling at him.

"Yeah…" Harris said.

"Yeah, what?"

"I don't know," Harris shrugged, as they neared the jet. "It was probably my imagination. It's probably nothing."

McKinley stopped walking. "What?" he demanded. "If it's about the JEMs, you'd better tell me."

Harris stopped and looked back at him. "It wasn't about the JEMs. Well, maybe it was, I don't know."

"What?" McKinley demanded again.

Harris sighed, put his hands on his hips. "I saw Sharley."

"You saw Sharley?! What do you mean? He was there? He's not dead?"

"Oh, he's dead, but don't forget that I can speak to the dead."

McKinley stared at him. "But that's in your dreams, right? When you're asleep, when your subconscious is—"

"Yeah, but I've been seeing dead people while I'm awake for a long time, McKinley."

"How long?"

Harris shrugged. "I started seeing Sibbie and Etta around the time of the Darwin mission. The more I opened myself up, the more I started seeing them while I was awake."

McKinley stared at him. "And you just saw Sharley? What did he want?"

Harris shrugged. "Nothing. I don't know. He just smiled. Creepily, like he does. *Did.* I guess he was just showing me how pleased he was that you and I were fulfilling his plans."

He glanced at the jet, then back to McKinley. "Now come on. We gotta get out of here and prepare to move the JEMs."

Carrie waited in the Red House boardroom for Harkowitz. She'd left the children in the apartment watching Mars TV with Novak and Sampson.

The president entered with Sentinel Beach by his side, who stopped to stand by the door. The president took a seat as one of his staff placed a tray of tea and coffee on the table.

"You've settled in your apartment?" he asked, as the staffer left.

"Yes. Thank you. It's lovely."

"Well, I want to ensure you're comfortable. Tea? Coffee?" He motioned to the tray.

Carrie nodded and looked at Beach. "Would you mind giving us the room, Sentinel Beach?"

Beach shook his head. "I am to remain at the president's side."

Harkowitz looked at Beach and nodded a dismissal. "It's fine. Please wait outside."

Beach gave Harkowitz a nod, then left, closing the door behind him.

Carrie looked back at Harkowitz. "How are your new Sentinels doing?"

"It's only been a week but they're doing fine so far. Between them and my usual soldier coverage, I'm not sure your services will be needed. It seems like overkill and, I must say, a little odd that you're here to protect me, while you have your own Sentinels," he smiled.

"My Sentinel protection is more for the kids than me."

Harkowitz sipped his tea, studying her.

Carrie smiled. "I know I don't look like much on the surface but—"

"You're the UNF's finest sharpshooter and the first female Alpha soldier."

She gave a nod, eyeing him curiously.

"Harris told me," he explained. "I'm not sure what attitudes you've had to put up with inside the UNF, but rest assured, I have no problem with a female bodyguard. So long as you do your job and keep me alive."

"About that term, *bodyguard*, how many people know why I'm here?"

"My staff and Sentinels know you're here due to the rising tensions, but I've not explained in what capacity yet. I was waiting for my cue from Harris on that."

"Good. We should tell everyone I'm here as a consultant for Mars-UNF relations. If they think I'm here in a political sense, they won't see me as a threat. If someone makes a move, they will soon see their mistake."

Harkowitz's eyes narrowed and he smiled, then sipped his tea. "I like it."

"So, first things first, do you trust your staff?"

Harkowitz placed his teacup down. "I thought I did."

"Whose attitude has changed, perhaps, in recent months?"

"My staff are nothing if not consistent. I haven't noticed anything specific. Outside the Red House, however, the tide seems to be turning."

"How so?"

"My staff usually keep me away from any unnecessary bad-mouthing in the press or on social media, but, since being notified of the threats, I've ventured online recently to see for myself. Some folks are questioning why the UNF doesn't remove me if I'm butting heads with them. Others say I'm their lackey. Some say I'm getting in the way of progress and that Regan Lotz will be more amenable to it. I saw another exchange where someone said that I have an ego, but that my heart's in the right place, and someone responded saying that a good heart won't stop the Zetas. Another said that the Harkowitz they saw when I first came to power is very different from the Harkowitz they see now." Harkowitz sighed. "Things have changed since the invasion. The whole universe has turned on its axis."

"I wouldn't pay much mind to a few comments on social media, sir," Carrie said.

He sat back in his chair. "I've had a good run until recently. The people wanted me here and I never had to fear things like death threats. It's a different world out there."

"An alien invasion will do that. The UNF finds itself in a similar position. We've ironed out our inner turmoil, now we're dealing with the people outside the gates. I guess it's the Red House's turn to iron out its inner turmoil. But if there's one thing we learned from the Command Uprising, sir, it's that you need to take these threats seriously or people *will* die. Not just you, sir. If someone gets to you in here, it's your staffers' lives, too. If they get you outside, it's your constituents' lives. If hostile sentiment is growing, you need to stamp it out fast before there are casualties."

Harkowitz nodded. "So, what is your suggested course of action?"

"Take me for a tour around Mars. It's been a while since I've seen your colonies, and I want to see the proxy-steel mining and manufacturing plants. The civilian ships that defied your orders and tried to kill that Zeta, off Atlas, they were miners, right?"

"Yes. Mostly."

"Then that, to me, sounds like a good place to start. Show me around under the guise of Mars-UNF relations. I'll get the lay of the land and study who you're up against."

Harkowitz studied her a moment, then nodded. "Alright. I'll have Laurelai arrange an itinerary."

Harris stared at Marchant through the transmission screen.

"Yes," he said, "and as we left, our scans picked up a camouflaged truck with four men aboard. It's definitely under surveillance and I'm *very* concerned, sir."

"Yeah, it's got me concerned, too," Marchant said, scratching his face in thought. "The general does not wish to enter negotiations with Russia, so we need to pull them out. Fast."

"Could we house the JEMs on Centralis?" Harris asked.

"Absolutely not! We'll need to keep them on the mainland. We have an underground facility in the mountains, about an hour away from Edwards Air Force Base that we can clear out for them."

"Okay, good. When do we start the transfer?"

"As soon as I can arrange the transport. You thinking one large aircraft, or a series of smaller jets?"

"A jumbo craft gets them all out in one hit. One mission. Smooth and fast."

Marchant nodded. "We'll send the jumbo with air support, including the *Aurizun*."

"Yes, sir," Harris said, before nodding at Hunter and Frazer. "We'll need to erase our UNF markers so the Russians don't know our involvement."

"Agreed," Marchant said. "We move fast, and friendly, and hope the Russians don't take offense to us taking assets out of their country."

He ended the transmission and silence sat aboard the jet as it sailed over the Atlantic, headed for Centralis Island.

"It's better this way," Harris said, nodding to himself. "Having them on US soil leaves them in our control. It was always a risk having them in Siberia, but Sharley set it up that way initially to keep the UNF out of it."

"What are your friends at the Command gates going to say when they discover what the JEMs are?" Frazer asked, looking at Harris with the answer in his eyes. "First the UNF protects the Zetas, now we're abusing children?"

"Yeah," Harris sighed, guilt stabbing him, "that's a big fuckin' problem."

19

Developments

Carrie stepped onto the proxy-steel platform, beside Harkowitz and Sentinel Beach, as red dust blew gently around them in their atmospheric suits. She'd left the children with their Sentinels, attached Archie's discs behind her ears, and flown in the deluxe presidential small ship, *Mars Force One*, to the main mining complex on Mars called Haides-1. Run by the Mercandez company, it was located some 700 kilometers from colony Brahe. Harkowitz told her the mine was named after the Greek god of the underworld, who was also the god of the hidden wealth of the Earth – from the fertile soil to the mined wealth of gold, silver, and other metals. It seemed an appropriate name for this site.

The Haides-1 complex was large and flat, and like most Mars infrastructure, built mostly underground from the shiny, silver proxy-steel. Though the meeting had been arranged quickly, Carrie noted that Mars Media was on the scene to capture the president's visit.

"Did your team arrange for the media to be here?" Carrie asked through their private comms channel.

"No, but the media tends to watch my transport like hawks. When I move, so do they," he answered.

"Interesting," Carrie said. "I only see Mars Media, though. There's no Universal Press outlet here?"

"They have a small presence in Elon. They obviously didn't think this was worth the journey," he smiled through his face mask. "Don't worry, the media won't be allowed access to the mine or plant, but they'll be waiting for us with questions when we depart."

Leaving a handful of Space Duty soldiers to guard the ship, they made their way inside the complex, through several atmospheric, temperature and dust controlled doors. Harkowitz told her the mines were not built under domes like the colonies as it was deemed too great a risk due to their mining efforts beneath the Martian surface. Though the domes were solid structures, the constant vibrations underground could lead to soil shifting, which in turn could cause stress fractures in the domes, which could result in a collapse.

Carrie was grateful for all safety measures, but the experience, so far, was reminding her painfully of her time in the Hell Town dungeon, and she was starting to feel claustrophobic and uneasy.

Once inside the complex and out of their atmospheric suits, they were greeted by a large man – in both height and girth – with a bushy brown beard and intelligent eyes.

"Mr. President," he nodded, shaking Harkowitz's hand, then held his hand out to Carrie. "Ron McCaulay. Haides-1 Ops Manager."

"Nice to meet you. I'm Carrie Welles-McKinley. I work for—"

"The UNF," he said, eyeing her Space Duty uniform. "So, I can see."

"I'm usually based at Command on Centralis Island," she smiled. "I work in the Zeta Strategy Division."

"She's here to see how impressive your proxy-steel operation is, Ron," Harkowitz smiled, on his best 'PR' behavior, then looked at Carrie. "Prepare to be dazzled!"

"I can't wait."

"I'll dazzle you best I can given this is a mining and manufacturing operation," Ron said. "But given it *is* literally a one-of-its-kind facility, it is pretty special, if I do say so myself. This way."

Ron walked off, and Carrie, Harkowitz and Beach followed.

*

Carrie stared at the 3D image projected from the center of the boardroom table. It showed a map of the expansive new seam of Martian ore recently discovered.

"That's… a lot," she said.

"Biggest ore discovery in human history," Ron told her.

She nodded to herself and looked at Harkowitz's gleaming eyes. No wonder he'd been so confident in pushing back against the UNF. The seam of ore was a war decider. An endless supply of material for new ships, general infrastructure, and even an army of Alpha-Mech soldiers. When she'd last visited Brahe, the factory producing the proxy-steel had been based in the colony, but due to the rapid expansion, it had now been housed in a neighboring facility close to the mine site.

"It's impressive," Carrie said to Ron. "Who knows about this? How much information is public?"

"The new seam was reported in the media," Ron told her, "but exact details of the size and such was not released. Outside of the Mercandez company, the UNF, and certain Heads of State, no-one else knows. We plan to keep it that way until we can put plans in motion to capitalize on it."

"And your security?" Carrie asked. "Have you had any attempts? Threats?"

"What? To take over the mine and plant?" Ron asked.

Carrie nodded. "Hacking attempts?"

"Not that I'm aware of. The Mercandez company runs a tight ship and we hire private security contractors. It's not a concern."

"It should be," Carrie said. "You're sitting on an incredibly important mine that the UNF needs. Whoever controls this seam, controls our fate if the Zetas return."

"The Mercandez company is happy to assist the UNF," Ron said.

"For a price?" Carrie smiled.

Ron shrugged. "It's a business. We paid for the mine license, and we've got workers to pay."

"Yeah, I get that. But, tell me, how many workers did you lay off in past years due to advancements in technology? How much of the mining and manufacturing plants are run by machines?"

Ron stared at her a moment. "No more than any similar operator on Earth. What's your point?"

"My point is, the UNF needs this proxy-steel to build ships and such, to save lives. We understand the Mercandez company wants to be paid for their toil, but extortion is a very risky move."

"Well, now," Harkowitz spoke up, "I'm sure that's not even on the Mercandez radar. This is good for everyone. I'm sure we can work out a deal that suits all sides."

"Hey," Ron shrugged again, "the truth is, I just oversee the mine and plant, right? You want to talk numbers, you gotta go up the line."

"Happy to," Carrie said. "Who should I speak to?"

"My boss is the CEO—"

"Is the CEO the top of the tree?" Carrie cut him off.

Ron stared at her again. "Technically, the top of the tree is the owner of the company, Jennifer Drew-Mercandez. She's based back on Earth. The top of the tree here on Mars is Miles Chiel."

"Which one owns the *Golden Orb*?"

Again Ron stared at her. "The *Golden Orb* is a Mercandez company asset, shared by the board directors, CEO, CFO, etc."

"Right," Carrie said. "Would you happen to have a log for who borrowed it for a few days, right after the incident off Station Atlas?"

Ron looked uncomfortable. He glanced at Harkowitz, then back at her. "I thought you came to tour the facility?"

"I did. As you know, I work for the UNF in our Zeta Strategy section and I'm here to bolster relations between Mars and the UNF. The *Golden Orb* followed a UNF group of ships escorting the Zeta ship to Earth. We'd like to know who organized that and what their motives were."

Rob shrugged. "You'd have to speak to them, but if I were to guess, I'd say it was to make sure that the Zeta ship stayed the hell away from Mars." His eyes turned hard as he stared at her. "A lot of people can't believe you voluntarily took that thing to Earth and are protecting it."

Carrie stared back at him. "We're trying for peace. We were thinking if this Zeta, which did not attempt to harm us in any way, wanted to communicate with us, then we should listen to it."

"They didn't bother to communicate last time. They just shot our ships out of the sky."

"Yes, they did," Carrie said, "but I'll let you in on a secret, Ron. There are different types of Zetas. The recent visitor is different from the ones that tried to kill us. You ever heard that saying: 'an enemy of my enemy'? This Zeta might give us important information which could help us either avert a war, or win one. Don't you think that opportunity is worth protecting?"

Ron didn't answer, but she saw his mind turning over.

"How many of them are out there?" he eventually asked her.

"Two that we've met," she said, withholding knowledge of the others.

"So, there could be more?"

"There's always been the chance of other life out there. That fact has never changed since the time of our forefathers," she said, standing. "Thank you for the tour of your facilities and your briefing on this new seam of Martian ore. We look forward to working with you. If you could give me the log details for the *Golden Orb*, we'll be on our way."

Ron stared at her again a moment, then glanced at Harkowitz, then stood from the table. "I'll need approval before I can do that. I'll send it through to you once I have it. Someone will be here shortly to escort you back to your ship."

Ron left the room. Carrie noticed Harkowitz staring at her in analysis as he stood.

*

"I don't see how pushing buttons is protecting my situation," Harkowitz said as they boarded *Mars Force One* again.

"I'm not pushing buttons," she said. "If we turn a blind eye to the dissent that's brewing, we'll be too busy fighting a civil war to be fighting off an alien invasion. One of the biggest foes we face these days is misinformation. If we don't stamp it out quick, it'll evolve into a beast that's too big to fight. Everyone thinks the Zetas are our enemies and they're wrong. So far, it's just the Priestess Zetas that are. If we can make an alliance with the other Zetas, we'll win the war if it comes. But we won't have an alliance if angry civilians are attacking our allies."

"I agree," he said, taking a seat, but leaning forward and lowering his voice, "but I can't have a new UNF face marching into Mars and laying down the law. I know these people and I know how the politics of Mars works. You need to trust me on that and let me do my job."

Carrie nodded, sitting opposite and lowering her voice, too. "I understand that, sir, but someone is sending you death threats. Maybe your handle on Mars politics isn't as strong as you thought it was. Maybe being Mr. Nice Guy has run its course. If they think you're weak, it'll make you a target. If they realize you are, in fact, strong with powerful allies they might think otherwise."

Harris leaned over the boardroom table at Command, staring at the projected plans, going over everything one last time. It was late, he was tired, but they had to act quickly.

He looked around the table at those gathered: McKinley, Morrell, Arken.

"This is a plan that requires smooth, swift action. Our team is lean, but that's because we don't want to draw too much attention from the Russians. We've got one shot at this mission to evacuate the JEMs safely. Admiral, is your transport aircraft ready to go?" he asked.

"It's fueled and on the tarmac ready to depart," Arken answered.

"And it'll carry 499 JEMs and their staff?"

Arken nodded. "We can fit 600 on that spacejet. Are you sure the Russians won't shoot us down?"

"No, but Siberia Nine tells me he's logged an incoming shipment through an electronic system Sharley set up. It lets the Russians know it's one of his and not to fire upon it." Harris turned to McKinley. "But if it comes to it, are you ready to defend that transport jet?"

"Yes, sir," he gave a nod. "The *Aurizun* and *Carcharias* crews are loading now into combat planes without UNF signatures, and will be ready for departure."

"Good. Morrell? Have you sent Earth Duty troops to Edwards to prepare for the safe delivery of our assets?"

Morrell gave a nod. "I've sent our most trusted teams on the mainland to the location. They'll be ready and waiting."

"Good," Harris looked at the plans again, then at his team. "Then let's do this. I want those JEMs tucked in a US bed by 0600 tomorrow morning."

McKinley watched the radar over Hunter's shoulder.

"Approaching target," the pilot said.

"*Carcharias* team?" McKinley said into his comms mic. "You keep your eyes in the sky, while the *Aurizun* team takes the ground."

"*Roger that,*" Ryker's voice replied.

Hunter brought their small craft in to land as close he could to the JEM facility, then the *Aurizun* team, in full combat gear, swiftly exited. McKinley motioned for Yughi and Evenssen to guard their ride, while McKinley, Brown, Steinberg and Tikaani made their way to the facility entrance. By the time they arrived at the door, Arken's behemoth spacejet had landed, rumbling the earth around it.

McKinley banged on the facility door, it opened, and Siberia Nine stood there.

"I need them on the jet in ten minutes," McKinley said. "Follow Brown and Tikaani. Move!"

Siberia Nine quickly stepped outside, then turned back to the facility and motioned those inside, forward.

"Just like we practiced," Siberia Nine ordered. "Fast, fast, fast!"

Brown and Tikaani moved for the jet, eyeing their surrounds and sweeping their weapons, as the JEMs began to jog out of the facility. Dressed in long, black, hooded cloaks which almost made them disappear into the night around them, and adorned with bulky backpacks, they moved with swift determination.

McKinley motioned for Steinberg to move, and he, Brown and Tikaani spread out to guard intervals along the running line like they'd planned. Brown was near the jet, while McKinley continued coverage on the facility end. McKinley saw the JEMs beginning to load onto the jet, then glanced back at the facility as more JEMs continued to pour out.

"Who's last in line?" McKinley asked Siberia Nine.

"I will be," he said, as he waved to his crew inside the facility. "Go!" he said to them. "Get to the plane. Now."

The crew nodded and began to run alongside the JEMs.

McKinley scanned their perimeter carefully with his Alpha eyes, as the sound of jogging feet filtered into the night air.

"Count's at 250," the transport pilot said over McKinley's comms.

"Roger," McKinley said. "Carcharias? How's the view?"

"*We've picked up four jeeps. They're spread out around the facility. So far they're just watching.*"

"Any long-range weapons?" McKinley asked.

"Not that our scans are picking up. We've been emitting a targeted pulse at them, which will disable any electronic devices anyhow."

"Roger that," McKinley said, "stay on 'em."

"They won't damage this cargo," Siberia Nine said to McKinley as more JEMs continued to race past. "If anything, they want it for themselves."

"Still a bad thing," McKinley said, checking his watch. "What's the count?" he asked through his comms.

"Three hundred and fifty," came the reply.

"Hunter, start the engines," McKinley said.

"Roger that," came his reply.

"Move! Move!" Siberia Nine said as the last of the JEMs exited the facility.

Siberia Nine reached back through the door and handed McKinley a bulky backpack.

"What's this?" he asked.

"Hard copy back-ups of Sharley's data and files," Siberia Nine said, pulling another backpack over his shoulders. "Everything else can burn."

Siberia Nine began jogging to catch up to the end of the line, as McKinley quickly slipped on the backpack and jogged after him.

"Carcharias, get ready," McKinley said through his comms, as he swung his gun back and forth looking for threats.

"Roger that," Ryker replied.

"Brown! Tikaani!" McKinley said. "Start pulling back to our jet."

"Roger!" Brown said, as he and Tikaani pulled back from the line and began moving back to their jet, while Steinberg and McKinley followed up the tail of the line toward the transport.

A small flash of light caught McKinley's periphery vision. He stopped and swung his gun toward it.

"Carcharias, report!" he ordered. "Did I pick up movement?"

"There's one approaching to your right. Doesn't appear to be armed."

At the treeline in the near distance to the right, he saw branches moving and a dark figure running away. He took aim, following the figure, but decided not to fire. He wasn't about to cause an international incident.

"He's running away," Ryker reported.

Seeing no other threat, McKinley continued running to catch up to the others.

As he neared the end of the line again, he heard Siberia Nine puffing, visibly struggling with the weight he was carrying.

"*Count is 450!*" the pilot said over his comms. "*Preparing for takeoff.*"

"Roger," McKinley said. "Stein—"

Siberia Nine tripped and fell forward.

"Shit!" McKinley said, darting out the way before he ran right over him.

The final JEM in the line stopped and turned around. He saw Siberia Nine pushing himself off the ground and stepped toward him.

"I can take the bag," the JEM said, his voice sounding older than it should, making McKinley's brain glitch as he looked at Jesse's face.

"No, JEM-1. I am fine," Siberia Nine said, catching his breath.

"Move!" McKinley barked to the child, pointing to the plane.

JEM-1 looked at him, then nodded. "Yes, sir!"

He turned and sprinted for the jet, and Siberia Nine and McKinley followed.

McKinley watched as JEM-1 leaped up into the transport hold, and turned back for Siberia Nine's bag, which he grabbed from the man and tossed back into the plane with ease, before reaching back once more for McKinley's bag.

"Sir," JEM-1 nodded at McKinley, waving his fingers for the bag.

McKinley swung the bag off his shoulder and passed it to him, as Siberia Nine got aboard.

"Buckle up," McKinley said to JEM-1, then banged the side of the plane. "Close up! Take off! Now!"

He waved Steinberg away from the plane and the two of them began to make their way back to Hunter's jet.

"Carcharias, report!" McKinley said, jogging and sweeping his weapon around.

"*The jeeps were moving closer, but they've stopped. They're still just watching.*"

"We're getting airborne," McKinley yelled over the noise as they reached their aircraft and began climbing aboard. "Stay sharp!"

Steinberg pulled the door shut behind them and McKinley looked to Hunter.

"Go! Go! Go!"

Hunter got their jet in the air, as McKinley got back on his comms.

"Siberia Nine? Now!"

"*Yes, major!*"

As they flew away they saw the bright flash of an explosion behind them, as Sharley's JEM facility was destroyed.

Harris sucked down a pouch of sugar solution as he paced the facility that would be the JEM home for the foreseeable future. It turned out to have been designed as a bomb shelter, and maintained for use in the event of a nuclear war. It had everything the JEMs would need. And anything it didn't have, they would soon put in place.

Despite some tense moments listening to Hunter's radio chatter when Russian jets took to the skies – just a little too late to cause any problems – as soon as Harris heard that the JEMs had left Russian airspace and were safely en route, he had boarded his own jet for the new facility. It was a last-minute decision. He hadn't intended to be here for their arrival, but his gut was pulling him to do so. As the JEM leader, he thought it would be crucial to be here and welcome them to their new home. It was another way to assert his leadership, but he was also there to satisfy his curiosity. He wanted to see how these boys would handle their new surroundings after living seven years in their underground facility in Siberia. Although, yes, they were coming to a new underground facility, he couldn't help but wonder what affect this might have on their psychology.

They'd never seen anything of the outside world before.

That said, he was also concerned about the facility's security and wanted to ensure that prying eyes did not witness this transfer. What Frazer said, had been niggling at Harris. What *would* the public say if they knew about the JEMs? Now that Harris was in charge, could he really stand by and let the JEMs continue to be raised this way? Or was it already too late? Had the damage to them already been done – several years of cold, calculated rearing? Then again, what could he do with 500 illegal clones? He couldn't exactly assimilate them into society.

"Sir!" a soldier jogged up to him. "They're coming!" He turned and pointed into the sky, and Harris saw the spacejet's lights twinkling in the distance. He felt a shiver run across his skin. This was important, he thought. He didn't know why, yet, but somehow he knew this was important.

He watched, eyes fixed on the large jet for the minutes it took to descend, a sense of relief washing over him when he saw the wheels smoking on the tarmac. Listening to the comms exchange, he saw Hunter's jet land shortly afterwards, while the *Carcharias* team continued to circle overhead, as instructed by McKinley, until the JEMs were inside.

Harris watched the door of the jet slide open, saw the familiar red head of Siberia Nine get out, as McKinley's team jogged over to meet them. Then, within moments, a line of JEMs sprung forth from the plane, jogging toward him in long, hooded cloaks, like small terrifying muscular wizards.

He stood, arms behind his back, his face a mask as the JEMs approached with Siberia Nine leading the way, panting and carrying a large black bag.

"Colonel Harris," Siberia Nine puffed, his pale gaunt cheeks flushed with pink as he came to a stop before him, "thank you for getting us out of there."

Harris gave a nod. "I think you'll find this facility will suit your needs."

"I'm sure we will," he nodded.

Harris held his arm out and motioned for them to move inside as he noted a bottleneck forming by Siberia Nine's pause.

The JEM instructor nodded and continued forth, waving the JEMs to follow him.

Harris watched as the line of JEMs got moving again, doing his best to make eye contact with each JEM. Though they darted their eyes about with wide curiosity, they were mostly focused on doing, and moving, where told.

As the end of the line approached, the *Aurizun* crew began to gather, spreading out and keeping their eyes peeled. McKinley kept close to the last in line, though, who slowed as he approached Harris.

Harris didn't know how he knew, but he could just tell this was JEM-1. The kid, carrying a bulky backpack like Siberia Nine, stopped before him and saluted.

"Welcome, JEM-1," Harris said.

"Thank you, sir! I am honored to be here." JEM-1 lowered his salute and looked over his shoulder at the clear open space and the surrounding mountains. "This is the outside world, sir?"

McKinley locked eyes with Harris.

"Your place is inside, JEM-1," Harris said firmly.

JEM-1 looked at him.

"For now," Harris added.

JEM-1 nodded. "Yes, sir," then ran after the others.

McKinley looked at Harris again. He saw a concern furrowing the major's brow.

"Everything alright?" Harris asked.

"He's different to the others," McKinley said.

Harris nodded. "Because he knows he's different. He's three months older than the rest. He was the successful test." He glanced back into the facility where the door was now sealed shut. "He's the older brother, and Sharley raised him to be their unit leader." He looked back at McKinley. "He knows he's different and he will act different because of that... We'll have to keep an eye on him."

McKinley nodded, his mind turning over.

"The evacuation ran smoothly?" Harris asked.

McKinley's attention turned back to him. "A little too easy. The Russians were watching us on the ground, then they joined us in the skies. But they just watched."

Harris stared at him in concern. "Tell me they weren't filming us?"

"The *Carcharias* was pulsing them. I think we're safe."

"We'd better be." Harris said. "If they have anything to blackmail us with, we're fucked."

Carrie sat at an elegant table in an equally elegant dining room at the Red House. President Harkowitz had arranged a private dinner with his staff and colleagues. It was a means to officially introduce Carrie to them, and she was going to use the opportunity to study them carefully. Among them: Laurelai, Colonel Samuel Greavy – head of security and the top soldier on Mars, and colony senators – Charlie Butten and Edgar Pope. The president's Sentinel, Aston, stood in the corner keeping watch.

The children also dined with them. At first Carrie considered whether to keep them in the apartment, but she decided to have them join her. She'd been thinking a lot about her role in the future war, and though her ultimate role was still uncertain, the role of her children was not. She knew it couldn't hurt for them to get used to the halls of politics sooner rather than later, despite only being 11 and nine years old. She'd also brought Archie with her to listen in, but opted to leave the discs in her pocket so as to not draw the attention of her fellow diners.

Most of the room was furnished with proxy-steel designs, from the elaborate table to the sideboards, even to the chandelier hanging from the ceiling. Harkowitz saw her studying its design, the delicate shards of proxy-steel dangling beside elegant crystals, and told her it was made by a renowned local artist by the name of Vera.

"Vera?" Carrie said, as a memory crawled back to her. "She has the Harmonia stall in Elon, right?"

"Well, I wouldn't call it a stall," Harkowitz said. "She has a store in the underground mall, but yes. You know her?"

"No, not really. I bought a necklace off her once when she just had a little stall." She glanced at Freya. "It was a beautiful piece made of proxy-steel and amethysts she called 'Freya'."

"Ah!" Harkowitz smiled. "And you named your daughter after it?"

"Kind of," Carrie said, smiling at her daughter. She didn't want to explain that it was also because "Freya" was the goddess of sex, fertility, war and wealth. Knowing Freya was the goddess of war, and being at war with Sharley at the time, Carrie had been drawn to the name.

"Vera's retiring soon," Harkowitz told her. "Her niece is taking over the store."

"I'll have to pay her a visit," Carrie said.

"Can I get a necklace like yours?" Freya asked excitedly.

"Well, I was going to give you mine one day," Carrie smiled.

"I can have two," Freya said. "A girl needs options, Mom."

Harkowitz chuckled. "Freya, you are born for politics and negotiation."

"Oh, no, Mr. President," Freya shook her head. "I'm going to be a Space Duty pilot."

"Is that right?" Greavy asked, amused.

Freya nodded. "Uncle Hunter's going to teach me when I'm old enough."

"Uncle Hunter?" Greavy asked.

"First Lieutenant Jacob Hunter," Carrie said. "He's the *Aurizun's* chief pilot."

Greavy nodded in recognition. "I heard he did some great flying down in Australia during the invasion."

"He did," Carrie said. "If it wasn't for his actions and that of his co-pilot Frazer, the team would be dead. And not just those in the ship when it was attacked by Zetas, but also Harris and McKinley. They were injured badly on the ground, and the *Aurora's* escape pod and the *Carcharias* helped rescue and airlift them out." Carrie paused thinking about it. "It could've been quite devastating," she said quietly.

"The *Carcharias* is often at the center of the action, isn't it?" Senator Pope said.

Carrie eyed him. "Are you referring to the Atlas incident?"

Pope gave a nod.

"I find the terminology, 'incident', rather interesting," Senator Button spoke up, brushing down his bushy mustache. "Everyone keeps referring to it as an incident, as though it was a *small* thing, when in fact it could've been a major catastrophe."

"But it wasn't," Carrie said firmly. "Thanks to Major Gold and the *Carcharias*, a major catastrophe was avoided."

"Was it though?" Button asked. "Our populace has been divided ever since."

"Our population has always been divided," Harkowitz said with a smile. "That's life. What's important is that we distill the facts from fictional conspiracy theories."

"Yes," Button challenged, "and what are they?"

"The facts are," Harkowitz said, "the Zeta did not attack us. It did not show aggression toward us in any way—"

"It fired up its—" Button began, but Harkowitz raised his finger cutting him off.

"It responded as any of us would have if weapons were armed and targeting *us*. The point is, it did not fire. And reports from Command so far show the creature as cooperative. You know politics as well as I do, Charlie. Information is power. If this creature can provide us with information to help stop any further invasions, I will support Command in this action and any further action it decrees, if it will save our people."

"How the tide turns," Senator Pope smiled. "You were baying for their blood not so long ago." He raised his glass of red wine to Harkowitz, then drank.

"I did." Harkowitz gave an awkward nod, glancing at Carrie. "They did the wrong thing and they have since apologized. I have learned that moving on and forgetting my ego is more important. Lives are literally at stake and the UNF need our ore and proxy-steel manufacturing facilities to save those lives."

"You realize it's only a matter of time before they start manufacturing the proxy-steel on Earth," Senator Butten said, "and Mars loses money."

"Is it?" Harkowitz said. "Mars is the only place in our known universe that has the particular ore which makes proxy-steel. It's not cost-effective to ship the ore to Earth to manufacture the proxy-steel there. We mine the ore here, we manufacture the proxy-steel here, we can build the ships and stations here. They need us. We are critical to their strategy, and that makes us the most important planet in the universe. So, you can tell your displeased businessmen constituents, Charlie, they have nothing to fear. Their businesses will not only boom, but they will be hailed heroes for helping to save the lives of billions."

Senator Butten smiled and raised his glass. "They will indeed be happy to hear that."

"So, Second Lieutenant Welles," Senator Pope said, "you're here to oversee the transition of this new *improved* relationship?"

"In a manner of speaking," she said. "The president is right when he said this relationship is critical to all our futures. The UNF very much want to nurture this relationship."

"And have you spoken to the incarcerated prisoners as yet?" Pope asked. "I hear you've visited Haides."

"Oh?" Carrie asked, surprised. "News travels fast."

"They say it's the dust storms," Pope smiled. "They carry everything far and wide."

"I see," Carrie smiled back. "I've not spoken with the prisoners yet. That's not typically my area of expertise, investigations and such."

"Oh?" Pope asked, mimicking her. "And what is your area of expertise? I'm quite curious as to why, and please no offense is meant by this comment, but why a mere second lieutenant has such a place in Zeta Strategy and is here to oversee things on behalf of the entire UNF?"

"Now, now, Pope," Harkowitz said. "Perhaps we should cut off your wine if you're going to be rude."

"Mom's the best sharpshooter in the entire UNF," Jesse said defensively.

"Honey," Carrie tapped his knee, "it's okay."

"A sharpshooter?" Pope asked.

"Sharpest in the universe," Brody said firmly, equally defensive.

"That's quite a feat," Pope conceded a nod to the boys, then looked at Carrie, "but that makes you qualified for political negotiations?"

"I'm not here to negotiate," Carrie said, then smiled. "I'm just here to observe and report back to Colonel Harris, who heads up Zeta Strategy."

"Indeed!" Harkowitz said. "And I did not call this dinner to put her under the Spanish Inquisition." He smiled at the senators. "Anyone would think you feel threatened in some way, gentlemen."

"Not threatened," Butten said. "Just curious. It's our job to interrogate things on behalf of our constituents."

"Indeed," Pope said, sipping his wine.

"Speaking of interrogation," Laurelai piped up, "I'd love to hear how your recent trip to the Moon colonies went, Senator Pope? Have you worked out a new trade deal?"

As Senator Pope regaled her with his exploits on the Moon, Harkowitz gave Carrie and her children a subtle smile for handling things well.

20

The Returning Past

Harris sat on the floor of a Zeta ship, waiting for Martha and DaJuan to join him in his dream. Now the JEMs had been safely moved, he had to turn his attention back to connecting with the Alma Mater. Dr. Serquey had provided updates on their behavior since he'd been gone. It seemed Tess was relishing being free of her restraints, and most intriguingly, further seemingly heated exchanges had taken place between the two Zetas.

On the one hand, heated exchanges were a good thing. It meant they were disagreeing over something. But what that was exactly, left him a little anxious.

DaJuan finally appeared beside him. They exchanged a nod and looked forward into the circle of darkness surrounding the space in which they sat. The minutes ticked by and nothing.

"I'll see if I can get her attention," Harris said. He closed his eyes and projected an image of Martha sitting with them.

In response, they heard a strange noise. Part "moo", part "bray".

Harris opened his eyes and she was there, standing before them, a little ways back. She eyed him down her snout, then DaJuan.

"This is DaJuan," Harris told her. "You've met in the flesh, remember?"

An image flashed inside his mind of Welles. For a moment he panicked, thinking if Carrie was asleep she might join them, but he quickly realized that wouldn't happen as Mars was on a different time zone. Besides, Dr. Bakshi had prescribed something to stop her dreaming.

No, this was an image projected by Martha. A question. She wanted to know where Welles was.

"What are you going to tell her?" DaJuan asked him, coming to the same conclusion.

Harris thought for a moment, then sighed. "The truth. She probably already knows."

He projected an image of Welles holding her temples, then projected an image of Carrie in the pod-bed on the *Aurizun* as Gregson cared for her.

He opened his eyes and saw Martha staring at him intently. Suddenly he saw falling grains of silvery Zeta Archelois soil. The ashes of their dead.

He shook his head. "No. No, she's alive." He projected another image of Welles on Mars. "She's just busy elsewhere for a while."

Martha projected an image of Welles sitting with them.

"She wants Welles," DaJuan said.

"She can't have her," Harris said. He projected an image of Martha sitting with him and DaJuan again. He opened his eyes. "We don't need Welles to talk. We can talk, just the three of us." He motioned to the three of them.

Martha stared at him. He sensed distrust.

Once more he saw Welles, only this time she was strapped down in a bed like Tess – and Harris was tightening her restraints.

"No," he said firmly to her. "I've not locked her away. She can't do this because of her brain."

Again he projected images of Welles on Mars, smiling. He opened his eyes and saw Martha staring at him.

He closed his eyes again and decided to just start talking. He projected images at Martha, ones that had been projected at him in a prior conversation. The images of war between the Zeta clans.

Martha gave a moo-bray in objection. He opened his eyes, looked at her, then closed them again.

He projected images from the dream he had with Sarai, of the Zeta ship flying overhead and the building rubble. Then he projected images of an argument between Martha and Tess. He opened his eyes again.

"Why were you arguing?" he asked. "Tell me about your civil war."

Suddenly he saw a series of projections flash inside his skull, making him breathe in deeply and DaJuan groan. They saw the Priestesses marching HH off their ships on Zeta Archelois. They saw arguments. They saw high-tech maps of Earth, images of future Zeta colonies. They saw more arguments. They saw images of the male Zetas. They saw the arguments between the female Zetas turn violent. It was chaotic and choppy, but Harris saw the Amphibia group siding with the Priestess group, saw the Alma Mater group standing with the Zisis, and he saw Salacia standing on their own, with neither side. Next the Priestess and Amphibia left with their HH slaves. The three remaining Zetas talked and argued. Salacia threw her scaly arms in the air and stormed out.

He opened his eyes and stared at Martha, before another image cut through his mind. It was of Zeta Archelois and its silver sands. The planet was fractured, and the silver sands were slipping through the cracks into space.

Then, suddenly, Welles was projected again sitting with them.

When the image disappeared, so, too, did Martha.

Carrie stared down the encrypted transmission screen at Harris.

"So you think the Zetas are fractured into three groups?"

Harris shook his head. "No, I see two groups with Salacia being Switzerland."

"But if it came to it, we could talk the Salacia over to join the Alma Mater and the Zisis."

Harris shrugged. "You're assuming they want to help us at all. Technically, this isn't their fight."

Carrie nodded and sighed. "Yeah. If we try to force her to choose a side, it could backfire."

"We have to proceed on our own, but just because Martha and her allies decide not to involve themselves in our war with the Priestesses does not mean they cannot still be our allies. They can provide us with information, and they could also provide us with weapons or tech. You never know."

Carrie nodded again. "So, what are we going to do about her wanting me there?"

Harris sighed. "The general still won't approve the interview with Finch. I'm running out of options."

"What about Sarai?"

"She's communing alright, but she doesn't know the right questions to ask and it looks bad if I feed them to her in front of Martha. Martha doesn't understand that I'm her father, that I'm trying to protect her. Martha thinks I'm trying to control her. I also think Tess has been planting seeds of doubt that I'm somehow controlling you, too, and we know how the female Zetas feel about that."

"So prep Sarai thoroughly beforehand?"

"You know what it's like in the dreamscape, Welles. Shit can happen that throws you off. I know she's almost ten, but it's a risk. I'm happy for her to watch and learn right now, but I can't make her be Earth's leader or put that pressure on her."

"Well, what about Colt? She was on the list for Zeta DNA, yeah? Maybe you could start working to develop the node in her. It's like a muscle, right? The more Colt uses it, the bigger it should get."

"Maybe, but it's going to take a while to get her going. You had a 57 percent match, Colt only had 29 percent."

"Yeah, and McKinley only had 14 percent and he's now dreaming."

"Because he died. We ain't killing Colt to get that result."

"You know…" Carrie's voice drifted off as another memory surfaced.

"What?" Harris asked, eyes fixed.

"When Colt was gone, when Harbourg had her captive…"

"What, Welles?"

"I've had dreams of Colt before. When she was missing, I dreamed she was hiding in the shadows, both terrified and terrifying… I thought it was just an ordinary dream at the time, my anxiety for her whereabouts, but… it came true. Colt escaped. When we found her she was hiding from us, and she'd been transformed into a Jumbo. She was both terrified, and terrifying… And I dreamed of Colt asking me whether I'd heard the news, when Sharley had escaped. I dreamed she asked me that before it happened. What if that was the Zeta in me, connecting with the Zeta in her?"

Harris stared at her. She could see his mind ticking over.

"Has Colt had any dreams she's told you about that have come true?"

Carrie shook her head.

"Look, Welles, I'm not saying let's *not* try this with Colt, I'm just saying we shouldn't get our hopes up. You may have just dreamed the future and Colt was part of that future. It doesn't mean she connected with you."

"Get Dr. Bakshi to do new scans of Colt's brain. See if the node has grown in her, and if not, see if you can get it growing."

"I will. How's the president? Do you have any thoughts so far?"

Carrie sighed. "People are... disgruntled. Just how far that disgruntlement goes, I'm not sure. I'm working on it."

"Good. And your CTE?"

"I'm seeing the president's doctor tomorrow for a check-up and some vitamin and mineral injections. Bakshi's going to join us over transmission."

"Alright," Harris said. "I'll speak to Colt, and I'll check in with you again soon."

Carrie gave a nod and ended the transmission. She sighed again and stepped out of the guest office she'd been assigned, and began to make her way back to her apartment.

"Sergeant?" she heard Laurelai call out.

Carrie turned as Laurelai approached.

"We've received a request for you."

"A request?" Carrie asked.

"Yes. You know ex-Colonel Harbourg? One of the Originals?"

Carrie felt a shiver run though her, given they'd just been talking about him. "Yeah, I know him. He's a current resident of Hell Town."

"It seems he's discovered you're planetside and has asked if you would pay him a visit."

"In Hell Town?"

Laurelai nodded. Her eyes held questions, but she was polite enough not to ask them.

Carrie wanted to tell Laurelai to tell Harbourg to go fuck himself, but she bit her tongue on that. "Why would he want to see me?"

Laurelai shrugged. "He just said he had matters that he would like to discuss with you."

Carrie stared at her, wondering what the Greenback was up to. She didn't want to pander to his every whim. He was the man who'd kept Colt captive for all those years. But at the same time, she knew he was a man with connections – he had brought the guards to assist her when she was attacked by Jules' gang in the Hell Town showers. And most importantly, he was a man who traded in information and favors, and had been here on Mars for several years now. What if he knew something about the vigilantes currently residing in Hell Town? Could he find out who was behind the death threats against Harkowitz?

"Shall I arrange for you to visit?" Laurelai asked.

Carrie considered things for a moment. "I want to speak with those involved in the Atlas incident. They're in Hell Town, right?"

Laurelai nodded.

"Please arrange that. If I have time, I'll see Harbourg then."

President Finn Harkowitz ascended the staircase to the Red House's grand reception with Sentinel Beach in tow. As the floor came into view, he saw Welles's son, Brody, standing alone, staring at the image of his grandfather.

Harkowitz paused, sensing the boy wanted this moment alone, but he needed to cross the floor to the boardroom. The child turned to him, somehow sensing him there.

"It's a great shot, isn't it?" Harkowitz smiled as he approached.

The boy nodded, turned back to the photo.

"I'll see you in there." Harkowitz motioned for Beach to go on ahead. He did so.

"I was on break from my schooling," Brody explained. "Thought I'd stretch my legs."

Harkowitz came to a stop beside the boy. "That's fine. I imagine, as an Alpha, you have a lot of energy to burn?" Harkowitz was guessing, of course. Given Welles was an Alpha and the children had Sentinel protection, he could only guess that they were Alphas, too. There was just something about them that made Finn suspect they weren't ordinary children. They had a certain 'presence' about them that ordinary children did not have.

The boy nodded, not realizing what information he was giving away. "Mom always sends us outside to run it off when we get too much."

Harkowitz chuckled. "I bet." He glanced out the front doors of the Red House. "I'm sorry you can't just walk out these doors and run around in the fresh air here, but we do have exercise facilities below ground. Did Laurelai show you those?"

Brody nodded, then glanced at his grandfather again.

"Did you know your grandfather well?" Harkowitz asked him.

Brody nodded. "He helped Mom a lot." He glanced at Harkowitz. "My real dad died when I was a baby."

Harkowitz gave a gentle nod. "Yes, I know. I'm very sorry that happened."

Brody looked at him. "How did you know? Did Mom tell you?"

"I'm given a dossier on every visitor, including children. From what I've read, it sounds like your father, First Lieutenant Walker, was a brave man."

"I guess. I didn't really know him."

Laurelai came walking quickly up the staircase. "We'll be late, Mr. president."

Harkowitz checked his watch. "Tell them I'm running late and I'll be there shortly."

"Sir?" Laurelai questioned, darting her eyes to the boy.

"I'll be there in a few minutes," he told her. "Warm them up for me."

Laurelai gave a confused nod, but proceeded toward the boardroom. Harkowitz looked at Brody.

"Come on, I want to show you something."

He led Brody down a corridor, lined with more photographs and artworks, then turned into his official presidential office. The lights came on automatically as he entered, and he saw the boy looking around.

"Is this your office?" he asked in awe.

Harkowitz nodded, moving to the wall opposite his desk.

"Cool," Brody said, eyeing the photographs on the walls.

Harkowitz approached a glass box affixed to the wall, swiped his hand over a console on the side and opened the door. He delicately pulled out another smaller box and flipped the lid open. Inside was his father's Blue Nova medal, awarded by the UNF for services to space colonization. He stared at it a moment with pride. It was small, fitting in his palm, a cluster of stars melded together in brass, sealed with a blue shimmering coating and adorned on a lapel pin.

He showed it to Brody. "Do you know what this is?"

Brody nodded. "A Blue Nova. My dad got one. After he died. Mom keeps it in a drawer."

Harkowitz gave a sad smile. "This one was awarded to my father." He handed it to Brody who studied it and touched it gently.

"What did he do?" Brody asked.

"Have you heard of the Inca Station disaster?"

Brody shook his head.

"It was our first foray into space settlement, our first civilian space station. It was small, populated by 485 people. But eight months into its existence, there was meteor shower, a one-in-a-million event where one small flying piece of debris punctured a station wall, causing a series of catastrophic failures, and unfortunately everyone aboard died. After that, space settlement programs were killed. *Until*, my father decided to lead the charge and try again. He helmed the build of Inca-2 Station, and it became such a success that he went on to lead others," Harkowitz said. "And here we are today. The UNF awarded him this Blue Nova for his bravery and services. Just like your father."

Brody stared at the Blue Nova. "My dad died saving me and Freya." He looked up at Harkowitz. "Some bad people tried to kidnap us."

Harkowitz, knowing the children were Alphas now and why that event might've occurred, gently squeezed Brody's shoulder in sympathy. "And you stand here today because of his actions."

"Did you know your father?" Brody asked him.

"I did. He was a very busy man, though, and spent a lot of time in space, while I grew up on Earth."

"James is a bit like that. He's my dad now. He's always away with Uncle Saul."

"Uncle Saul? Colonel Harris?"

Brody nodded. "He's not my real uncle. He's my godfather, but we call him uncle."

Harkowitz couldn't hide his surprise. "You're a lucky boy, surrounded by such great men. Having an Original for your grandfather, your birth father a Blue Nova recipient, your living father being the hero of the Command Cleansing, and your godfather being Colonel Harris... Not to mention your mother being the sharpest shooter we have serving."

Brody nodded, looked at the Blue Nova again and passed it back.

Harkowitz stared at Brody, detected a sadness inside, like the boy was lost. He could sense the pressure the kid felt. It was a pressure Harkowitz understood all too well.

"It can be a hard thing living up to the memory of a hero father. I know what that's like."

Brody looked at him. "Did everyone expect you to be a hero, too?"

Harkowitz nodded. "Nobody more than myself." He studied the Blue Nova in his hand. "My father was a good man and I was proud of what he achieved, but it's taken me a long time to finally understand that I am not him, and the only person who can pull me out from his shadow, is me. I need to be my own man. My own hero. I am not him and I can never be him. I can only just be me. And that's okay, because I have talents that he did not. I will use them in my own way and I will cast my own shadow." He reached out and squeezed Brody's shoulder again. "And you will, too, in time."

Brody watched as Harkowitz locked the Blue Nova back in its glass display case. "Mom keeps telling me I'm a born leader, but I don't know."

"What don't you know?"

Brody shrugs. "What I'm going to be. A leader? A sharpshooter? Space Duty? Earth Duty?"

"You're not supposed to know yet, Brody. You're still young. What your destiny is, it will become clearer to you, when the time is right. You'll know when you know."

"Did you know you wanted to be president?"

Harkowitz smiled. "I knew I had a gift for leadership, knew my interest was in space colonization, and I knew Mars could be something special. I didn't know I was going to be president, until suddenly the stars aligned. The UNF announced they were seeking to establish a Mars presidency and I was in the right place at the right time." He glanced around at the historical photographs in his office. "It just felt right... And I feel privileged to be counted among these heroes that adorn the walls of the Red House." He looked back at Brody. "Including your grandfather."

Brody smiled.

"I have no doubt that one day your mother, and McKinley, and Harris will also adorn the walls of history," Harkowitz said, then patted Brody's shoulder again. "And maybe even you and your siblings, too."

Harkowitz checked his watch. "Now, I am rather late. I'd better go before they fire me from being president."

Brody laughed, and Harkowitz ushered him toward the door.

Harris studied the three leaders before him. McKinley and Morrell sat on the opposite side of the desk, in his office, while Gold appeared by transmission from Atlas. Given everything that had happened of late, Harris was behind on notifying the teams about the nodes and the radiation.

"What are the tests for this time?" Morrell asked.

"We need to do regular tests to monitor the Alpha virus, and given the events of the invasion, we don't know what complications, if any, may result from the Zeta's heat weapons. Any long-lasting effects, for instance," he said, ensuring he talked in general terms and didn't out Gold's news. "Though Colberge is still studying them, he has confirmed that the ships are giving off small amounts of radiation, and he's advised that he can't rule out this having adverse consequences for our soldiers. We also just want to keep an eye on things given our proximity to the Zetas. I mean, Morrell, Tess literally had her claws inside you."

"They've been making me take blood tests to check for any nasties. So far, I'm clean," he said. "Besides, you'd know that with the Zeta scars you got down your arm."

"I know, but we also need to consider their Thought-Biology and the impacts it could be having on us."

"Such as?" Gold asked.

Harris glanced at McKinley, then looked back at the other two. "Dr. Bakshi believes she has discovered a dormant node in some of our brains that have... reawakened."

"Nodes?" Gold asked.

"Who?" Morrell asked, brow furrowed.

"Me and Welles, for at start," Harris said, "but we've been interacting with Tess, so it makes sense. We just need to check that it's not spreading."

"Is the node a good thing or bad thing... like cancer?" Gold asked carefully.

"So, far we think it's a good thing," Harris said. "We're thinking it's just evolution in action. We have the ability to communicate with them, and we think it's due to this node."

"I've had the *Carcharias* team tested to check heat ray effects, like you asked," Gold said.

"Any results yet?"

Gold shook his head. "Due any day."

"What tests are we talking?" Morrell asked.

"Blood tests, biological scans, precursor checks," Harris said.

"Precursor checks?" Morrell's brow furrowed again. "That's for cancer and stuff right?"

Gold sighed subtly. "I guess they'll find out eventually, colonel?" he said to Harris.

Harris gave a nod for him to proceed.

"I tested positive to a cancer precursor," Gold nodded. "It's new. I didn't have it when I joined the UNF, so it's developed since."

"You think those things are giving us cancer?" Morrell asked Harris.

"Not the Zetas, no," Harris said, "but we can't say for sure about exposure to the heat ray."

"What?" McKinley asked.

Harris held his hands up to halt them all. "Right now, we don't think the smaller hand-held rays are responsible, but there's a chance the bigger rays from the ships might."

"So, unless you were in a firefight in the sky and got hit," Gold said, "you should hopefully be alright."

"But the *Carcharias* and *Aurizun* teams were," McKinley said.

"Yeah," Gold nodded.

"Shit," McKinley said.

"Look," Harris said, leaning forward, "nobody panic just yet. Let's start with this round of testing to check for any radiation or cancer-precursors, as well as testing for node growth, then we'll take it from there."

"What happens if we got this node thing?" Morrell asked.

Harris looked at him. "If you have the node, we're taking that as good thing and you will join a special program to see if we can develop it."

Morrell stared at him, clearly not happy with that possibility.

"How're things outside the fence?" Harris asked him.

"Much the same. They're still there and hurling abuse, but not much else."

"Gold, how're things on Atlas?"

"Stable. Connolly's been sent back to Earth and there have been no more visits from unfriendly civilians."

"And the crew?" Harris asked.

"Stable," Gold said. "I trust Lieutenant Batoya and she's been keeping a keen eye on everyone and all transmissions. There's been no other signs of dissent."

"Heard from Welles?" Morrell asked Harris.

Harris nodded. "They've got some protestors at the Red House, but so far there's been no danger to the president. She visited the Haides-1 proxy-steel facility and is waiting on information as to who took the *Golden Orb* out for a spin when it followed us to Earth."

Morrell nodded and looked at McKinley. "That why you moved into Command? Because Welles is on Mars?"

McKinley paused briefly, but nodded at Morrell.

"He's trying to get a handle on his inner mech," Harris said. "We're undertaking some intensive training and I want him to focus." He looked at Gold. "If there's nothing else, Gold, you're free to go."

"Thank you," he nodded and ended the transmission.

Harris looked at Morrell. "Any update on the JEM army?"

"I'm told they're settling in well enough," Morrell said, giving him a strange, almost accusatory look.

"I know, Morrell," Harris said. "It's a fucked-up thing that Sharley did."

"But we're rolling with it, anyway?" Morrell said, eyes pinning his.

"Yeah," Harris said, "and I don't need to remind you how fucking confidential it is, right?"

"Oh, I get it. That's why you cut Gold loose before talking about it."

"I'm not happy about it, Morrell. And already too many people know about it. I need you to ensure your soldiers keep their mouths shut. Understand?"

"Yes, sir," he said, giving a slightly mocking salute.

"If there's nothing else, you can go," Harris said. He wasn't going to admonish Morrell. If anything he wanted to shake the man's hand for having the ethics to question it.

Morrell glanced at McKinley. "Guess you get to stay for all the updates."

"I *am* head of Alpha soldiers," McKinley replied.

Morrell smirked and stood.

"Hey, Morrell," McKinley said, "apparently the *Aurizun* team is still waiting on a date for an Alpha UNFer Bowl. Why you stalling?"

Morrell's smirk turned into a grin as he moved to the door. "You'll have a date by the end of the day."

They watched Morrell leave. Harris looked at McKinley.

"I've been thinking… I'm not sure the UNFer Bowl is a good idea right now. Like you said before, we're wearing thin. I can't risk my Alphas getting injured."

McKinley shrugged. "We need some camaraderie, and we need an outlet."

"We? Or *you*?"

McKinley stared at him.

"How's your training going?" Harris asked him.

McKinley shrugged. "I haven't had much time for it."

"Why?"

The major shrugged again. "Well, just when I get started, something crops up. Suddenly I'm on Mars, then Atlas, then I'm guarding Zetas, then we're handling the JEM situation."

"Do I need to ground you until you sort things out?"

"I guess that depends on whether you want me to lead the Alphas."

"You can still lead the Alphas from the ground."

"What about the *Aurizun* team?"

Harris shrugged. "Hunter could step in, if needed."

"He's the pilot, he needs to focus on the ship. Besides, I'm best when I'm busy."

"When you're busy? Or when you're avoiding things?"

"I'm fine."

"Are you?" Harris arched his eyebrow. "Had any dreams lately."

McKinley shook his head. "Nothing that makes sense."

"You writing them down?"

"They don't make sense."

"I'm telling you to write them down," Harris said firmly, then laid his arm across his desk. "Hold my hand."

McKinley looked at Harris's hand awkwardly.

"Get over yourself, McKinley," Harris said bluntly. "You're not my type. Now hold my goddamn hand. With your *real* hand. I want to see if I feel a buzz."

McKinley reached out with his left hand and clasped Harris's. Harris closed his eyes and concentrated.

He felt nothing. He let it go and sat back.

"Your node is growing. I should feel something."

"I'm not one of you," McKinley said.

"No, you *weren't* one of us, but then you died and something happened, and now your dreaming and your node is growing. I'm feeling nothing when I hold your hand because you are so damn closed off to this."

"Look, I can't do this now. I gotta focus on getting my new arm working, like you said. I gotta sort the physical stuff first. I can't lead your soldiers if I don't."

"McKinley, do you know how powerful a weapon it could be if I could transmit my thoughts to you on the battlefield. It could save lives."

"Maybe so," he said, as he stood, "but when it comes to saving lives, I start with my hands." He turned and headed for the door, as an angry fire surged though Harris.

"McKinley!" Harris quickly stood.

McKinley turned around as Harris, Alpha swift, hurled his coffee cup at him.

Alpha swift, McKinley raised his mech arm in defense and the ceramic cup smashed against his proxy-steel appendage, shattering into pieces.

McKinley glared at Harris as the Alpha reared within. Harris strode around his desk toward him, his own Alpha energy very present, as he stopped right in front of the major.

"There's nothing wrong with your arm, McKinley. It's your head that's the problem. Forget the gym, forget the range, forget the physical stuff. You do nothing else until you clear that mess inside your head. Understand? You do *nothing* but talk to that shrink. That's a fuckin' order."

Harris stormed past him, leaving McKinley alone in the room.

21

Conversations

Carrie watched as Mars Maximum Security Prison, aka Hell Town, came into view. She felt a shiver race across her bare arms as she eyed the silvery-gray complex sitting beneath its puri-grav domes and spanning 20 city blocks. She focused her Alpha eyes on the ground surrounding the facility, wondered if the dungeons were still there underneath. Knew they would be.

She glanced over to the left of the facility, her eyes tracking to the ridge in the distance. Wondered where exactly the entrance to the dungeon was, as memories flashed through her mind. Memories of exiting from that tunnel into the dull Martian sunlight with Hunter by her side. Freed from her captivity, but uncomfortable in that freedom, knowing Doc and McKinley had still been inside the dungeon at the time. Doc, unconscious on that operating table; McKinley, a mess of bandages in their small, feral cell.

"Iron Bird, preparing to land," the pilot spoke into his comms.

"*Roger that, Iron Bird,*" the Hell Town comms officer responded. "*Clearance to land.*"

"Roger. Over."

"You alright?" Colonel Greavy asked, green eyes studying her. Though Carrie had arranged the visit through Laurelai, Greavy had stepped in and offered to escort her on his designated craft, to speak with the vigilantes. He had, of course, asked why she wanted to speak with them and what this had to do with Mars-UNF relations. Carrie had simply told him that she was trying to capture the temperature of the Martian people and these vigilantes were pissed, so she wanted to understand why.

Carrie nodded at Greavy. "Yeah. Just remembering when I was here before."

Greavy looked out the windows. "Must've been an experience being inside those walls. And surviving."

Carrie glanced at him, then looked back at Hell Town. She saw the outer wall of the prison, and as they flew nearer, saw the inner wall and, in between, the electric moat, which sparked currents of blue and silver. Of course, Greavy was referring to her time as an inmate after she killed Sharley. She wondered if he knew about the dungeon beneath it and what she'd been through there.

They landed safely beside the dome, waiting for the connecting chute to engage, then began to make their way through the various walkways and security clearances to enter the complex. Once inside the walls, as they walked along the protected path to the building, Carrie scanned her eyes over the grounds, searching the faces of the inmates in the yard for any sign of Zico Cavelera, the ex-*Aurora* soldier who betrayed Carrie, Doc and McKinley to Sharley. The betrayal which led them to being held captive in those dungeons. The last time Carrie had been here, she'd left instructions with Colonel Harbourg to fuck Cavelera up. She wondered whether he had, and smiled.

But her smile faded, suddenly wondering whether the Carrie before CTE would've taken such glee in brutal punishments. She made a note to herself to work harder to ensure the CTE didn't rule her life, that instead she ruled the CTE. If not for herself, then for her children and McKinley. If she became too brutal and cold, would they stop loving her as they have?

With Greavy by her side, they entered the central building, passed more security measures, then finally made their way to the visitation rooms where she would question the civilians who attacked the *Carcharias* and Atlas.

Greavy left her in a small room that had proxy-steel walls, while he went to fetch the prisoners. Time alone within these walls made more memories surface. The fight with Jules' gang. The time in the dungeon when she'd felt her tracking device emitting its signal. The hole in the wall and Cavelera's angry brown eye, promising he was going to fuck her up. He had been the one to send Jules and her gang after Carrie in the showers.

She felt a little agitated and alone, wishing Archie was with her, but given Hell Town security, she would not have been allowed inside with her AI.

The door to the room opened and Carrie paused at who walked in.

Ex-Colonel Harbourg, aka the Greenback.

He looked much the same as the last time he'd seen her, except maybe a little older, a little plumper. He moved over to the spare seat across her table and took a seat.

"I'm not here to see you," Carrie said bluntly.

He smiled. "Yes, you are." He nodded to the guard who'd escorted him in. The guard tapped at a screen on the wall beside the table, then left the room.

Carrie tensed.

"Relax," Harbourg said. "The guards leave me because they know I'm not a threat. Well," he smiled more broadly, "I'm not a threat if they don't fuck with me."

A face appeared on the screen via transmission.

Roxy Harbourg.

"What is this?" Carrie asked.

"What's she doing there?" Roxy asked her father, brows knitted in a scowl.

"Both of you shut up," Harbourg said. "You're both here because you're both too stubborn to meet of your own accord."

"I've been busy," Carrie said.

"And I don't care," Roxy said.

"Well, you need to care!" Harbourg snapped. He looked at Carrie. "Why has the UNF not rolled out their Alpha program yet?"

"That's classified," Carrie said plainly.

"They need to roll out their program and get to training now or it'll be too late."

"We have a strategy. It's in hand," Carrie said calmly.

"Strategy? You mean wasting time trying to communicate with an alien race that wants to annihilate us."

"Not all of them do," Carrie said.

"What do you mean, not all of them?"

Carrie shrugged. "Their race is a lot like ours. It's fractured."

"But they're still gunning for us?" he asked.

Carrie shrugged again. "Some of them, possibly."

"If the UNF fuck this up, if they don't arrange soldiers in time," he pointed to Roxy. "You'll need her."

Carrie looked at Roxy's face on the screen. She stared at the peroxide-blond for a moment, then looked back at Harbourg. "Why?"

"While the UNF sits on their hands, the Harbourgs will take care of business."

"Do you mean forcing people against their will to have children?" Carrie asked.

He sliced his hand across the air to silence her.

"What's she talking about?" Roxy asked.

"Your dad didn't tell you all the gory details of what he did?" Carrie asked.

"The UNF failed to do their duty. We were all gonna die if I didn't do something."

"So you thought you'd take a black woman, hold her captive, impregnate her and force her to carry and raise children she did not want?"

"What the *fuck* is she talking about?" Roxy demanded. "Why is she here?"

Harbourg stared at Carrie. "How *are* the children?"

Carrie stared back at him. He had no right to know how Malik and Casim were doing.

He smiled. "You forget, I saved you in those showers."

"I was handling Jules and her gang just fine."

"No, you weren't," he said, "because that little shit, Cavelera, had a fail-safe. If Jules' gang failed, the guards were supposed to finish you and make it look like it was Jules. I stopped those guards from touching you."

Carrie stared at him, wondering whether that was true. A shiver ran down her spine making her think he was telling the truth.

"Why?" she asked. "Because my dad was an Original?"

He nodded. "I told you. We didn't see eye to eye much, but I respected him. And he did not deserve to die at the hands of the Zetas in the invasion. We've wasted too much time. This is our chance to right wrongs."

"Right wrongs?" Carrie asked. "You can never right the wrong you did to my friend."

"Maybe not. But we can still save the world. So, I am telling you," he said then looked at Roxy on the screen, "and *you*, that you don't need to get along. Just like me and your old man," he said to Carrie, "didn't get along. But when we were Originals, when we were in the field, we had each other's backs."

Carrie looked at Roxy. "What could she possibly offer me in the way of assistance."

"When you're back on Earth, go look her up. She'll show you."

"Dad—" Roxy went to object.

"No, Roxy! Enough time has passed. They've invaded us once and now this new Zeta is here. It's only a matter of time before more come." He glanced back and forth between them. "Suck up your pride and do what needs to be done, like your fathers did."

A knock sounded on the door. Harbourg looked at it, then stood.

"We're out of time," he said, fixing his eyes on Carrie. "When you're back on Earth, look her up." He turned to Roxy. "When she comes, *you* let her in."

Harbourg walked to the door as Carrie locked eyes with Roxy. The woman scowled and ended the transmission.

"Harbourg?" Carrie called.

He looked back at her.

"How *is* Cavelera?" she asked.

"He's dead," Harbourg said, as the door opened.

"What?" Carrie asked, shocked. "How? I said fuck him up not kill him."

"I didn't. The kid thought he was a puppeteer. Thought he could maneuver into a position of safety in here. He fucked over the wrong people and they ended him. I tried to warn him. He didn't listen."

Carrie stared at Harbourg, unsure how she felt.

"I look forward to hearing how your visit to Roxy goes," Harbourg said as he left the room.

Within moments Colonel Greavy entered, ushering in a gray-bearded man with accusing eyes and a mouth twisted in anger. Greavy sat him down in the chair opposite Carrie, giving her a curious look.

Had Greavy seen Harbourg leave the room? Had Greavy been in on it? Was he in Harbourg's pocket? Or was he suspicious about the exchange?

"Who the hell are you?" the inmate spat at her.

"Second Lieutenant Welles-McKinley," Greavy said, "meet Carson Beckett, captain of the *Yorke* and leader of the vigilante group."

McKinley eyed the elderly woman sitting across from him. Her name was Dr. Elspeth Getty and was his new designated psych. She reminded him a little of his mother, but her disposition was different. This woman had a look about her that said she was in control. In control of her life, of her emotions, and of her position as head UNF psychologist.

"Make yourself comfortable," she said. "This is a safe space. Nothing is being recorded by camera and no-one is watching or listening but me. This is just a conversation between the two of us. I will take notes, for myself to look back on, but that is all."

McKinley nodded.

"Make yourself comfortable, Major," she said again, a little more firmly.

McKinley glanced at her, then sat back on the couch. She smiled.

"I'm sorry if that sounded forceful, but I've found that soldiers respond best to orders."

McKinley nodded. "I guess."

"I have a relaxant I can give you with your permission. It's a mild sedative that helps you to shed inhibitions. You will still be in full control, you will just be less self-conscious about whatever you need to unload. Would you like this, or would you prefer to speak as you are?"

"You offer the drug before we even try to speak?" he asked.

She smiled again. "I've done this job for a long time. Only in this particular position since Dr. Scavesci, er, passed away, but many years working with soldiers and I've become somewhat of a pro at knowing which ones need the drug."

"And what is it about me that tells you that?" he asked cautiously.

"You don't want to be here. It's all over your body language. You were ordered here. I've read your file, have seen your history, starting with the murder of your father, your mother's mental collapse, your troubled youth, then seeing how you excelled with military guidance, only to suffer a relapse when you were forced into the Jumbo program. Then your brush with death during the invasion, and your struggle to deal with being an Alpha-Mech, then your recent struggles with PTSD and the incident with your wife."

McKinley's eyes sharpened on hers. "What does it say in the file about that?"

"It's listed as an incident. The incident was logged by Lieutenant Welles's AI." She smiled gently. "Relax... the AI listed it only as a PTSD incident, albeit a serious one."

McKinley looked at his Alpha-Mech hand, made a fist.

"It is important we ensure it is not repeated," she said calmly.

McKinley glanced at her, then darted his eyes away. He nodded.

"Would you like the drug?" she asked.

He looked back at her. "You mean the truth serum... I don't know. What do you recommend?"

"I guess it depends on how much time you have," she said. "I'm more than happy to work like this every day until you learn to trust me and let out all that you need to. Or, if you want to sort your problems out sooner rather than later, this drug helps to speed up the process. The sooner you tell me what's on your mind, the sooner I will know how to treat you. The sooner I can unlock the troubles in your mind, the sooner you can return to your family."

"You just listed off all the issues I've had in my life. You can't diagnose a solution from that?"

"I listed *incidents* in your life that will have caused serious emotional effects, but what effects exactly, I can't predict. Do I need to help ease your anger? Or is it your self-esteem that's the problem? Or is it abandonment issues? Or is it the pressure you place upon yourself to handle things and be the tough hero? Or do we need to work through the fact that your childhood was cut short?" She gave another gentle smile. "Or is it all of these at once? The list goes on. I can only help you once you tell me what you need."

McKinley looked back at her, as his mind turned over. "Then I guess you're going to need to give me that needle, because I have no idea where to start."

Harris entered Colt's cabin.

"Long time, no see," she said.

"Yeah," he sighed. "I'm sorry about that. Busy times."

"So Brown tells me," she said, then folded her arms. "You here to check on the kids?"

"No, I came to speak with you."

"Yeah?" she asked curiously.

Harris nodded. She eyed him a moment then motioned for him to sit at the table.

"I see you're back working in our weapons division?" Harris said.

Colt nodded, taking the seat opposite. "Yeah. The kids are old enough now and I'm happy to be back into things, doing my bit to help win this future war."

"So, you're good?" he motioned to her head, her mind.

She nodded. "As much as I'll ever be. I've done years of therapy now. That's why I'm back at work."

"That's good to hear," he said, then laid his arm out on the table. "Give me your hand."

She looked at it. "What?"

"I just want to try something."

She gave him an odd look, but placed her hand on his. He took her hand and squeezed it while she gave him a curious look. He closed his eyes and concentrated.

He felt nothing.

He opened his eyes again, let her hand go.

"Is this to do with your gift?" she asked.

He nodded, studying her carefully. "Do you believe in it?"

Colt studied him back, then nodded. "Yeah, I believe you've got something going on."

"Did Welles tell you about her condition?"

Colt nodded. "CTE."

Harris nodded back. With Brown's boxing history, it was no doubt something they'd come across, perhaps occurring in some of his heroes.

"Her brain is fragile, right now," Harris said. "It means she can't help me connect with the Zeta."

Colt glanced at his hand. "What, and you think that I can step in?"

"I'm exploring all options. Your DNA markings matched 29 percent with Zeta DNA."

"What?" Colt pulled a face like he was crazy.

Harris held his hand out calmly and explained the Zeta markers in the DNA, their theories about the past colonization, and how the Zeta communication worked. Colt listened, a little shocked at first, but eventually her face smoothed out with understanding and, perhaps, because of Harris's calmness and the educated manner with which he spoke. He filled her with ease.

"The Zetas are a female dominant race," he said. "At least, the ones we're dealing with. They're... hesitant in speaking with me and DaJuan. My daughter..." Harris paused, found he had to swallow. "My daughter has the gift, but she's young, Colt. She's been connecting with them, but I'm just exploring all options before I have to officially throw her in the ring. The general won't let me go wide with this just yet, so I'm scouring those already in the know, to see if they can help out."

"So, you want me to see if I can replace Welles?"

Harris nodded.

"I don't know, sir," she shook her head and sat back in her seat. "I don't know if this is me. My specialty is bombs."

"We didn't think it was our specialty either, but it became one."

Colt stood and paced slowly around the room, her mind turning over.

"All I'm asking is that you give it a try, Colt. If it doesn't work, I can rule you out and look elsewhere."

She looked back at him. "What do I have to do?"

"We start by getting a fresh scan of your brain to check the node."

Carrie stared at Carson Beckett, captain of the lead vigilante ship, *Yorke*, seated across from her. According to his file, he was 57 years old, one of the Haides-1 mine team leaders, and a resident of Mars since shortly after its settlement. He stared at her with coolly defiant eyes, the kind that knew his legal rights.

"So? What do you want?" Beckett asked.

Carrie stared at him, unable to stop her Alpha reacting to his attitude. "I want to know why you think you have the right to fuck up everything we've worked for?"

He scoffed. "I see your Space Duty uniform, but you are not part of the local Mars force that polices this planet, so I have *nothing* to say to you."

"The local Mars force is a part of the UNF. Part of Space Duty. Of which Colonel Greavy, here," she motioned to him, "is a part of. I have been authorized by the president himself to interview you."

He scoffed. "Like that puppet has power."

"Puppet?"

"Harkowitz bears the title president, but we all know who really rules this planet." He looked down his nose at her uniform.

"The UNF settled this planet. You are here because of them."

"The UNF did not settle this planet alone. There were many scientists, engineers, and yes, *miners* who helped colonize this planet. I was one of them."

"And you were paid for your work, yes?"

He stared at her.

She sighed, pushing her Alpha back down. "Why don't we both save our time and you just tell me exactly what it is that you want? Do you feel you were underpaid? What?"

He leaned over the table toward her. "I helped make Mars the planet it is today. I moved here to make this place my home. I have a comfy little hab, underground at Brahe, but everywhere I look, I don't see freedom. I see a lie. The hab I own, I don't really own. The UNF could take it away from me tomorrow if they wish. All of this, *everything*, they think it's theirs. They make us think we have a say, that we can vote in the president and live like we were on Earth, but that's not the truth. I am sick of living under UNF rule and having them make decisions for me and my planet."

"Decisions like protecting the Zeta?"

"You're *goddamn* right!" he said sitting back and folding his arms.

"You don't want peace with them? You'd rather war?"

"We're already at war," he said. "They came and they killed hundreds, if not thousands."

Carrie nodded. "One race of the Zetas did, yes. But just like with humans, there is more than one race. You would declare war on all of mankind for that which *one* race did?"

He stared at her. "The truth is, I don't even care that much about the Zetas. I just want the UNF to pull back and let us live our lives here in peace."

"You want the UNF to get off your lawn?"

"Yes," he said, unfolding his arms and placing his hands on his hips.

"So, you leading that charge to kill the Zeta wasn't really to save mankind, it was simply to tell them and the UNF to fuck off from Mars?"

Again, he stared at her, his eyes analyzing.

"Like many here, we believe in Martian independence," he said. "The ore is ours. The proxy-steel is ours. And if the UNF wants it, you gotta pay. It's business. You don't just get to walk in and take it or tell us what to do."

"We're not just taking it. We're paying for it," Carrie said. "And we're not telling you what to do, we're trying to work *with* you and advise you in matters where we know best, such as planetary safety against possible invaders."

Beckett grunted a laugh. "Yeah, invaders like the UNF."

Carrie sighed. She could sense this guy wasn't going to budge from his position. She looked at Greavy. "I'm done. Send the next one in."

Greavy nodded to a second guard who grabbed Beckett and led him toward the door.

"Be careful in here," Carrie said to Beckett as he passed. He glanced back at her and smiled.

"Oh, don't you worry, I'll be safe in here."

The guard led him from the room and for a brief moment Carrie wondered whether Beckett knew Harbourg. And then another thought sprung to mind. How did Harbourg feel about the president? Was Harbourg frustrated like others at his lack of action against the Zetas?

She looked at Greavy.

"Is what he saying true?" she asked. "Is there a growing sentiment of resentment for the UNF? It's not just Harkowitz they're against? Do people really want Martian independence?"

Greavy considered his answer then nodded. "The abuse our soldiers face on the colony streets is increasing. There's been a spike since the Atlas incident. We've been on heightened alert, but the truth is, many of my soldiers agree with it all."

"They do?"

"Yeah," he nodded. "A lot of 'em lost friends and family on ships during the invasion. Word spread that Harkowitz was pissed with the UNF afterward. A lot of people thought that maybe he would make a push for independence, then suddenly he's in alignment with the UNF again. Some folks out there think he's backflipped on promises. He's lost the trust of some people."

"And you? Has he lost your trust?"

Greavy stared at her. "My job is to serve Mars and the president."

"Smart answer," she studied him. "Your soldiers do realize that if we can broker peace with the Zetas, we'll save many lives in the long run?"

He nodded. "That may be, but Martian independence is very much on the table. It's not going away. Regan Lotz has been forming a political party and they'll be there at the next election."

"I thought he was an independent? He has a party behind him now?"

Greavy nodded. "He claims he wants to protect Martian resources and wants a free Martian people. Folks are listening."

"Do you think he has the numbers?"

"I guess we'll see when the time comes."

The door opened and the guard returned with a younger man bearing a hard glare.

"Dominic Faber," Greavy said, taking the man and sitting him down. "Captain of the *Alexi*."

"The ones who fired upon a UNF ship," Carrie said, piercing the man with an Alpha stare.

Harris stared at Marchant and Berger as they sat in the general's office.

"I've spoken with them and gave my orders for the series of tests to explore both the node and any possible radiation or other effects from being around the Zetas and their ships."

"And if your soldiers start showing cancer precursors?" Berger asked.

"Then we're fucked, sir," Harris said. "If our current stock of soldiers get cancer, there's no telling if they'll be around when the Zetas come. Between that and Welles's CTE, everything we've done, everything we've been through to get to this point will have been for nothing."

"Not necessarily, Harris," Berger said. "We have the First Gens and the JEMs. Everything you and your teams did, ensured their survival."

"They will all be in their early to mid 20s, if my predictions are right," Harris said, then sighed and shrugged. "I mean, that's when I predict the war, but with Martha showing up like she did, who knows what else might happen between here and then. When the war comes they'll be strong, they'll have stamina, but will they have the strength of mind to do what needs to be done?"

"Let's not get ahead of ourselves," Marchant said. "We do the tests, and take it from there. Like you said, you and McKinley were potentially exposed to less radiation than the *Carcharias* team."

"That doesn't make me feel any better. I do not wish for the *Carcharias* crew to die. Nor the *Aurora* team who were also exposed to blasts in the invasion. Besides, what if the buried ships give off radiation of some kind. Me, Welles and Yughi have tried to connect with them. Physically touched them. Hunter and McKinley have been inside them with me. Even Dr. Ross has spent a large amount of time inside them."

"There's also the exposure to civilians where the ships crashed," Berger said.

Marchant held up his hand. "Like I said, we do the tests and take it from there."

Harris sighed and ran his hand over his scalp. "I can't believe we might survive a war, only to die from its radiation."

"We'll be stepping up analysis of the heat ray weapons and look at how we can reinforce our ships with radiation shielding. There's still time," Marchant said.

"Yeah, for future fighters, but what about my guys from the invasion?" Harris said.

"We're doing what we can," Marchant said.

"I can't wait for the results," Harris said. "I need to play around on those Zeta ships."

"Why?"

"I want to earn Martha's trust. I want to escort her to one of the buried ships, see if she can show me how to get inside. I mean, I saw her connect with hers in my dream, but I want to see her do it in the flesh. Maybe the way I dreamed it, was different to the actual reality of it."

"And if she awakens a ship?" Berger asked.

"Imagine the intel we could get," Harris said.

"And if Martha uses the ship against you?" Berger asked.

"Why would she? She knows she's outnumbered here."

Berger shrugged. "Maybe she'd rather die knowing she took you out first?"

Silence sat for a moment as their minds mulled things over.

"We need to try it," Marchant said. "Any intel from an awakened ship could be a game changer."

Berger considered this a moment, then relented. "I agree, but you'll need back-up in case things turn bad."

Harris gave a nod. "That's what the *Aurizun* team is for."

"I hear you're going to try Colt with Martha?" Berger said.

Harris nodded again. "I'm running out of options. If she doesn't work, I *absolutely* must do that interview with Finch, sir."

"We've still got protestors at our gate," Marchant said.

"We'll have them as long as Martha and Tess are here," Harris said. "That ain't going to change. I'm sorry, general, but I mean it. If Colt doesn't work, I'm doing the interview and I'm putting a call out for people like me."

"Harris—" Berger began.

"General, I can't help it if the Zetas are sexist bitches who don't like dealing with men, but this is where we are. Me and DaJuan will only get so much from her. I need a female. Then she'll fully trust me. If you want to win this war, this is what we need to do."

Berger stared at him, then exchanged a consultative look with Marchant.

"Try Colt first," Marchant said.

22

Ship to Shore

McKinley lay back on the couch, it felt like he was floating on a soft cloud. A memory surfaced of Carrie joking about the UNF having the good drugs. He smiled.

"Now you're relaxed," Dr. Getty said.

McKinley nodded. "So where do we start?"

"Why don't we start at the start. What's your earliest memory?"

McKinley cast his mind back. It was hard at first. His childhood seemed so long ago, buried under so much rubble. A memory broke through, however.

"My father coming home with bruises on his face."

"Had he been in a fight?"

"He worked undercover for the DEA. Every now and then he'd come home with bruises and scratches, or torn clothes, or looking like he'd been up all night."

"How did your father handle the situation with you? Did he tell you where the bruises came from?"

"He'd make light of it, say the other guy looked worse. He'd say there were bad guys out there and he was doing his best to stop them."

"How did that make you feel?"

McKinley thought on this. "I thought he was cool. A real life superhero. Wanted to be just like him."

"And how did your mother deal with it?"

McKinley sighed. He tried to remember the last time he'd seen Grace. With everything going on, it had been a while. He'd called her occasionally or sent emails, but he hadn't seen her in the actual flesh for some time. He felt the guilt pool in his belly at that, but since the invasion it's not like he'd had much time for social visits. "She pretended like the bruises weren't there and everything was fine…. But I could see the worry underneath."

"How was your parents' relationship?"

He shrugged and looked at the wedding ring on his left hand. It had once belonged to his father, while Carrie wore his mother's wedding band. "They loved each other, but she hated his job. His last case undercover, the one before he died, was a hard one. It was taking a lot out of him and I'd see her watching news reports about gangland killings. She begged him to leave the DEA or switch to a desk job. He wouldn't. He kept saying he was close to nailing the guy. He felt like it was a duty, you know, to stop these guys and keep the streets safer. But you take one down, another steps up in their place. Always. The threat never ends."

"Do you want to talk about your father's murder?"

He ran his hand over his face. "Not really… What's there to say? He hurt the gangs, they hurt him back."

"Do you want to talk about your mother's collapse?"

"Even less so."

He saw Getty studying him out of the corner of his Alpha eye.

"I think we need to start with your father," she said.

"Why?"

"Because I imagine what you saw that day when the package arrived at your house, the one your mother threw to the ground… seeing your father's head and hands spill out onto the ground, must've have left an awful scar on your 13-year-old psyche that was never treated."

"Oh, it definitely scarred. But it was a long time ago. The scar has healed."

"The scar has healed on the surface but beneath the skin the infection remains."

"I sucked the poison out. Never looked back."

Getty studied him a moment and McKinley could see the doubt in her eyes.

"Your own recent wounds must've been a stark reminder of what happened with your father," she said. "He lost his head and hands. The Zeta's heat ray caused you to lose your arm, your ear and your eye, left permanent scars over the right side of your body."

McKinley twitched involuntarily, then shifted his body as though it had been intentional.

Getty studied him in silence again. "How did your mother react when she heard the news about what happened to you?"

Despite the soft cloud around him, McKinley shifted uncomfortably again. "I never told her."

"Why not?"

"Because."

Getty waited patiently for him to answer. McKinley looked at her.

"She always thought that I'd end up like my father. She was right."

"Is she? I see you here before me alive and well. Physically well."

McKinley looked away again. "If I told her I lost my arm, that I died… she'd have another breakdown and I'm not sure it's one she'd recover from."

"She must've known you would've been fighting in the Zeta invasion?"

McKinley shook his head. "She has a carer who checks on her daily. They're careful with what she's exposed to. They try to keep things light, avoid the news. She'd be virtually oblivious to it, out there in Phoenix."

"When did you last visit her?"

"A while ago. Before the invasion."

"I see… Let's go back to your father."

McKinley sighed and rubbed his face.

"You don't want to talk about him," Getty said carefully. "Do you not see why?"

McKinley looked over at her again. Her face was soft and caring. Motherly.

"No," he said, "enlighten me."

"I suspect we might find that your untreated childhood trauma is the reason for the issue you're experiencing now. You're an Alpha, yes, but you have anger management issues underneath, and they're understandable. You're angry your father was butchered and taken from you. You're angry your mother had a mental collapse and left you without a functioning parent. You're angry that your parents were fallible, that your superhero father wasn't a superhero after all. You're angry the world left you to fend for yourself. You're angry that you finally found a home and a family among the military, but then elements within that military betrayed you. Just like your father was betrayed by one of his colleagues. They sent you to Station Darwin to be captured. They forced you to become what was then known as a Jumbo. Then fatherhood was forced upon. You grew up without parents, and I suspect you were terrified that you didn't know anything about fatherhood. Then, things finally seemed to go well for you. You'd found love with Second Lieutenant Welles, had another child of your own making, but elements within the military used your son's DNA for experiments without your knowledge." He glanced at her. *She knew?* "Then the invasion occurred and the Zeta took your arm, your ear, and your eye, and you were forced to become an Alpha-Mech. And then, more elements within your military family betrayed you once more and tried to kill you and your wife. Then, through accident, from the pent-up frustration and trauma over the years, your actions led to the discovery of your wife's CTE. You feel like you are your father all over again, inflicting mental anguish on your wife. You've had so much to deal with, major, that you have just buried things, and buried things, and carried on because that's how you survived when you were young. That's how you survived when you had no other choice. But it's catching up with you now. So many things have happened without your free will, that you are now struggling with your own free will. You didn't want to be an Alpha-Mech but you're being forced to accept it. Forced to perfect it. And I believe that all of this, becoming the ultimate soldier, winning the war and saving humankind will mean nothing to you, if the love of your life, Carrie, the one who stood by your side through thick and thin and never deserted you, who gave you the family that you never had growing up, is not by your side at the end of it."

McKinley suddenly felt very awake. His heart was thumping hard in his chest, his breathing short and stilted. He looked away from her, his real eye stinging with emotion, yet stunned. Getty had just summarized his whole life, everything that had ever happened to him, everything he'd ever felt, everything he'd never been able to express himself. Just like that.

"H—how... do you know all of that?"

She smiled. "Colonel Harris declassified most of your file in order to help me to treat you." She leaned forward in her chair. "The fact that you've managed to survive and be sitting here today is an absolute testament to how utterly strong you are, major. But do you know what will make you even stronger?"

"What?"

"If you allow yourself to release it all."

McKinley stared at her.

"We will talk through everything," she said, "and through talk we'll heal and we'll release. And through release, you will have less blockages in your mind and more space to deal with what you need to. No longer will you be lacking free will. You will have full control of your free will. Of your body. Of your life. Of your anger and your frustration. Finally. And you will be able to reclaim your place within your family."

McKinley sat numb for a moment. Numb on the inside, while his external body shook. The real parts of it anyway.

He eventually sighed and looked up at the ceiling. "That's gonna take a long time, doc."

"It's just as well we started today, huh?" She smiled.

Harris sat on the silver sands waiting. DaJuan was beside him and Martha stood a ways off, staring at them.

"I don't think Colt's gonna show, man," DaJuan said.

"It's her first time. It might take a while to sleep."

"I may not be a Sense'er like you, but even my gut is telling me the truth. This isn't for Colt. She's not strong enough. If she was, you would've known it before now."

Harris ran his hands over his face, sighed in frustration. He knew DaJuan was right. The latest scan of Colt's brain showed no progression of the 'shadow' Dr. Bakshi believed was a potential node.

"Time is of the essence, man," DaJuan said. "You know she's not right for this. Listen to your gut. What is it telling you?"

Suddenly Sarai stood before them.

"Dad?"

"Sarai?" Harris said, glancing at Martha, who eyed her keenly.

DaJuan looked at Sarai, then back to Harris. "She's the one," he said. "Until you convince the general to go wide, she's all we got."

Martha stepped forward, studying Sarai. Harris's daughter turned around and stared back at Martha, then gave a smile.

"Hello," she said, tentatively. "My name is Sarai."

Harris stood, maybe a little too quickly because Martha took a step backward. Harris held out his hand, motioning for calm. He moved up beside Sarai and held his daughter's hand.

"She's my daughter," he told Martha. "I will protect her with my life." He gently pulled Sarai backward to stand partially behind him.

Martha studied them both. Sarai hugged Harris's arm, while giving Martha a friendly smile.

"He's my dad," Sarai told Martha.

"I'm going to project something," Harris told them all. "Close your eyes."

Harris projected an image to Martha of him holding Sarai at her birth, kissing Taya's forehead. Then he projected another image of Sarai at her third birthday, blowing out the candles on her cake and hugging Harris as she giggled.

Harris opened his eyes. "She's my daughter," he said again. Martha stared a moment, then gave a slow nod.

"She understands," DaJuan said.

"Okay," Harris said. "Let's get down to business."

He projected an image of Martha on the buried ship near the Carlsbad Caverns. He pictured himself, Sarai, DaJuan and Yughi with her. He pictured Martha pressing her hoofed hands into the console, then, for some reason he pictured all of them doing the same in unison. All of them, hands sinking into the console.

Martha gave a mooing grunt. An image struck Harris's mind of only Martha with her hands in the console.

"You don't want us to touch it?" Harris said. "Okay, but can we watch you?"

Martha stared at him.

He closed his eyes again and pictured the images on the Egyptian ship. Images of HH being marched as prisoners onto the ships. Then he pictured the Priestess Zetas dead on the ground outside the ships, pictured the ships empty.

Martha grunted again, and he opened his eyes. She looked as though she was unsure whether he was making a threat.

"No," he said, shaking his head, which he felt she understood now – what shaking his head meant. "This happened. We need to know why they died. Why didn't they leave on these ships? Why did they leave these ships behind?"

He closed his eyes again, pictured an ill Priestess communicating with the console, then dying. Then he focused on the console and whatever report the Priestess had made. He opened his eyes again.

"We don't want you to get sick," he told her. "Information is power. Help us and help yourself."

Sarai stepped out from Harris's side. "We won't hurt you. I promise."

Harris looked at Sarai, then back at Martha.

"We won't hurt you," he said. "I promise."

Carrie sat across the desk from Harkowitz in his office, while Sentinel Aston waited outside the closed door.

"It seems there's a growing contingent of your constituents who want a Mars independent of the UNF," she told him.

"Yes, I'm aware," he said.

"Apparently you were the poster boy for their movement at one point."

Harkowitz glanced at her, then moved his eyes to one of the screens on his desk. "I won't lie. After the invasion, I was thinking heavily about it. With each passing year, the UNF were supposed to be taking a step back." He looked back at her. "That's why they called the presidential elections in the first place, and that's why I took the job. They were supposed to leave Martians to rule Mars, similar to the HOS on earth."

"But given your history in universal politics, you must've known the UNF would still be very present and take an active interest in Mars' decisions. The exact same has happened on the Moon. They have their own president, but the UNF is still very involved."

"Yes. And I see Moon President Gillet has finally announced he's hanging up his boots. Word is, based on Senator Pope's recent visit, is that he's being pushed out by the UNF. That wouldn't have anything to do with his ties to certain elements within the UNF who fell out of favor, would it?"

"I can't comment as I know nothing about that, but I do know it's important to have friends in high places."

"Is that what my presidency is to become?" Harkowitz asked. "A puppet on the UNF's strings, exchanging favors?"

"Colonel Harris does not wish for you to be a puppet. In his brief before I left, he told me that he values your leadership because you'll do what's right for the people, not what's best for you. So, quite the opposite, actually. He knows that you now understand the right thing to do is work with UNF, not against it."

Harkowitz stared at her with a slight smile on his face. He sat back in his chair as he continued to analyze her. "Harris must think highly of you to put you in this post, to be his spokesperson. To be my *protector*."

"Like I said, he values you."

Harkowitz sat forward again. "We seem to have that in common. He went to great lengths to free you from Hell Town."

Carrie nodded. "So, let's not let him down. I'm here because you're not sure who you can trust. I mean, how did folks find out you were unhappy with the UNF in the first place? Your private complaints must've been leaked, right?"

A guilty look shot across Harkowitz's face.

"Who did you voice opinions to?" Carrie asked, sensing something was up.

He sighed and leaned back. He stared at her a moment while his mind ticked over. "I was angry after the invasion. I shared my thoughts with Sam."

"Colonel Greavy?"

He nodded. "But I also may have said things to Senators Butten and Pope and some others."

"What things?"

He sighed again, rubbed his forehead. "There was an event celebrating the opening of an extension of the Mercandez mine. I'd had a few drinks and I... may have voiced some opinions that I shouldn't have."

Carrie nodded to herself. "Opinions against the UNF?"

"Opinions in support of an independent Mars," he admitted. "I was angry I'd been left out in the cold. President Gillet knew about the Zeta threat and I knew nothing. It left me looking powerless in front of my constituents."

"Who was there? Who heard these opinions? Who may have been excited by this, then angry when you changed your tune and toed the line with the UNF?"

"Sam, Senators Butten and Pope, Lotz, a handful of other businessmen."

"Lotz? As in the guy who keeps running against you for president?"

"Yes," Harkowitz gave an awkward nod. "Like I said, not my finest hour."

"Can you give me a full list of the names?"

Harkowitz studied her. "You don't honestly think one of them is behind the threats?"

Carrie shrugged. "What about the soldiers? I've heard there's some dissent among the ranks. Would Greavy be sharing your opinions with his men? How else would they find out?"

Harkowitz shrugged. "Mars is a small place. Word travels fast."

"So, your private gripe to this small group of men at this event, would easily travel through the civilian population?"

Harkowitz nodded. "Most likely."

"We need to stabilize Mars," Carrie said. "You may have swayed people in the wrong direction, so you now need to pull them back. That's one issue. We still have the issue as to who in your camp leaked the news of the Zeta ship off Atlas. And, more importantly, we need to find out whether they were simply providing an inside scoop for monetary gain, or whether they support this vision of an independent Mars and were looking to take you down from the inside."

"Having me ousted is one thing. But death threats?"

Carrie shrugged. "Politics can send some people crazy. All I know is that the Mercandez company just discovered a huge seam of Martian ore that will provide the much needed resources to produce the proxy-steel we need. They have a stranglehold on the market and they want to maximize their profits. A Mars independent of UNF rule will ensure this profit. They don't want to see a friendly president brokering a deal with the UNF to make that ore more affordable for the good of all mankind. If someone's angry enough, they'll take you out to make way for a president who will stand their ground against the UNF. Maybe even blame *us* for not protecting you. They could use your assassination to distance Mars from the UNF."

"It just seems so extreme."

"After the Atlas incident, tempers are flaring. I spoke to the vigilante leaders up in Hell Town. They border on extremism."

"Extremism?"

"Maybe they're not *quite* there yet, but they're close. They left Mars against *your* orders and fired upon the Zeta, and upon our soldiers against *our* orders. That's not a weak threat. That's a *very* real, very extreme threat."

"I understand that, but it's the job of my team to report on and monitor such threats. I've been briefed on the political group Lotz has been forming, seeking Mars independence, and I've heard whispers of those preparing to bear arms if needed. Just like those vigilantes did."

"What if it's more than whispers? What if it's very real and someone inside your camp intentionally kept it from you? The growing extremism? What if they want you to have a blindspot to make you a weaker, easier target." Carrie sat forward. "Mr. President, you have been around politics long enough to know that it's about strategy, and often about smoke and mirrors. I know you don't want to believe in betrayal, but I'm telling you it could be a reality. People can be bought."

Harkowitz sighed. "The only two who would have the reach and the authority to keep any known real extremist threat from me, is Laurelai and Sam. They're the ones responsible for my political and security briefings. Everything goes through them." Harkowitz looked her in the eye. "But I just don't see Laurelai doing that, and Sam has already warned me of the whispers of this armed group. Why would he do that if he wanted them to enact their plans?"

"You can't afford to give anyone the benefit of the doubt, sir. It's not worth your life." Carrie stood. "From this moment on, you cannot be alone with either of them. They may not try to harm you physically themselves, but they can allow others to get close to you who can. If I can't be by your side, then my Sentinels will be."

"I already have Sentinels," he said.

"I'm not trusting anybody. You'll have mine too."

"What about your children?"

"As far as I'm aware, no-one's gunning for them." She headed for the door. "I'm going to dig into your staff and follow up on the *Golden Orb* details again. Haides-1 are being very uncooperative."

Harris walked slowly beside Martha while DaJuan trailed behind, as they approached the *Aurizun*. Despite it now being the early hours of the morning, and the protesters at the gate were small in number, the path they walked was shielded by a canvas covering erected the day before, to protect Martha from the prying eyes of any airborne media with super-zoom lenses. The last thing they wanted was for people to follow them to Carlsbad where the buried ship lay.

They arrived at the entrance to the *Aurizun*, where McKinley waited. They exchanged a nod, then Harris looked at Martha and motioned to McKinley.

"You know you can trust him."

Martha was hesitant to enter. Harris stepped forward and led the way, DaJuan followed him. Martha cautiously stepped aboard the ship, looking about. When her eyes fixed on the UNF Pegasus symbol – the winged horse rearing over the Earth Duty and Space Duty shields – she paused, fascinated. Maybe she recognized herself a little in the Pegasus, or perhaps recognized it as an amalgamation of the Alma Mater and Zisis. Harris realized that so far, she'd only seen humans. He should show her the other mammals of Earth. Perhaps that would encourage her to seek peace, to protect the life on this planet.

"When we're done with the ship, I will show you more of your kind," he said her to her calmly, taking his PDP off his belt and using it to bring up images of cows, horses, sheep, monkeys. Martha stared at them curious. "Your kin," he said gently.

Still fascinated, she followed Harris to the flight deck where the rest of the team were gathered in their seats. They turned to stare at her when she entered. Martha tensed, hesitant again, uneasy at being outnumbered in such a small space. She'd no doubt seen them all while they guarded her at the cells, but outside of her interaction with Evenssen and Yughiarto, she'd not mingled with them before.

Yughiarto slowly got up from his seat and moved toward her. He bowed gently in greeting and held his arm out to motion her toward a seat. Martha stared at him a moment. She looked at Harris and suddenly an image flashed inside his mind, of Yughi on the Zeta ship's flight deck, guiding Harris and Carrie as they tried to connect with the ship.

Harris nodded at Martha.

"Yes," he said, "Yughi's been on the Zeta ships before."

"I saw that…" Yughi seemed surprised, but mostly contained it.

"She projected?" Evenssen asked. "She did that with me too."

Harris realized he needed to share the news of the node with the team, sooner rather than later. Just not now. He smiled. "She likes you, Yughi. That's good."

Martha looked back at Yughi, then followed his outstretched arm.

By the time Harris attempted formal introductions to all his team members and settled Martha in a seat, Morrell had arrived.

"Special delivery," he said, with Sarai by his side.

"Dad?" she said nervously as Martha looked around at her.

Harris moved to Sarai and hugged her. "Hey, honey." He crouched down in front of her. "Thanks for coming. We're going to board a buried Zeta ship today and see if Martha can help us connect to it. I might need you. Is that alright?"

Sarai nodded.

Harris glanced at Martha and saw she was staring at Morrell. The Earth Duty soldier noticed, and stared back at her.

"Tess has told her a lot about you," Harris said to Morrell.

"No doubt," Morrell responded, as Harris looked back at Sarai.

"Everything's going to be fine," Harris told her, "but if anything bad should happen, you don't have to worry because my soldiers will protect you with their lives. Okay?"

Sarai nodded.

Brown, sitting nearby, gave her a wink. "We got you, girl."

"Amen," said Tikaani. "Ain't nothing gonna touch you, honey."

Sarai smiled, as McKinley stepped forward.

"You wanna sit in the captain's seat?" he asked.

Sarai's grin grew wider and McKinley held out his real hand. She took it and he led her to his chair and strapped her in.

"Captain Sarai Harris," McKinley smiled. "It's got a nice ring to it."

Harris looked to his pilots. "Alright, Hunter, prepare for takeoff." Then he looked at Morrell. "Retract the covered walkway before Hunter incinerates it."

Morrell gave a nod and departed.

Harris moved to Martha, whom he'd intentionally seated beside another woman, being Tikaani, and projected an image of the ship taking off. She gave a nod in understanding.

"Alright," he said, strapping in beside her. "Let's do this."

Carrie sat in her small designated Red House office. Harkowitz had granted her access to his employee records, so Carrie was perusing the files and quietly listing names for Archie to start his own files on. She'd opted to carry Archie's discs in her pocket again, much preferring that to wearing them in her neck, despite his protestations otherwise.

A knock at the door startled her and she shut down the screen. Colonel Greavy entered.

"You got a moment?" he asked.

"Sure," Carrie said.

He entered and closed the door behind him, approaching her desk. "You made an enquiry at the Mars Docking Station for records on the *Golden Orb*?"

"Yeah," she said.

"I thought the Mercandez company was supplying that?"

"So did I, but after repeated requests I've received nothing, so I took matters into my own hands."

"You didn't think to run this by me first?" he asked.

"Why should I?"

"Because I'm the ruling soldier on Mars."

She conceded a nod. "I understand that, but Colonel Harris, who although of the same rank, actually rests higher on the totem pole than you, asked me to look into something for him, so that's what I'm doing."

Greavy stared at her. "You're asking a lot of questions about things that go beyond simple Mars-UNF relations."

"As I said, I'm looking into something for Colonel Harris."

"I oversee Mars and the president. It's my job to be across things. What's this about?"

"As a soldier you know that some things are classified whether we like it or not."

"What could be classified about Mars that I don't already know?"

Carrie sat back in her chair. "That's a very good question..." She studied him a moment, wondered whether to play her cards. "Do you know who was on the *Golden Orb* the day we escorted the Zeta back to Earth?"

"Last I checked it wasn't illegal to fly to Earth."

"Don't you think it's odd they were following a Zeta ship? And this occurred right after a series of vigilante ships attacked Atlas?"

Greavy shrugged. "Major Gold oversees Atlas. That's outside of my control."

"But Mars isn't. And the vigilantes came from Mars. You just told me it's your job to be across things here. What are you doing about the rise of the independent Mars movement?"

Greavy put his hands on his hips like he was bored. "Just like on Earth, it's not against the law to create your own political party with your own policies, no matter how questionable they are."

"What about those preparing to take up arms for the cause?"

Greavy stared at her.

"You're being very blasé about this," she said. "You just said it's your job to ensure Mars remains peaceful and that the president is protected."

"He currently is. You sticking your nose in and stirring things up without my knowledge puts that in jeopardy."

"What about the death threats?" she asked. "They were there before I came along."

"Is that why you're here?" he asked, eyes narrowed.

Carrie stared at him, but didn't answer.

"The president has received threats for some time," Greavy said. "Nothing has ever come of them."

"But you felt the need to put Sentinels on him."

"Yes. Because it's my job to ensure he remains safe."

Carrie sat forward. "Something's not aligning here. You're talking the talk, and walking the walk, but I feel like something's missing."

Greavy dropped his hands and stepped right up to her desk. "I have known the president for a long time. He is a friend. I do not take his safety lightly. Understand? If anything, *he* does."

"In what way?"

"He often tells me I'm overreacting about his safety." He leaned over the table and lowered his voice. "After the invasion, he wanted to pull away from the UNF and *I* was the one who pulled him back. A Mars Colonial Force sounds great until you look at the numbers. If the Zetas came back we'd be annihilated."

Carrie studied him a moment. "And, in the future, once Mars does have the numbers?"

Greavy stared at her for a moment, his eyes cold as steel. "That's a long time away," he said, then raised his PDP. "Now, you enquired about the *Golden Orb*?" He tapped at his PDP, then sent her the information. She felt her own PDP chime as the information hit. He looked back at her. "You may be working for Colonel Harris, but if you do not respect my authority here on Mars, we're going to have a problem. Like you said, I'm in charge of the president's safety and if you're not going to share information about what you're doing here, then I will be forced to remove you from the Red House."

Carrie stared back at him with equally cool eyes. "And do you think the president and Colonel Harris will agree with you?"

"I will not have a second lieutenant order me around on my own turf. Understood? Know your place!"

He turned and left the room, closing the door firmly behind him.

Carrie looked at her PDP and pulled up the MDS record of the *Golden Orb*'s departure and its list of passengers.

Kellan van Pelt – Mars Media.

Two pilots – Glenn Carlton and Hope Fisher.

Orb crew – Mark Abrams, Costya Ware, An Sun, Foster Tessier.

Carrie read the names quietly to Archie. "Do a search on those names," she ordered. "I want full employment records, criminal records and any possible links to those on the president's staff or the vigilantes."

"*Yes, lieutenant.*" Archie replied. He'd been calling her that ever since they'd been in the Red House, as opposed to the usual "Miss Welles" that he did in the privacy of the Fortress.

Carrie heard laughter, yelling and running footsteps. It was Jesse's voice. She walked to the door, opened it and saw Jesse and Freya were sprinting down the corridor. Jesse tackled Freya and they skidded to the ground, while Brody watched on, laughing. Freya grabbed Jesse, holding him down and tickling him. Jesse screeched.

"Hey!" Carrie called out to them. "*Hey!* Not up here! You want to play, go play in the apartment!"

"We were just exploring," Brody said.

"Playing hide and seek," Freya said.

"We're bored," Jesse said.

"No," Carrie said firmly, "this is the Red House. This is not a place for playing. Downstairs. *Now.*"

They slumped their shoulders and walked away.

Carrie started to wonder if she'd need more help. Usually her Sentinels would be watching the kids and keeping them in line, but right now she only had two and she'd shifted their remit to watching over the president when she wasn't with him.

She sighed and headed back to her desk, feeling unsure about her conversation with Greavy. He was being guarded, but she understood his reaction with someone coming on his turf and keeping him out in the cold. And if what he said was true, that it was him who had pulled Harkowitz back from the idea of separating from the UNF, then was Greavy *not* the one betraying the president? Or did he just pull Harkowitz back because the timing wasn't right? Because it was too early?

She turned back to her screen, reopened the staff files, and continued to dig.

23

Natural Habitat

Harris tempered his frustration, squeezing Sarai's hand and giving her a smile, noticing that faint vibration again. It was taking a painfully long time to get Martha anywhere as she was naturally very hesitant and cautious, but also very curious, taking in everything she saw, fascinated.

They'd held their breath mid-flight when Martha had stood from her seat and moved right up to the flight deck console. Harris reminded everyone to stay calm as she literally peered over the shoulders of Hunter and Frazer to study how they flew the ship, probably finding the *Aurizun* somewhat archaic in comparison to the advanced Zeta fleet. The pilots kept their cool, exchanging a glance between themselves, but carrying on as normal until Martha, satisfied, returned to her seat.

It then took more time to get her moving from their landed ship in the dark of night, where Dr. Ross and Lieutenant Colberge met them, eager to witness the Zeta connect to its ship. With more and more humans around her, Harris could sense the tension in Martha, so he took his time to introduce her to these new faces, to assure her she was safe and they meant her no harm. Ross wore a plain, button-up shirt, and cargo trousers, whilst Colberge stood tall and lean in his Space Duty uniform, pushing his round glasses up the bridge of his nose.

Harris left Brown and Tikaani guarding the *Aurizun* while the rest of them led Martha into the mountains, then to the secret passage where the tunnel entrance was located, which led to the buried ship. Harris had then left Evenssen and Steinberg to guard the tunnel entrance, as the rest moved down the sloping tunnel toward the ship, Martha continuing to be very cautious, absorbing everything.

If they didn't hurry it would soon be daylight.

They finally reached the ship's entrance. Dr. Ross had hurried ahead to ready things for their arrival, lights illuminating the scene. Not that the Alphas needed that, but the humans – Ross, Colberge, Sarai and DaJuan – did, and as far as they knew the Zetas couldn't see in the dark either, something he made a note of to ask Dr. Serquey when he saw her next.

"McKinley," Harris said, "you stay out here. The rest with me."

Martha stopped at the door, looking around at Harris hesitantly. He passed her with Sarai and entered the ship, motioning for Martha to follow. They stepped aboard and DaJuan paused, taking in the sight of the strange Zeta ship.

"Holy shit," he whispered, "this is radical, man."

Harris smiled. "It's quite a sight, huh?"

"It's awe-inspiring," Colberge smiled. "Such amazing technology."

DaJuan nodded, blue dreadlocks rattling, as Frazer and Sarai, also seeing it for the first time, gaped.

While Martha took her time examining potential threats, Harris had his team spread out as best they could in the small flight deck. Harris wanted their thoughts afterward, if Martha connected with the ship: Hunter and Frazer as his pilots, Yughi as his comms-tech, DaJuan and Sarai for a second pair of "eyes" in case Martha projected, and Ross and Colberge for their existing knowledge of the Zeta ships.

Martha stepped inside the crowded flight deck carefully. Harris, still holding Sarai's hand, moved over to the console. He ran his fingers across the surface, seeing the faint blue light beneath his fingers.

"Whoa..." Colberge said in amazement.

"You haven't seen that in the ships you're studying?" Harris arched his eyebrow in question.

Colberge shook his head. "We've not been able to restore power to any of the crashed ships, and I've not seen anyone do that to any of the buried ones."

Harris looked at Sarai and motioned for her to do the same. She did, the light much more vibrant beneath her small fingers.

"Brighter than Welles," Yughi said quietly.

Harris nodded. "And mine."

"She's got the Xs we need," Hunter said.

Colberge stepped up to the console lip and touched it with his fingertips. The console remained gray and lifeless. He looked at Harris. "It must respond to you because of whatever gift you have that enables you to communicate with the Zetas."

"Something like that," Harris said, watching the brighter light emanate from beneath Sarai's fingertips.

"We'll definitely need female pilots to crack these," Hunter said, watching Sarai, too.

"Female pilots with the Zeta DNA," Harris said.

"How many female pilots you think we've got with that?" Frazer asked.

"Not many," Harris said. "If any."

A thought struck Harris. He pictured Freya and suddenly wondered whether she'd inherited the node from Welles. She was already showing a natural affinity for piloting. Could she fly one of these one day? He'd have to check on her node and DNA markers.

Martha studied the light beneath Sarai's fingers. The Zeta stepped closer to her. Again, everyone held their breath, wondering how Martha was going to react to them trying to connect with the ship. After all, in their dreams, she'd been against it.

Martha moved closer again to the console, staring at Harris. She projected an image of a Priestess at the helm of the ship in which they stood.

"Yes," Harris said to her, "this belonged to a Priestess."

Martha projected the same image. Sarai looked at him.

"I think she's trying to tell you, this isn't her ship."

"I know," Harris said, "but—"

Another image flashed inside his mind. The green leathery hands of a Priestess on the console. Harris looked back at Martha as Sarai placed her hand on the console again. Martha brayed vehemently at her. Harris pulled Sarai's hand off, as the team stared at him for answers.

"I just saw a Priestess' hands on the console."

"What does that mean?" Frazer asked.

"Maybe she can't get inside?" Yughi said. "Maybe only a Priestess can?"

"*Any* Priestess?" Hunter asked. "Or only the one that flew it here?"

"It could be coded to their specific DNA or handprints," Colberge nodded. "Or even their specific Thought Biology."

Martha appeared uneasy as she looked around.

"She really doesn't like it here," Harris said.

Ross stepped forward. "What if it's to do with the illness?" he posited. "What if she detects the illness here that killed the Zeta who flew on this ship?"

Harris looked at him curiously. Ross glanced between him and Martha.

"She's wary," Ross said, "that's all I know."

"We need to try and connect," Harris said. "Sarai, get on the opposite side to me from Martha." She did. "Put your hands on the console. Close your eyes. Yughi is going to help us meditate and see if we can't get inside. I wanna see if Martha joins in." Harris glanced around at the others. "Hunter, Frazer, keep an eye on her. If she looks like she's going to attack…"

Hunter nodded, subtly took a step closer, placing his hand on the tranq gun he carried. Frazer did, too.

Harris placed both hands on the console and Sarai mirrored him. They closed their eyes as Yughi began to meditate with them.

Minutes passed as Harris and Sarai pressed their hands against the console.

"Picture your hands becoming one with the console," Yughi said quietly. "Breathe in… Breathe out…"

"She's moving closer," Hunter said quietly.

"You are one with the console," Yughi continued. "Breathe in… Breathe out…"

Harris felt Martha's hot breath against his cheek.

"Picture yourself inside the Zeta console," Yughi said calmly. "Look for a way to connect…"

Martha gave a whine. Harris couldn't tell if it was through excitement, fear, or anger.

"Find a way to communicate with the ship," Yughi said. "Breathe in… Breathe out…"

"Her hands are on the console," Ross said quietly.

"I'm going to project," Harris told them. He pictured Martha connecting with him and Sarai in the console, pictured star maps, pictured the Zeta ship flying.

Martha projected back. He saw her fellow Zetas standing on their silver sands. Then he suddenly felt as though he were falling. Deep, deep down into blackness. Next, he and Sarai were standing on the flight deck beside a Priestess. Several Priestesses. The ship was shaking, throwing them about as though they were experiencing an earthquake, then everything stopped. The spaceship door opened and he saw a wall of rock, and grains of sand and small rocks tumble inside. He saw blasts of a powerful heat ray, and a tunnel was cleared. He watched as the Priestesses left the ship and walked down the tunnel toward sunlight. Then, he felt time passing. He didn't know how, but he saw or felt the Earth spinning and the sun rising and lowering beneath horizons. Repeatedly, swiftly. Then suddenly a Priestess returned. She looked ill, but managed to lay traps outside the door, before locking itself inside. Holed up on the ship, the Priestess became more ill, before she collapsed on the flight deck floor. Then, Harris watched, horrified, as the creature immolated itself, turning its heat ray weapon inward until all that remained was the blackened charred remains. Next, more time passed, as he saw the Priestess slowly decompose into the silver sand, mixing with the Earth sand already spilled on the floor.

Then he saw, clear as day, Martha there. She stood over the pile of sand and looked at him, her eyes, questioning.

Then her eyes went wide and she gave a frightening mooing bray.

Harris flicked open his eyes, saw Martha's hoofed hands rise in the air over his head. In a flash, Hunter's tranq gun was out.

Harris waved him down. "No! No!"

Martha turned and charged toward Hunter, who held his gun firm.

"Hunter, move!" Harris yelled, as McKinley appeared in the doorway at the commotion.

Hunter swiftly slid aside, and Martha bent over the spot where the silver sand had been.

Harris, panting, looked at Ross. "When you found this ship, was there a pile of sand here?"

"I—I..." Ross stuttered with fright, trying to remember, as Martha paced agitatedly. "I believe there was rock debris. Thought to have been carried in from outside when they cleared the tunnel."

Harris held his hands out calmly to Martha. "It's okay. Stay calm," he told her, then looked at Ross. "It wasn't debris. It was the remains of the Zeta this ship belonged to. Where is it now?"

Ross' face paled. "Er, I believe most was swept outside. But a sample would've been collected and stored away."

Harris looked at him. "Study that sample and you might find just what killed this Zeta, though be warned, it turned the heat ray on itself."

Ross nodded with surprise as Martha continued to pace, agitated, in her confined space.

"Dad?" Sarai said.

Harris looked at his daughter as she pushed past him and moved carefully to Martha.

"Sarai, be careful," he warned her.

"She's just worried," Sarai said, moving up to Martha and holding out her hand. "It's okay. We didn't mean to scare you."

Martha studied her outstretched hand, calming a little.

"We just want to help," Sarai said.

Martha continued to study her hand, before slowing raising her own. Everyone held their breath, watching as Martha placed her hoofed-hand on Sarai's.

Sarai suddenly gasped and her eyes went wide. Martha's, too, as they connected.

"Close your eyes," DaJuan urged Harris, "join them!"

Harris closed his eyes, but before they could connect, Sarai cried out. His eyes flashed open and he saw Sarai on the ground.

He rushed toward her, placing himself between the two. "Sarai!"

His daughter latched on to him.

"It's okay!" he said, glancing back to ensure Martha wasn't coming for them.

"It was the connection," Yughi said quickly. "It wasn't Martha hurting her. It must've been powerful."

Harris scooped Sarai up and quickly passed her to Frazer. "Get her back to the ship."

Frazer nodded, took her and left.

"Martha didn't mean to hurt her," Yughi said.

"No," DaJuan agreed, "the connection was strong. It surprised them both. She didn't expect that from our race and not from a child."

"What does that mean?" Harris said, eyeing Martha carefully.

"It means there's great potential for Sarai," DaJuan said in awe.

"That's great," Colberge said keenly. "We haven't learnt anything new about their ships, but maybe Sarai can find out for us?"

"Maybe," Harris said. "We might not have learnt anything more about their ships, but we might've learnt more about what killed them."

"I'll recall the stored sample immediately," Ross said, "compare it with the findings on the skulls."

"Good," Harris said.

"Do you…" Ross swallowed, staring at Martha who still appeared agitated. "Do you think we could ask Martha about these?" He pulled up a series of images on his PDP and showed Harris. He saw the metallic coin, the marble idol and the gold chain. Harris took the PDP and moved carefully toward Martha and showed her.

"Did these come from your people?" he asked her.

She stared at the images, then looked back at Harris.

An image shot into his mind. He saw a Priestess holding the coin, placing it on the body of a dead alien creature on some faraway planet. Then he saw other coins, left on other bodies, the shine of the metal gleaming here and there across a battlefield, across a planet. He suddenly wondered whether that coin was made of the Zetan metal. He was certain of one thing, though.

"It's not a coin," he told Dr. Ross. "It's not money. It's… I think it's a calling card of sorts. Or a marker to lay claim to what's theirs. I just saw the Priestess leaving them on the dead bodies of their victims."

"And the idol?" he asked.

Harris pointed to the marble idol, in which he could definitely see the resemblance to Martha's kind.

Another image thrust into his mind. He saw the idol being passed to a Zeta child. An Alma Mater child.

"It was a gift," Harris said, as the image played out in his mind. "Given to a child."

"A doll of sorts?" Ross thought aloud. "Human-like behaviour. The chain?"

Harris showed Martha the chain next. She looked at it, then back at him her face blank, no images thrust into his mind.

"She doesn't know," he said.

"A mystery," Ross said.

"Perhaps we should be asking Tess about that?" Yughi suggested.

Harris nodded. He saw the time on Ross' PDP, then glanced around. "We better get Martha back before daylight and someone sees us."

Carrie walked beside President Harkowitz as he did the rounds, shaking hands, at the grand opening of a new hab complex on the outskirts of Brahe, located near the colony's dome wall. She found it interesting that Regan Lotz was behind the development, yet the president had been invited to cut the ribbon.

The complex was definitely an upgrade from the digs Carrie had stayed in the last time she was in Brahe with Harris, McKinley and Steinberg, some 12 years ago, after the Pegasus mission. This new complex had a nice modern reception area that led to elevators which took residents underground to where the apartments were. All the underground habs were two-bedroom apartments, built around the elevator and a stairwell core. Simply furnished, each apartment came with a periscope that enabled residents to check the outside weather on their TV screens. After all, the miners, engineers, and scientists needed to know what was going on outside those domes. If a dust storm was coming, they needed to be prepared. Regardless, this complex marked a notable shift in Mars colonization. No longer was the accommodation being designed to suit Fly-in/Fly-out workers, but now the colony was established enough, it was ready to welcome the workers and their families permanently. And as Harkowitz said in his brief opening speech that night, it signified a new era of Mars. A shift away from the Wild West stereotype it had been stuck with, to one of a welcoming, family-friendly community, no different from that on Earth.

As they made their way through the small crowd, Sentinel Aston stuck close to them, his eyes constantly surveilling everyone around them, while Sampson hung back at Carrie's request. Carrie did much the same as the

Sentinels, glancing around at everyone, and she was surprised when Harkowitz made a beeline for Regan Lotz, the man who wanted his job.

"Regan," Harkowitz smiled, extending his hand to shake with his competitor. "Congratulations on the hab complex. It looks fantastic."

"Thank you," Lotz shook his hand. "I like to put my money where my mouth is and deliver a future the Martian people want."

Harkowitz smiled politely, his eyes sparkling with competition. "As do I," he said, "which is why you invited the president here to give you the seal of approval before the constituents."

Lotz laughed politely, those around them doing likewise, as Harkowitz moved on to the next person. Carrie watched Lotz's face. She saw his eyes narrow as he watched the president move off, saw loathing flash in his eyes, but they cooled quickly when his gaze met hers.

She extended her hand to him. "Second Lieutenant Welles-McKinley."

He shook her hand. "Regan Lotz."

She gave a nod, as they dropped hands. "Owner of the All Mart *and* Space Mart franchises now, I hear? Not to mention a successful businessman in other affairs, such as this apartment complex, presidential candidate, *and* married to the heiress of the Khalid fortune."

"You've done your research."

"I have."

"As have I," he said. "You were recently released from Hell Town where you were on a murder charge, laid by the UNF. Now you're in great favor with the UNF and residing in the Red House under the guise of UNF-Mars relations. Why is that? You must have some dirt on them?" He smiled.

Carrie smiled back. "It's simple. I was incarcerated hastily and erroneously, and hence, swiftly exonerated."

Lotz studied her. "And you're married to Major McKinley," he said, with a curious tone. "The hero of the Command Uprising."

She smiled. "He was *one* of the heroes, yes."

"That must've helped with your new status, being married to a hero."

Carrie chuckled. "Well, you know that old saying: behind every great man there's an even greater woman. I mean, isn't that true for you and your wife, and her money?"

Lotz chuckled back. His eyes narrowed again. "Touché, Mrs. McKinley."

"Welles-McKinley," she corrected him.

"Daughter of Original, Jeffrey Welles," he said.

"Yes," Carrie nodded, wondering if the guy knew the size of her underwear, too. He'd done as much research as she had.

"I'm sorry for your loss," he said. "I heard he was killed during the invasion."

"He was. But thank you for your condolences."

"Can I buy you a drink?" he asked. "You have me intrigued."

"And you, I," she said, glancing over to catch Sampson's eye. She motioned for him to continue to shadow Harkowitz with Aston, then turned back to Lotz.

"Champagne?" he asked.

"Vodka," she said.

He quirked an eyebrow then turned to a waiter and placed an order. He turned back to Carrie.

"So, what brings you to Mars? I mean, I know it's UNF-Mars relations, but what does that mean exactly?"

"What?" Carrie feigned shock. "You haven't found that out yet?"

Lotz laughed. "No, but I have my theories."

Harris sat on the side of the bed in McKinley's quarters on the *Aurizun*. Frazer and McKinley had put Sarai there to keep her away from Martha. Frazer was now back on the flight deck, preparing to take them back to Command, while McKinley stood watching Harris and Sarai from the doorway.

"Where is she?" Sarai asked, looking scared and very much a child, filling Harris's heart with guilt for exposing her to the dangerous Zetas.

"She's on the flight deck. We'll keep you two apart for a while. Tell me what happened when you connected?"

Sarai looked down at her hand, rubbing it with the other. "It hurt."

Harris nodded. "Was it like a zap of static electricity?"

Sarai nodded. He took her hand in his and felt a sharp zap, had to stop himself from gasping at the sensation. He'd felt the tingling before with Sarai, but nothing this strong. Again, the guilt smacked at him. What had he just awakened in her by letting her touch Martha?

"Did you see anything, Sarai?" he asked.

Sarai thought for a moment. "I don't know."

"Describe it to me?"

"I'm not sure it was anything… It was all black. And there were green vines. No… green *veins*. And lightning. Cracks of light in the distance."

Harris trawled his mind as memories surfaced. He recalled a dream he'd had with sparks of lightning.

He nodded. "You know, when I came into the realization of my gift, I had a dream like that. Sparks of lightning." He hugged Sarai. "I don't think it's anything to be worried about. I think it's just like a doorway opening."

"A doorway to Martha?"

"A doorway to your gift," he told her. "Those sparks of lightning, I think, is the electricity in your brain awakening your gift more fully. Like…" Harris thought for a moment, "like when your conscious mind becomes aware and realizes what your subconscious has known all this time."

"And the green vines and veins?"

Harris thought for a moment. "Maybe that's the connective tissue. The neurons talking to each other."

"And awakening the node," McKinley said from the doorway.

Harris looked at him.

"Sarai's never had a scan has she?" McKinley asked.

Harris shook his head.

"If you want to track what connecting with Martha is doing to her, you'd better get a scan so you can set a baseline."

Harris nodded. "We need your kids done too. Especially Freya."

McKinley gave him a questioning look.

"She's Welles's daughter," Harris said simply. "If there's a chance she's inherited the node, we need to boost it."

McKinley nodded in thought, and Harris looked back at Sarai. He gave her a warm smile and hugged her again. "You did good today, honey. Real good. What's happening is nothing to be scared of. It just means you're becoming more like me."

Carrie listened with interest as Lotz spoke of his dreams for the future of Mars. He was passionate, she'd give him that, but there was something about his passion that left Carrie a little cold. It was obviously the same thing that Harris sensed too, that made him want to keep Harkowitz in the president's seat. Lotz was passionate about the future of Mars, but Carrie could draw clear lines to how each of Lotz's businesses would benefit as a result of what he was proposing. She heard him talk of buildings and construction and mining, and on paper it would look like a prosperous Mars. But the truth is, it would also mean a prosperous Lotz. He wanted to build an empire – his *own* empire. Harkowitz had no personal business empire, he was a "lifer" in politics. Harkowitz building a better Mars would be for the benefit of everyone.

"That sounds very interesting," she told Lotz. "You have grand plans for Mars."

"The quicker we shed this Wild West image the better. Mars needs a makeover to attract a better clientele to become a more prosperous place to live." His eyes caught on someone and waved them over.

Carrie turned to see a solidly-built man, in his late 40s, approaching. It looked as though he'd been talking to Ron McCaulay, the Ops Manager from Haides-1. McCaulay saw Carrie and gave a nod. She nodded back, before he disappeared into the crowd. She wanted to yell after him that she got the records for the *Golden Orb*, no thanks to him, but left it alone.

Lotz's associate shook hands with him.

"Jensen Faber, this is Second Lieutenant *Welles*-McKinley," he said, emphasizing the Welles.

Faber looked at her, then held out his hand.

"Faber?" she asked, shaking his hand. "Any relation to Dominic?"

"He's my son," he said dropping her hand. "I believe you met him recently?"

Carrie nodded, her mind turning over. "I did. In Hell Town."

"You should be giving my son a bravery medal, not locking him up like a criminal."

Carrie glanced at Lotz. "Was this a setup?"

Lotz shrugged. "We all must answer hard questions sometimes. I believe he deserves some answers."

Carrie smiled. "Well, as part of the UNF, I don't owe your son anything after he fired on our soldiers."

Faber stepped toward her, leaning closer to her face. "They nearly killed my boy in order to protect that alien."

She smelled the wine on his breath. "The UNF was forced to take action because your boy tried to kill an alien who came here in peace."

"Bullshit!" he said leaning back. "All these rumors that the UNF can communicate with them. *Bullshit*! Fuck these scientists. What do they know?"

"Quite a lot, actually," Carrie said.

"We can all gather the proof we need to support our arguments."

"Scientists gather data and facts, not—"

"The governments and the military will parade science around when it suits their needs. They hide behind it, but we know they're lying. It's to control the people. They want to control Mars, so they are coming up with these bullshit stories to get us into line. Well guess what? We're not falling for their bullshit!"

Carrie glanced at Lotz, then back at Faber. "So, let me guess… Mr. Lotz, there, is the answer you're looking for. If he becomes president, you'll get the independence you want?"

"Damn straight. He's the only one trying to develop Mars for the people."

"For a price."

Lotz feigned an arrow to the chest. "Come now, we all have to eat. Is a man not allowed to make a profit while helping pull this planet out of the shit pile?"

Faber pointed at her. "You need to release my son and the others, or there will be problems."

"Is that a threat, sir?" she asked.

"No, it's a promise. You think I'm the only one unhappy about what happened. There are *many* of us. Enough to swing the vote Mr. Lotz's way. Harkowitz is on borrowed time. And when Lotz gets in, you and the UNF will be out." He hiked his thumb sideways.

"That definitely sounds like a threat," Carrie said. "Do you think it's wise to threaten a member of the UNF as well as a president?"

"Now, now," Lotz said, playfully slapping Faber's back. "Jensen is just being passionate. It's the red wine talking."

"Oh, I'm serious," Faber said. "We're done listening to the government's lies and its pandering to the UNF. Word is, Harkowitz knew shit when that invasion happened. He's not in control here. He's a puppet. A 'yes' man. We're not stupid and we're not eating up your lies. Feel free to tell the UNF that."

Faber walked off into the small crowd, knocking Carrie's shoulder as he did, though she saw it coming and held Alpha strong. She didn't move, but Faber did – around her, with a surprised look on his face.

"I can see where Dominic gets his sunny personality from," Carrie said to Lotz.

"Like I said, passionate," Lotz said.

"No, he's not. He's an idiot. And I did not take a smart man like you to be associating with idiots."

"A constituent is a constituent, and they all deserve to be heard."

"Or used for votes to gain power," Carrie said then stepped closer to Lotz. "But answer this, Mr. Lotz. What happens when they get you into power, and you fail to deliver on the crazy things they want you to do? I'll tell you what, they'll turn on you. Just like they're turning on Harkowitz now because he's not doing what they want." She stepped back. "It's a dangerous move, Mr. Lotz. You lay down with dogs, you're gonna get fleas."

She turned and headed for Harkowitz.

McKinley and Harris stood in the Command elevator taking them below ground, to what they had taken to calling "the Alpha suites". They were also taking Sarai for a brain scan with Dr. Bakshi.

They stepped out of the elevator and began walking down the corridor when McKinley saw his psych, Dr. Getty approaching them quickly.

"Major McKinley," she said, her face serious.

"Did I miss an appointment?" he asked curiously.

She darted her eyes to Harris and Sarai. "I need a word. I have some news regarding your mother, Grace."

Harris shot them both a glance, then continued on with Sarai, glancing back over his shoulder.

"What is it?" McKinley asked Getty.

"Let's find a room—"

"What's happened?" McKinley asked firmly. "Just tell me."

Getty softened her eyes. "We received word that she's suffered a stroke." She reached out and clasped his shoulder. "She's not good. They think you should head to see her immediately."

McKinley felt his face fall. He stared at Getty, numb.

She squeezed his shoulder gently. His real shoulder.

"Go, lieutenant," she urged him. "Go while you can. If the worst happens, you'll be glad you did this."

McKinley nodded vacantly, but stood there. He glanced down the corridor, saw Harris had stopped and was staring back at him. Harris whispered something to Sarai, then left her and headed back to him.

"What's wrong?" Harris asked, looking from McKinley's face to Getty's.

When McKinley didn't answer, Getty did. "Major McKinley's mother has had a stroke. It's serious. He should go and see her. Immediately."

"Fuck," Harris exhaled, looking at McKinley. "I'm sorry. Go. Do what you have to."

McKinley felt the blood rushing out of his body, felt his real arm starting to shake. "What about... about everything we just did... we gotta do?"

"I'll handle it," Harris said firmly, looking him in the eye. "Go."

"I'll call you later to check in, major," Dr. Getty said, then left.

Harris stepped closer and squeezed McKinley's upper arm. "Go. I dropped everything when my mother was on her deathbed and it was the best thing I did. Go. Trust me. You only get one shot at this before it's too late."

McKinley nodded, a strange sense of déjà vu washing over him. Harris had said similar words to him when Freya was born. And he'd been right.

He nodded, then turned and headed for the elevator, feeling as empty as a ghost.

24

Phone Home

Carrie sat in the *Mars Force One* spacecraft as it zoomed back toward the Red House from Colony Brahe. She watched as Laurelai debriefed with Harkowitz and he gave her instructions on who to set meetings up with, based on his conversations that evening. Laurelai gave a nod and disappeared into the back of the craft, leaving Carrie alone with Harkowitz. She glanced back after Laurelai and saw Sentinel Aston through the doorway, sitting in the next cabin, watching her.

"So, I saw you talking with Lotz tonight," Harkowitz said. "How did you find him?"

Carrie turned back to Harkowitz, thought for a moment. "Ambitious."

Harkowitz chuckled. "Yes, he is absolutely that. It's why he's been so successful. When he started no-one thought he'd ever dominate Charles Mortimer in the space service station business, but *boy*, did he ever. Enough to drive Mortimer to retirement."

Carrie nodded. "I hope his success is down to his smarts and not just a lot of promised favors and underhanded dealings."

"What do you mean by that?"

Carrie sighed. "There's been plenty of leaders on Earth who've come into power because they promised a lot of things to a lot of people. For their own gain they've come into power, and they've wound up screwing over most of the population because of the stupid promises they made to get there."

"And you think Lotz falls into this category?"

"I don't think he's stupid… but I do think he needs to be careful of the supporters he's gathering."

"Such as?"

"I met Jensen Faber tonight. He's Dominic's father. The captain of the *Alexi* vigilante ship."

"Yes, I've been told they've been donating to the Mars Independent Party. It wouldn't surprise me if Lotz was using their zeal to push some negative press my way."

"It's not just negative press you should be worried about. These are the kinds of guys who, when given too long a leash, will resort to violence if they think they can get away with it. If they think they'll be protected by those in power."

"You're thinking they're behind the death threats?"

"I don't know yet, but they fit the profile."

Harkowitz sighed and loosened his tie. "Lotz is ambitious, but I don't think he'd resort to violence. It's not his style. He wants to humiliate me, run me through the mud. That would give him more satisfaction than seeing me dead. He wants to win the presidency in his own right, whether that involves a smear campaign or not," Harkowitz shrugged, "that's politics, that's the game play. I don't think he'd want to win by default because I was murdered. He's the kind who likes to conquer, to be the victor while the loser watches. Like he's had to do that past two times he ran against me."

Carrie studied Harkowitz, wondered herself if maybe he was becoming too soft, too comfortable. If he was going to remain president he needed to be a tiger. A *charming* tiger, but a tiger nonetheless. "Exactly. Lotz has tried and failed a couple of times now to win the seat. He can't afford to lose again, or *he* risks serious humiliation. You say he wants to see you lose face, but he's the one who keeps losing face and missing the seat. Who knows just what lengths his ego will go to finally get his win."

Harkowitz stared at her, his mind busy. He didn't respond, but she could tell he was taking her words under consideration.

Laurelai came back into the main cabin. "Mr. President? The contracts are ready for you," she tapped the datapane she carried. "In your portal, sir."

"Thank you," Harkowitz said, standing. "Excuse me," he said to Carrie and moved into the rear cabin.

Laurelai took a seat and continued tapping at her datapane.

"How do you think tonight went?" Carrie asked her.

Laurelai looked up. "Good. It's important the president be seen supporting progress."

"Do you think it's strange that he was invited given Lotz's involvement in the project?"

"Not at all," she smiled. "Mars might be growing but it's still a small place. They run into each other all the time. It's unavoidable. They're amicable in public."

"And what do you think of this Mars independence movement? Do you think it has legs?"

Laurelai considered this a moment, then shrugged. "If you'd asked me before Lotz agreed to head them up, I would've said no, but now? Anything is possible. People change. Societies change. Minds change. That's unavoidable. The cold hard truth is, we adapt or we die."

"And what happens to you if Harkowitz loses his seat?"

Laurelai paused and looked at her curiously. "We're not going to let that happen."

"But if it does?"

She considered this seriously. "I'd like to think I have a lot to offer. I'm still young enough to have a long career ahead of me. I'll land on my feet."

"Between you and I," Carrie said, lowering her voice and leaning toward her. "Has Harkowitz lost power? Do you think he's lost steam with the people?"

"Lost steam?"

"You've worked for him for a long time. You know him well. Know the man he was when he first became president. Know the man he is now. As you said, times have changed. Is he the kind to sail with the wind, or is he fighting against the inevitable?"

Again, Laurelai considered her question. "Times have definitely changed, but it's our job to move with it, not against it. The president relies on me to help grease the gears when they start to seize. So, we grease the gears when they need it, we pivot when we must, and we forever look to the future and plan as best we can to ensure we stay the course."

"What if you don't agree with the set course?"

"We serve the president. Not the other way around."

"Has Lotz ever approached you to switch sides?"

Laurelai appeared taken aback by the bluntness of her question. "Lotz would never be seen to make an offer like that."

"Never be *seen*…?" Carrie pondered.

"To be seen groveling to the opposition's staff," Laurelai elaborated.

"What about off the books?"

Laurelai stared at her.

"Behind closed doors," Carrie said. "From what I can gather, he is a fan of exchanging favors to get what he wants."

"Well, I assure you, lieutenant, I'm not so cheaply bought." She stood with her datapane. "And I take offense at any insinuation otherwise."

Laurelai walked back into the rear cabin.

Carrie watched her go, locked eyes with Aston again, then turned to look through the ship's portal at the vast, orange-brown ground below.

Harris entered General Berger's office, where he and Marchant awaited an update. Harris sighed as he sat down.

"You heard about McKinley's mother?" Marchant asked.

Harris nodded.

"We thought it best if Getty delivered the news. She tells us she made good progress with him in their session."

He nodded again.

"You look beat, Harris," Berger said.

"I am," he said. "This thing with McKinley's mother is just another setback in a line of setbacks. I should be used to it by now. One step forward, three back."

"You had Sarai scanned?" Berger prompted him.

Harris nodded. "She's been connecting with Martha and I believe it's triggering her node. I felt a huge zap when I touched her today after she physically connected with Martha."

"And the ship?" Marchant asked. "Dr. Ross is pulling old samples out of storage for testing?"

Harris nodded. "Turns out what they thought was soil on the flight deck, was actually a decomposed Zeta. We think it may have been dying from natural causes, but it chose to immolate itself with its heat ray. Hopefully, the remains might give us some clue as to whether those natural causes came from here on Earth."

Marchant nodded. "That's good."

"Don't get too excited," Harris said. "There may be no organic matter left to find."

"And you didn't connect with the Zeta's ship?" Berger asked. "Colberge learned nothing new about flying them?"

"No. Martha was hesitant to touch it. It could be because of the illness, or maybe because it was DNA coded to a Priestess. I have no idea, yet, but we'll work on it," Harris said, rubbing the back of his neck. "Are the results in from the *Carcharias* crew medical checks?"

Marchant nodded. "Most are now showing the cancer precursor who, like Gold, did not have this when they joined the UNF."

"Most?" Harris asked. "But not all?"

"One of the crew isn't showing the cancer precursor because they weren't on the *Carcharias* at the time of the invasion. They came aboard after Gold left. One other isn't showing the cancer precursor, who was aboard at the time. So, it's inconclusive at this stage."

"Inconclusive?" Harris said. "All but one have the cancer precursor who were aboard at the time. I'd say that's pretty conclusive."

"We've noticed something else of interest," Marchant said, eyes fixed on his.

"What?" Harris said feeling a shiver roll down his spine.

"We've rolled the testing out to other groups who were on ships at the time of the invasion and who were exposed to the heat ray radiation. No human soldiers are showing the cancer precursors. Only Alpha soldiers are."

"What?" Harris felt his face furrow with confusion.

Marchant nodded. "It makes sense. The Alpha virus was designed to strengthen the human body right down to a cellular level. It was also designed to be adaptable, to allow changes into the DNA, to accept them and strengthen them, too. That's why soldiers were always given the virus first, then the senses were implanted. The changes the virus made to the cells made them more adaptable. In a way, this made the Alpha bodies akin to sponges for cellular changes like these."

"For the planned improvements, yes, but not illness or things that could kill us."

"When Sharley designed this program, he didn't know about the Zeta's heat rays. He couldn't predict this," Berger said.

"No, but I don't believe for a second that Sharley didn't consider the negative effects of his program," Harris said, "of what this virus could do."

Marchant held his hand up to Harris, calling for calm. "Our best are working on this. We'll know what this means for our Alpha soldiers soon."

"What it means?" Harris said, unable to hide his frustration. "It sounds like it means we're all gonna get cancer and possibly die because our bodies are absorbing radiation from the heat ray at a faster rate than other humans. What about the *Aurizun* team. Same results?"

"So far, yes," Berger said.

"They have the cancer precursors?" Harris asked, feeling his chest sink.

"Yes," Berger said.

"But there might be hope—" Marchant began before Berger cut him off.

"Don't give false hope," Berger warned.

"No, give me hope," Harris said, "I need it."

"We're doing further testing," Marchant said carefully, "but it appears that the Alpha soldiers with the stronger matches to Zeta DNA are the ones who are not yet showing the cancer precursor."

Harris darted his eyes between the two, as his mind rolled this information around and he tried to make sense of it.

"So, being an Alpha soldier raises your risk of radiation, but the Zeta DNA lowers it again?"

"We're still studying this, but yes, quite possibly."

"And the human soldiers who were exposed, but don't have the Zeta DNA?"

"They're not showing cancer precursors yet."

"Just the Alphas?"

"Just the Alphas."

"So, I don't have the cancer precursor?" Harris asked.

Marchant shook his head.

"And Yughi and Evenssen? They got hit on the *Aurora*."

"The results for Evenssen are unclear. You and Yughiarto do not have the cancer precursor. Based on this, we are exploring the idea that anyone with 35 percent match and higher are safe."

"But the rest of the *Aurizun* team have the precursor?" Harris said, his voice came out weaker than he'd wanted it to.

Marchant nodded.

"Fuck..." Harris said, placing his head in his hand. "What the hell do I tell them?"

"Nothing yet," Berger said firmly. "We've got work to do and we need their heads in the game."

"You want me to lie to them?" Harris asked him. "I can't do that, sir."

"Just hold off telling them until we investigate this further," Marchant said. "When you tell them this, you want a plan of action at hand to ease their worries. Just remember, right now they're just showing a cancer precursor. They don't yet have cancer."

Harris looked down at his feet for a moment, soaking it all in. He looked back up at Berger and Marchant.

"How does this align with the nodes?"

"What do you mean?" Marchant asked.

Harris shrugged. "It's in the brain. Does it emit hormones or anything that might combat the radiation? Where does McKinley sit in all this? He's got the node growing, but Zeta markings were low."

"He seems to be an anomaly," Berger said, checking his screen. "He's not showing the cancer precursor, which could mean that the node means something, but it could also be due to the fact of the amount of medical procedures he had after exposure to the heat ray. We cut away all the exposed tissue and replaced it. He had multiple blood transfusions and a whole raft of other treatments including the bacteria that ate the dead tissue, like you did on your exposed arm. We may have destroyed his radiated parts before it could spread to other cells throughout the body."

Harris glanced at the scar along his left arm. His mind turned over, then he nodded to himself and looked back at them.

"We've run out of time. I need to do that interview with Finch."

"Harris—" Berger began.

"No, sir. Look at us. We are falling apart. We're getting older. We're getting tired. Some of us could be dying. Maybe only slowly, but it has begun. We may be Alphas but we cannot pretend that we are invincible. We need younger, fresher, legs. We need to start preparing now. You know it and I know it, when the war comes, the *Aurizun* team won't be out there in the field. We might be the ones leading the battle, but not out there fighting it."

"Don't be so sure," Berger said.

"Oh, don't get me wrong, if we are attacked the *Aurizun* team will fight with everything we've got, but where possible you will need us in the control rooms, giving orders, because it is *us* who will know the Zetas best."

"How does an interview with Finch change this?" Berger asked.

"We need a direct line with the public to earn their trust. If they trust us, they will join us."

"You're talking about the See'ers again," Berger said.

"Yes, but I'm also talking about finding the soldiers who will make the best Alphas, as well as the ones we know now won't be affected by the radiation. It will take time to transition them all. We focus on those 20-35 years old. They'll still be good in 10 to 14 years' time. And every year we roll out more."

"If the ship radiation is a problem, we'll only be able to have human soldiers in space," Marchant said.

Harris nodded. "The Alphas were always going to be the last line of defense on the ground. They'll fare better in hand-to-hand combat against the Zetas and the HH."

"The question is, do we roll out more of the JEMs?" Berger asked.

"No," Harris shook his head, "we don't even know if they're right for us yet."

"Yes, we do," Berger said. "They were born to die."

Harris stared at him, shocked by his bluntness.

"That's what Sharley designed them for," Berger said. "They were always going to be the blanket we threw on the fire to snuff it out. We never expected to get that blanket back."

"No," Harris said firmly, shaking his head.

"Harris—"

"No, sir," Harris said more firmly. "I will raise soldiers to fight and if necessary give their life, but I will not raise soldiers solely to die like pieces of meat."

"Agreed," Marchant said. "That's not the UNF we signed up for."

Berger stared at Marchant. "We do what we have to."

"We're dealing with the fallout of what Sharley created," Marchant said, "we're continuing that, but I can't stand by and condone creating any others. Not when we can create Alpha-Mechs or androids to fight in their place."

"You realize I was the one who signed off on the JEMs creation," Berger said.

"I know," Marchant nodded, "but it was a mistake, and we cannot repeat it."

Berger continued to stare at him. "I agreed to their creation to save our human soldiers."

"I know," Marchant nodded. "Regardless, we can't create more. At the end of the day, it's no different to sending our human soldiers into battle. They risk death, but we do everything we can to get them back alive. No-one wants to be part of an army that sends soldiers into battle with no regard for seeing them return alive."

Berger sighed and seemed to relent. "I'm not the emotionless asshole you think I am, you know?"

"I know," Marchant said. "You're a man who must make hard decisions and you cannot let emotion sway you either way. I understand that, sir."

"Let's focus on our Alpha soldiers," Harris said. "It will take time to build trust with the people, so we need to start building that trust. Let me do the interview with Finch."

Berger sat back in his chair as he studied Harris.

"There's never going to be the perfect time," Marchant backed Harris, looking at Berger. "He's right. We need to open the gates. The *Aurizun* and *Carcharias* teams can't carry the load anymore."

Berger studied them both, then sighed and leaned forward on his desk. "Alright," he said, "but not live. You can pre-record the interview, but I approve it before it airs."

"Thank you, sir," Harris nodded. "I'll check on the JEMs, see how they're settling in their new facility, and as soon as I return, I'll do it."

Berger nodded and Harris stood.

"I'll keep you updated."

Harris left Berger's office, snapped the PDP off his belt and made a call.

"*Colonel Harris?*" Finch answered, surprised.

"Miranda," he said, "I'm ready for your interview."

There was silence for a moment. "*Er... you are? When?*"

"In a few days. It won't be live. It must be pre-recorded and vetted by General Berger himself."

"*Deal. You want to do it at Command?*"

"Yes, they'll want full chain of carriage with the footage. Just get ready. Send through your proposed questions. I'll be in touch when we can record."

Carrie accepted the transmission as soon as it came through. She smiled as she waited for it to connect, keen to see McKinley's face. As soon as she saw it, though, her smile disappeared.

She quickly studied the background. He wasn't at Command. She saw red rocks, knew in her heart he was back in Arizona. She looked back at his pale face, saw his real eye was red with emotion.

"What happened?" she asked, but as soon as she spoke those words, she knew.

"Grace is dead," he said.

The wind rushed out of her. "Oh, god... I'm so sorry." She wanted to reach through the screen to touch him. Frustration swelled within that she couldn't, that she was days away on Mars, while he was all alone, dealing with this. "What happened?"

"She had a stroke," he said quietly. "A bad one. I came as soon as I could."

"Did you make it in time?"

He nodded, sniffing. "She was too far gone... I don't think she knew it was me."

Carrie's heart ached. She knew McKinley hadn't seen Grace since before the invasion. He hadn't wanted her to see him as an Alpha-Mech. Though he looked quite normal, except for the plate on the side of his head, he'd told her that he knew Grace would see right through him, know his eye wasn't real, his arm…

"I'm coming home," Carrie blurted. "Me and the kids, we'll be there—"

"What about the president?" he cut her off. "Is he safe?"

"We can find others to cover him, McKinley. I need to be with you."

"Do you know who you can trust?"

Carrie hesitated, then relented. "No. But—"

"Then you have to stay."

"McKin—"

"Carrie, we've just repaired his trust with the UNF. If we fuck that up now, if something happens because we took our eyes off him…"

"I know that, but you can't ask me to choose the president over you."

McKinley looked away from the screen, off to the horizon. He sniffed again, wiped his real eye, then looked back at her. "It's okay," he said, nodding as though to himself. "Grace… she's better off this way."

"McKinley—"

"No, Carrie, she is," he said firmly. "She was a mess my whole life, and the stroke was… bad. Trust me. She's better off dead. She's not suffering anymore. And I won't have to suffer anymore either."

Carrie felt a tear run down her cheek as she stared at him. She reached out and touched the screen, as though touching his cheek.

"She was never going to survive the war," McKinley said. "It's better she died this way. And she didn't die alone. I was there, I held her hand… Whether she knew it was me or not." He looked around again, sniffed and wiped his eye. "It's time," he said, looking back down the screen at her. "It's time I bury her and move on."

"I will come to you in an instant, you know that right?" she said. "If you want me there, I will come to you. Just say the word."

McKinley shook his head. "You gotta protect the president. He needs you more, right now. And we need Mars. You can't jeopardize that."

More tears ran down Carrie's face. "God, I want to be with you so much right now."

"It's okay," he said, clenching his jaw. "I actually think I need to do this alone."

"Yeah?" she asked him, surprised.

He nodded. Wiped his eye again as he looked at the surrounding red rocks. "Mom's been dead for a long time, Carrie. It's time to let Grace go... I gotta leave the past behind me. I can't carry it around any longer."

Carrie studied him carefully. "You're handling this so well."

McKinley nodded, inhaled deeply and seemed to pull himself together. "Yeah. My psych called earlier, we talked. Maybe she's doing me some good after all." He looked back down the screen and flashed a cheeky smile.

She touched the screen again. "I love you," she said. "And so do the kids."

"I know," he said, "that's why I'm doing okay... If you weren't in my life, I'd be fucked." He gave a short laugh, sniffed again.

She gave a sad smile.

He let out another big sigh that was part groan. "It is what it is... So, go do what you need to. Secure Harkowitz's safety, and I'll see you when you're back."

Harris walked along the new JEM facility, doing an inspection of the repurposed nuclear shelter. The facility itself was not quite up to the standard of the purpose-built one in Siberia. That said, they hadn't needed to do much to the dorms – they were fine for the JEMs – but the other living areas needed to be cleared to make way for training facilities. The last-minute move meant they were still changing and fixing things while the JEMs lived amongst it all. He could sense the upheaval and the activity around them was distracting.

"The JEMs look antsy," Harris said to Siberia Nine, narrowing his eyes in study of a group of them milling about close by.

"They are," he nodded. "We've taken them from order to chaos. It's a disruption we did not need in their lives. One that Sharley would not have been pleased with."

"Well," Harris said, "these are the cards we've been dealt. We gotta play them best we can. Besides," Harris glanced at him, "at some point we were going to have to let them out to fight. Maybe it's better we get them used to the outside world now. We don't want them distracted with other things when the Zetas come."

"Perhaps you're right. Shall we?" Siberia Nine said, motioning for Harris to move into their makeshift training facility.

He nodded and entered the room which was effectively the size of a basketball court. "You're training them in groups now?" He arched his eyebrow.

"Yes," Siberia Nine said, "because we cannot fit 499 JEMs in here. Even training them 100 at a time is difficult in these confines."

"Any concerns?" Harris asked.

"Well, it is preferential to train them together as one large unit. Fracturing them into smaller groups could result in more permanent fractures in the JEMs as a whole. JEM-1 is the anointed leader, but if we continue training them in these smaller groups, it is only natural that this will result in other leaders forming."

"Is that such a bad thing?" Harris asked. "They may be of more use if we can send them out in smaller teams to do what we need."

"And if we need all 499 to amass on one area?"

Harris looked at him in consideration. "JEM-1 still leads. We need to be ready for all outcomes. As a whole, and divided with separate targets."

"Then we must continue to also train them as a whole, as well as in the smaller groups," Siberia Nine said.

Looking around at the JEMs squeezed into the room, even Harris felt claustrophobic.

"I have a suggestion, sir," a voice sounded from behind.

Harris turned to see a JEM before him. Again, though they all looked the same, he just knew which one it was. The one who seemed that bit older than the rest. Harris's skin prickled, wondering how much of the conversation he'd been listening to.

"JEM-1," he gave a nod. "What is your suggestion?"

"On our way inside this facility, I saw much room outside. Could we not train outdoors?"

"You must first acclimatize to your new home, JEM-1" Siberia Nine answered.

JEM-1 looked at Siberia Nine, then turned back to Harris. "We need more space, to train as one. Surely the battlefields we'll fight on will be larger than this room? If we are to fight the Zetas out there, shouldn't we become accustomed to fighting out there?"

"It's not safe outside, JEM-1," Harris said.

"We can protect ourselves," he said.

"Maybe so, but you're our secret weapons, which means you need to be kept a secret."

"We have been trained for stealth," JEM-1 said confidently.

"Yes, stealth of sound, and where possible visual stealth, but here is very different from your old home. We cannot ensure the outside world is not watching you here. And the outside world is not ready for you."

"I cannot run or swing my fists in that room," JEM-1 said with a furrow in his brow. "This is no way to fight. We have Alpha energy to burn."

Harris studied him. It was true, they needed space to burn their energy. As they grew into teenagers and beyond, that small training room would indeed fail to contain them, and their hormones, and their flaring tempers.

Siberia Nine stared at Harris, awaiting a response.

Harris studied JEM-1 one again, the seven year old muscular man-child. Part of him knew he should stick to Sharley's plan, that to derail it now would cause instability in the subjects. But that was the problem. Harris had already caused them upheaval, and he found it hard to view them as subjects and not human children. After all, they weren't much younger than Sarai. Frazer's and Morrell's comments remained ingrained in his brain, because they were right.

And Sharley was dead. Harris had control now.

He sighed, then looked at Siberia Nine. "Have plans drawn up for an external, protected yard to be built. Large. Covered with spy-glaze so they can see out, but no-one can see in."

"Thank you, sir," JEM-1 said, then ran into the room to join his brothers.

Harris watched him. "Do you educate them? Or only teach them to fight?"

"They are given basic education. They must be able to interact and receive orders and understand certain things about society."

Harris's mind turned over as he looked at Siberia Nine. "Keep an eye on JEM-1. I'm concerned by his growing interest in the outside world."

Siberia Nine nodded. "Yes. I have noticed this too."

"All he knew before was that underground warehouse. Now he's seen there's more to the life than what he knew existed. He's curious. It's natural. But it could be a big fuckin' problem if he decides he no longer wants to be a JEM, and instead decides to fight for his freedom, and worse, if he convinces the others to follow him. He's still a kid right now, but once they're full grown, you won't be able to hold them back."

Again Siberia Nine nodded. "I know," he said quietly. "It worries me too."

25

Clearance

McKinley sat on those red rocks in Sedona, Arizona, and studied an old photo of himself that he'd taken from his mother's house. The photo was of his teenage self on the trip to Myanmar to help rebuild villages decimated by a mudslide – his escape from juvey at the time. It was a photo that his mother had printed and framed. She'd kept it in the drawer beside her bed. She'd wanted him close. She did care. She just didn't care for the career he'd chosen after what had happened to his father. But little did she know, due to her condition, his career had actually saved his life and kept him from going under.

He looked at the tall, skinny teenager in the photo, standing beside Colonel Jesse in the wild Myanmar countryside. If only that kid knew what was in front of him. That moment, if he recalled correctly, was after target practice when he'd hit his first bull's-eye. The local villagers had dubbed him the "White Warrior" and presented him with a woven leather band, and later a special silver band stating those words in their language. It was the very first day of the life that he now knew. He hadn't known at the time, but Colonel Jesse knew about the Zeta signals and the UNFASP program, and had been actively recruiting soldiers showing promise. After that trip, Colonel Jesse had gotten him fast-tracked into the military.

He looked down at the leather cuff on his wrist that Freya had made and inscribed with "White Warrior", then he thought of the tattoo Carrie had gotten on her right wrist of the "White Warrior" silver band he'd lost, along with his arm, in the Zeta attack. He smiled.

So many years had passed since that Myanmar trip. A lot of wild times. A lot of bad times. He went from spending his life with an absent family and getting into trouble, to joining the military, then eventually the *Aurora*, and once he'd lowered his guard, had found a new family. Harris, only 11 years older, had become a father figure. Hunter, so different to McKinley in many ways, a best friend.

He recalled his first mission on the *Aurora*, how a simple call for assistance had turned bad, Doc had been stabbed and McKinley had saved his life – shooting Doc's attacker from down the corridor. He tried to imagine a world where he hadn't saved Doc's life, and it was a world that didn't make sense. Doc was a guy McKinley had wished he could be, but never thought he could. He thought he was too damaged to ever be that guy, the *snowflake*. And it became painfully obvious when Carrie came into their lives and fell head over heels for Doc.

He recalled the day she came aboard the *Aurora* for the Darwin mission. She was attractive, but he also thought she was a bit of a princess. His curiosity was piqued when he first saw her shoot – and she beat him – but he still didn't take her seriously. He tried to recall how and when things changed. Memories surfaced of seeing her gasping for breath in Doc's arms after Grolsh's attack. McKinley had felt guilty at the time that he'd missed seeing Grolsh slip out of the mess hall. It was the mission that changed everything; the trajectory of every one of their lives. He saw himself trying to save Smith from bleeding out. He recalled seeing Hunter unconscious in a pod, wondering what he was going to tell Leilani if he didn't make it. McKinley felt the spray of Oxer's blood as Carrie saved his life.

While the Darwin mission had changed their lives in general, it had been the Pegasus mission that had changed the trajectory of his relationship with Carrie. What they went through in the Hell Town dungeon together had forged a bond between them that hadn't been broken since. After they were pulled out of the dungeon, he'd found it hard not to think about her. Memories of her nursing him through his painful Jumbo transition were etched in his mind, the kindness somewhat alien to him. The beatings, the torture, being stripped to their underwear, the truth about their murdered parents coming to light. All barriers between them had been forcibly removed down in that dungeon. And she just seemed to be stuck there in his mind afterward, like a splinter. Not one that hurt, just one that he could see wedged beneath the skin. It wasn't supposed to be there, but it was now a part of him. A part he gave up trying to remove. And he'd felt conflicted about it because of Doc.

He'd tried everything he could to erase her from his mind, and it mostly worked. That is, until she went missing from the *Vortex*, seeking revenge on Sharley. Suddenly, she was in his mind again, and that splinter started to hurt, made worse by the note she'd left him, longer than Doc's or Harris's. The bond was there. The tie between them, laid out uncomfortably in words, no longer a secret or a lie he'd told himself. Hunting high and low for her on Meridian, he felt the tension in Doc and tried to pretend it wasn't echoed within himself.

Then she suddenly returned, bursting through the *Aurora*'s mess hall door, outing Cavelera's betrayal. Relieved, for a brief while, McKinley had felt like maybe they could all move on, but then the bombshell of her pregnancy hit. Just when he was hoping to break free, he was suddenly tied to her more than ever. One of the kids she was carrying was his.

And he couldn't run. He'd wanted to. He'd tried to. But she'd found him and pulled him back in. He went back to Centralis, to the *Aurora*, not just for her, but because he knew that Harris, and Doc, and Hunter, and the team – *his family* – needed him. He was the only full Alpha with the senses. He was their asset. He was their secret weapon…

So, he did everything he could to keep his distance from her and Doc, but it was hard. Damn hard. Forced to guard her, watching her abdomen grow, trying not to think about one of those kids being his. Then she'd given birth. When McKinley had held Freya, that was probably the most scared he'd ever been in his entire life. What the hell did he know about being a parent? Surely Freya would've been better off without him around. But Carrie had nursed him through that too. Forced it on him at the start, but she was patient, and, *boy*, was Doc patient. McKinley wasn't sure he'd be so understanding with another guy hanging around like that. But Doc wasn't going to deny him seeing his child.

Then came the attack. McKinley recalled the thick smell of Carrie's blood as he used his Alpha senses to find her body. Her life hung by a thread, and the twins were missing. His daughter, stolen. His own blood was like boiling ice – frozen numb by all the emotion he'd felt and that he'd denied – but boiling with rage and the need for revenge. His fight with Quint had been cathartic. To take on a Jumbo and fight to the death, and win. To feel Quint's neck when it cracked, vented so much from him. Then Carrie and the twins had pulled through. And once again, he felt like maybe they could all move on.

Then Doc died. And despite everything he'd been through in his life up until then, he wasn't sure he'd felt grief like that. Grief for Doc, for a guy who truly deserved to live. Grief for Carrie, to see her so utterly shattered, to see glimpses of his mother and what Carrie might become, to have that bring up his childhood grief again... He had to do everything in his power to ensure his daughter did not go through what he'd gone through.

He often thought about the day that Doc died. How he'd had a choice – help Doc, or help Carrie. He hadn't had time to stop and think about a choice, he could only react in the moment. Doc was physically stronger, Carrie was weaker, it was an obvious instinct. But something always niggled him about it. He knew deep down that he didn't save her because she was weaker. And it wasn't even because she was Freya's mother. He'd saved her because he just couldn't imagine life without her. Whether she was his, or not.

But fate had taken a turn neither of them had expected. When Doc collapsed and died in Carrie's arms, McKinley had felt the biggest gut punch. He'd felt guilty for being alive in Doc's place. The man who'd deserved to live. The man who'd been a great father to Freya, when McKinley had failed.

And that's when everything *really* changed. McKinley stepped in to be a father for the twins, because he owed Doc that. He owed Brody a father, like Doc had been Freya's when McKinley couldn't. His relationship with Carrie deepened through co-parenting, but it also deepened because Doc was no longer there. The ultimate barrier between them. The line neither would've dreamed of crossing, was gone.

Everything McKinley had done since, was to earn his place. To earn his life. Doc died to save their kids. McKinley had to live to keep saving them.

Man, how he'd changed. The McKinley from 12 years ago would not recognize the man he was today.

His heart ached at the thought of Carrie being on Mars. What he would give to have her there with him right now. She was the best friend he needed, the lover he longed for. Hell, she was sometimes even the nurturing mother he'd needed too. She was everything to him.

A peace settled over him as he looked out at the sunset bathing those red Sedona rocks, thinking about Grace's body being taken to the crematorium. Thinking about the day Doc died when McKinley had to make a choice between saving Carrie or saving Grace. He'd been numb at the time, so Harris had chosen for him. And he'd chosen right. The threat on Grace had been a decoy. The threat on Carrie and the kids had been real. And he still had Carrie and the kids today because of Harris's decision. The right decision. Grace had been gone a long time now. She was his past, and it was time to lay it to rest.

Carrie was his now. His future. His always.

He would choose her and the kids, and move forward. And never look back.

Carrie was glad to throw herself into work, to try and stop herself from thinking about McKinley and the fact that she couldn't be with him. After their transmission, she'd gathered the children and told them about Grace's passing. They were sad for their father, but the truth was, Grace had always been somewhat estranged from their family, so they never really knew her. McKinley had, over time, told them bits and pieces about her, so the kids had always just known her as their grandmother who lived on the mainland, who was too sick to travel. It left Carrie with a stab of guilt. The only grandparents they had left now were Ellen and David Walker, Doc's parents. And even then, they were technically only Brody's grandparents. It was odd that Doc had died so early, yet his parents were the only grandparents her children had left. Carrie made a mental note to take Brody to visit them once they were back on Earth.

Archie had dug up information on those aboard the *Golden Orb* the day it followed the Zeta ship to Earth. Her AI submitted full employment records for each, had found one criminal record, but no obvious links to any Red House staff or to the vigilantes.

Kellan van Pelt of Mars Media was named as the only 'traveler' on the manifest, with the rest being the *Golden Orb*'s crew. Kellan had a clean record, good university grades, and media internships on Earth, finishing with his latest employment with the Mars Media organization. The two pilots, Glenn Carlton and Hope Fisher, also had clean records. Carlton had trained in commercial space flight, while Hope came to the *Golden Orb* after a career in the Canadian Air Force on Earth and a stint on Earth Duty before a few years on Space Duty. The rest of the *Golden Orb* crew, Mark Abrams, Costya Ware, An Sun, and Foster Tessier, had varied career paths to the ship that ranged from commercial flight, Earth armed forces, and mechanical and engineering degrees. The only one with a criminal record was Costya Ware, who had been charged with the theft of some cargo and banned from working cargo flights since. Other than that, nothing stood out as suspicious. They were just regular ship crew who flew wherever the Mercandez company directors and associates wanted them to. In this case, they'd been hired out to Mars Media, who had an obvious interest in the Zeta ship.

Carrie could, of course, draw links to Regan Lotz as the owner of Mars Media, but that still didn't stand out as anything out of the ordinary. Lotz was also a major shareholder in the Mercandez company, but again, nothing raised her suspicions. He was just a rich guy leveraging his assets.

Carrie closed the file down and opened a new message that had appeared in her portal. It was from Colonel Greavy. Earlier that day, she'd requested the information he had on the death threats Harkowitz had received. In total, he had been sent 15 death threats to date. Greavy's team had traced some, but not all, to three different people: Boyd Larson and Leslie Byrne, miners based in Brahe, and Roman Augustyn, a proxy-steel manufacturing worker, also based in Brahe. Each had been paid a visit by Greavy and his men, issued with warnings that if they continued to make such threats, formal charges would be laid against them. By law, they should've been thrown in jail, but Greavy opted for leniency if they cooperated and backed down. Each did, and they accounted for eight of the threats that had been made publicly, or sent to the Red House. Which meant, seven of the threats had not been attributed to any person as yet. Carrie was hoping to fix that.

"Archie?" she said.

"*Yes, lieutenant?*" Its voice issued quietly from the discs in her pocket.

"Given you're a Command-issued AI, do you have any extra access that Greavy's team wouldn't have?"

"*I'm not sure, but I can check, lieutenant. I, and my AIS siblings, can have full access to everything. Most data we can interrogate without approval, and any that we require approval for is generally granted swiftly, depending on who seeks the information and why.*"

"Good," she said, "I want you to look into the seven unattributed death threats and see if you can trace them to their source."

"*Yes, lieutenant.*"

"And see if the three identified threat senders raise any new links to any parties on our lists."

"*Yes, lieutenant. Will that be all?*"

Carrie scrolled through the information one last time. "One other thing. Can you get a message to Colonel Harbourg in Hell Town for me?"

"*Yes, lieutenant.*"

"Good. Tell him I need a favor. Ask him to find out what he can about Dominic Faber, as well as this independent mars group. I'm not talking about the official political party Lotz is fronting; I'm talking about the rumors of the armed one that's off the books. I want to know if Harbourg will help us, or whether he's on their side."

"*Yes, lieutenant,*" Archie replied. "*May I make a request of my own?*"

"Sure," she said.

"*I would prefer it if you wore my discs and did not carry them around in your pocket. I cannot analyze your health this way.*"

"My health is fine right now, Archie, and I'm currently confined to the Red House. It's unnecessary."

"*I disagree.*"

"If I leave the Red House again, I'll wear them. Okay?"

"*Yes, lieutenant.*"

McKinley stood on the Command indoor shooting range, staring at the target. He'd just gotten back to Centralis after attending his mother's cremation, and was still deciding whether to sell the house or leave it as a holiday home. Part of him wanted to show the kids Arizona, but another part of him never wanted to see it again.

Harris was on his way back from the JEM facility, so, feeling antsy, McKinley started walking the corridors of Command and ended up at the range. Target practice was something he often did when he needed distraction, or time to think. Right now he just wanted to kill time and shake this restless feeling off while he waited for Harris to return. He could only put the antsy feeling down to the fact that his life would be different now his mother was gone from his life. Like carrying a heavy weight for a long time and then suddenly being free of it – the muscles shaking from the lightness and relief as the blood flowed freely again.

He moved to collect a pistol to use, but stopped before he picked it up. He stared at it, suddenly wondering whether it was a good idea. He was rusty, yes, but he knew how to shoot with a handgun. What he didn't know how to do was to shoot with the gun that was inside him, the one he needed to control with his mind.

He turned away from the rack of guns and moved over to the target range, stopping at the firing point. He stared at the target at the end of the range. Took a breath in, then out, then raised his arm and flexed his hand back to expose the wrist.

"It's time to shoot, you useless bastard," he muttered to himself, before internalizing his thoughts. *"If you can't shoot, you got no place being in charge of Alphas."*

He took another breath, focused hard.

"Open…"

Nothing happened.

"You did it before, involuntarily. You can do it now voluntarily. Just breathe, and shoot…"

Arm outstretched, hand flexed back, he stood waiting.

Nothing happened.

He sighed, lowered his arm, looked at the ground.

"Don't let it defeat you," he told himself. "You can do this. You need to do this. They're counting on you."

He thought of Grace's coffin entering the fire, felt the scar at his right mech shoulder burn at the memory. He recalled the weight of her ashes in the little jar. His past. He thought of Freya, and Jesse, and Brody, and Doc.

Didn't want to let them down. Then he thought of Carrie, felt a weight lifting off his shoulders, knew she believed in him like no-one else did.

He looked back up, quickly raised his arm and flexed his hand back, curling his fingers into a fist. Pictured the barrel of the gun extending from his exposed wrist.

And he heard it: a mechanical noise inside his arm. He sensed a vibration, movement.

He tilted his arm slightly, saw the barrel of the gun projecting from his wrist.

He did it.

Eyes wide, he looked ahead at the target.

He focused. And fired.

Startling himself, his arm bounced around firing like he was scattering confetti.

"Whoa!" he said, as he stopped firing, grabbing his mech arm with his real one to control it.

He looked at the target. He'd hit just about everywhere along the wall, except the target. Even hit the one in the next lane – laser burns wafting smoke here and there.

"Shit!" he said. He quickly glanced about, saw Sidney, his physical rehabilitation coach, walking swiftly toward him.

"Sorry!" he called out to the man. "It was an accident."

"Why are you sorry?" Sidney said coming to stand beside him, eyeing all the hits at the end of the range.

McKinley looked at him. "I shot the place up."

Sidney turned back to him. "You sure did," he smiled. "You *shot*, McKinley. You didn't use the remote. You shot with your mind. That's great!"

McKinley looked at the erratic scattering of holes across the two ranges. "I normally shoot a lot straighter than that."

"But you shot. Whatever it is you've been doing, it's removing the block in your mind." Sidney eyed him. "You'll be shooting straight in no time."

McKinley stared at the target, still wide-eyed and a little shocked.

"Let's see if you can do it again," Sidney said.

26

Freedom

Harris was dreaming. He walked along the silver sands with Sarai and DaJuan. They came to a stop, then slowly sat on the ground, waiting.

Tess made herself known first. The hiss sounded before she appeared. No longer was she strapped down in her bed, but pacing her glass cell, glaring at Harris while she rubbed the stump of her half-arm. Harris felt gooseflesh ripple across his scarred arms. There was something about her. Her venomous energy was still there, but there was something about the look in her eyes, something that spoke of assurance, of cunning, of calm.

Now she was freed from her bed, she had grown in confidence.

"You feel that?" DaJuan said quietly, looking down at the gooseflesh rippling across his own arms.

Harris glanced from him to Sarai, who shivered.

"You alright?" he asked his daughter.

She nodded, staring at Tess. "She wants out."

Before Harris could respond, images from the invasion flashed through his mind in a frenzy: heat rays, ship fire, explosions, crashes. He blinked, shook his head and looked over to see Martha standing there. "What's wrong?" he asked her.

More flashes, this time of dead Priestesses laying on their ships, turning black, then into silver sand.

Tess hissed again.

"They've been talking," DaJuan said quietly.

"I think that came from Martha," Harris said, studying her.

He projected back, sending images of the Priestesses stealing the HH and enslaving them, marching them onto their ships.

Martha stared back at him. Images flashed of Zeta ships falling from the skies during the invasion.

Harris projected images of the Priestess fleet opening fire first on human ships.

"They started it," Harris told her. "*Every* time, they started it. They started it with the HH, and they started it again when they came back. What do you expect our people to do?"

Martha stared at him, while Tess hissed, then the bright lines, dots and swirls flashed in the air. Harris darted his eyes between the two Zetas.

"Don't listen to her," Harris told Martha. "Whatever she's saying, don't listen. What I've shown you is the truth."

Suddenly Welles flashed inside his mind, of a time past when they communed with Martha. Then, an image of Harris with DaJuan flashed inside his mind. Then Welles again.

"She wants to know where Welles is again," DaJuan said. "Martha thinks we've done something to her."

"Welles is fine. She's alive," Harris said to Martha. "I told you this."

Martha motioned to Sarai, as though in question.

Harris thought for a moment, then swallowed. "She's our real queen," he said, motioning to Sarai. "Welles was a decoy. But I remain the royal guard and Zeta liaison."

Martha studied Sarai, then an image flashed through Harris's mind, of Welles lying dead, turning to silver sand.

"No," Harris shook his head, projecting an image of Mars, then of Welles in the Red House with Harkowitz, "she's still there."

Martha projected an image of Welles's brain, of the dark patches the CTE has caused. Harris stared back at Martha, agape.

"She knows," DaJuan said. "She could tell Welles's brain was glitchy."

"We're fixing her," Harris told Martha, projecting an image of Welles receiving treatment, surrounded by doctors and nurses, their hands on her head.

Martha mooed a grunt, stomped her foot in disagreement.

Suddenly Harris saw Welles on Archelois, surrounded by Zetas, receiving *their* treatment. He saw the dark patches in her brain receding.

Harris stared at Martha. "You can fix her?"

Tess hissed tetchily, as though telling Martha to hurry.

Martha glanced at her, then back at Harris. Then, she projected herself and Tess leaving Earth, being set free.

"I..." Harris stuttered. "I'm not sure I can arrange that."

He saw an image of Tess tied to her bed, of Martha too.

Harris shook his head, motioned to the image of Tess pacing her cell. "She's not restrained anymore."

Another projection pierced his mind. He saw Tess's locked cell door. That image, he knew, came from Tess.

Harris countered with images of what Tess had done to Morrell and to his soldiers, then projected images of Martha being peaceful, trying to explain why Tess was locked up.

Martha mooed an angry grunt and stomped her foot again. She projected more images of Tess and herself, and this time, Welles, leaving Earth for Zeta Archelois.

"I can't do that," Harris said, shaking his head.

Sarai looked at him. "If you don't let Martha go, you're holding her prisoner like Tess. She wants to leave, Dad."

"We've so much more to learn from each other," Harris said, standing and stepping closer to Martha. "You can't leave yet."

Martha projected another image of her returning to Zeta Archelois, to her sisters, then another of Tess and Welles with her.

Harris sighed. He looked down at the ground, mind turning over.

DaJuan looked at Harris. "If you keep her here, your good blood may turn bad."

Harris stared at Martha, then at Tess.

"You want to try for peace, yes?" DaJuan said. "We need to keep Martha on side. We've not caused her any harm. Don't you want her to tell her sisters that?"

"We haven't caused her harm, but we have harmed Tess. What if her sisters side with Tess?" Harris asked him. "If we let Martha go and they tell them that, we might just start the war."

"Martha wants to know more about our world," Sarai said, "but she has to return to her home."

Harris looked at her. "How do you know that?"

"She's been talking to me."

"What?!" Harris said, urgently. "When?"

"Since we were at the ship."

Harris moved to Sarai. "What have you told her?"

"Nothing, Dad. She wanted to know about our world, so I showed her."

"Showed her what?" he said, clasping the tops of her arms.

"I just showed her flowers, and animals, and cartoons, and Mom's cupcakes, and Ty's basketball," Sarai shrugged. "I just showed her our life."

Harris looked back at Martha. She stared at him evenly, her eyes glancing to where he held Sarai's arms. Harris let her go.

"She doesn't want to hurt us, Dad," Sarai said. "She just wants to go home. I think maybe she's homesick."

"This could be a good thing, man," DaJuan said, looking at him. "Sarai has shown Martha a world of peace. We want her to tell her sisters that, right?"

"What if they think peace means we're a weak target?" Harris asked, before sighing again. He ran his hand over his face. "I need to make sure she knows where we stand." He looked back at Martha, then closed his eyes and projected himself with Sarai, DaJuan and Welles, standing among other humans on Earth, standing with the Zetas, peacefully, shaking hands."

He opened his eyes again. Martha stared at him, then gave a slow nod.

Again, she projected herself flying away with Tess and Welles.

Harris shook his head. "No. You can't take Welles, and you can't take Tess." He projected an image of Martha going to Zeta Archelois alone and returning with her treatment for Welles.

Martha grunted again, stomped her foot. And this time, Harris heard her talk. Talk in her language. The humming, buzzing and clicks. He felt his whole body shiver at the sound.

"That's her language," Sarai told them. "That's how they speak."

"What are those colored lines and dots then?" DaJuan asked.

"That's also their language," Sarai told him. "They have three. The spoken, the written, and the projections."

"Whoa," DaJuan said, nodding impressed.

Harris saw Welles holding her head again, saw Welles collapsing, laying on the ground, eyes vacant, dead. He watched as her skull caved into silver sand.

Harris studied Martha. Deep in his bones he believed she wanted to help Welles, but he couldn't let Welles go out there to Zeta Archelois. It was too dangerous. Firstly, it would take years. Secondly, despite Martha's presence, he just didn't trust Tess.

He projected the image of Martha going alone.

Tess hissed, moved angrily about in her cell. Martha glared at Harris, motioned to Tess, stomped her hoofed-foot again. Then the other hoofed-foot. He saw an image of Tess freed from her cell.

Harris projected an image of Tess with her claws in Morrell's gut.

Martha projected an image of her standing beside Tess, as though vouching for her.

"She wants you to release Tess," Sarai said. "She won't leave without her."

"I know," Harris told his daughter. "But I'm not sure I can allow that."

"Do you trust that Tess won't rip your throat out if you let her go?" DaJuan asked.

Harris thought about it. "I trust Martha. Tess wants out, and she may just behave if it means a ticket out of our captivity." Harris looked at DaJuan. "I tell you one thing, though, the general may just rip my throat out if I promise them both freedom."

"Yeah," DaJuan nodded, "but if it's peace you really want, he may just have to roll with it."

"How do I project to her that I need time to clear this?" Harris asked.

Harris saw an image flash in his mind of Harris, Sarai and DaJuan conferring, then turning back to Martha.

"Who did that?" he asked.

"I did," Sarai said.

"Stop talking to her, Sarai," he said. "I do the talking, understand?"

Sarai slumped a little.

Martha stomped her hoofed-foot again, motioned to him and Sarai.

"I know you don't like men so much," Harris told her, "but I'm her father. She's a child, she's not an adult."

Tess hissed angrily then, smacking her reptilian hand against the glass wall, startling them.

Martha grunted at Tess, then whined at Harris.

"Alright!" Harris called, holding up his hand to Martha. He closed his eyes, projected him conferring with a group of soldiers, including Welles and McKinley. Then he reopened his eyes.

"I'll be back with an answer," he told Martha.

Carrie sat in her Red House apartment, cleaning things away from dinner. She could hear the kids laughing and panting in their bedroom, still running around, play-fighting, and getting up to mischief.

"I don't hear much homework being done!" Carrie called out.

The laughter turned into giggling and whispering. She heard Freya tell her brothers: "We need to practice our stealth."

Sampson emerged from the Sentinel bedroom, scratching his head and Carrie felt guilt flush through her.

"I'm sorry," she said, "did they wake you?"

"Nah, it's all good," he smiled. "I gotta get up anyway. It's time to relieve Novak from president watch."

She smiled. "Can I make you some coffee?"

"Thanks," he said. "I'll make it."

"Please, Sampson," Carrie waved him off. "Sit."

She moved over to switch the coffee machine on and listened to it softly purr as it heated up.

"*Lieutenant?*" Archie sounded from the discs in her pocket.

"Yes, Archie?"

"*I have an update on the death threats I think you should see,*" it replied.

She snapped the PDP off her belt and opened her portal. It was a file on all the known threats made against Harkowitz.

"What have you found?" she asked Archie.

"*Firstly, as you know, Dominic Faber was high on our list of suspects,*" he replied. "*See the date of the last known threat?*"

Carrie's eyes skimmed across the data. "Two days ago."

"*Yes,*" Archie replied. "*While our vigilantes were locked up in Hell Town and unable to transmit.*"

"So, it wasn't him."

"This last one wasn't, no, but all the seven unaccounted threats have been sent in an identical fashion, using a sophisticated encrypted system called EncryptTych, which implies the same person, or the same group of people are sending them. However, as far as I can trace, their origin comes from different servers."

"Meaning what?"

"I've managed to narrow down the milliseconds between the sent files and the receive files, for four of them, and I can confirm that all four have been sent to the Red House from the vicinity of Mars. The encrypted system means I can pinpoint the location of the different servers but not who has been sending them. With government approval, I could—"

"How did Greavy track down those behind the other eight threats?"

"Quite easily, as they did not use an encrypted system. Byrne and Augustyn sent theirs, three apiece, from their personal email addresses. They each made similar threats for President Harkowitz to stand aside or they would move him aside, but no actual mention of death or killing was mentioned. The third person, Larson, made comments on social media posts relating to Harkowitz's announcement that he would host the Heads of State meeting for the UNF. Larson specifically said in his comments that if the president won the next election, then someone had to take him out."

"Okay," Carrie asked, pouring Sampson his coffee and handing it to him, "so it's likely those three people were just blowing off steam with little intention to actually follow through, but those behind the encrypted threats could actually be very real."

"We shouldn't rule any out, lieutenant," Archie said, *"but as the known three are being watched, it's unlikely they could make an attempt on the president without us knowing and stopping them."*

"Tell me about the servers. Where were they located exactly?"

"Two I have traced to Colony Brahe. One I have traced to Colony Elon, and one I have traced to the Mars Docking Station."

"Okay, that's four. But we had seven unaccounted threats?"

"Yes, I am still tracing the last three, but I thought it of interest that the very last one I am yet to trace, is new, and it was sent after Dominic was imprisoned in Hell Town, which means it wasn't him. However, I have surveillance footage that places Dominic in the vicinity of Elon and Brahe at the times those encrypted threats were sent."

"Yeah, but a lot of other people were in those colonies, too, Archie. We'll need more than that. I assume you're also looking at his father?"

"*Yes, lieutenant. One other thing I find interesting,*" Archie said, "*is the ease with which I have discovered this information to date. Colonel Greavy told you he hadn't been able to trace all the threats as yet.*"

Carrie paused as her mind turned over. "When he sent the files he said his team hadn't been able to."

"*From what I've been able to gather, his team did not engage AI assistance to search.*"

"Why wouldn't they do that?"

"*Either they were lazy and assumed they were much like the other minor threats, or—*"

"They didn't want to find the answers," Carrie said, locking eyes with Sampson who sipped his coffee.

"*Yes.*"

"So, where does this leave Colonel Greavy?" Carrie asked. "Is his team just incompetent? Or are they screwing him over? Or were they withholding information on his orders?"

"*That I cannot say,*" Archie said.

"Alright," Carrie said, "keep working on it. Has Colonel Harbourg supplied any information yet?"

"*Not as yet, no.*"

"But he agreed to look into it?"

"*Yes, lieutenant. My message was accepted, and he responded stating that you owed him.*"

Carrie grunted. "I don't owe him anything." She checked the time on her PDP. "Okay. Harris has called an extraordinary ZAEP meeting, so I'm about to log in. I'll let them know we're getting closer."

"*Lieutenant?*"

"Yeah?"

"*I suggest you impress upon them that the threat against the president is still real and very present. Dominic and his father were not alone in their desire for an independent Mars. I've been tracing online activity associated with them, as well as keywords that align with the movement, and I have traced this activity beyond Mars to sources on the Moon, several stations and Earth.*"

Carrie stilled, glancing at Sampson who had remained quietly listening as he sipped his coffee. "Why would people outside of Mars want Harkowitz removed?"

"I would need to dig further but my guess is that they may have a stake in the Mercandez company and interests in proxy-steel."

Carrie nodded to herself. "Let me know as soon as you have something. If this goes beyond Mars to something wider, we've got a big problem on our hands."

"Yes, lieutenant."

Carrie sighed and looked at Sampson.

"Are you really surprised?" he asked her. "It always comes down to greed. Shareholders will do anything to protect their money."

"But kill a president?" she asked.

"It's happened before," Sampson shrugged. "Let's hope it's just a bluff. A little blackmail to get him to do what they want."

Carrie nodded in thought. "The problem is, some people don't think blackmail is enough."

"What are you going to do?" Sampson asked.

Carrie checked her PDP again. "Right now, I gotta go join the ZAEP. *You*, however, stay sharp and make sure Aston stays sharp too. Let me know anything unusual, no matter how small. And tell Novak I want him and Beach to do the same."

Sampson gave single nod, his eyes focused and mind turning over quickly as the coffee took hold.

Harris watched Welles join the ZAEP onscreen, alongside Gold.

"Welles," he gave a nod, then looked at those around the Command boardroom table. "Alright, let's get started. Thanks for joining this extraordinary ZAEP meeting. I have something important we need to discuss." Harris inhaled subtly, and exhaled just the same. "I'm just going to cut straight to it. The last time I connected with Martha, she told me she wants to leave."

"Command?" Dr. Serquey asked.

"No," Harris shook his head, "Earth. She wants to go home."

"But she can't," Serquey said quickly. "I have more tests I need to run. You asked Dr. Ross and I to get to the bottom of what killed the Priestesses when they were here last."

Harris turned to Dr. Ross. "Do you have the results from the sand found on the ship?"

"It's being analyzed," he replied.

"How long will it take?" Harris asked Serquey.

She shrugged. "It could take days or months. At the moment we have nothing conclusive as we are struggling to find any biological matter in that sand sample. I've worked up a biological profile on Tess, but I still have much work to do with Martha. As she is not captive, I can't just take what I need. I try to communicate with her best I can, but ideally I need you or DaJuan present to help explain that I'm not trying to hurt her. This takes time."

Harris shrugged back at her. "What can I say, Martha's made it clear she wants to leave. Like you said, she's not our captive."

"Then we make her one," Berger said.

"No, sir," Harris said firmly. "We can't do that. We want peace, remember? She's our key to that. If we show her we're not a threat, she'll tell the others."

"You can't be sure of that," Berger said.

"My gut is sure of that, sir." Harris said. "She knows we don't want war."

"And what about the Priestesses?" Morrell asked.

"I don't know about them," Harris said, "but if the Zetas are going to attack us, I'd prefer it if the Alma Mater, Zisis, and Salacia stay out of it."

"Like you said, she's our ally," Berger said. "Can't you ask her to stay longer and help us? We need her here, like Tess."

"That's just it, I'm suggesting we let both go," Harris said.

All the faces around the table stared at him in astonishment.

"Ask DaJuan and Sarai," Harris said quickly, "they were there with me. Martha wants to go and she's pushing for Tess's release as well. I have assured her we want peace, but if we refuse to let Tess go too, then she won't believe that."

"You let that thing go, she'll kill us all," Morrell said firmly.

"I think Martha will hold her back from that," Harris said.

"And if she doesn't?" Marchant asked. "If people die?"

Harris took a breath, steeled himself. "Then I'll take full responsibility. But Martha wants this, and I feel I must agree for the sake of a chance at peace. I need her to tell the others that we don't want war."

"Dr. Pullman," Marchant said, "what are the sky scans telling us?"

"They've been clear. There's been silence for some time. It's been eerily quiet."

"Eerily quiet?" Marchant asked.

"Obviously there is some distance between us and the Zeta Archelois system, so large gaps of silence are to be expected as the signals transfer, but with the invasion, and with Martha's visit, we now know that does not determine the real distance the Zetas are from us. We may have been genuinely communicating with those on Zeta Archelois, but we've learned that the Zetas are not confined to that galaxy. They've been present in ours this whole time."

"So, the threat is very real that they could appear in our skies tomorrow?" Berger asked.

Dr. Pullman nodded. "Of course. It's happened twice now. It would be foolish to think it won't happen again. Knowing what Colonel Harris does now about their fractured society, those who remain on Zeta Archelois may be friendly, but those roaming our galaxy may not be."

"My gut tells me we've got time," Harris said. "And now we've got the Deep-Star satellites out there, there won't be any surprises. They worked when it came to Martha's visit."

"Why are you fighting for peace when you've always told us that we're going to war," Arken asked. "You've told us it was inevitable."

"That was before I met Martha. She's given me hope that we can either avert a war, or minimize the strength of the army against us."

"Tess doesn't want peace," Morrell said. "I have the scars to prove it."

"I know," Harris said, "and if I'm honest, my gut tells me that she will never try for peace. She only wants revenge."

"Then why release her?" Marchant asked.

"Because," Harris said, looking around at all of them, "like I said, I'm doing this for Martha. She wants to go home and as a gesture of goodwill she wants us to release Tess. I believe she has honor and I believe she will respond to my honor when I let Tess go."

"And if Martha's playing you?" Arken asked.

"That's what the kill switch is for," Morrell said.

Berger shot him a stern look.

"Kill switch?" Serquey asked confused.

"You're asking us to give up our greatest weapon in this coming war," Berger said to Harris, moving the conversation along. "Information."

"I know," Harris nodded, "but I trust that Martha wants peace. And if there's a chance she can talk to her Zeta sisters and they, in turn, can talk the Priestesses down from waging war and reclaiming Earth, or us as slaves, then it will be a risk worth taking."

Berger looked at the screen. "Welles?"

"Yes, sir?" she said.

"You've spent time with her. Do you trust Martha?"

Welles considered this and nodded. "Yes, sir. She never once threatened or attacked us. We proved to her that we're not enemies. I believe she wants peace, but I did feel that she was conflicted at being free while Tess was our prisoner. I agree with Colonel Harris that we should honor Martha's request and that, in return, Martha will keep Tess in line."

"Until Tess is off planet," Morrell said.

"Then we'll be ready for her," Welles said. "Just so long as Martha goes back to Zeta Archelois and puts in a good word for us."

Harris looked back at Dr. Serquey. "If I get Martha to sit one last round of tests, can you get what you need?"

"Well," she said, a little flustered, "yes, I can get *some* answers, but studies are best run over time to see progress or decline."

"I understand that, and I understand you're a scientist, but you were the one pushing to release Tess from her restraints. How much testing can you realistically do without knocking her out all the time? I know you'd like longer, but this is war. Sometimes we don't get what we need, so we make do with what we have."

Dr. Serquey sighed in defeat and waved her hand as if to say "fine".

"What about the dreams?" Marchant asked him. "The world, the rest of their tech, all the other information we won't get to find out because she won't be here to dream and project with you?"

"Like I said, we'll have to make do," Harris shrugged.

"Make do?" Berger said. "That's not how to enter a war. If we have options we should exploit those options."

"We do have options," Harris nodded. "We have the option to release the Zetas and hope that brings peace, or we incarcerate them and *absolutely* go to war. I know we'll be giving things up if we release them, but if there is a chance for peace, no matter how slim, I have to give that a chance," Harris said, trying to restrain the passion and pleading in his voice, though it was hard to do. "Every war is a matter of 'make do'. We prepare as best we can, then we pivot as necessary. Thanks to the work we've already done, we can now detect their ships, we have matched the metal of their weapons with the proxy-steel, and we're understanding how their heat rays work. We can openly communicate with them, we know the basics of their history and their civil war, we know about the nodes, the DNA, and we even know a bit about their languages." He looked around the table again. "We have enough to work with. Martha wants to go and every day I force her to stay here is another day that Tess turns her into an enemy. We *cannot* risk that."

Silence sat around the table as minds turned over.

"To Morrell's point," Berger asked with narrowed eyes, "how do we know that Martha hasn't gotten inside your head?"

"Because I'm telling you she hasn't. I would know. I would feel it in my gut if she was playing me. She isn't. I am Head of Strategy. You need to trust me. If I'm wrong, then I'm wrong, and you can do with me what you will. But I'm not alone in thinking this, that Martha is truthful. Like, I said, DaJuan, Sarai and Welles have communicated with Martha and they believe this is the right course. Sarai connected with Martha separately from me. I'm still going over their exchanges, but there may still be more to learn from this after she's gone, when I extract it from Sarai."

"What if Sarai told Martha things we don't want them to know?" Berger asked concerned.

"Like what? It's not like she knows our nuke codes. All she showed it was that we wanted peace, not destruction. Like most kids do."

The silence sat as they each contemplated the decision.

"If Colonel Harris believes this is the right course of action," McKinley spoke up, "then he has my vote of confidence."

"And mine," Welles said. "I believe Martha wants peace."

"He has mine too," Gold said.

The remaining ZAEP members looked at each other, still contemplating.

"If there's a chance for peace," Dr. Ross said carefully, "then I believe we should take it."

Serquey sighed heavily. "I want to keep studying the Zetas, but if releasing them means peace, then I have to go with that option."

Dr. Pullman nodded. "I strongly believe we must proceed with caution and remain vigilant, but I'd much prefer them as allies than enemies. I agree."

Harris noted that the scientists were on board, but many of those in military uniform were still quiet. But he understood that. If things turned bad, *they* would be the ones responsible for fighting the war and saving civilians. Half of the ZAEP were idealists and hopeful, the other half were realists.

"What are those people on the gates going to do when they see us releasing them?" Morrell voiced silent thoughts in the room.

"I don't know, but whatever it is we'll manage it," Harris said. "The general has approved me doing an interview with Finch, which I will do asap. We will have that interview go live during their release to distract civilians. Hopefully, my interview will give the people reassurance that we are doing the right thing."

"And if it doesn't?" Admiral Arken asked.

"Then we manage the fallout," Gold said. "Just like we did on Atlas."

"We trust Martha," McKinley said, "and if we earn the people's trust, they will trust her too."

"I don't want to go to war, and I'll do everything I can to avoid it," Harris said, "but I assure you, if it comes to it, I will do everything in my power to fight it. *Everything*. If the Zetas try to hurt us, I will hurt them back, tenfold. You have my word."

Marchant nodded to himself in thought and looked at Berger. "We give peace a chance," he said. "And if that doesn't work, we go to war."

Berger stared back at him. "We prepare for war regardless." He turned to look at Harris. "Alright, we'll go ahead with your plan. We'll release the Zetas while the interview goes live. We bolster security everywhere and hope to hell we don't sink into our own civil war over this."

"Thank you, sir," Harris nodded. "Let's prepare, everyone."

"Sir," Welles said, "may I have a word with you and our military component?"

Harris nodded and watched the scientists leave, then turned back to Welles. "What is it?"

"We believe the threat against the president remains real. There is a growing movement for an independent Mars, which Archie tells me is not limited to Mars civilians, but one that extends to Earth, the Moon and our stations. There are a lot of people with their fingers in the proxy-steel pie who don't want to hand it over to the UNF without earning a hefty price."

"Is it a good idea to proceed with the HOS and Stage One Atlas launch?" Gold asked.

"Yes," Berger said. "We need to assure both the HOS and civilians that we've got things under control and we will be ready for the Zetas if they return. Delaying the HOS or this launch will look bad. Your station is ready to go, is it not?"

"Yes, sir," Gold nodded. "We're ready."

"Then we proceed as planned. Not only were we launching the Stage One completion, but we were also going to show off the *Barbican* returning to service. The HOS will be nothing if not impressed with the UNF. So, we hold the HOS meeting at the Red House, then we travel to Atlas for the launch, letting them see the *Barbican* nearby, and we make damn sure everything runs smoothly."

"We should increase security for the HOS," McKinley said. "If the threat against Harkowitz is real and they want to make a statement, disrupting the HOS or the Atlas launch is the way to do it."

"Agreed," Welles said.

"See it done," Berger said.

Carrie made her way to the president's office and found Sampson standing guard out front with Aston.

"He's in?" Carrie asked motioning to the door. Aston nodded and knocked on the door.

"*Yes,*" Harkowitz sounded from inside.

Aston opened the door, Carrie entered and closed the door behind her.

Harkowitz looked up from his portal screen. "How was your ZAEP meeting?"

"Good. There are some developments, though."

"Yes?" Harkowitz asked, leaning back in his chair.

"Firstly, they're going to release both Zetas."

"Release them?! As in, allow them to roam on Earth or return home?"

"Return home."

"You can't be serious?" Harkowitz said leaning forward again.

"Martha wants to leave. If they don't let her go, it could make her an enemy and hasten war. Releasing Tess is a sign of goodwill."

Harkowitz stared at her for a moment. "You realize when the people find out there'll be anarchy."

"We're trying to broker peace, not stoke a war."

"Some people won't see it that way. They'll see it as a sign of weakness. They'll think Harris has been seduced by them."

"And you, seduced by Harris and the UNF," Carrie nodded.

Harkowitz sighed and ran a hand over his face.

"We're doing what we can to manage the fallout. Harris is about to do a full interview with Miranda Finch. It will air while Martha and Tess are being released."

"The vigilantes will gun for them, you know this."

Carrie nodded. "And like last time, we will stop them long enough to ensure Martha leaves our solar system."

Harkowitz sat back in his chair again, loosened his tie. "What else?"

"The HOS meeting and Atlas Stage One launch are going ahead as scheduled."

Harkowitz thought for a moment. "It will take place after they're released?"

"Yes, if everything goes according to plan, the Zetas will be long gone."

"But civilian anger may be high."

"Possibly, but if they watch the interview, I think many will approve of us trying to broker peace and avoid a war."

"The HOS could be a prime target for action."

Carrie nodded again. "We handled insurgents last time. We can handle them again."

"Are you sure about that?"

"Yes. We're increasing security and this time, the *Aurizun* team will not be prisoners like they were at the last HOS. We have our freedom and we have power. We will prevail."

"Spoken like a true soldier."

"Mr. President, I have communicated with Martha before. She means us no harm."

"And Tess?"

"Tess… is smart. I think she'll cooperate to gain her freedom."

"And once she's free?"

Carrie shrugged. "We'll have to wait and find out."

Harkowitz stared at her. "If she turns on us?"

"She won't turn on us alone."

"So, we send her out there with information on us to gather her troops and return."

"Quite possibly. But we, too, have information on them. And, instead of fighting the entire five races of Zetas, we may only have to fight one or two. I prefer those odds, sir."

Harkowitz sighed and nodded. "Very well. I guess I have no choice."

"We all have a choice, sir."

Harkowitz eyed her. "Yes, and I'm choosing the UNF."

"Thank you, sir." Carrie checked her PDP. "It's late. You should get some rest."

"I should," he said, "but I should probably revisit our plans for the HOS meeting, too."

"It'll still be there tomorrow, sir, when your brain is thinking more clearly. Goodnight."

Carrie left the president's office and glanced at Aston and Sampson.

"The Heads of State meeting is proceeding as planned. Let's meet at the shift changeover to go over security plans."

27

Risk Factor

Harris stood outside Tess's cell, staring at her through the glass wall. Tess stared back and Harris thought he detected a smile on her face.

She knew she was about to be released.

He'd connected with Martha the previous evening and projected an image of her being released, along with Tess, under escort from UNF ships. Martha had given him a slight bow, her eyes pleased. Tess had just hissed. Martha, once more, had projected Welles traveling with them, but again Harris shook his head and declined. He tried to project images that showed Archelois as a very long way away, then projected an image of Welles with McKinley and their kids, though he'd tried his best keep their faces blurred. Martha had stared at him without response. Tess, again, just hissed at him. He wondered whether they thought he was controlling Welles, keeping her away from them. He guessed it was true, he was, but it wasn't because he was trying to dominate her, it was because he was trying to keep her alive. Even if Zeta technology could fix Welles's brain, it was too great a risk to send her out there alone with the two Zetas. It wasn't just the length of the journey and the fact she'd miss a large chunk of her kids' lives, but for whatever reason, his gut just wouldn't abide it. It was too dangerous. He wasn't even going to mention it to Welles.

As if on cue, his female ancestors had appeared to him and they gave him a nod, confirming his decision. Next, Martha had suggested taking Sarai with them. Harris did not respond to this at all, and Martha took that as his answer. When Tess hissed again, Harris made a point of projecting images of Harris holding Welles's hand and Sarai's.

"I'm not trying to control them," he'd said. "I'm doing it to protect them. Don't mistake me for your male Zetas."

Of course, then Sarai had appeared, alongside DaJuan, in his dream.

"Is it happening?" DaJuan asked.

Harris nodded. "Very soon."

When he'd awoken after that dream, he'd felt a sick feeling in his stomach, and Sibbie, Etta, and Maeve were standing there at the foot of his bed, staring at him in his waking mind.

"I don't trust Tess," he said aloud to himself, in his Command quarters, "but Martha wants this, so it must be done."

He threw his sheets back and his female kin disappeared. Within minutes he was dressed and sipping coffee as he headed for Tess's cell, and he stood there now, staring at the Zeta who had once tried to kill him.

Harris closed his eyes and projected an image of them leaving peacefully. He opened his eyes and Tess just stared at him with her black eyes. Harris closed his eyes again and pictured Tess attacking a faceless soldier. He then pictured himself killing Tess, and opened his eyes again. Tess hissed.

"Behave," he said quietly, "or I will take you out."

Martha flashed into his mind then. He turned and saw her walking toward him. Her face was slightly tilted as she studied him.

He turned to her and slowly held his hand out to her, palm up. She looked down at it, then placed her hoofed hand on his with an electric zap, shocking them both. He closed his eyes and projected the images he had just projected to Tess – a warning that if Tess attacked anyone, she would be killed. He opened his eyes, and Martha gave a slow nod in agreement.

He looked back at Tess, reinforcing the warning once more with his Alpha eyes, then turned to Dr. Serquey as she stepped forward. Harris projected to Martha the series of tests that Dr. Serquey wanted to do to her, taking blood and the like. He opened his eyes again and stared at Martha for her answer. Tess hissed and for the first time he heard her speech – the humming, the buzzing, the clicks. She was becoming bolder, more open. Martha returned the sounds back to Tess.

"Don't listen to Tess," Harris said to Martha, then projected her sitting through Serquey's tests, unrestrained.

Martha studied him again for a long moment, then gave a nod. He motioned to Dr. Serquey, who ushered Martha to her consulting room, under the watch of Yughi and Brown, while Harris followed to keep Martha calm.

Miranda Finch sat waiting patiently for Harris to arrive. She was in an interrogation room where one wall was lined with one-way mirrors. Julie's camera was set up in the corner and Julie stood beside it playing with sound levels.

Miranda checked her notes, reading through her questions one last time. Most of her suggestions had made it through. The general and his team had only struck two from her list. Ones that veered a little too close to specific strategies they were working on, namely the Alphas, but also their ships and weaponry. Everything else, it seemed, was fair game – with one or two word tweaks.

The door opened and Harris entered. She stood and extended her hand. Harris shook it.

"Thank you for this interview, colonel," she said.

"Thank you," he said. "You'll be pleased to know that we want this interview turned around fast and on the air tomorrow."

"Really?" she asked. "Why the urgency?"

"Because it's overdue, wouldn't you say?" he said, taking a seat and motioning for her to take hers again.

Miranda sat, eyes narrowed with curiosity.

"Shall we begin?" Harris asked, clasping his hands in his lap.

"Yes," she smiled, pulling her notes closer. "I have a lot to ask you."

Carrie stood in the Red House boardroom looking over plans for the HOS meeting with Greavy, Novak, Sampson, Beach, Aston, and Laurelai.

"We'll position soldiers at various points along the route from the Mars Docking Station to here," Greavy said. "Along with the military escort, that should deter any attacks along with way."

"Possibly," Carrie said, running her eyes over the map.

"We'll also space out arrivals so there're no bottlenecks when they're processed into the Red House, which we'll do as quickly as possible."

"And those left waiting at the Mars Docking Station?" Carrie asked.

"They'll stay on their ships until the escort is ready for them," Greavy answered.

Carrie nodded. "Okay. So, let's turn our focus to here. Once they arrive, they will be secured in this boardroom for the meeting, then escorted straight back to the MDS, then shipped to Atlas, where they'll stay."

"Yes, that's correct," Greavy said. "We'll call in all available ships to help with the escorts to Atlas."

"It's a strong military presence," Novak said, nodding in approval.

"It sure is," Greavy said. "I haven't seen anything like this on Mars before."

"Okay," Carrie said. "My AI needs to see the personnel files for every soldier involved."

"*Every* soldier?" Greavy asked. "We're talking hundreds. They've previously been vetted otherwise they wouldn't be wearing the uniform."

"Yeah, well, I learned in the Command Cleansing that you can never be too sure who to trust. I need those files asap, please, colonel."

Greavy stared at her, but bit his tongue on the response his eyes told her he wanted to give. "Alright."

"Thank you, sir," Carrie made sure to acknowledge his authority.

"Beach? Aston?" Carrie looked at them. "As the president is playing host, he'll be leaving Mars last. You need to stay sharp, understood?"

"Yes, ma'am."

"And I want you to be extra vigilant these next few days."

"Why's that?" Greavy asked.

"Because Colonel Harris is doing an interview and it may draw some folks out the president needs to be wary of."

"What's the interview about?" Greavy asked.

Carrie glanced at the Sentinels and Laurelai. "You're dismissed."

They looked to Greavy for their orders. He gave them a nod.

They left and Carrie looked back at Greavy, wondering whether she could trust him.

"He's doing a full interview about everything," she said. "Why he's prioritizing peace with the Zetas. We need to be on alert."

Harris walked the corridors of Command toward General Berger's office, as his shadows followed. He dialed Ty's number.

"*Hey, Dad,*" he answered.

"Ty, where are you?"

"*Playing ball with some guys I met.*"

"I need you to get back here to stay with Sarai."

"*Why? She's got a Sentinel with her.*"

"I've just done an interview about what's been going on, and until we know how people will react, I need you to hole up with the Sentinels. Understood?"

"*What'd you say in the interview?*"

"Nothing you're not already aware of, but the public won't be. There's bound to be some blowback from conservatives, so I want you to get your ass indoors and stay safe."

"*I can protect myself.*"

"Ty," Harris said firmly, "I know you can, but I want you to protect your sister, understood?"

"*She's in Command. No-one can reach her in there.*"

"You'd be surprised," Harris said, "and this isn't up for debate. Get your ass here. *Now.*"

Ty sighed. "*Why? We live in the same building, but we still never see you. At least, I don't. Sarai gets to see you more than I do.*"

"I've had a lot going on as you can imagine and Sarai is helping me with that. It's work. We'll do dinner again soon, I promise."

Ty was silent.

"Ty," Harris said, "I'm doing all this for you." He paused for a moment, lowered his voice, suddenly felt the urge to say it. "I love you and Sarai, and I want you to be safe. Please, come back to Command now."

Ty hesitated, but then spoke. "*Alright, alright. I'm heading back.*"

Harris arrived at Berger's door and hung up the PDP. He took a breath, steadied himself and knocked on the door.

It opened and Marchant waved him through. Harris took a guest chair and looked at Berger.

"Have you watched the interview? Are we good to go?"

"I have," Berger said.

"What's wrong with it?"

"I'm just a little uncomfortable with how much you reveal, Harris."

"We're walking a fine line, sir," Harris said. "The people will smell bullshit from a mile away. The only way to do this is to be completely transparent. No holds barred. I lay my cards on the table and hope that the people appreciate the honesty and our call for help."

Berger sat back in his chair and swiveled it to look out the window over Fort Centralis, the skies were pale gray, the seagulls sailing on the wind.

"He's concerned we'll look weak," Marchant said, "and that is not something a military force should ever do."

"I understand what you're saying," Harris said. "I do. But I don't think I give that impression. I tell them that we don't have all the answers, but I assure them that as soon as we do, we will step the fuck up and deliver their safety."

Berger swiveled back to him. "I'm concerned there will be backlash against our Head of Strategy using unorthodox methods to defeat our enemy. Being so open about being a See'er, it's just—"

"Governments have had psychic programs running covertly throughout history," Harris said. "This is not a new concept."

"I understand that, but it is also not a concept many believe in," Berger said. "Some will think we're ensuring their deaths by spending time on this avenue of defense."

"Look, I know you struggle to believe in this. You can't explain much of what you've seen me do with the Zetas, and still something in your brain won't let you believe it. I get it, and I know there're people like you out there. But there are also people like *him* out there," he pointed to Marchant. "Those willing to believe what their eyes are seeing. I know I won't connect with those like you out there, general, but I will connect with those out there like him. That's who I'm appealing to. The already-believers, and those willing to believe. I think they'll have the numbers I need to make this work."

"What if..." Marchant said, mind turning over as he stroked his bottom lip. "What if Finch interviews us too," he said, looking at Berger. "We can report what we've seen and you can clearly state that you're not sure that you believe, but you can't deny the results Harris has yielded, therefore, you are prepared to back him."

"We have to show a unified front," Berger said. "I can't go out there saying I don't really believe."

"So, say you believe, then," Harris said. "Say you believe, because of the dreams Welles and I had, because we saved your life."

Berger stared at him, unable to formulate an argument to that. The general's mind seemed to turn over, thinking it through one last time.

"Run the interview as is," he said. "If needed, I'll back you up in a second interview."

"Thank you, sir," Harris said, standing. "I'll tell Finch she can air it."

President Harkowitz sat glued to the screen in the Red House boardroom. With him, equally glued, were Laurelai, Sam, Lieutenant Welles, her children, and the day-shift Sentinels, Beach and Novak. On the screen, credits rolled from a prior show, ahead of what was promised to be an exclusive interview between reporter Miranda Finch and Colonel Harris, who would shed light on the Zetas, and UNF plans. It was airing on the World News Network, something that would, no doubt, be aggravating to both the Universal Press and Mars Media. Harkowitz allowed himself a small smile at picturing Lotz's face. It quickly faded, though, as he wondered what the world's reaction might be.

"I hope he knows what he's doing," he said, trying not to let the nervousness within show.

"He does," Welles said, though he noticed her eyes showed concern.

"Why do you look worried, then?" he asked.

"Because," she said, "I trust that *he* knows what he's doing, but I don't trust how people will react."

"Uncle Saul's a hero," Brody said. "The people have to believe him. He's fighting for us."

"I wish it were that easy, Brody," Welles said.

"Why isn't it that easy?" Freya asked. "What's wrong with people?"

"They don't have all the knowledge that we do, honey," Welles said. "We have the privilege of knowing the truth and the finer details about the Zetas. Everyone else out there only knows rumors, conspiracy theories and scaremongering. That's why Uncle Saul is doing what he's doing. They'll have access to the truth, so they'll know what we're trying to do. Hopefully, they'll support us and stop protesting and calling for the death of the Zetas."

"People are stupid," Jesse said.

"Misinformation is a big problem," Harkowitz told him. "That's the biggest battle we have to face, trying to distinguish between lies and the truth."

"They're on!" Freya yelled.

Their attention turned to the screen as brief introductory music played. Miranda Finch sat in a plain room, looking into the camera.

"Good afternoon, and welcome to this *exclusive* interview, where the United National Forces have granted me unprecedented access to the colonel at the heart of the Zeta invasion and the Zeta solution." She turned her face and the camera pulled back to reveal Colonel Harris sitting opposite her, with a small table between them. "Thank you, Colonel Harris, for allowing me this interview. I know you're very busy and the people have a lot of burning questions they'd like answered, so I appreciate your time."

"Thank you for agreeing to host this interview," he said. "I've been wanting to provide the people with answers for a long time, but unfortunately universal security meant I could not."

"So, why now?" she asked. "Why has the UNF agreed to declassify information at this point?"

"Because," Harris said, turning to look straight into the lens of the camera, "we need your help."

Harris and DaJuan stood outside Tess's cell. Martha was beside him and Dr. Serquey nearby. He heard footsteps and looked over his shoulder to see McKinley and the *Aurizun* team approaching, minus Hunter and Frazer who waited on the ship. They were armed with tranq pistols, ready to escort Tess and Martha to Martha's ship.

"If she tries anything," Dr. Serquey said, eyeing Tess, "I'll gas the room. It means you'll go down with her, but at least you'll be alive."

Harris gave a nod. "Stand back behind my team," he told her, then looked at DaJuan. "You, too." He turned to McKinley. "Spread out. Line the pathway back to the elevator. If she runs, tranq her."

McKinley nodded and made hand signals to the team with the instructions. Steinberg and Evenssen moved back to the elevators, while Brown and Tikaani positioned themselves down the corridor a little, and Yughi stood near McKinley. Gregson disappeared back into the elevator to wait for them on the ground floor.

Harris walked up to the door of Tess's cell, under the fixed stare of Martha. He looked at the Alma Mater, closed his eyes and projected the pathway they would take to her ship, under armed guard. He made it clear that his soldiers were there to protect them, not hurt them, showing her images of people trying to attack and his team taking them down. He opened his eyes and Martha gave a nod. He closed his eyes again, projected an image of Tess attacking his soldiers and his soldiers taking Tess down too. He opened his eyes again and Martha stared back at him.

Harris pointed to Tess, then to his men, and shook his head at Martha. Again she stared at him a moment, before an image appeared in his mind of Tess attacking McKinley, and Martha stepping in to help. Harris stared back at the Alma Mater. She understood, and like Harris, she would stop any attack.

He gave her a nod in thanks.

Harris took a deep breath and looked at Tess.

"You saw all that, right? You know what I'm gonna do if you fuck with me."

Tess hissed quietly, but her face was passive. She may hate humans, but she wasn't stupid. She knew she had a way out if she toed the line.

Harris turned to Dr. Serquey. "Can I open the door from here?"

"I can release it from here," Serquey suggested.

"No," he said, "it's the symbolism. I want her to see *me* releasing her. I want her to know I am responsible for her freedom. Maybe that way, she won't fuck with me or my men because I'm her ticket out of here."

Serquey nodded and called out a code that Harris punched into the data pad beside the door.

A yellow light flashed overhead, then, with a hiss of hydraulics, the glass door unlocked and popped open. Harris grabbed the handle, locked eyes with Tess again, then pulled the door open.

He stepped inside and looked over his shoulder to see Martha moving with him. He hoped it was because Martha was prepared to protect him and he wasn't about to be jumped by them both. He looked past Martha to where McKinley stood, eyes fixed on the cell and his hands clasping the tranq gun ready to raise and fire.

Harris looked back at Tess who stood in the corner of her cell. She hissed quietly again, her skinny tongue poking out to taste the air, to smell him.

Memories flashed inside his mind. He was suddenly back in Australia, McKinley was lying on the ground groaning in agony, and the attacking Zeta was smelling Harris.

He heard Martha give a gentle mooing grunt, saw she was looking at Tess, who had turned her stare to McKinley. Harris and Martha looked back at McKinley too.

"What?" McKinley asked, noticing their stares.

Martha placed her hoof-like hand on Harris's arm with static zap. Strangely enough it was his right arm, the one scarred from the Zeta claws. He felt his arm vibrating slightly, knew Martha was trying to reassure him.

"Nothing," Harris told McKinley and turned back to Tess.

He locked eyes with her and held his arm out, ushering her to the open doorway. Tess didn't move but stared at him, and the whole floor of Command was so silent he felt like he was in a vacuum.

He stepped backward to give Tess room and watched. She continued to sniff the air, black eyes rolling across everyone as she assessed for threats.

Martha looked at Harris and motioned to the door.

"I think she's telling me to get out," he told the others. Harris moved backward out the door, not turning his back on the two Zetas.

Martha and Tess stared at each other, having some conversation that Harris wasn't privy too. He felt the hairs stand up along his arms and neck. Suddenly he saw his female ancestry there, standing along the back wall of the cell, behind the Zetas.

The Zetas can control their conversations, he whispered in his mind to his kin. *They have the power to shut people out.* Sibbie, Etta and his mother nodded back at him, closing their eyes as they did.

Harris was pulled from his thoughts as Martha looked around at him. She stared at him a moment, then turned to look at the back wall of the cell where his female kin were standing.

Martha looked confused. Curious.

Because she didn't see them.

Because she couldn't talk to the dead.

Harris locked eyes with DaJuan.

"Your ancestry?" DaJuan asked quietly. As they hadn't been in a dream state, DaJuan hadn't seen them. Harris nodded.

"And they can't see them," DaJuan said, eyes shining with Harris's secret. "But Martha must've detected activity in your brain."

Harris felt a warm sensation slide down his spine, and for a moment he felt powerful. Knowing he could do something the Zetas couldn't.

Martha walked to the door, eyes fixed on Harris curiously, as Tess continued to survey for threats, rubbing the stump of her half-arm. As Martha exited the cell, Tess started to follow.

"Here we go," McKinley said, glancing back at his soldiers along the corridor. "Stay sharp."

"Tess might need assistance," Dr. Serquey said.

"Stay back," Harris warned. "You're the face that kept her in restraints. In fact, we don't need you anymore. Go to the elevator and wait on the ground level. If we need you we'll come get you. You too, DaJuan."

McKinley waved Dr. Serquey and DaJuan toward him and they obeyed.

"Yughi, take them topside, wait with Gregson."

Yughi escorted them down the corridor. Harris heard the elevator ping and the doors close again as they disappeared.

Martha gave another gentle mooing grunt and held her hoof-like hand out toward Tess. Tess ignored it, and slowly made her way to the door of her cell.

The *Aurizun* team began to move backward down the corridor. As the elevator returned, McKinley motioned for Steinberg and Evenssen to head topside. They did, and Brown and Tikaani took up their positions at the elevator as McKinley moved down the corridor, and Harris and Martha waited for Tess.

Tess slowly stepped out of her cell, tongue whipping around in a sensory bonanza. When she was sure it was safe, she moved in the direction of Martha's outstretched arm, all the while keeping her shiny black eyes on Harris.

An image shot into his mind of Tess coming under threat from the soldiers and her ripping McKinley's head off. Harris stared back at her unaffected. He wondered why she singled out McKinley. Perhaps because of his earlier flashback, but as he thought about it, he recalled showing her images of McKinley wounded during Decima when he'd first begun projecting with her, some time ago. Perhaps Tess sensed a weak spot in Harris. That weak spot being McKinley. He would not let her see that she was right.

The elevators returned and McKinley motioned for Brown and Tikaani to head topside.

"Go with them," Harris said to McKinley.

"No, I'll go with you."

"I'll be fine," Harris said.

"You can't be left alone with them."

"I can and I will. Go," Harris said firmly.

McKinley clearly didn't agree with his tactics but knew better than to argue. He exhaled heavily in protest, but slid between the closing doors of the elevator and disappeared.

Harris stood there for what felt like hours, alone on a deserted subterranean floor of Command with two Zetas. One of which he was sure wanted to kill him.

Tess hissed menacingly at him, but Martha turned to Tess, huffed through her nostrils and stomped her hoofed-foot. Looking at the two, Harris wasn't sure who would win in a fight. Martha was broader, looked stronger, but Tess looked flexible and agile and downright mean. The only thing working in Martha's favor at the present was that Tess was missing half an arm. And, perhaps, the size of their nodes. Dr. Serquey had informed Harris that Martha's node was larger than Tess', which could indicate that she was stronger of mind. Regardless, Tess wasn't stupid. Between the stocky, strong Alma Mater and the Alpha Harris, Tess wouldn't stand a chance. She had to know this.

Finally, the elevator dinged and the doors opened. Harris looked at the two Zetas, and held his arm out to usher them inside. Martha entered and turned her back to the wall. Tess hesitated, staring at Harris as her tongue whipped around tasting the air. Once again he heard her speech, the humming, buzzing and clicks. Tess was bestowing her parting words to Harris and he had no idea what she said. He looked at Martha, hoping to read her face, but she gave nothing away. Harris looked at Tess as she moved inside the elevator, with what he was sure was a sly smile on her face.

If Harris was a betting man, he wouldn't put money on her wishing him well.

He joined them in the elevator and as the doors closed, locking him inside with the two taller, somewhat terrifying Zetas, he fixed his eyes on Tess once more.

Carrie paced along the boardroom, darting her eyes from the interview playing out on one screen with sound, while Archie fed security footage from Command through to another.

A middle-aged staffer came in with a tray of homemade biscuits, tea and coffee.

"Thank you, Helen," Harkowitz said, sitting up. "Kids, you must try these biscuits. Helen always keeps a supply in the kitchen for me when I'm working late at night and need a snack. They're the greatest biscuits ever."

They each grabbed one and took a bite, moaning with delight.

"Good, huh?" Harkowitz smiled.

Carrie declined the biscuits. She was too tense. It felt weird to hear Harris's voice talking about the Zetas on one monitor, while on the other, he walked through Command's quarantine area with DaJuan close by, leading the two Zetas toward the UNF Space Dock.

"We have a chance at peace," Harris told Finch. "A real chance. The Alma Mater has not displayed any threatening behavior toward us. *At all.* She's been trying to understand what happened here during the invasion."

On the other screen, Harris continued to walk slowly toward the *Aurizun* team spread out ahead of them. Harris looked over each shoulder at the Zetas, pausing to stare at Tess a little longer. "I've conveyed to Martha, the best I could, that the attack was unprovoked. That *we* were the victims. And I have conveyed as best I could to her, that if we are attacked again, we *will* fight with everything we have."

Harris stared at Tess. He swore he could see that sly smile across her leathery lips again as she made an overt glance to McKinley, then back to Harris. He stopped walking and turned to Tess.

Harris closed his eyes and replayed the scene from the invasion, of him and McKinley cheering the *Barbican*'s return. Then the bright flash of light and the heatwave that threw McKinley into Harris, essentially, protecting him from the blast. He saw McKinley writhing on the ground in sheer agony. Pictured himself hiding from the Zeta, before standing and facing it.

"What's wrong?" McKinley asked, disrupting his thoughts.

Harris held his hand up to silence him. He focused again, showing Tess what happened next. How he lunged at the Priestess and killed it with his bare hands, caving its skull. When the memory finished playing through his mind, he opened his eyes and stared at Tess again. She glanced down to where the claw scars protruded beneath his shirt sleeve.

She hissed slowly, quietly back at him. Harris projected a quick flash of what the Priestess' head had looked like once he had finished with it.

"That's what happens when you fuck with me or my team," Harris told Tess, his muscles bulging with Alpha energy. "Understand?"

Tess didn't respond this time, but he was sure he saw that sly smile again.

He heard Martha moo calmly. Harris turned to look at her, but saw she was staring at Tess. The Priestess hissed quietly back at the Alma Mater, another private conversation they were blocking Harris from.

"What's going on?" McKinley asked, approaching them.

"Stay back," Harris pointed McKinley away.

"What's going on?" McKinley asked again firmly.

"Nothing," Harris told him. "Tess is just playing mind games and you're at the center of it. Swap places with Steinberg."

McKinley looked at Tess. "Does she want to go back to her cell?"

Tess hissed at him viciously.

"Swap with Steinberg now," Harris ordered, then glanced back at Tess. "I'm just taking her obsession away."

"I'm not afraid of her," McKinley said, his blue eyes turning cold.

Harris gave him an Alpha piercing look back. McKinley understood it, then headed toward Steinberg. Harris then turned to DaJuan.

"You pull back now. You're not coming with us. I want you here on Earth in case I need you."

DaJuan gave a nod, then turned back for the Command building.

Carrie stood still like a statue, utterly fixated on the security feed.

"What was that about?" Harkowitz asked, brow furrowed.

"I don't know," Carrie said, mind turning over. "He made McKinley swap with Steinberg. He was giving Tess an Alpha pose. Maybe she's threatening McKinley and Harris is separating them. The fucking *bitch*."

"Mom!" Jess gasped, smiling.

"Sorry, honey," Carrie said, eyes still fixed on the screen. "That's one for the swear jar."

Brody looked at Harkowitz. "Mom's Australian. They swear a lot."

Harkowitz fought a smile. "That's why we British banished the riffraff down there to Australia in the first place."

Carrie glanced at him, amused. "You'll keep, Mr. President." Then she turned to Brody. "And, by the way, your father swears his fair share too, you know, and he's American. We're both riffraff."

Harkowitz chuckled.

"They're headed out to the space dock!" Freya said, pointing at the screen.

Harris felt a breeze blow across his skin as he walked toward Martha's ship, beneath the canvas sheeting they'd erected. Though Martha kept his pace, Tess moved slower, looking around at everything, gathering information, seeking threats.

Harris paused again and looked around at her.

"I gave you my word you would not be harmed if you didn't harm us," he said. "Your freedom awaits." He held out his arm and gesturing the way to Martha's ship. Tess looked ahead, then began moving again.

Harris glanced around and saw Morrell in the distance, watching. Harris caught his eye and gave a subtle flick of his hand and motioned him away. He understood why Morrell would want to see the creature one last time in the flesh, perhaps to witness it leave Earth for good, but he'd warned Morrell to stay out of sight of Tess.

Unfortunately, Tess sensed Harris's movement and turned to stare at Morrell. Her shoulders instantly hunched and she hissed loudly.

"Don't!" Harris said, stepping around her into her line of sight. He raised a pointed finger at her. "You wanna go, then go. Don't fuck yourself, or us, for revenge."

Martha gave a mooing grunt and stepped up to them. Harris projected the vision of Morrell maiming Tess, then he projected Tess ramming her claws into Morrell's gut.

"You're even," Harris told Tess. "So, go."

Images suddenly projected inside Harris's mind of Morrell beating him in front of the restrained Tess. Harris saw his own bloodied and bruised face staring back at him. Tess hissed as though making an exclamation point.

"Yeah, he did," Harris nodded, "but I forgave him." He projected an image of Harris and Morrell shaking hands. He stared at Tess. "It's called peace."

Martha held her hoofed-hand out and gave a gently urging moo. He saw himself shaking hands with Morrell again. Harris looked at Martha's hand and understood what she meant. He placed his hand over hers, feeling the static zap, then Martha looked at Tess. Tess stared at each of them, tongue poking in and out in thought, before she raised her leathery hand and placed it on Harris's. He felt another, painful, static zap, as though being pricked with needles from above and below. But he clenched his jaw and arm muscles, and kept his hand in place.

"We should move," Yughiarto said. "It's not safe out in the open."

"Agreed," Harris said, relieved to pull his hand back. He looked at the Zetas, then motioned to the ship again. "You gotta go."

28

Release

Carrie watched the security feed as Harris led the two Zetas toward the ship. She had so many questions for him, wondering what the McKinley switch was about, then wondering what the other pause on the tarmac was for, and what happened when all three touched hands. She had an uneasy feeling and didn't know why. Was it just because she wasn't there to help watch their backs, that she wasn't part of the mind-melding, because she felt helpless here on Mars? Or was it something else?

She took a seat at the boardroom table, closed her eyes, placed her head in her hands and focused, wondering whether she could pick anything up, despite being on Mars. She pictured Harris and Martha, and even Tess, searching for a connection.

"So," Miranda Finch continued on the other monitor, "you have this ability to communicate with them, through projecting images."

"Yes," Harris answered.

"And it's a form of ESP?"

"Of sorts, yes. My female ancestry had similar gifts. They were See'ers and Sense'ers. My grandmother would have dreams about the future, of things that would come true, and I have inherited this gift."

"And did you dream of the invasion?"

"Yes."

Finch nodded carefully. "I have to ask you, why didn't you warn us?"

"Because, at first I didn't believe it myself. I fought and I fought not to believe in this gift until too many things had happened that I couldn't *not* believe. But still, who was going to believe me? I could've told the UNF about these dreams, but I feel I would've been removed from service and sent off for a pysch evaluation immediately. So, I did what I could to stay in service, so that when the time came, I could do everything in my power to try and stop it."

"Do you consider us overcoming the invasion as a victory?"

"No, I do not. The Zetas were outnumbered. We were always going to win the battle per se, but the cost of that win was great... I lost my w—" Harris's voice caught. He paused cleared his throat and continued. "I lost my wife in that invasion. The mother of my children... the love of my life." Harris stared at Finch. "I have to live with that. But I will not make that mistake again. That's why I'm doing this interview. I am laying my cards on the table and I want the people to know everything they can. Though I am trying to broker peace with the Zetas, I cannot promise it. If they come back and we go to war, I will fight them with everything I have. We have learned a lot about their ships, their weapons, and most importantly their, what we're calling, Thought Technology, their Thought Biology. I have learned to communicate with them, and I believe this will be a key factor in our success, should any war take place." Harris looked back into the camera. "And that is why I am doing this interview today. Because I *cannot* do this alone. And I do not believe that I am alone in my gift. There are others out there like me, and I would like them to come forward and join me. Many hands make light work, and I believe that many minds will make victory easier to achieve. So, if you are like me, then you will feel it in your bones, you will know it in your soul. And you will know that you are being called to step forward. You will know it's safe to come to me. Now is the time."

McKinley watched in awe as Martha opened the door to her ship with her mind. Tikaani and Brown flanked him.

"Start loading onto the *Aurizun*," McKinley told them. "We need to leave as soon as they do."

"Roger that," Brown said, then turned and waved the team to follow.

McKinley remained watching as Harris said his farewells to the Zetas.

Martha stood before Harris and they just stared at each other. To the unfamiliar, it would look odd, but McKinley had seen enough now to know they were having a conversation through projection.

McKinley shifted his eyes to Tess. He saw her looking around the space docks at the ships, the building, the soldiers. He didn't like it. She was assessing their defense. They should've kept the dock completely clear.

"*Arizona*," Hunter said over his comms, "*the team is loaded and ready to go. Just waiting on you.*"

"Roger," he replied. "I'll be there as soon as these two get on their ship and Harris is safe."

Harris stood silent and still, doing everything in his power to assure Martha that she would be under safe escort to the edge of the Belt. He also did what he could to reiterate that they wanted peace. It might be his last chance to do so.

Martha gave a nod. She, too, projected images of peace. From what he gathered, in her projections and all that she'd told him so far, she would return to Zeta Archelois and confer with her sisters on all that had happened. It gave him some reassurance.

With one last static touch of her hoofed-hand to his, and a projected image of Harris holding Sarai, who smiled, she turned and entered her ship.

Harris then looked to Tess who remained still, scanning around her.

"You're free," he said, ushering her into the ship. "Go."

Tess took one last look around, tongue darting in and out. He was sure she was seeking Morrell again, before turning her eyes to McKinley, then to Harris again.

And he swore he saw that sly smile slipping across her leathery lips again, before she turned and entered the ship.

He stepped backward as the canvas sheeting overhead was pulled clear from the ship. He stood in the sunshine, staring at the ship's entrance, empty but for shadows. He saw nothing but darkness within like a black hole, and he felt the hairs raise across his arms and the back of this neck.

"*Saul?*" he heard a voice call. He recognized it as Sibbie's.

Suddenly he was standing in that dream, the one he'd had the morning he got the call for the Darwin mission. He was standing in that field, the sunshine on his skin and he was turning around in circles looking for whoever called him.

He paused, came back to the present, and watched as the ship's door closed. He felt a sudden, overpowering urge to beg Martha to stay, but he fought it.

She didn't want to stay. He couldn't make her. It was time for her to go.

"Move back!" McKinley called to him.

Harris glanced around, then began moving backward toward McKinley while staring at the ship and picturing Tess's sly smile.

McKinley watched from the captain's chair as the *Aurizun* took flight after the Zeta ship. The *Carcharias* and *Benevolent* joined them, and the *Aurizun* moved to the point position, leading the ships on the two and a half days to Station Atlas, where they would part ways.

"Looks like our friends on the *Golden Orb* are back," Frazer announced, studying a screen on the flight deck console.

"How'd they know?" Evenssen asked.

"They'd have eyes on the Space Dock," Hunter said.

"As long as it stays out of the way, there's nothing we can do," Harris said from beside him.

"At least we didn't have any trouble from civilians as we left Earth," Tikaani said. "Looks like airing your interview was a good idea for distraction."

Harris nodded. "Yeah, but things will perk up once they realize the Zetas have been set free and they've heard what I said in that interview."

"Morrell will handle Command, and Welles will handle Mars," McKinley said.

"I'm sure they will," Harris said, "but I can't help being worried about Ty and Sarai while I'm gone."

"Marchant and the Sentinels will look out for them," Steinberg said.

"Maybe," Harris ran his hand over his buzz cut. "I still feel like shit for leaving them, though. They need me, but I need to be here in case Martha needs to communicate."

"You're worried," Yughi said, studying him, "about something else. Something aside from your kids."

Harris nodded, mind turning over. "I just hope Martha knows what she's doing."

"What was that shit back at Command?" McKinley asked. "Why'd you send me away?"

"Tess identified you as a target to get to me," Harris said, looking at him. "That was my fault. A memory surfaced of the Zeta attack and you on the ground."

McKinley lowered his eyes, then returned them. "So, she saw me as weak?"

"I don't know. But she's wrong if she does. Besides, I showed her what I did to the Zeta that attacked you. Broke my goddamn hand on that Zeta's face. She held back her threats after that."

The soldiers on the flight deck sat silently contemplating the discussion.

"If you think it's a mistake to release Tess," Evenssen said, "then why are we doing it?"

"Because Martha wanted it. If I refused, I risked making an enemy of her. I couldn't do that. We need her as an ally."

"What difference does it make," Brown shrugged. "If Tess comes back with friends, we'll be ready and waiting for her."

"Yes," Steinberg said, "but Harris is the one who will need to live with the decision to release her, when he could've killed her." He looked at Harris. "I don't envy that decision, sir, but it was the right one. Peace with the Alma Maters is more important than war with the Priestesses."

"Agree," Yughi said. "The course has been set. It is as it's meant to be."

Harris sighed. "Let's hope I don't regret it."

McKinley turned his eyes to the flight deck console, focusing on the footage of the Zeta ship following them. "I, for one, welcome the return of Tess. I'm looking forward to showing her just how weak I am."

He held out his mech arm, flexed his wrist back and felt the muzzle of his inbuilt gun protrude.

"Holy shit," Harris said, straightening. "You got it working?"

McKinley nodded. "Kind of. Can't shoot for shit yet, but I can bring the damn thing out now."

"You'll be shooting aces in no time, Arizona," Hunter smiled.

"Let's hope, Kiwi. Let's hope."

Carrie's head began to ache as she watched the news break of the two Zetas being set free. She looked over to Harkowitz who fidgeted as the adrenaline took hold. Laurelai, too, looked antsy.

Harkowitz stood from the boardroom table and buttoned his jacket.

"I need to get out and see the people. Reassure them."

"I don't think that's a good idea," Carrie said. "I think you should give it time to settle."

"Absolutely not," Laurelai said. "He can't look like he's formulating a response or hiding. He needs to respond immediately and let people know that he knew this was happening. Now is *absolutely* the time to speak."

"I want to go live as soon as possible," Harkowitz said.

"Yes, sir," Laurelai said, "we're ready when you are. We have Universal Press and Mars Media reps on standby."

"Who?" Carrie asked. "Who from Mars Media?"

"Kellan van Pelt," Laurelai answered.

"But he was on the *Golden Orb*," Carrie said, "and they're following the *Aurizun* as we speak."

Laurelai looked back at her and shrugged. "He might've been on the *Orb* on the way to Earth, but he's not on there now."

Carrie's PDP beeped. It was a private message from Archie, who'd been listening from the discs in her pocket:

>>> *I will investigate who is on the* Golden Orb *and trace van Pelt's movements.* <<<

Carrie clicked her PDP back on her belt.

"There's no need to panic," Harkowitz told her. "We'll film the live Q&A from here in our press briefing room, then I'll take personal meetings with influential people of note to reassure them these are the right measures and that I support them."

"Requests are already coming through," Laurelai said, studying her datapane.

"Then let's get to work." Harkowitz left the room with Laurelai in tow. Sentinels Beach and Novak moved with him.

Greavy stood and headed to the door. "I'll have soldiers patrol the colony streets to ensure things stay calm. Last thing we need is trouble before the HOS meeting."

"Sampson, take the kids back to the apartment and rest," Carrie ordered. "We'll need you later."

Sampson gave a nod and as soon they had swept from the room, Carrie used the boardroom facilities to make a private transmission to Gold.

"Welles," he gave a nod in greeting, "what's happening?"

"You've seen the interview and know the news has broken that the Zetas have left Earth?"

Gold nodded. "Yes. They'll rendezvous at Atlas and the *Carcharias* will remain stationed here after that."

Carrie nodded. "I just want to warn you that Harkowitz has decided to go on a PR blitz. Hopefully, there will be no issues, but I just want to warn you."

"No problems."

"I'm nervous about the HOS and the visit to Atlas given all that's been going on. We need to ensure our security is tight."

"We will. We're running everything by the book, checking everyone and everything, and running drills daily. After what happened with Connolly, I'm not taking any chances. Atlas will be impenetrable to any terrorist attack."

"Good," Carrie said. "That gives me hope for the launch. I just have to make sure we make it through the HOS first."

"Trust no-one and you'll be fine," he smiled.

"Yeah, I already operate on that."

"How's the head?" he asked. "It can't be easy with this stress upon you."

"It's okay," she smiled.

"If you need a hand or even just a second opinion, don't hesitate to reach out. Got it?" Gold said. "We're in this together."

"I will. Thanks," she said. "It's nice to have a friendly face in the vicinity."

"Agree."

"Talk soon."

She ended the transmission, then made her way to the press briefing room.

Morrell watched the news report which showed the gathering crowds at UNF and government buildings around the world. The faces carried a mix of emotions. Some were clearly angry, calling for Harris's blood, for the UNF to answer for releasing the Zetas, while some were professing to share his "gift" and insisting they speak to Harris, while others just looked lost and didn't seem sure what to think, just hoping for some clarity on it all.

Morrell had limited sea and air traffic to Centralis Island, shutting down commercial transport and only allowing official and military approved travel and shipments. It meant the crowd at the Command gates hadn't grown overnight, which was something at least.

"How's the situation on the mainland?" Marchant asked coming up beside him.

"As we expected," Morrell said.

Marchant studied the screen.

"What's the situation on Mars?" Morrell asked.

"Colonel Greavy has a UNF presence on the colony streets. Time will tell."

"I hope Gold and Welles are ready."

Marchant nodded. "They will be."

Carrie watched as Harkowitz undertook his Q&A with Kellan van Pelt, and Ari Vasker from Universal Press. Though Kellan, who Carrie guessed was in his late 20s or early 30s, was throwing some hard questions at the president, Harkowitz was answering them calmly, with ease and confidence.

Carrie's PDP vibrated against her hip. She pulled it off her belt and saw it was a message from Archie:

>>> I must talk with you urgently <<<

She clipped her PDP back on her belt and locked eyes with Novak to let him know she was exiting the press briefing room. She stepped into the corridor, taking one of Archie's discs from her pocket and holding it to her mouth. "What is it, Archie?"

"I have extremely concerning news, lieutenant. My scans picked up a report from Hell Town. Colonel Harbourg is dead."

Carrie paused. Her blood rushed down to her feet. Her breathing stopped. "W—what?" she said, getting her brain to work again.

"He was found dead in his cell. His throat had been cut."

"No, no, no…" Carrie breathed. "How? This can't be right? Harbourg had everyone in his pocket. He had the guards on side."

"Someone must have paid them more."

Carrie felt her body begin to shake. She looked down the corridor saw a junior staffer entering the briefing room.

"Fuck," Carrie hissed, turning away and keeping her voice low. *"Fuck!* He was looking into the independent Mars group for us. That has to be why, right?"

"Quite possibly," Archie replied. *"Unless his other dealings got the better of him."*

"No," Carrie shook his head. "He didn't survive all this time because he made bad calls or sided with the wrong people. This was *us*. He was killed because he was helping *us. Fuck!"* She started to pace. "Has Roxy Harbourg been informed?"

"She will be soon."

"Shit!" Carrie hissed again. "She's going to blame us."

"What are you going to do?" Archie asked.

Carrie started walking back to the briefing room. "I'm gonna stay close to the president, his threat level just went up. Keep going with your searches. We need to find out who's behind this."

"*Yes, lieutenant.*"

Carrie stepped back into the briefing room as Harkowitz stepped off the podium. Colonel Greavy entered the room behind her, walked straight up to the president and began whispering in his ear. Carrie saw Kellan looking on with interest, so she walked over to him and held out her hand, to distract him.

"Second Lieutenant Welles-McKinley," she said.

He looked down at the hand, then shook it. He was handsome, with sandy-blond hair and chiseled features, very smooth, though his brown eyes were filled with ambition. "Yes. I believe you're here consulting for the UNF?"

"I am."

"And what exactly are you consulting on?"

"Security mainly. As you know, we have the Heads of State meeting within days."

"Of course. I'm looking forward to it."

"I see you're missing out on taking another ride on the *Golden Orb*?"

"I'm sorry?"

"Oh, it's just that you were on it last time when it tailed the Zeta ship to Earth."

"You accessed its passenger manifest?" he smiled.

Carrie smiled back. "The UNF was curious."

"Well, unfortunately one has to make a call as to where to be, and I chose to stay close to the president while another colleague took over the *Orb* transit."

"Not a bad play given there's only two reporters here," Carrie said, glancing around at Vasker who was packing up. "You might just get the scoop."

"Do you like sport, lieutenant?"

"Sometimes," she shrugged.

"Well, just like in rugby, we can either choose to be in the scrum where the perceived action is, or we can hang back and grab the ball when it comes rolling our way. That's what I've chosen to do. Mars and its proxy-steel is the real story here. It has the power to make or break a war."

"And which side are you on?"

"Which side?"

"Do you think they should hold the proxy-steel hostage for ransom? Or do you think they should help the UNF defend our territories?"

"I'm a reporter, lieutenant," he said confidently with a smile. "It's my job to remain objective."

Carrie saw Greavy trying to catch her eye. She looked back at Kellan.

"Well, that's good to know. We need more objective reporters. It was nice to meet you."

"And you," he said.

Carrie walked over to Greavy. "What is it?"

He ushered her outside the press briefing room into the corridor, where Harkowitz whispered with Laurelai.

"I got word from Senator Butten that the mine is shutting down in protest and the workers are going on strike. Word is, some are on their way here to protest."

Carrie nodded. "So, we will be ready for them."

Greavy nodded. "I'm going to increase the soldiers on patrol in Brahe and Elon, and put more outside here, which should hopefully encourage some to stay home, but the president disagrees. Please talk some sense into him."

"Disagrees? With what?"

"No," Harkowitz shook his head as he approached them, while Laurelai moved to speak with the junior staffer. "Pull the soldiers back. If they think I'm turning Mars into a military zone, they'll revolt. *No.*"

"If you let them think they run this fucking planet, there'll be anarchy and you'll wind up dead!" Greavy spat.

Carrie placed a placating hand on Greavy's arm and moved him back, making sure to lock eyes with him in warning. She wasn't necessarily a fan of the guy, but he was walking a fine line that could lead to automatic dismissal for talking to the president like that – despite their friendship.

She looked back at Harkowitz. "We need to find a happy medium, sir. A medium that says the soldiers are there to prohibit violence, not to enact it."

"When people are angry you need to let them vent. If you don't release the valve, they will explode and the fallout will be bad."

"I understand that," she said, "but if you just let them go for it and things boil over, your civilians may wind up hurting each other. Worse, you may not get them under control again without a heavy hand. If you do not want to show them a heavy hand, then you need to show them a firm, but nurturing hand now."

Harkowitz stared at her, considering her words.

"Besides, I have news," Carrie said, glancing at Greavy. "I've just been informed that Colonel Harbourg was found murdered in his cell."

Harkowitz's mouth fell open in surprise. He looked at Greavy. "Did you know this?"

Greavy nodded. "Why do you think I'm telling you to be careful."

"Why? You think this is related to my death threats?" Harkowitz said, then shook his head. "You know Harbourg was mixed up in a lot of things. It's no surprise it finally caught up with him."

Carrie locked eyes with Harkowitz. "I asked him to look into the independent Mars group. Now he's dead."

Carrie stepped closer to Harkowitz and lowered her voice. "If you don't take your safety seriously, you are endangering everyone around you. What if someone guns for you and hits Laurelai instead? Do you want to explain to her family that she died because you didn't listen to your security team?"

Harkowitz glanced at Laurelai down the corridor talking on her PDP. He sighed and placed his hands on his hips. "What, then, is this happy medium?"

"Increase the soldier presence on the colony streets and outside," Greavy said. "Just to let them know we're here. If there's any trouble, my soldiers will move folks along quickly and as calmly as they can."

"And you stay here inside the Red House until after the HOS," Carrie added.

"What?" Harkowitz said, then shook his head. "No, I need to visit the mine and speak with the people there."

"Sir, I—" Carrie began.

"No," Harkowitz said firmly, "we need the proxy-steel. The UNF needs the proxy-steel. It's why you're here. We need to sort that out as a priority. We need them on side."

"Agree," Carrie said, "but you can do that over a transmission."

"I need to show my face in person, to show I care enough to go to them. They already think I'm a coward. I need to prove them wrong."

"Try the transmission first, sir," Carrie said firmly. "If that doesn't work, I will personally escort you to the mine. Either way, Harbourg is dead and we're raising the threat level against you."

Harkowitz stared at her in analysis, glancing at Greavy. "We need to maintain peace ahead of the HOS. I don't want all those Heads of State coming here to a shitshow. I want them coming to a pivotal planet that's under control. And it *will* be as soon as I smooth things out with the miners. I get them on side, the rest will follow suit. The miners hold the power."

"Understood," Carrie said firmly. "Try the transmission first, sir."

Harris stared down the transmission screen at Sarai.

"Your Sentinels are close by?" he asked her.

She nodded. "They're right outside my door. I heard them talking to Mr. Marchant earlier."

"Marchant?" Harris asked. "What did they talk about?"

"They told him the apartment was secure and Ty wasn't here."

"What?" Harris asked, straightening. "What do you mean he's not there? I told him to go stay there with you."

"He came and checked on me, then left again."

Harris clenched his teeth so hard he thought he was going to break them. He clenched his fists too.

"I wasn't supposed to tell you that," Sarai said guiltily. "He said you had enough on your mind and I shouldn't worry you."

"Did he say where he was going?" Harris asked.

Sarai shook her head.

"I'm gonna kill him," Harris muttered.

"You know what he's like, Dad," Sarai said. "He doesn't listen."

"Yeah, I know," Harris said. "He's just like his Uncle Terence was. That's what worries me."

"I think he feels left out," Sarai volunteered.

Harris studied her over the transmission screen. "Left out of what?"

"This," she shrugged. "The Zetas. The war. He knows I've been communicating with them. With you. I think he feels useless. He wants to do something, to be helpful. He wants to avenge—"

"Your mother's death."

Sarai's face fell. He studied his daughter, realized he'd never asked her an important question.

"Sarai?" Harris asked quietly.

She looked at him with eyes that seemed much wiser than her nine, almost ten, years.

"Did you see your mother pass?" he asked her.

Sarai's eyes flooded with tears, her mouth scrunched. She shook her head. "I went to sleep when the building collapsed. When I woke she was on top of me and she didn't wake up." Sarai started crying, and in response Harris felt tears spilling from his own eyes.

"I'm so sorry, Sarai," he managed. "You never should've been in that position... I should've been with you."

Sarai wiped her face. "It's okay... When I was sleeping I dreamed of great-grandma Sibbie and she told me I would be okay. And that's when I saw Carrie." She sniffed. "I dreamed she came for me, and she did."

Harris felt a surge of emotion rush through him. He lowered his face, covered his mouth, tried desperately to block the sudden release of grief, but for a moment it was uncontrollable. He heard Sarai crying just as hard in response. It took a few moments, but he managed to take hold of his emotions and rein them back in.

"You're so strong, Sarai," he said between breaths and sniffs, "so much stronger than I'll ever be." He studied her. Sarai had seen pictures of Sibbie and Etta before, but had obviously never met them. She hadn't even met Harris's mother, Maeve, having been born after her death. Yet, through their gift and connection with the dead, Sibbie had appeared in a dream and shown Sarai her future.

"Aunt Holly always told me to listen to my dreams," Sarai said, sniffing. "She said they would always guide me to what was right, so I knew that Carrie would come."

Harris wiped his face. "I'm so sorry I'm not there with you right now, honey."

"You need to make sure Martha's safe."

"I do," he nodded, "and as soon as we reach Atlas, I will return to you as fast as I can."

She nodded, wiping her face too.

"When you see Ty again," Harris told her. "You tell him to stay put, alright? You tell him, I'm begging this of him. Tell him to do this for me. Okay?"

Sarai nodded, looking at him cautiously as her mind ticked over.

"What?" Harris asked.

Sarai thought some more then looked back at him. "I'm worried Tess will hurt Martha."

"Did Martha say something to you?"

Sarai shook her head.

"Did Tess ever try to contact you?"

Sarai nodded. "But Martha would always appear and Tess would leave again."

"Martha was protecting you," Harris allowed himself a smile. "When Martha left, she showed me a picture of you. Of me hugging you. I think Martha was telling me to protect you."

Sarai seemed to think about this. "They would look at me as though they were looking right into me. I was scared."

"They could tell your gift was strong," Harris said, nodding to himself as he thought about it. "Martha knows you are an asset to be protected. She knows if there's any chance that our two races can cohabit this universe, then we need to communicate and you can do that well. You're our new queen, honey."

Sarai blinked down the screen at him, her mind expanding with the knowledge.

"And you're just a kid, Rai," Harris said. "Imagine what you'll be like when you're an adult? How strong your gift will be."

They sat in silence for a moment before Harris checked the time on his PDP. "Honey, I gotta go. I'll be home as soon as I can, but until then, you don't leave Command or your Sentinels side. Understood?"

She nodded.

"Keep dreaming, honey. I'll see you soon."

He ended the transmission, and another transmission immediately came through. It was Marchant. He answered it.

"Sir?"

"Harris, we just got word that Colonel Harbourg was found murdered in Hell Town. Apparently, Welles asked him to look into the independent Mars movement. Now, we don't know if that's what got him killed or whether it was something else, but… it's concerning."

"Fuck. What's Welles doing about it?"

"They're boosting security. Apparently, the miners have gone on strike and folks are letting Harkowitz know they're not happy with the UNF."

"Well, we knew there would be some blowback."

"Harkowitz is going to try and talk them down. I'll keep you posted."

Harris gave a nod and the transmission ended. He sighed heavily, rubbed the back of his neck.

There was a lot going on, but right now he couldn't think of anything else until the Zetas were safely gone from this solar system.

29

The Edge

Carrie sat quietly off-screen while Harkowitz spoke with Ron McCaulay, Ops Manager at Haides-1.

"What are their demands?" Harkowitz asked him.

"They're demanding justice for those who died in the invasion. They believe they've been robbed of that justice due to the UNF allowing the Zetas to leave."

Harkowitz nodded. "Did they watch Colonel Harris's interview?"

Ron nodded.

"They saw him say that the Zetas appeared to want peace?" Harkowitz said.

"Yes, he said they *appeared* to want peace. They think the UNF are fools for trusting the Zetas, and they think you're a fool for trusting the UNF."

"All of them?" Harkowitz asked. "You're telling me that every single one of your workers feels the same way? That none are capable of individual thought?"

"Who's gonna speak up when the loudest are screaming for blood?"

Carrie leaned forward into frame. "Who's screaming for blood?"

Ron stared at her. "There're too many to name. Look, as I told Senator Butten, I think it's just talk right now, but like you, I want them to get back to work, so anything you can do to help push that forward would be great."

Harkowitz gave a nod. "Find me the leader or someone willing to be the spokesperson and have them wait for me in your boardroom. I will come and speak with him personally."

Carrie shot him a look, but Harkowitz leaned forward and ended the transmission.

"What are you doing?" she asked.

"My job," he said. "In order for me to support the UNF, I need the people to support me. Right now, I'm at risk of losing that. I've got Butten and Pope on my ass for answers. The quicker I quash this little rebellion, the quicker we get back to normal."

"Do you want to die?" Carrie asked him.

"No," he said, "I don't. So, the fewer enemies gunning for me the better." He pressed his desk comms. "Laurelai?"

"Yes, sir?"

"Prepare the jet for a journey to Haides-1."

"Yes, sir."

He released the comms and looked back at Carrie. "I'll have you, Beach, and Novak by my side. I'll be safe," he said. "These miners don't know you're an Alpha and what you can do."

"An Alpha can't do much against a bomb, or a sniper shot."

"That's what your senses are for, are they not?" Harkowitz said.

Carrie's brow furrowed, confused.

"Harris told me enough about the Alpha program for me to feel well protected, lieutenant."

"I only have the Alpha eyes, not the rest of the senses you think I do."

Harkowitz paused briefly. "You'll still be enough."

"And if you take one risk too many that I can't save you from?"

Harkowitz stared at her a moment. "Then that's on me. But I must try this. With or without you."

McKinley sat on the flight deck, watching the *Carcharias* and the Zeta ship behind them. With pockets of trouble promising to flare out of control around the universe, it had felt like a long, slow journey so far, and they still had a day and a half to go.

Harris sat beside him, his mind seemingly elsewhere.

"Everything alright?" McKinley asked him.

Harris waved him off. "I told Ty to stay at Command under guard, but of course he's gone elsewhere."

"Get Marchant to send soldiers to find him."

"I left messages for him. If he doesn't respond soon I will." Harris looked at him. "I gotta give him breathing space."

"Fuck that. You're his father. Tell him to get his ass home."

Harris chuckled. "He's an adult. I can't tell him what to do no more. Just wait until your little Alphas are teenagers, then adults, McKinley. You'll find out what it's like then."

McKinley groaned. "Alpha teens…"

"Sir!" Frazer said. "Transmission from Welles."

"Put her through here," Harris said.

Welles appeared across the observation window.

"What's up, Welles?" Harris said, studying her serious face.

"I'm just letting you know that I'm about to escort the president to Haides-1. They're striking, upset the UNF let the Zetas go."

"Is that a good idea, given what happened to Harbourg?" Harris asked.

"No, but I can't talk the president around, so we're going."

"What are the colonies like?" McKinley asked.

"I'm waiting on an update from Colonel Greavy, but he was putting a stronger presence on the streets. The numbers of civilians outside the Red House gates are swelling a little."

"Their suits will run out of air eventually," Brown said.

"Honestly, they're the least of my problems right now," Welles aid. "I gotta go."

"Stay safe," Harris said before the transmission ended. "Frazer, get me Gold."

"Sir," Frazer said, punching in the transmission code.

Gold appeared. "*Aurizun* team," he said. "What's up?"

"All's well here," Harris said. "The Zeta ship is on course. How're things with you?"

"All's well here, too. We're counting down to the HOS and launch."

"I want you to keep an eye on Mars as well, if you can," Harris said. "Welles is about to escort Harkowitz to the Mercandez mine and there seems to be some unrest."

"Yeah, I've been keeping one eye on it," Gold asked.

"I'm concerned with the little fires burning everywhere that one might get missed that turns into an inferno. Get my drift?"

"Understood. I'll put two eyes on it."

"Good," Harris said and nodded for Frazer to end the comms. "Now, get me Morrell if you can."

It took a while to track him down and get him to a transmission screen, but eventually Morrell appeared with a blood-splattered shirt.

"What the fuck happened?" Harris asked. "Is that blood?"

"Yeah, some asshole started hurling glass bottles at us on the gate."

"You got hurt?" Harris asked.

Morrell shook his head. "No, but *he did* after we dragged him out of that crowd."

"Tell me you didn't do this in front of the media?"

"Don't know. I wasn't looking for cameras. I was just trying to stop him before he injured more civilians. Some of the bottles went astray and hit innocents."

"How bad did you work him over?"

"Not bad," Morrell said. "Just one or two cracks to calm him down."

Harris ran his hand over his face. "Alright. I know it's hard out there, Morrell, but I need you to stay calm and rein that shit in. Now is not the time."

"I *am* reining it in. I wanted to beat the living shit out of him, but I didn't. And it's hard, you know, because I kind of agree with them."

"I don't care about your personal preference for the welfare of the Zetas, Morrell, I care about you following my orders. Understood?"

"Yes, sir," Morrell said placatingly. "Anything else? Because I need to get back out there."

"No," Harris said lightly. "Just be the guiding light for your soldiers. Go forth."

The transmission ended and Tikaani chuckled. "He's a character."

"There's no room for characters in the military, Tikaani," Harris said. "It's a fuckin' hard job trying to maintain peace while not being seen to exert your authority. It takes restraint. One false move and we're all over the news as villains. We can't have that. Especially not now."

"The sooner the Zetas are gone from our solar system, the better," Brown said.

"Out of sight, out of mind, huh?" Steinberg asked him.

"They'll be out of sight, but they'll never be out of mind," Yughiarto said. "There's too much trauma from the invasion for people to ever forget."

"The Zetas will be safe," Hunter said, "but we'll be left to pick up the pieces."

"I don't want to have to look over my shoulder for our own kind as well as the Zetas," Evenssen said.

"We're going to have to," Harris said. "So, let's do everything in our power to keep the peace, huh? Even if we want to crack skulls, we stow it."

Gold flicked between security feeds showing various views over the streets of Mars, as well as the Mars Docking Station. The Red House was, of course, a dead zone. No-one was allowed to have access to or hack into security footage of that area. The Haides-1 site was a dead zone, too, but everything else was up for grabs.

From what he could see things looked mostly calm. He saw a noticeable Space Duty presence: driving around in MaPVs, walking the streets. Here and there were small gatherings of crowds, but nothing that looked like it was out of control or couldn't be handled. The smaller Mars population had that going for it, at least. The Martian soldiers had less people to deal with than Earth forces right now.

Having watched Harris's interview and the subsequent news breaking of the Zetas' freedom, Gold knew that some people would be angry about the release and angry that they were distracted by the interview when it happened, but he also knew that those who listened carefully to Harris's interview would know his true intentions were trustworthy and in humankind's best interests.

But he also knew that a disruptive minority could make it hell for the majority.

He checked the Carcharias's electronic logs, keeping track of the journey toward Atlas, then he checked the MDS logs to ensure no more vigilantes were departing to cause more trouble. They'd ensured the MDS was locked down this time and it was working.

So far, so good. But he knew how quickly things could change.

Carrie sat in the Mercandez boardroom with Harkowitz, waiting for the strike leader to appear. Beach stood in the room with them, while Novak stood outside.

"They're keeping us waiting," she said to Harkowitz. "Intentionally."

"Let them have this one," he said quietly.

The door opened and Ron entered with a well-built, clean-shaven man who looked like he should be in an advertisement for weightlifting supplements. Harkowitz stood and extended his hand to the man.

"You must be Angus White," Harkowitz smiled. "It's nice to meet you."

White shook the president's hand then took a seat at the table alongside Ron.

"So," Harkowitz said, "I believe your workers are on strike and I'd like to see if I can help end it."

White stared at him a moment. "I'm listening, Mr. President."

"Your strike, what is the core issue behind it? Is it my dealings with the UNF, or is it the fact that the UNF released the Zetas?"

"Both," White said, sitting forward and resting his big arms on the table, clasping one fist in the other.

"Okay," Harkowitz nodded. "Well, with regard to the UNF releasing the Zetas, it is a play for peace with their race. Killing or keeping captive two Zetas won't stop more from coming, but releasing them unharmed is a gesture of goodwill which *could* stop more coming."

"Goodwill? They killed innocent people when they attacked us, unprovoked."

Harkowitz held up a finger to stop him. "Only one of those Zetas attacked us. The other came in peace and never once threatened violence."

"It doesn't matter."

"It doesn't matter? So, if two separate people from out of town walk into this mine, and only one of them starts a fight, you'd kill both? For what? For merely being from out of town?"

White stared at him. "The Zeta that attacked us should've been killed."

"*That* Zeta landed on Centralis Island and attacked and killed only Command soldiers. If anyone should be angry about that, it's the UNF. Yet, they are the ones pushing that aside and trying to broker peace for *all* of us."

White leaned forward. "Out of respect for those dead soldiers, that Zeta should've been killed."

"So, your strike here at the mine and manufacturing plant is a protest against the UNF for not avenging their dead soldiers?" Harkowitz stared at him. "And if they *did* kill the Zetas and triggered a universal war that resulted in millions of humans being killed, would that justify it?"

"If you show weakness, they will exploit it."

"I understand your point of view, and I admire your passion and courage, Mr. White—"

"Don't patronize me."

"—but I believe you know less about warfare than the UNF, and should trust they know what they're doing."

"*Blindly* trust the UNF?" White said, sitting back in his chair and folding his big arms. "You might prefer to do that, sir, but we don't wish to."

"I am privy to a lot more sensitive information than you are," Harkowitz said, locking eyes with the man. "To you it may look like I'm blindly following them, but I assure you, I am a smart man who studies the facts, and I wish to see Mars succeed, and exceed expectations. We have valuable resources here, resources that the UNF need, and the smart move is to work together with them, not against them."

White moved his pale-blue eyes over to Carrie, looked her Space Duty uniform over, then looked back at Harkowitz.

"Why is she here?"

"The UNF would like to help resolve the qualms with your miners."

"What assurance can you give my workers that this won't become a UNF-run mine?"

"It won't," Harkowitz said. "The Mercandez company hold the lease. It's theirs. If Mars is going to succeed, we need a thriving economy. Our resources are a key part of that and the UNF will be our biggest client."

"May I ask a question?" Carrie piped up, looking at White. He shrugged back at her, nonchalantly.

"What's the difference between the UNF running the mine and the Mercandez company? Either way, it's a monopoly."

"The difference is that Mercandez pay well and they don't carry guns. If the UNF take over, it'll become a slave camp."

"That's a little extreme," Carrie said. "The good news is that the UNF is not interested in taking over the mine or the manufacturing plant. We *absolutely* wish to buy the resources off you, but we have no interest in working the mine or plant. Our business is in peacekeeping. It's in the security and defense of mankind, and that is where we will focus *our* resources. You mine the ore, and create the proxy-steel, we'll buy it off you and build our ships and weapons, and if the Zetas come back, we will annihilate them on your behalf. That's the circle of life."

White stared at her and a smile curled his mouth. "You ever been to war, sweetheart?"

"Have you?" Carrie smiled back at the patronizing bastard.

He continued to stare at her with challenging eyes.

"I've been in more than my fair share of battles," Carrie told him, "and I have the head injuries to prove it. I was there during the invasion. My fellow soldiers were killed. I watched my father, a founder of Mars, die."

White's smile fell away as she mentioned her father.

"Second Lieutenant Welles's father was the Original, Colonel Jeffrey Welles," Harkowitz explained to White.

White darted his eyes between the two. "An Original, huh? Is that supposed to win me over, bringing the daughter of a celebrity here?"

Carrie felt her Alpha rise abruptly without warning. "I'm not the daughter of a celebrity. I am a soldier who has taken beatings, fighting people and things you couldn't even dream about because you'd wake in the middle of the night crying like a baby!"

"Lieutenant," Harkowitz said firmly, but friendly. "Thank you. Would you please wait outside."

White stared at her, curious at her outburst. "You have a big mouth for a small package."

Carrie stood and walked slowly to the door. "I've fought bigger guys than you before and lived to tell the tale, so spare me the tough guy routine."

As Carrie left the room she heard Harkowitz sighing. She stepped outside and motioned for Novak to head inside, while she took up his position.

As Novak moved inside, she stood by the door and felt her skull beginning to ache with the tension.

*

Carrie sat opposite Harkowitz as they journeyed back to the Red House in *Mars Force One*. He'd said nothing to her as they'd left and the air felt stifling as they sat alone with Beach and Novak. She'd felt bad, of course, losing her cool like that when they'd been trying to resolve the situation. She'd been like a bull with red flag. And it worried her. While she'd been standing outside the room, all she could think about was her brain and the CTE, wondering whether she would be up to the task of protecting the president if it came to it. Would the CTE make her too cavalier? Make her miss something she shouldn't? Take risks she shouldn't? If the president died on her watch, the repercussions would be immense for the UNF.

"Alright, let me have it," Carrie said to Harkowitz, wanting to clear the air. "I'm waiting."

Harkowitz studied her. "You didn't help things. Well, you did, you were doing great until you lost your temper."

She nodded. "I've been known to be hot-headed, and especially so when people attribute my success as being due to who my father was."

"Oh, I understand that more than anyone," Harkowitz said. "But that's the difference between me, a politician, and you, a soldier. I am trained to use words very carefully. You are trained to be physical. You follow orders and expect others to follow *your* orders, and when they don't, you resort to violence because it's what you're trained at."

"Sometimes words don't work."

Harkowitz conceded a nod. "But they did in that room."

"How did it end?" Carrie asked. "Is White just making a cry for attention, trying to show off his dick to the workers?"

Harkowitz chuckled. "Well, I wouldn't have used those words but, yes, I think he's just flexing his muscles. I have assured him that the UNF will not interfere with the mine," Harkowitz locked eyes with her, underlining the point, "and I think he felt somewhat reassured."

"And the anger over the release of the Zetas?"

"That, I don't know. I can't change people's opinions on that. If Harris's interview didn't sway them, nothing will. We'll have to wait and see if White gets the miners to head back to work."

"My AI traced some of your death threats back to Colony Brahe where most of your miners reside."

Harkowitz nodded. "I'm not surprised. That's why I'm keen to reassure them that I care, and why I wanted to show my face. I want them to know they have nothing to fear from me, that their jobs are secure."

"Harbourg's death worries me," she said, feeling the pressure in her skull again. "If he died because of what he was looking into—"

"Colonel Greavy has been briefed to obtain a full update on what happened. Let's wait until we know more."

Carrie didn't feel reassured, still unsure whether she could trust Greavy.

"Relax," Harkowitz said, ever the leader. "If we keep clear heads, things will calm down soon enough."

"Things will calm when the threat against you has been dealt with."

Beach glanced at her, then Harkowitz. "We'll keep you safe, sir. No-one's getting through our wall of protection."

"I should hope not," Harkowitz smiled back.

Harris entered McKinley's office aboard the *Aurizun* and took the transmission from Marchant that he had stated was to be private.

"Sir?" he said, upon seeing Marchant's face. "What's wrong?"

Marchant sighed. "I found Ty."

"Is he alright?" Harris asked, heart leaping into his throat.

"He's fine," Marchant reassured him, "he's just in jail."

"What?"

"Some MPs picked him up. There was a fight at a bar."

"Is he hurt?"

"No, Ty's fine. The other guy is still unconscious, though."

"Fuck," Harris breathed. "Can I speak with him?"

"I thought you might want to. I'll send you the details. You want us to send him back to Command?"

Harris thought for a moment. "Normally, I would say a night in a cell might make him think twice about doing that again, but I can't risk his safety with everything else going on. Send him to my quarters and handcuff him there if you have to."

Marchant nodded. "Will do. I'll look after Ty, you just keep your mind on the job up there, you hear?"

"Yes, sir."

Harris sighed and waited for the transmission details to come through. As soon as they did, he entered the code.

A uniformed MP with a five o'clock shadow answered.

"I'm Tyson Harris's phone call," Harris said.

"Colonel. Just a minute."

Harris waited for Ty to appear. As soon as he did, Harris said nothing, but eyed him over.

"The other guy gonna wake up?" he eventually asked his son.

"The punch wasn't that hard."

"But was the ground? Skulls don't beat concrete."

"Hey, I did it protecting you!"

"From what?" Harris asked. "Words? I asked you to stay with Sarai not just for her, but to protect *you*. To save *you* from *this*."

Ty exhaled annoyance.

"Why'd you disobey me?" Harris asked.

"Because I can take care of myself."

"Can you?"

Temper flared in Ty's eyes. "Why are you calling me? Don't you have more important things to do like free those Zetas."

"Yes, I do have important things to do, Ty, but I will always make time for you."

"Oh, really?" Ty's eyes popped and he gave a laugh, before scrunching his face in thought. "I don't recall you doing that when I was younger."

"You're right, I didn't," Harris said. "I've seen the error in my ways, and I'm trying to change."

"Hey, don't sweat it. I turned out fine without you."

Harris felt a slash across his heart with those words. "You turned out fine because of your mother, but she's not here anymore, Ty, so you are left with me."

Ty looked away from the screen, then back at it. "You don't even wanna know what they were saying about you?"

"No," Harris shook his head. "I'm going to ignore it, like you should."

"Well, it's hard to do that. It's everywhere."

"And it will be for some time. You wanna join the military? You need discipline, Ty, and it starts here."

Ty studied him a moment. "So, you're really supporting my application?"

Harris thought for a moment, released a controlled sigh. "Yeah, I guess I am."

"Why? What changed?"

"Nothing changed. I don't want you to, but I see that you do, and I know you're stubborn, just like your Uncle Terence. And I know, that if I try and stop you, you'll do it anyway. Just look at tonight."

"Why is it that you'll let Sarai be involved, but not me? Why don't you want me near you?"

"What?" Harris's brow furrowed. "I do want you near me, Ty."

"No, you don't. You keep pushing me away!"

"I was pushing you away from joining the military because I don't want you to *die*!" He snapped.

"But you let Sarai—"

"Sarai has a gift that I know she can use in the safety of a bunker somewhere, Ty. You'll be out there on the front lines."

"Yeah, like many others, Dad. You kept the Zetas secret from people. You can't let your kids sit back in a safe bunker while others die."

Harris took a deep breath, swallowed, looked back at the screen. "I know. That's why I'm not stopping you."

Silence sat for a moment between them. It broke Harris's heart that Ty wanted to join, but he knew his son's mind was set. Besides, the more and more he thought about it, the more he thought the discipline of the military might be good for him. Maybe it was the course correction Ty needed to avoid becoming too much like his Uncle Terence.

"You might not want to listen to your dad," Harris said, "but if you want to join the military you better listen to your CO's orders. Do you understand me? This shit, these bar fights, this trouble, your *attitude*, it's got to stop or they won't take you."

Ty stared at him.

"Right now, I'm your dad, Ty, but once you join up and make it to Earth or Space Duty and you wanna become an Alpha, I *am* your fuckin' CO. You don't listen to *my* orders then? I'll kick you the fuck out. Understood? I don't take this attitude from my soldiers and I sure as *fuck* won't take it from you either."

He could see the temper flare in Ty's eyes, the glimpses of Terence there, but the flames quickly smoked out.

Ty nodded, his face softening. "Yes, sir."

Harris stared at him a moment longer to reiterate his point like he would with a soldier, then he gave a nod.

"Someone is coming to get you and take you to Command. You go there and you stay there, or you will *never* see a uniform. Are we understood?"

"Yes, sir."

"You wanna be a soldier, start by protecting your sister."

Ty nodded.

Harris took another breath, then softened his features. "I love you, Ty. I'll see you and Sarai soon."

Carrie awoke suddenly. Her head ached as fevered fragments of dreams bounced around her skull. She saw images of Harris, of Martha, then the sound of an alert broke through her half-asleep brain.

"*Lieutenant!*" Archie's voice sounded from her discs, sitting on the bedside table.

"What?" Carrie said, through slurred sleep.

"*I'm sorry to wake you but I've made a critical discovery.*"

Carrie glanced at the time, saw it was 1.37 a.m. "What is it?" She rubbed her face.

"*Together with my AIS siblings, I have cracked the encryption and traced the source of the final and most recent death threat.*"

"Where did it come from?" she asked, feeling slightly more awake.

"We traced the server to an All Station franchise located on Eureka Station, the halfway point for civilian travelers between Earth and Mars. Accessing surveillance footage from around the time the message was sent through the encrypted system, I located the Golden Orb on station at that time."

"Did you trace the flight logs?" Carrie asked, fully awake now.

"Yes. I have the crew manifest, and facial recognition systems have identified Costya Ware in the All Station at the approximate time of transfer."

"Does he have links?"

"Yes, lieutenant. Classified documents from the Universal Intelligence Agency have identified Costya Ware in photographs alongside members of a possible anti-military group. They are being watched as potential risks for terrorist activity due to online anti-military speech."

Carrie rubbed her face as though trying to make the information sink into her brain. "So, the *Orb*'s Costya Ware has been hanging with potential terrorists? Who is on this watch list?"

"A man by the name of Taylor Mallet is believed to be a member of this armed anti-military group, and he is a known associate of Dominic Faber."

"So, Dominic's behind it after all?"

"My analysis, and that of the UIA Master AI, has led me to believe that both Dominic and Costya were being groomed by Mallet to become members of this group. However, that is not why I've woken you. I've woken you because I've discovered, after looking further into Taylor Mallet, that he is a second cousin of Andrew Aston."

"Aston?" Carrie sat up. "As in the president's Sentinel?"

"Yes. Now, I must warn you, I haven't been able to find any evidence that Aston is involved with this armed group, nor that he's had any contact with Mallet, but it is a risk and I wanted you to know immediately."

Carrie threw back her sheets and swung her legs out of the bed. Her mind raced. Aston was placed on the president's detail not long before Carrie came to Mars. He was a new addition, handpicked by Greavy. Was it a coincidence? If he was working for this group, why hadn't he moved on the president yet? Or was he just biding his time until he received the order to proceed?

"How did the UNF not know this?" Carrie asked. "How did he become a Sentinel?"

"The UIA runs completely separate from the UNF, lieutenant. Agencies only share information when there is a need to, when conspiracy can be proven or active terrorist plots become apparent. The UNF was not aware of the link, nor aware of the existence of this potential terrorist group."

Carrie felt the Alpha adrenaline begin to surge through her. Greavy put Aston on the president's detail. Whether Greavy knew or not, someone, somewhere paved the way to make that happen. She couldn't trust either of them.

"Contact Colonel Greavy," Carrie ordered Archie. "Have him arrest Ware, but say nothing about Aston. I'll warn the president now myself."

"Yes, lieutenant."

Carrie got out of bed, quickly dressed, found her pistol and checked it was loaded, then holstered it on her belt. She swiftly moved to the apartment's bathroom and washed her face, her mind processing how to approach this. Aston had links, but they were familial. He couldn't exactly help who his second cousin was, or what the cousin was involved in, but it was just too close for comfort. Thoughts of Greavy circled her mind again. He'd told her his people hadn't been able to trace the threats, yet Archie confirmed no attempts had been made to trace them. Was someone setting Greavy up? Or was Greavy setting Harkowitz up?

"Fuck," Carrie said. She needed to be able to trust Greavy. He controlled all the troops on Mars. If she couldn't trust him, she was on her own.

Right now, that didn't matter. Right now, she just had to warn the president, and get Aston as far away from him as she could.

Carrie left the bathroom and marched with intent toward her apartment door.

"Mom?" Freya asked. "What's going on?"

Carrie turned to see her daughter in the kids' bedroom doorway wiping her sleepy eyes, with Brody standing beside her.

"Nothing, honey. Go back to bed. Stay here."

Carrie locked the door behind her, then stepped out into the corridor.

30

Freeze-frame

Harris lay in bed drifting off to sleep. He needed rest, but he also felt a pull to check in with Martha.

As he drifted off to sleep, Welles swirled around in his mind. He opened his eyes and pushed the thoughts away. As they were nearing Mars, the last thing he wanted to do was bring her into his dreams. Not with her brain the way it was. He had to work hard to block her out like Martha and Tess did with him at times.

He breathed deeply, in and out, forcing himself into a state of relaxation and sleep, picturing himself pushing Welles away whenever she appeared. Before he knew it, he was walking along the silver sands, then standing on Martha's ship.

She stood alone on the flight deck, gave him a nod.

He pictured Tess, questioning where she was, and Martha motioned to another part of her ship.

He studied Martha a moment, tried to project an image that represented trust between the two Zetas. Martha seemed to understand and gave a nod. She projected an image of him traveling back to Earth, a smile on his face, peaceful.

"You're telling me not to worry," he said.

Martha stared at him, projected the image of him going back to Earth again.

"You want us to leave you?" he asked.

Martha projected an image of her ship jumping, vanishing into the deep, dark of space.

Harris nodded. He projected back an image of the *Aurizun* escorting them as far as Atlas, then her ship jumping.

"Let me do that for you at least," he said.

Martha thought for a moment, then gave a bow.

Harris looked around the flight deck, moved up to the lip of her console.

"You never did show me how to fly one of these things."

She stared at him as he traced his fingers along the lip, the blue lighting up beneath his fingertips. He looked back at Martha.

He projected an image of her touching the console back on earth, then projected an image of her watching Hunter and Frazer fly the *Aurizun*.

"You saw ours, let me see yours," he said.

Martha stared at him, but her body and thoughts remained silent.

"Drawing the line there, huh?" he smiled.

She projected an image of Station Atlas in the distance, then projected her ship blinking out of existence, reiterating their plans.

Harris nodded, then turned and stepped off the Zeta flight deck.

He suddenly found himself standing in a cemetery. It was one he recognized. One he'd been in before. With Doc.

At the thought, Doc appeared, and Harris realized that he was standing in the New Orleans cemetery. The one his long-ago kin were buried in. Memories flashed through his mind of being drunk and asking Doc why Taya hadn't visited his dreams yet. He recalled Doc saying: *Do you really want her to see you like this?*

He looked at Doc, who smiled. The medic was suddenly standing among his female kin. A shiver tore up his arms as they parted.

And there she was.

Taya.

Harris's mouth fell open.

"Tay?" he managed, his body suddenly feeling as though it was filled with air and not blood.

She smiled and nodded.

"It's really you?" he asked, as tears pricked his eyes.

She nodded again. Doc smiled wider.

"Why now?" Harris asked, confused.

"You broke the seal," Sibbie told him, "with Sarai."

"You let your grief flow," Etta smiled.

"You're healing your rift with Ty," Maeve said.

"It's time to let it flow, Saul," Doc said. "You've opened the door, now keep it open. We'll always be here for you."

Harris stared at Taya as tears rolled down his cheeks. He walked toward her, arms outstretched.

She smiled and opened her arms to him.

And suddenly he was in bed, staring at the ceiling, embracing himself, his face and neck drenched with emotion.

Carrie made her way to the president's apartment. Neither Aston nor Sampson were posted on the door. She knocked, no answer.

She pulled her gun, opened the door and looked inside, listened. It was empty. Perhaps Harkowitz was still working in his office?

She tucked her gun away again, then moved carefully up the spiral steps to the Red House reception. Most of the house lights were on, but that was normal. Often the staffers worked late, but she saw and heard no-one.

She headed for the president's office. When she arrived, she found the door open, the room lights on, and his desk screens alight, but it was empty.

Where could he be?

She walked back toward the boardroom. It, too, was empty. She suddenly recalled him telling her children about snacks in the kitchen when he was working late, so she decided to head there.

She crossed to the other side of the Red House, heading for the kitchen tucked away in the far corner of the complex. As she neared it, she saw Sampson standing guard in the corridor and heard voices inside. Sampson looked at her, surprised. Carrie raised her finger to her mouth. Sampson saw she was armed and he tensed, his eyes questioning.

Carrie moved alongside him and listened. She heard Harkowitz talking about his grandmother's sticky date pudding.

"Is Aston in there?" Carrie whispered to Sampson. He nodded.

"What's going on?" Sampson asked, his dark eyes concentrated.

"Archie found a possible link to Aston."

Sampson's eyes popped. "What?"

"Just stay calm. I need to get the president alone."

Carrie moved to the doorway and peered in. It was a large, rectangular room with a countertop along the rear and side walls, and a large rectangular island in the middle of the room, topped with marble. Aston and Harkowitz stood in the far right-hand corner, diagonally opposite the doorway. They noticed her and looked over, surprised.

"Lieutenant?" Harkowitz said. "You're up late?"

"As are you, sir?"

"Yes, well Senators Butten and Pope are demanding a briefing tomorrow. I've been reviewing what Laurelai's done but I need coffee to continue," he said, pottering around a coffee machine on the kitchen bench.

Carrie stepped into the room and moved to her right, along the wall without any countertop. She glanced at Aston who studied her curiously. The Sentinel was tall and athletic, his eyes sharp, exactly what you'd expect from a presidential bodyguard. Carrie looked back at Harkowitz.

"Sir, may I have a word alone with you for a moment?"

Harkowitz glanced at her. "Fire away."

"Alone, sir," Carrie said, glancing at Aston.

"The Sentinels hear everything anyway," Harkowitz said.

"I'm sure they do, but I would like to speak with you alone, sir."

Harkowitz looked at her, sensing the importance, then at Aston and shrugged. "Fine. Andrew, would you mind?"

"If this relates to the president's safety, I should know," Aston said to Carrie.

"Sampson?" she called out. He appeared in the doorway. "Please go with Sentinel Aston back to the president's office. Wait for us there. I'll escort him back."

"Yes, ma'am," Sampson said, stepping into the room to usher Aston out.

Aston looked at Sampson like he was an annoying fly. "You don't tell me what to do with the president's security, thank you."

"Andrew, relax," Harkowitz said. "Go wait in my office."

Aston glanced at him, then Carrie, then straightened his jacket and walked to the door. As soon as he and Sampson left, Carrie moved right up to Harkowitz as he raised a coffee cup to his lips.

"My AI found a link between an armed anti-military group and your Sentinel Aston," she said quietly.

Harkowitz swallowed his mouthful of coffee, as his eyes popped a little.

"He could be working with this anti-military group," Carrie said, "to help the independent Mars movement, or the group could be working alone to undermine the UNF. We don't know."

"What's the link?" Harkowitz asked.

"Aston's second cousin is a known member of this group. The UIA have been monitoring them due to their anti-military talk, but as they haven't carried out any specific terrorist plots yet, nor said enough to get them on conspiracy charges, they haven't shared the information with UNF."

"A second cousin?" Harkowitz furrowed his brow. "If the UNF didn't know, then how did your AI discover this?"

"He's part of a special network of UNF AIs that have access to a lot of data, and any data they can't access, they can request access to. My AI has been tracing your threats and managed to access this UIA information."

Harkowitz stared at her, his mind turning over.

"The last and most recent death threat against you," Carrie continued, "was traced to an All Station franchise on Eureka Station, sent by a crew member of the *Golden Orb*. That crew member has been photographed with a member of this anti-military group who is Aston's second cousin."

"But how does that implicate Aston?"

"Sir—"

"I just want to be sure," Harkowitz said firmly. At least he was taking this seriously.

"There's no *direct* link, sir, but that's what places him in a good position to get close to you. His cousin is part of this armed militia and he should not be your *goddamn* Sentinel, the risk is too great."

Harkowitz's face paled. "He's been guarding me for weeks now. He's done nothing out of the ordinary, been extremely professional—"

"To gain your trust," Carrie said, "so that you will be comfortable being alone with him."

"A president should be comfortable being alone with his guards." Aston's voice sounded from the doorway, startling them both. They looked over at him as he entered the room.

"Where's Sampson?" Carrie asked.

"At the office. I wanted to come back and check on the president."

"Sampson wouldn't disobey my orders."

Aston shrugged, walking around the left-hand side of the island and coming to stand a few feet from them both. "Take it up with him. Would you like to tell me what's going on, sir?"

"No," Carrie said, "go bring Sampson here."

"I don't take orders from you."

"Er, look, Andrew," Harkowitz said. "If you could step outside, this is a private matter."

Aston stared at Harkowitz.

"I'm told your second cousin is a member of an armed anti-military group," Harkowitz said calmly.

Carrie shot Harkowitz a pissed glance, but Harkowitz held his hand up to calm her.

"What's this got to do with me, sir?" Aston asked, his brow slightly furrowed.

"You cannot work for the president with those links," Carrie told him. "You should *never* have worked for the president with those links."

"I am not my cousin," Aston said.

"Good to know," Carrie said. "You still can't work for the president. So please leave. Now."

Aston looked between the two of them, his brow furrowed further in confusion, maybe offense. Perhaps anger.

"Sampson?" Carrie called out. There was no response. She felt a shiver down her spine, looked back at Aston as she placed her hand on her gun. "What did you do to him?"

"I told you, I left him the office..." Aston said, sounding concerned as he looked over at the doorway. Carrie's eyes followed.

But they shouldn't have.

Aston swung a fast fist at her. Carrie saw the movement in her Alpha periphery and tried to pull back from it, but it still connected with her jaw and the force spun her around into the kitchen countertop along the wall.

Harkowitz yelled "No!" and dropped his cup of coffee on the floor, as Aston's big hands grabbed the back of Carrie's neck and threw her to the floor.

"Run!" she yelled to Harkowitz.

Harkowitz foolishly threw himself on Aston's back and tried to pull him back from Carrie. "Stop it!" he yelled.

Aston swung a hard elbow into Harkowitz's side. The president groaned and curled a little. Aston snatched a large knife off the bench and ran it deep into the president's gut. Harkowitz gasped, and his eyes went wide as his hands clasped at the knife inside him.

"Noooo!" Carrie yelled, pulling her gun.

Aston kicked it out of her hand, then threw another kick. Carrie ducked it, then leaped to her feet with Alpha prowess and rage, knocking Aston over.

They fell to the floor, instantly wrestling, punching, and trying to end the other.

Sampson opened his eyes and saw the ornate decoration on the Red House ceiling. His head ached and an intense pain burned around his ribs. He looked down, saw all the blood and remembered. He and Aston had walked back to the president's office, where Aston had suddenly shot him with a silencer, then hit him across the head.

Sampson felt for his comms gear, but it was gone. He rolled over, in pain, and moved for the comms panel on the wall beside the door, as blood dripped out of him like a heavy leak.

He pulled himself to standing, smearing blood over the wall, and hit the guard comms. Pressed it again, and again, until he heard Beach's sleepy voice.

"What is it?"

"Aston's attacking the president. I think they're still in the kitchen."

Sampson's bloodied hand slipped off the comms button and he collapsed back down to the floor.

Carrie groaned as Aston landed a hard punch to her face that felt like it reverberated around her skull. She momentarily loosened her grip on his neck as black spots flashed in her vision, but gathered herself and slammed her fist into his face. He groaned, looking a little surprised by the strong fight she was putting up. He was a well-trained fighter. She was glad she was an Alpha.

He threw her off and she banged into the kitchen cupboards, while he stood, pulling out his gun and raised it to her.

But he suddenly looked toward the door, then dropped down behind the island bench as Beach's voice yelled, "Drop it! Now!"

Carrie quickly scuttled around the corner of the island toward Harkowitz whose belly was pooling with blood and his face had turned an ivory white. She felt for her discs but realized she'd left them on the bedside table. "*Shit!*" she hissed.

She grabbed a tea towel and wrapped it around the base of the knife protruding from Harkowitz and pulled it out. He groaned again, but gunfire rang out from Beach and they instinctively ducked. She placed Harkowitz's hands over the top of the tea towel as more gunfire rang out and Aston and Beach shot at each other from their covered positions – Beach from the doorway and Aston from behind the island bench with a silencer.

"Hang in there," she said to Harkowitz, locking eyes with him.

"Go," he managed through the din of gunfire. "Get out while you can."

"No," Carrie shook her head vehemently. "It's my job to protect you."

She left Harkowitz and scuttled over to where her gun had ended up after Aston had kicked it away. Just as she was about to reach it, movement through the doorway caught her eye.

Beach was there in his sleepwear, firing. But as he retreated around the doorway, Carrie saw Brody back a little, staring in at her from a crouched position. Beside him, Freya and Jesse.

"Go!" she mouthed angrily waving at them to leave. "Get Novak!"

Beach leaned out from his covered position again, but a clean shot from Aston saw Beach's head blow apart.

Blood and brains sprayed as Beach's body fell to the floor before her three kids.

"NO!" Carrie yelled at them. "Go! Get Novak!"

Aston peered around the corner of the island, gun in front. He fired, she rolled Alpha quick, he missed. Aston stood and came toward her. Harkowitz grabbed Aston's ankle and he tripped, hit the floor. Carrie swung her leg out and kicked Aston's gun away. She turned, reaching for her own gun again. Aston kicked Harkowitz's hands away and sprang to his feet.

Carrie grabbed her gun and swung it back to Aston as he lunged. He grabbed her wrist as she fired. It hit the ceiling. She tensed her Alpha muscles, saw Aston straining against her strength as they fought to control the gun. He straddled her and threw his full weight against her, pressing her arm down to the side. With the gun pointing toward the children, who still huddled, shocked, in the doorway, Carrie loosened her grip and took her finger off the trigger. Aston sensed the moment of weakness, gave another hard punch to Carrie's face and her blood went flying across the kitchen tiles.

Aston snatched the gun from her hand. She suddenly saw Jesse ram into Aston like a wounded bull.

"Jesse! No!" Carrie yelled as Aston dropped the gun, grabbed her son and threw him into the wall. Jesse hit it with a loud bang and screamed in pain.

"NO!" Carrie yelled at Aston, slamming a fist into his gut. Aston groaned, swung another, weaker, punch that Carrie blocked, as Freya lunged at him this time, screaming like a wild child as she got Aston in a choke hold.

"Freya! *No!*" Carrie yelled again in desperation, wanting her kids to stay out of it.

Carrie strained to reach the gun as Aston, still straddling her – his thighs holding her in a vice-grip – reached back for Freya, grabbing her long hair and tearing her off him. Freya screamed in pain, falling to the ground beside them on Carrie's right. Carrie threw a hard punch toward Aston's throat, but missed as he moved and hit his collarbone instead. His face screwed in pain and he swung a punch back at Carrie. She felt the crack across her cheekbone, saw Freya getting up and moving back toward them, but Carrie threw her arm out and pushed her daughter away.

"No!"

Aston grabbed Carrie's jaw and turned her face toward him. The gun was back in his hand. She grabbed his wrist, fighting him with everything she had to stop him turning the gun on her. Aston, frustrated with her strength, bent down and rammed his skull into hers.

Lightning flashed across Carrie's eyes, as pain ricocheted around her skull. She heard her kids crying and screaming for her.

And she froze.

It was only for a second, but the terror of a catastrophic brain injury froze her.

Her arms weakened, briefly. Just for that instant, but it was all Aston needed to shove the gun in her face.

"Die, you *bit—*"

A shot rang out from the doorway, and Aston's head flew back, spraying blood through the air. He swirled briefly, before his body slumped half over Carrie and half on the floor between her and Freya. Carrie blinked his blood and brain matter from her eyes, saw he was dead, saw Freya's shocked face, then looked over in the direction the gunfire had come from.

And there, in the doorway, she saw him.

Brody, her son, with Beach's gun in his shaking hand.

Carrie froze in shock. She looked back at Aston's head, then shoved him off her, and scrambled, dizzily, to Brody.

Her son's eyes were wide, his arm was still extended and shaking, the gun still pointing where Aston had been.

Carrie immediately took the gun from his hand, put it aside, and pulled him into a hug.

"It's okay," she said, rocking him as much as herself. "It's okay. It's gonna be okay." Her mind raced, trying to comprehend what just happened, her own body shaking as much as his. "It's okay… It's okay…" she told him, as she tried to think a way forward. "I shot him… I shot him. Okay?" She pulled Brody back, cupped his face in her hands, locked eyes with his. "I shot him. Okay? *I* shot him!" Brody stared at her, still wide-eyed, his mouth unmoving. Carrie shook him a little. "Honey? It's going to be okay. Alright? I shot him. Okay? *I* shot him. It wasn't you, it was me. It's going to be okay."

She heard movement and turned around to see Freya crying and scuttling over to cradle a sobbing Jesse who held his arm like it was broken.

Then she saw Harkowitz peering around the corner of the kitchen bench, having dragged himself there. His eyes darted between her and Brody.

"I shot him!" she said firmly to Harkowitz. "*I* shot him!"

Harkowitz glanced at Brody again, then back to her. He nodded, his eyes drooping with blood loss. Carrie pulled Brody tight against her, then moved him over to Freya and Jesse. She hugged and kissed them both, smearing hers and Aston's blood on their skin.

"I shot him," she whispered to them, looking each in the eye, as she felt her own left eye swelling like a balloon. "Got it? I shot him." They nodded and Freya hugged Brody tight. "Don't leave him," Carrie told Freya, then turned to Jesse. "Lay down, honey, don't move that arm." She quickly checked their wrists for the AI bands, but none wore them. She silently hissed, then scuttled to Harkowitz, pressed against his wound, fighting the dizziness that wanted to overcome her, closing her eyes briefly to stop it spinning.

When she opened them again, Harkowitz pointed to a console on the wall. "Sam," he managed. "Alarm… Call Sam."

Harris rushed onto the flight deck with the *Aurizun* team in tow, dragged from his bed by Hunter with news there'd been an attempt on President Harkowitz's life by one of his own Sentinels.

Harris took his seat, not liking the feeling in his gut, as Colonel Greavy appeared onscreen.

"How bad?" Harris asked, skipping formalities.

"The president's been rushed into surgery," Greavy informed them. "He was stabbed. Took a kitchen knife to the gut. One of his Sentinels, Beach, was killed, shot to the head, and your Sentinel Sampson was injured as well. He's also being rushed into surgery. He was shot."

"Welles?" McKinley asked quickly, eyes fixed on him.

Greavy seemed to take silent breath in. "Some concussion, maybe. They fought, but she killed Aston. Saved the president."

"Fuck," Harris muttered, relieved, yet wound tight. "Take Welles to hospital immediately," he told Greavy. "Don't listen to what she says, tell her it's my order. She needs to get checked. A concussion on her is different to others. It's potentially deadly."

"Will do," Greavy nodded. "Uh, Major McKinley, you should know your children were there when it happened. Your son, Jesse, broke his arm in the incident."

Harris saw the blood rush out of McKinley's face.

"What the fuck were they doing there?" McKinley asked.

"I don't know, but other than the broken arm, they're okay. Mostly bruises and shock. Jesse's broken arm is the worst of it."

"How the *fuck* did this happen?" McKinley hissed.

"I'm still getting the full details, but somehow Welles got wind of a connection between Aston and the death threats. She went to warn the president immediately. I guess the children followed her."

"I want a full report, asap," Harris said, "and medical updates as soon as you have them."

"Yes, colonel," Greavy nodded, and ended the transmission.

"*Fuck!*" McKinley hissed in anger.

"I know. I hear you," Harris said, feeling McKinley's tension in his own bones. "Let's just see off the Zeta ship, then we'll head straight to Mars to see them, alright?"

McKinley nodded, still silently seething.

"You got strong little kids, man," Tikaani reassured him. "They're fighters."

McKinley looked at her, but didn't respond.

"Hunter, how long until we hit Atlas?" Harris asked.

"About half a day, sir."

"Get us there as soon as you can. The sooner we see the back of the Zetas, the better."

Carrie sat in Laurelai's office with her children. After Carrie raised the alarm with Greavy, Freya had run to wake Novak, who took control over the situation until Greavy arrived. Carrie had been in no state to do so. Her head and heart were numb, and all she could do was hug her children.

Laurelai entered her office with blankets, her hair loose and bedraggled from bed. "The president and Sampson are both in surgery," she told them, unfolding and placing blankets over each of them. "The ambulance will be back soon for you," she smiled at Jesse. They'd given him some painkillers and he was a little doped out, laying on the floor with a pillow, waiting it out. Her strong boy.

"Thank you," Carrie said to Laurelai.

"Thank *you*," she said, with worried eyes, looking at Carrie's swelling face. "For saving the president's life."

Carrie gave a weak smile, and Laurelai left them alone, closing the door behind her.

Carrie looked at Brody, sitting beside her, leaning against her. He hadn't said a single word since it happened. She kept feeling his body shaking intermittently with the shock that still rattled through him. Freya sat on his other side, holding her twin's hand. Her daughter was equally shocked, yet somehow Freya had been her rock through all this. While Carrie nursed her aching head and her two boys – one physically wounded, one psychologically wounded – Freya had helped them all.

Brody shivered again and Carrie kissed his forehead. "I'm so proud of you," she whispered. "You saved my life. You saved the president's life."

Brody looked up at her and it was Doc's eyes that stared back. Tears stung Carrie's eyes. What would Doc think of this? Carrie putting Brody in this position. What kind of mother was she?

"Honey," she took Brody's face in her hands and looked him deep in his dazed eyes. "I know you're scared. I know you're in shock, and it's all my fault. I'm sorry." The tears broke their banks and rolled down her swollen cheeks. "I'm sorry you had to do what you did... but I'm glad you did, honey."

"You saved Mom's life," Freya said, sniffing back tears. "She'd be dead otherwise."

Carrie brushed a hand over Freya's hair, then reached out and did the same to Jesse. "You were so brave today." More tears rolled down her face. "You *all* saved my life... and you should *never* have been put in that position... I am *so* sorry." Carrie tried to hold back her sobbing, but it was hard. It was also very painful – her head felt like it was in a vice.

"It's okay, Mom," Brody's quiet, husky voice sounded, making Carrie stop. She looked at him. He was still curled into her side, but he stared at the wall ahead. "He was going to kill you…" He looked up at her. "I would do it again, if I had to."

Carrie burst into tears again, and hugged him tightly. "I love you so much, honey." She rocked him. "I love you all so much."

They rocked in silence for a few more moments, before a knock sounded on the door and Colonel Greavy entered.

Carrie tensed. Could she trust him?

He walked up to them and eyed Jesse. "Let's get you to hospital to fix that arm, huh?"

Carrie nodded carefully, wiped her face. She and twins got to their feet and Carrie swayed a little, needing to lean on Laurelai's desk.

"Harris has ordered that you be admitted too," Greavy said, studying her and taking her arm. "Said it was nonnegotiable."

Carrie looked at his hand holding her arm. She looked into his eyes. "Can I trust you?"

Greavy stared at her, an offended look crossing his face.

"You put Aston on the president," she said.

"I know," Greavy said, a look of guilt crossing his face, along with something else. Dismay. "I plan to find out how he came to be recommended to me."

"And why your team couldn't trace the threats when my AI could."

Greavy nodded. "Thank you for what you did."

Carrie stared at him, trying to read his demeanor. She sensed he was genuine. She leaned off the desk and swirled again with dizziness.

"It's okay," Greavy said, steadying her. "You can trust me. I serve the president."

Carrie considered him, then nodded. Harkowitz trusted him, so until her mind was thinking clearly, she was going to have to trust him too.

"My kids stay with me," Carrie said firmly.

A medic came in with a trolley for Jesse. They loaded him on and began to wheel him outside. As they stepped out into the corridor, Greavy tugged Carrie gently back toward him, away from the others.

"The security footage was wiped," he whispered.

Carrie looked at him, confused.

"In the kitchen," he said, locking eyes. "President's orders." He gently squeezed her shoulder, then walked off as a medic took over.

Carrie watched Greavy for a moment, then turned to follow her kids down the corridor, under escort from the medic.

Martha stood at her ship's console, closing in on the human structure where she would finally be set free. Free to return home to her sisters and share all that she'd learned.

Something snagged at her mind, however. She turned her eyes to the nearby planet. She felt a familiar connection there and suddenly pictured the female warrior of this race. The one she had previously communicated with. She was still alive, it seemed. The male had told the truth.

Something was wrong, though.

The connection was unstable. The warrior's brain was flawed.

Carrie walked toward the transport alongside the medic. As she did, an image of Martha suddenly pierced her brain – the Zeta just staring at her, before she reached toward Carrie's head, her hoofed hands disappearing inside her mind.

Carrie felt intense pain in her skull, cried out, then fell into blackness.

Martha stamped down her frustration, knowing the warrior's brain could be healed if she joined Martha on her journey.

Still, they had made their choice. The warrior would remain.

All Martha could do was send help back from Zeta Archelois. The warrior would just have to wait.

Gold watched carefully as the *Aurizun* came to a stop beside Station Atlas, and the Zeta ship approached.

"Update from the MDS?" Gold asked Batoya.

"All flights grounded," she replied. "No-one has broken the embargo."

"Good," Gold said. "Everyone hold steady as the Zeta ship passes. It's behaved so far, there's no need to suspect it would kick things off now with the *Aurizun, Carcharias* and *Benevolent* out there."

"Yes, sir," Batoya nodded, and turned back to her console.

The ops deck sat quietly, watching as the Zeta ship paused momentarily beside the *Aurizun*, then continued past it. Their eyes turned to the scanners and watched as it continued for a few minutes, then suddenly blinked out of existence."

"Report!" Gold called.

"I have no reading of it, sir," Khatri said, checking his screens. "Matter displacement reading zero. It's not there. It's gone." He looked at him.

Gold nodded. "It's jumped. Just like it told Harris it would." Gold clicked on his comms. "*Aurizun*, this is Atlas. Confirming Zeta-1 has jumped. Over."

"*Roger that,*" Hunter said. "*Confirms our readings. Over.*"

Gold ended the comms, staring out at the deep black space before him.

"So, what now, sir?" Abioye asked him.

"You keep watch," he said standing, "while the rest of us prepare to welcome the HOS."

"You think that will go ahead after the attempt on Harkowitz?" Batoya asked.

"I don't know," Gold said, "but I'm about to find out."

Harris watched as Gold appeared over the transmission screen in McKinley's office.

"Sir," Gold nodded. "How's the president?"

"Stable. He's out of surgery and recovering. He's going to be okay in time. As is Sampson, I'm told."

"That's good news. I, er, heard Welles's kids got hurt?"

"Yeah. They'll be okay, we're on our way there now."

"You're not stopping by Atlas?"

"No. As you can imagine it's taken everything in my power to hold McKinley at bay. I need to let him off to see them."

"Understandable," Gold nodded. "Will the HOS be proceeding?"

"I need to speak with Berger and Marchant, but we may need to postpone. Harkowitz won't be up for traveling and it's his show. I think we might need to let the dust settle. I'll let you know."

"Yes, sir."

"Just keep watching those skies and let me know as soon as anything pops up."

"Will do."

Harris ended the transmission, then headed back to the flight deck. He was feeling antsy and he didn't know why. Was it Martha? Was it Welles? Was it something else?

The truth was, he needed to get off the ship as much as McKinley did.

Carrie opened her eyes… well, mainly one eye as the other was swollen and half closed. She realized she was in hospital. She immediately tensed and looked around. She saw Brody and Freya laying on the bed next to hers. They looked at her.

"What's wrong?" Freya asked.

"Where's Jesse?" she asked looking about for him.

"Here," Laurelai's voice sounded, wheeling Jesse into the room in a wheelchair. "Arm's now set in a gel sling."

Carrie felt relief shoot through her and she collapsed back onto her pillow as her head throbbed.

"How're you doing?" Laurelai asked her with concern.

"Alright, I guess. How long have I been out?"

"A few hours," she said, helping Jesse out of the chair. She tried to usher him toward Brody and Freya, but Jesse pulled away from her and climbed onto Carrie's bed. She grabbed him and pulled him alongside, studying his gel cast.

"Does it hurt?" she asked. He nodded, dopey and grumpy as he snuggled against her. She hugged him and kissed his head. "It will heal soon."

Carrie looked back at Laurelai who placed the chair by the wall. "The president? Sampson?"

"They're in recovery."

"Can I see them?"

"Soon," Laurelai said. "For now, the doctor says you need to rest, or that concussion will knock you out again."

Carrie nodded, knowing just how true that statement was.

"If you need me, call," Laurelai said. "I'll be here until the president wakes."

31

Bloodlines

Harris walked the small Elon hospital's corridor toward Welles's room. McKinley stalked ahead of him, a man on a mission. He'd been relatively contained when they'd arrived, but upon hearing that Carrie had collapsed, he was immediately tense again.

They found her room and saw Welles and the kids sleeping across two beds. Brody and Freya slept on one, while a swollen-faced Welles and Jesse lay on the other. McKinley immediately moved to Welles and Jesse, and ran his hand over Jesse's hair, eyes studying his gel sling.

"Dad!" Freya said, waking. She jumped out of bed and ran to McKinley, immediately crying and hugging him. "He hurt us! He tried to kill Mom! He ripped my hair out!"

"Whoa, whoa, whoa!" McKinley quickly hugged her as the room awoke. "It's okay, Frey, I'm here now. You're safe. Alright?"

Jesse started crying then, holding his arm and Welles looked about in a daze – or tried to, one eye was almost swollen shut – and tried to settle him.

Harris looked over at Brody alone on the other bed and moved to him.

"You alright, champ?" Harris said, squeezing his shoulder. Brody also burst into tears and hugged him. Tightly. *Desperately.* "Hey…" Harris hugged him back, as a worried feeling swirled in his gut. Their reactions were worse than he thought they'd be. They were traumatized. How much had they actually seen?

"What happened?" McKinley asked Welles quietly, pushing past Freya and Jesse to kiss her forehead and caress her less swollen cheek.

Welles looked at him with her one good eye, tears spilling down her cheeks. "They saw everything. They came to help me."

"Saw what?" Harris asked.

"Aston shot Beach right in front of them."

"Shit…" McKinley said, hugging Freya again.

"He threw Jesse into the wall," Freya said. "I tried to get him off Mom, but he ripped my hair out." She showed him her scalp, and McKinley stroked her hair as she started crying again, burying her face into his stomach.

"Just as well he's dead," McKinley said with tempered rage, "or I'd *fuckin'* kill him."

Harris noticed Brody was shaking like a leaf in his arms. "Hey… it's alright," he said, rubbing his back as though trying to warm him.

"I did it," Brody whispered, looking at McKinley.

"You did what?" Harris asked him.

"I did it," Brody said to McKinley, who looked back at him. "I killed him. I—I killed Aston."

"Brody!" Welles said, stiffening.

McKinley looked between them, confused.

"Freya, close the door," Welles ordered. Freya left McKinley's grasp and quickly closed the door. McKinley looked back at Brody in Harris's arms, then moved toward him. Brody looked up at him, tears rolling down the kid's shaking face.

"I killed him," Brody whispered, as a waterfall of tears now ran down his face. "He was going to kill Mom…"

McKinley looked around at Welles to see if it were true. More tears burst down her face as she nodded.

McKinley looked back at Brody, his face white. He pulled Brody from Harris's arms and hugged him tight.

"It's okay," McKinley said in shock, locking eyes with Harris. "It's okay." McKinley took Brody by the arms and looked into his eyes. "It's okay. Alright?"

"I shot him just like you taught me," Brody said to McKinley.

McKinley immediately pulled Brody in for another hug, the major winded by the news. Harris stepped back and tried to get his brain moving through his own shock.

"Who knows?" he asked Welles.

"Harkowitz and Greavy. That's it."

Harris nodded, mind spinning. "We need to fix security footage and—"

"It's done," Welles told him. "Greavy took care of it. I did it. I shot Aston. They all know. I was the one who shot Aston."

"Fuck," McKinley breathed.

"I'm sorry," Welles said to him. "I left them in the apartment. They came to see if everything was alright. I—"

"He was going to kill Mom," Freya said. "He had a gun in her face."

"And he hurt Jesse and Freya," Brody said quietly.

McKinley squeezed Brody tight, then looked him in the eye again. "It's alright, Brody. You did good. You hear me?" He cupped the boy's face with his real hand. "You did the right thing."

"It's alright," Harris said firmly to the room. "We got this. Alright? It's our secret." He squeezed Brody's shoulder and looked his godson in the eyes. "I got you, Brody. You hear me? We've all got you."

Carrie looked at McKinley who brushed his real hand down the good side of her face.

"What'd they say about your head?" he asked her.

She glanced at the kids, sleeping across two beds beside hers, then looked back at him. "It's in a bad way."

He glanced down at the bed, clenched his jaw.

"I can't fight anymore," she told him, as more tears threatened her tired eyes.

He looked at her, empathy in his gaze.

"I know I'm an Alpha, but I just can't. Every hit now… I froze," she told him. "Aston hit me hard and the pain in my skull… I froze. All I could think about was a catastrophic brain injury and my kids losing their mother."

She clasped her hand over McKinley's. "I froze… and Brody had to finish the job for me."

McKinley squeezed his eyes closed, and rested his forehead against hers.

Tears ran down Carrie's cheeks. "I can't fight anymore," she whispered.

McKinley pulled his face back and stared at her with those piercing blue eyes of his: the real one and the mech one.

"So, don't," he said. "You don't have to. I'll fight for you."

He pulled his body back from hers, held out his arm and tilted his wrist. Carrie heard a noise and saw the muzzle of his Alpha-Mech gun protruding from his arm.

"You did it?" she said with surprise.

McKinley nodded. "My shooting's off, but I can get it out."

Carrie smiled. "You never had any trouble with that."

McKinley smiled back, then leaned forward and kissed her. He glanced at the sleeping kids, then back to his arm as he retracted the gun. "Sounds like I should get lessons off Brody."

Carrie stared at McKinley, tears pricking her eyes again. She raised her hand and caressed his real cheek. "It was a great shot, in a split-second window," she whispered sadly. "A *really* great shot."

McKinley nodded, the smile disappearing.

Harris hung up his PDP. He'd heard the whole story from Welles, then helped McKinley settle the overtired kids, then Harris had left McKinley with Welles to make a call to Greavy.

Greavy had confirmed that his Space Duty units, in coordination with the UIA and Earth Duty units, had undertaken a series of raids across Earth and space, and that people with links to the anti-military group were in custody, being questioned. Greavy advised they had also brought in a couple of UNF contacts for questioning regarding Sentinel Aston's posting, and he was sure they had found everyone they needed, as identified by Archie, or at least enough of them to scare the rest into hiding. Harris had thanked him and posed the question whether the leaks to the media were related to the attempt on Harkowitz's life or not. Greavy had informed Harris that he and Laurelai had been working behind the scenes to get to the bottom of it and they believed Senator Butten might have been the source of the leaks. When Harris asked if Butten was a threat, Greavy had told him that Butten had disagreed with some of Harkowitz's decisions, but he did not believe the man wished the president dead. Greavy felt that the leak served only to apply pressure on Harkowitz to steer Mars on a course that Butten agreed with. Greavy had forced the Senator to go on 'leave' until Harkowitz could decide if he would allow the man to continue in his role. Greavy was still looking into Harbourg's murder in Hell Town.

Harris watched as McKinley exited the hospital. The major came to stand beside Harris, hands on his hips.

"Welles alright?" Harris asked.

McKinley shrugged. "Her head's messed up. She can't fight anymore. She can't cope with it. She told me so herself. She's done."

Harris nodded. "Understood. She's a liability now."

McKinley clenched his jaw. "She could've died tonight… and the only reason she didn't is because our kids stepped in. Our *kids*! Nine and 11 years old, for fuck's sake!"

Harris exhaled. "I know," he said gently. "And there're no words I can offer that'll make it better for you."

McKinley clenched his jaw again and Harris could tell he was fighting off emotion.

"Brody…" McKinley began, "he shouldn't know what that's like. To kill someone. Not at his age. *Fuck*… I want to take that away from him so bad."

Harris nodded softly. "But you can't," he said. "Just like I can't take away Sarai's pain for lying there under rubble with her dead mother on top of her. I want to turn back the clock and be there for them, but I can't."

McKinley looked at him, his real eye shining with emotion.

"They're alive, McKinley," Harris said gently. "They're fuckin' traumatized, but they're alive." Harris walked up to him. "And they're alive because you and Welles taught them how to survive."

McKinley continued to fight the emotion building up inside his chest, inside his throat.

Harris stepped right in front of McKinley. "They're alive, because they're survivors. It's a cold, *hard* fuckin' world out there, McKinley. I'm sorry they had to learn that so young, but it is what it is, and we can't take it back. All we can do is move forward. We support those kids with everything we have. We continue to train them to survive at all costs." Harris's eyes bored into McKinley's. "And if we're lucky, those kids will save the world one day."

McKinley nodded, choked on his emotion. He turned away from Harris.

"No, don't," Harris said, grabbing his shirt and pulling him back. "Let it out."

McKinley looked at him, confused.

"Let it out," Harris said. "It's like poison if you don't. It's taken me a long time to learn that, but I know it's right. Get it out." Harris pulled McKinley into a hug. "You lost part of yourself in that invasion, you just lost your mother, and you almost lost them. Grieve. Get it out." Harris felt tears welling in his own eyes. "I should've grieved a long time ago, but goddamn, it's freeing to get it out now." He squeezed McKinley tight, then slapped his back. He pulled back to see the major's face wet with tears. One side at least.

"Fuck you," McKinley said, quickly wiping his face, trying to hide it.

Harris laughed, wiped his own face. "Aren't we a bunch of hard-asses."

McKinley smiled, wiping his nose. "Don't tell anyone. We have an Alpha reputation to uphold."

"Fuck our reputation," Harris said. "We're humans first and foremost and it's healthy to be emotional sometimes."

"God, I wish I'd been there," McKinley shook his head. "I would've fuckin' *annihilated* him."

"Yeah, well, save that feeling and annihilate the next one."

Carrie knocked on the door to Harkowitz's room. Laurelai answered and ushered her through.

Harkowitz lay in his bed, an array of tubes poking out of him and bloodied bandages across his belly. His face was pale, but he smiled on seeing her.

"There she is. My hero."

Laurelai smiled at her. "She is indeed a hero."

Carrie tried to smile, but couldn't. She felt like a phony taking credit for something Brody had done, despite wanting to protect him.

Harkowitz looked at his assistant. "Would you mind, Laurelai?"

"Of course not," she said, leaving them alone.

"They've released you?" Harkowitz asked her.

Carrie nodded. "We're leaving. Harris is going to take us back to Earth on the *Aurizun*."

Harkowitz nodded in understanding.

"I've looked over Greavy's reports, as has Harris," Carried continued, "and we're satisfied they've rounded up everyone with any connection. Between that and the media reports about an attempt on your life that involved injured children, well, even Mars Media is being sympathetic to you."

"So Laurelai tells me." Harkowitz motioned to a basket of exotic food on the table. "From Lotz himself."

"Really?" Carrie asked, surprised.

"We scanned it for bugs. It's clean." Harkowitz smiled.

Carrie chuckled.

"I know Lotz wants this seat," Harkowitz said, "but I never believed he'd have me killed for it."

"He may have stoked the fires, though," Carrie said. "Encouraged people to be angry that he really shouldn't have."

"Perhaps," Harkowitz said, "but I guess that's blown back in his face. Laurelai has offered Universal Press an exclusive on the known ties to this assassination attempt. I'm afraid Lotz appears in some of the photographs with the accused."

Carrie smiled, then sighed. "As horrible as this all is, I think it might actually work in your favor."

Harkowitz's smile faded. "I wish it hadn't cost Beach his life, or traumatized your children."

"No," Carrie said, glancing at the floor. "Sir, about that. I need your assurance—"

"You have it," he said. "I've established a Mars Medal of Honor, and you, Beach and Sampson will be the first recipients." He gave a sad smile. "You saved my life, Welles."

Carrie nodded, trying to find the words to reply. "Thank you, sir. My Sentinel, Novak, will stay behind for a bit to oversee the transition of your new Sentinels. We'll be ensuring the right ones are picked this time. The *Carcharias* team will also be sticking close to you for a while. And Sampson, too, albeit from a hospital bed. When everything's settled, Novak will escort Sampson back to Earth."

"I know. Go," Harkowitz said, "and take this with you." He pulled an envelope from beneath his pillow and handed it to her. It was addressed to Brody. "Take your children back to Earth, where they belong."

Harris watched as Welles and her children boarded the *Aurizun*.

"Here they are!" Hunter greeted them. "The bravest First Gens in the universe!"

Freya smiled and hugged him, while Jesse gave Hunter's waiting hand a high-five.

Brody stuck close to Welles, Harris noticed, or maybe it was the other way around.

"Can I sit at the flight desk with you when we take off?" Freya asked Hunter.

"You sure can," he said. "I need you to watch Frazer and make sure he's doing things right."

Frazer chuckled. "You're lucky there're children aboard, Kiwi."

Hunter grinned at him, ushering Freya forward.

"Look at that gel cast," Brown said, studying Jesse's arm. "Bet that hurt."

Jesse shook his head. "Nah, it's okay."

"Wow, you're tough," Tikaani nodded. "I'd be howling."

"C'mon, Brody," McKinley waved him forward. "Come sit next to me."

"Yeah, take your seats," Harris said. "It's time to go home."

Brody Walker sat in his father's room on the *Aurizun*, staring at the letter in his hand. His mom had just handed it to him, then left him alone to read it in peace.

It felt heavy. Lumpy. Like more than a letter was inside.

He opened the envelope carefully, slid the lumpy letter out and unfolded the paper to see three proxy-steel medallions, engraved with an image of Mars. Each was inscribed with names: Brody Walker, Freya McKinley. Jesse McKinley.

Dear Brody,

There are not enough words in the English language for me to express my gratitude to you and your siblings for what you have done. I can only apologize for you being caught up in these traumatic events, and extend every offer of support should you need it.

I know my father shines down upon me with pride for what I have achieved, and I have absolutely no doubt that your father does the same with you. As hard as it can be to stand in their sunshine, we must remember that it is there to warm us, to teach us how to shine our own light onto others just as brightly.

You and your siblings are brave, and smart, and I will follow each of your careers with interest.

On this note, I am proud to bestow upon you all a gift. Enclosed you will find the very first Mars Medals of Honor ever produced. Though your names will never be seen in the official records, know that you are there in my mind and in my heart.

I continue to be Mars president because of you.

Until we meet again, stay safe, look toward the future, and let your warmth shine – casting your own shadow.

Finn Harkowitz.

Brody held the medallion up and studied it in the room's lights. Images flashed through his mind of Jesse hitting the wall; Freya screaming as she was dragged by her hair; seeing that gun swing into his mother's bloodied face.

He couldn't remember firing at Aston. It was like a blank hole sat in his memory. Like someone else did it. All Brody remembered was Aston's dead body, his mother's blood-streaked face, and the gun shaking in his hand.

And, now... he just wanted to forget it.

★ ★ ★

Carrie stood in the mess, staring out the observation window, wondering how Brody was doing with the letter. She'd read it first, of course. Brody was 11 and a half and she wanted to ensure he would cope with whatever was inside it. She'd been touched by the medallions, was almost sad her son couldn't take the credit for what he did. The shot he'd made, under those circumstances, in the fraction of time he'd had, had been an ace shot. He had inherited her aim, and Doc's patience to wait for the right shot.

She pulled out her PDP and checked her portal. There were the latest reports from Greavy's interrogations, news reports on the Mars protests calming down, and an outpouring of support for Harkowitz.

She turned her attention back to Earth – glad she could return to it now the two Zetas were gone – and saw a report from Morrell that he'd reopened the commercial sea and space docks at Berger's orders. UNF facilities on the mainland were starting to send folks to Centralis who claimed to share Harris's gift. Though Carrie's head hurt, she felt a tingle of excitement in her belly. Had Harris's interview worked?

She saw a message from Dr. Bakshi who, having read the Elon hospital report, stated that Carrie was to see her immediately upon return. That was no surprise, and the truth was, Carrie still felt dazed and incredibly tired. Carrie sighed and continued scrolling and found an earlier notification from DaJuan that she had missed with everything else going on. She opened it and saw it was a report on her ancestry.

She scrolled over his findings, smiling at seeing that parts of her father's lineage went all the way back to the Vikings, noting she'd have to share that news with McKinley. As she read on, she felt a little shiver run through her as she saw her mother's name. DaJuan advised there were gaps in her mother's ancestry that required further research. He noted, however, that everyone with the node had ancestry that he'd traced back to the most ancient peoples on Earth.

Another shiver washed over her, as she thought of who her mother's ancestors could be.

Harris cleared quarantine with his team close behind.

"About time you got here," Marchant said, waiting for him, looking a little anxious.

"What's going on?" Harris asked.

"I think you'd better take a look."

Harris and the team left their bags with quarantine and followed Marchant through to the grand reception of Command, beneath the glass pyramid. The noise, of voices chattering, was deafening as they turned the corner and saw the cause.

Harris paused and stared, in shock. Welles and McKinley soon flanked him, glancing at each other in confusion.

"Who are all these people?" Harris asked Marchant.

"They're here for you," Marchant said. "You called them, they answered."

Harris glanced at him in surprise. "They all claim to have the gift?"

Marchant nodded. "There are more outside. These are just the ones we've processed that we don't believe are a security threat."

"Fuck," Harris said, scanning them all.

"What do we do?" Welles asked.

Harris looked at her. "*You* go rest. You're not using your head here."

"You're going to need a hand with this," she said.

"Take your kids home, Welles," he said.

McKinley looked at her, reiterating Harris's order, and she nodded, knowing he was right. She squeezed McKinley's hand, then gathered the children.

"Take the back entrance," Marchant told her. "I have a car waiting."

She nodded and headed off, as the rest of the team gathered around.

"How do you want to play this?" McKinley asked Harris.

Harris shrugged. "One by one, I guess. Where's DaJuan?"

Marchant pointed to where he stood in the distance talking to a crowd member. "I've put him to work already, trying to vet them."

Harris nodded and moved toward him.

*

Harris stood beside DaJuan.

"I've weeded out a few, man," DaJuan said, "but I don't know. What does your gut tell you? How should we handle this?"

Harris sighed, looked at the time on his PDP, then sighed again. "I guess I just talk to them one by one. We can't rush this. We've got to be sure."

Movement through the crowd caught his eye. A large Southeast Asian man was making his way between people, parting them like the Red Sea, occasionally looking over his shoulder at something behind him. He came to the front, looked at Harris, then stepped aside to reveal a tiny Southeast Asian woman who looked to be in her early 70s. She stepped forward, gave a slight bow, then began talking in a language he didn't understand.

"I don't understand," he told her.

Yughi stepped forward. "It's a Chinese dialect."

"That one of the languages you speak?"

Yughi nodded and began to converse with her, listening carefully. The woman kept glancing at Harris and motioning to him.

Yughi looked at Harris, surprised. "She said she's been waiting a long time for you to call her in."

Harris felt a shiver roll down his spine.

He looked back at the woman, stepped toward her, then crouched down so his face was level with hers.

"Hello," he said, extending his hand. "I'm Colonel Saul Harris."

She touched his hand and the static zap was so intense, Harris gasped and immediately pulled back. A nearby soldier raised his weapon at her, people screamed and ducked, and Harris yelled at him, "No! No! Put it down!"

Steinberg quickly stepped up and disarmed the soldier.

The tiny old woman looked at the soldier, a little startled, then back to Harris.

He glanced at his hand, still tingling with a vibration, then he looked back at the woman and smiled.

"I've been waiting a long time to meet you, too."

While Yughi translated, Harris turned to Brown. "Take her and her escort through to a room. Keep them somewhere safe and guard them with your life."

Brown nodded and motioned them to follow.

"She was powerful, huh?" DaJuan asked.

Harris nodded, scanning over the crowd. "We don't need to interview them all. I just need to touch them. Tell them to hold out their hands."

Carrie stood in the silence of the Fortress, glad to be home.

She'd tried to keep everything as normal as she could for the children – dinner, homework, TV, bed – but she knew things would never be the same for them again.

She reminded herself how resilient they were. They had survived the invasion. They had seen war and carnage before. They had lost their grandfather in a blast, and they had almost lost their father. This was just more trauma piled on the last. All she could do, was watch and wait to see how things shook out. She had accepted this fate now. Until her brain was healed, she couldn't fight and she couldn't mind-meld. So, for now, she was going to focus on her kids and make them as strong as they could be. Right now, that was the most important thing she could do. Ensure their survival.

If anything, the attempt on Harkowitz had taught her that.

She stared out at the space dock alight in the night, and thought about McKinley, and of Grace's death. Then she thought of her mother's hidden heritage, and of the secrets she took to her early grave.

And as she stared out the window, she saw her own reflection. The swelling had reduced and she could see out of her eye now, but the bruises remained. She thought of Brody firing that gun, thought of her sharpshooter father, then her mind turned to Colonel Harbourg's murder, and his daughter Roxy.

And she wondered just what would be going through Roxy's mind right now.

Devastation? Or revenge?

Roxy Harbourg lifted the bottle of vodka to her lips and took a swig. The bottle was half empty, but she wasn't drunk enough yet. She needed more.

She was holed up in her office at the Hell's Gate bar. The bar had been established by her father, in an old church, and she was now the sole owner of it because of his demise.

Demise…

Roxy snarled to herself.

She hit play on the video again. She'd been watching it on replay for hours now. Her father had sent her this footage some time ago. She'd watched it once when he'd first given it to her, then shoved it aside and forgotten about it. At the time, she thought her father was just being an asshole, rubbing Carrie Welles in her face *yet* again. It was something she never understood. Despite Colonel Welles being the one to take Roxy's father into custody, her father still had respect for the Welles family. And since Jeffrey Welles died, Roxy's father wouldn't shut up about Roxy meeting with Carrie.

Roxy hated her. Jealous, perhaps, that her own father seemed to respect her so much. More than his own daughter? Roxy had taken over the bar when he was sent to Hell Town, and she'd taken over his underground fighting ring too. She'd even been slowly rolling out the secret virus, turning her key fighters into Alphas. And yet, all her father could talk about was Carrie-damn-Welles. How could Roxy not be bitter?

Then there was this video, taken from security footage in Hell Town of the female shower block. Roxy had all kinds of questions about the legality of that, but given what she saw on the video, she guessed they needed the security in there. Not that it had stopped the white supremacist bitches attacking Carrie. Then, of course, Roxy's father had come riding in on his horse with his paid guards. She wasn't quite sure why her father wanted Roxy to see Carrie's brutal fight. Was it to rub in, yet again, how great Carrie-damn-Welles was, and how Roxy wasn't her?

Now, with her father's slaying, she'd felt the need to rewatch it. Her father was a game player and often kept things on a need-to-know-basis, or he spoke in code. Just like the rabbit hole she'd had to go down just to get her hands on the virus, from stuffed childhood toys to secret safes to damn freezers. Was he trying to convey another secret message to her by sending it? But what?

Roxy wasn't sure whether it was the alcohol, the bitterness, or the grief, but she was slowly becoming obsessed with watching it. The more she watched it, the more in awe she became of Carrie Welles, her strength, her fighting ability. But, the more she watched it, the more she also hated her. And so Roxy kept coming full circle, over and over again. Was her father trying to tell Roxy to become more like her? Why wasn't she good enough as she was, after all she'd done for him?

She put her big black boots up on the desk and took another swig, glancing at the security footage on a second monitor of the back room where her Alpha fighters trained.

She flicked her eyes back to the naked Carrie Welles doing battle in the showers of Hell Town, spilling blood over the clean white floor.

She took another swig.

She thought of her father lying dead on the floor of his cell, his throat slashed ear to ear, his blood everywhere.

Roxy clenched her teeth. When she found out who it was, she was going to make every one of the motherfuckers pay. Whether Hell Town staff, the UNF, or independents, they were dead folks walking. Roxy was going to be there when they met *their* demise.

Maybe Roxy herself would even be the one to end them...

Her eyes flicked to her fighters again, training in the back room, then flicked back to Carrie Welles fighting for her life in those showers.

And a thought occurred to her then. An idea that bubbled to the surface of her drink-addled brain.

Perhaps she would grant her father one last wish. If he wanted her to be more like Carrie, then she could be.

She picked up her phone and dialed her fight doctor, Francisco.

"*Roxy,*" he answered, "*I heard about your fath—*"

"Come down to the club," Roxy said, taking another swig as she stared at Carrie Welles fighting. "You're adding a new Alpha to the lineup."

"*I am? Who is he?*"

"Not *he*," Roxy said. "*Me.*"

Harris sat in a guest chair in Berger's office, beside Marchant.

"Forty of them had this zap thing?" Berger asked, brow furrowed.

Harris nodded. "I processed hundreds today and felt it with 40 of them, but only a few were particularly strong."

"And who were they?" he asked.

"The strongest was a little old woman from the Bayanbulak Grasslands in China," Harris said, staring at the general. "You realize the significance?"

Berger nodded. "That's where one of the Zeta ships was found."

Harris nodded. "The others, from what I can tell, come from a line of ancient peoples. There're Africans, Incans, Native Americans, Indigenous Australians, and a Norwegian teenager with bright orange hair, who I think is the one my daughter once dreamed of."

Berger and Marchant stared at him.

"So, what's next?" Berger asked.

Harris locked eyes with him. "The Zetas have their hive mind. It's time to build ours."

Epilogue

JEM-1 stepped outside the bunker. He felt the cool air brush his skin as he stood beneath the crude tarpaulins erected to shield them from spying eyes. And from the rain, too, he thought, as he heard the pitter-patter upon the structure. He found it fascinating, the rain. He'd been told about it before but, of course, had never actually seen it, or smelled it.

He was happy they now had an area outside to exercise and train, but he could only see black tarpaulin, overhead and all around, the crude structure a temporary measure until something more permanent could be built, something that allowed them to see the outside world. The only glimpse of the outside provided to them now was through a small doorway that rarely opened.

He moved toward it, curious as to why they were to be kept from the outside world, when all this time they'd been training to face it. The Zetas. To fight them. To destroy them. JEM-1 looked forward to his mission and the battle that lay ahead, and he wanted to succeed more than anything. But if he was going to fight out there with his brothers, he wanted to train out there with his brothers. The urge to stretch his Alpha legs in the open space was overwhelming.

He moved right up to the door and pressed his eye to the tiny crack that ran alongside. He saw fields and a mountain, and the slightest glimpse in the distance of what Siberia Nine had told them was the Edwards Air Force Base. To be so close to a military base and to not be able to engage with its soldiers left JEM-1 disappointed. Still, Siberia Nine told him this had to be the way. As soon as the JEM army were thoroughly prepared, they would be unleashed upon the Zetas, able to mix with their military brothers then.

All JEM-1 could do now, was work hard, and wait. His time would come. And when it did, he would destroy every Zeta he saw.

"JEM-1?" Siberia Nine's voice sounded behind him.

JEM-1 turned to face his master.

"What are you doing?" Siberia Nine asked, motioning to the door.

"I am imagining what it will be like to fight and kill Zetas, sir."

His master studied him carefully, then gave a nod.

"Good," he said. "Now, come. We must begin our training."

JEM-1 returned the nod, then jogged toward his gathering brothers.

Martha stared at the console before her, her hands deep within and flowing with blue light. She felt her heart sink at what she saw, but her mind and her gut remained calm.

She pulled her hands from the console and turned to stare at her Zeta sister, who smiled with a hiss of victory.

Martha turned back to the console, knew there was little to be done. She was surrounded by a fleet of Tess's kin.

She felt the suction as one of their ships joined with hers. The door opened and Tess moved toward it.

Martha gave her one last look, but did not bother with words. There were none to be said.

Tess left her ship. The door closed, and the ship pulled away.

Martha had but moments.

She thrust her hands into the console in a desperate attempt to make contact with her sisters.

But it was no good. The small fleet surrounding her had blocked Martha from using the Zeta mainwaves to send a message.

She could not warn her sisters.

But she could, perhaps, warn another.

Her console sounded a warning. Their heat rays were coming online, her ship their target.

Martha closed her eyes, used every effort within her to picture all the faces she thought might receive her projected message of distress.

It was all she could do, before the Zeta ships fired and turned her into silver dust.

Harris bolted upright in his bed, eyes wide.

Sarai, who lay beside him, bolted upright too. They looked at each other, panting in fear.

His PDP rang. It was Welles.

"Harris," she part slurred, part groaned. "Martha—"

"I know," he cut her off, as an urgent knocking sound on his door. He stood and moved toward it, PDP still to his ear, as he opened it to reveal DaJuan panting like he'd been running.

"Tess betrayed Martha," DaJuan said. "She never made it to Archelois."

"I know," Harris said, swallowing his rising fear. "We're going to war."

Join the next action-packed Aurora adventure with book 9 – coming soon!

If you enjoyed reading *Aurora: Atlas* (Aurora 8), let people know! Leave a simple rating or write a brief review wherever you can. It means a lot to the author, and really helps with making this book visible to others.

Keep up to date with new releases here:
www.amandabridgeman.com.au

Acknowledgements

Thanks as always to the wonderful *Aurora* fans who eagerly await each book, and the extra-dedicated ones who reread the entire series before each new book comes out. You're amazing! Regardless of how much I love writing the Aurora/Aurizun team, they become so much more special because of the love you have for them too. The passion is shared and that is a fabulous feeling!

I really appreciate your patience in waiting for this book to arrive. I know it was a very long wait due to various reasons – namely COVID, my Marvel/Pandemic/Warhammer offers, film and tv project opportunities, and also personal reasons, such as my father's passing, and a little bit of burnout, which all played havoc with my schedule. I will try very hard to ensure the wait for the final book isn't as long. Yes, final book! There *should* only be one book left to go in this series, and it's going to be a massive one – which will take some time.

Thanks, as always, to my family and friends for their support and understanding of how hard I work, and of how little time I have sometimes. Life is short and I am chasing my dreams, but I will always carve time out for you.

Thanks to the publishing team who always help me bring these books to you. My editor, Stephanie Smith, I've lost count of how many books we've done together now. The *Aurora* series would be truly lost without you!

Thanks also to Pat Naoum (Red Tally Studios) for another fabulous cover. Pat's done the *Aurora* covers since *Aurora: Eden* (Aurora 5), and they've all been amazing.

Again, I really appreciate the support from my readers. If you've enjoyed this book, please leave a rating or review at wherever you purchased this from. It lets me know that you're enjoying what I do and that you want more.

And I do have a potential idea percolating for a trilogy of novella spin offs…